"I want you," Griffin wh
close to her ear.

His warm breath in her ea
all she could manage.

"Care to take a stroll?"

Julia turned to him in surprise. Griffin pointed beyond the workmen to the heavy curtain of canvas that protected St. Martin's precious artwork. Julia's breath caught in her throat. He wanted to take her beyond the curtain to kiss her. How did he dare? Hadn't they said only a week ago that they couldn't risk discovery. Did *she* dare?

Julia started toward the workmen, Griffin following. When the curtain fell behind them, she felt Griffin's hand on her waist. He spun her around to face him and his blue eyes glimmered with a mixture of amusement, and something darker. Passion.

He kissed her, but this time their mouths lingered. Their tongues touched and Julia stifled a groan of pleasure. Suddenly she didn't trust her own judgment. Her heart was racing, every nerve in her body quivering. She wanted him so badly.

"We can't do this," she insisted as she allowed him to back her against the nearest solid wall. She delved her tongue into his mouth, knowing she was losing her sense of good judgment to her desire for this man. "Griffin . . . Griffin," she groaned as he lifted her skirt and slid his hand up her bare thigh above her stocking, then higher.

His fingertips brushed, taunted, teased, then retreated. He kissed her breathless.

"If we are caught, we are dead," she whispered. "Both dead."

"Shhh," he soothed, trailing a jagged line of kisses down her neck. "We won't get caught . . ."

Books by Colleen Faulkner

Forbidden Caress
Raging Desire
Snow Fire
Traitor's Caress
Passion's Savage Moon
Temptation's Tender Kiss
Love's Sweet Bounty
Patriot's Passion
Savage Surrender
Sweet Deception
Flames of Love
Forever His
Captive
O'Brian's Bride
Destined To Be Mine
To Love A Dark Stranger
Fire Dancer
Angel In My Arms
Once More

Published by Zebra Books

ONCE MORE

Colleen Faulkner

Zebra Books
Kensington Publishing Corp.

http://www.zebrabooks.com

ZEBRA BOOKS are published by

Kensington Publishing Corp.
850 Third Avenue
New York, NY 10022

Copyright © 1998 by Colleen Faulkner

All rights reserved. No part of this book may be reproduced
in any form or by any means without the prior written consent
of the Publisher, excepting brief quotes used in reviews.

If you purchased this book without a cover you should be aware
that this book is stolen property. It was reported as "unsold
and destroyed" to the Publisher and neither the Author nor the
Publisher has received any payment for this "stripped book."

Zebra and the Z logo Reg. U.S. Pat. & TM Off.

First Printing: September, 1998
10 9 8 7 6 5 4 3 2 1

Printed in the United States of America

Hatred stirreth up strifes, but love conquereth all sins . . .
                    Solomon
                    Book of Proverbs

Prologue

The Cliffs of Dover, England
September, 1660

Julia closed her eyes and felt the bitter wind against her face. It tore at her unbound hair and whipped at her new wool and ermine cloak, a costly gift from her betrothed.

She felt numb. Was it because of the teeth-chattering cold or because, as she stood here on the precipice, she felt her hopes, her dreams, dying? All these years through the war, she had imagined that one day she would be rescued from her father's decaying house by a handsome lord. His lordship would marry her, take her away to a foreign land, and love her more than life. She knew it was just a dream, a girlhood fancy, but it was difficult to let go of that dream just the same.

Steadying herself with one hand on the crumbling wall, she hesitantly slid one foot and then the other forward, until the toes of her kidskin slippers hung off the edge of the tower floor. Chunks of deteriorated mortar fell and hit the rocks below.

Colleen Faulkner

She did not hear them splash as they made their final descent into the ocean far below.

Julia held her breath and imagined that she was one of those ill-fated bits of mortar. She wondered how easy it would be to let go of the disintegrating wall and drop into the cold depths of the waves. Did the mortar feel terror, or dull acceptance? Was there, at the last moment, a certain sense of relief before death?

The ermine lining of her new cloak ruffled in the wind, brushing the sensitive flesh of her throat. Instead of feeling soft as it should have, it felt as abrasive as spun steel. She hated the cloak. She hated he who sent it. She hated her mother for making her wear the cloak. She hated her mother for making her marry him.

"I would miss you if you went away to our Lord Jesus . . ."

The sound of her younger sister's voice startled Julia, and she gripped the wall tightly. Fearing she might lose her balance and plummet off the tower ruin, she took a step back and opened her eyes. "Lizzy! What are you doing up here? You'll catch your death in this cold!"

Lizzy drew her patched brown woolen cloak tightly around her shoulders. "You wouldn't do it, would you, Sister? You wouldn't leave me."

Julia had always wondered how Lizzy had the innate ability to read others' thoughts. Her mind damaged since early childhood, after an exceedingly high fever, she barely had the sense to get in out of a hailstorm, yet Lizzy was exceptionally sensitive to the feelings of others. Sometimes she seemed to understand Julia's thoughts better than Julia understood them herself.

Julia offered her sister her cold hand. "I just came up here to think . . . to say goodbye."

Lizzy narrowed her pretty eyes. "Not to jump into the ocean and go to Lord Jesus?"

Julia thought a long moment before she replied. Had she climbed the crumbling tower steps to contemplate suicide? Had she actually considered the choice of death over marriage to the Earl of St. Martin? Had she thought herself willing to abandon her sister and mother to the perils of poverty, rather than marry a man she did not like?

Julia lifted her lashes and gazed into Lizzy's blue eyes, eyes as blue as the heavens. "Silly chick." She squeezed her sister's petite hand in her own. "I wouldn't leave you."

"Not ever?"

"Not ever. I just came to say goodbye to the ocean. There's no ocean in London, you know."

"London? Is that the house?" Lizzy's yellow blond hair fluttered in the wind, framing her oval face.

How Julia envied her sister's perfect blond hair. Her own hair had too much red in it; her father had called it strawberry. "No. London is the place, the city. Bassett Hall is the house. That's where we'll be living, you and I."

Lizzy thrust out her lower lip. She was strikingly beautiful, even when she pouted. "But you'll no longer sleep with me. St. Martin will sleep in your bed, and I will have to sleep with Drusilla and her cold, bony feet."

Julia laughed and hugged her sister as she turned her around. "Better to sleep with Drusilla and her feet than Mother and her snoring."

The sisters laughed in unison, Lizzy's voice the higher-pitched of the two.

"Race you down the steps," Julia dared.

"And ruin my slippers? I think not!"

But the moment Julia darted down the winding stone steps, Lizzy bolted after her.

"Mother says the coach is ready," Lizzy called. "Race you to London."

Running her hand along the cold stone wall, Julia descended the steps as fast as she could, her heart pounding. It was time to say goodbye to the disintegrating walls of the home of her childhood, the home of her father's childhood, and of his father's before him. She was bound for London and a new life, bound for Bassett Hall and her new husband.

Julia's grandfather, now dead and buried in the churchyard, had always said that in life, each time a door closed, another opened. She prayed feverishly that he was right.

Chapter One

Bassett Hall
London, England

The Earl of St. Martin stood at the window of his new gallery overlooking his gardens. He watched intently as two young women followed a stone path toward a fountain. Both wore heavy cloaks to ward off the October chill, but strands of hair escaped their wool hoods and silk bonnets and fluttered in the wind.

Annoyed by the vexatious sounds of chewing saws and banging hammers, Simeon glared at the carpenters. He clamped his jaw tight and ground his teeth. Didn't these maggot brains realize they were disturbing his concentration?

He considered ordering a halt to the construction, just so that he might better enjoy his picturesque autumn garden, but instead, chose to take a deep breath. Inhaling the chilly air, he slowly exhaled warm breath, forcing himself to calm. With this great control, he was able to block out the noise so that he might better enjoy the vision of the sisters.

His eyelids fluttered at the sight below. He crossed his arms over his chest and brushed his lips with his own perfumed fingers.

One woman was quite an ordinary blond, but the other, Julia, his betrothed, was simply exquisite. In all his worldly travels, Simeon had never seen hair the color of his beloved's. It was like spun fire, as golden and red as the setting of a Caribbean sun, a sparkling jewel in the midst of the dead garden. Now that fiery hair was his. Those sparkling blue eyes were his. Julia—heart, mind, soul, and body—was his. All his.

He let out a small sigh of satisfaction and felt his hot breath on his fingertips. He was glad he had agreed to honor the betrothal agreement signed many years ago with the wench's father. Though she was now poor, this connection with her family name would be advantageous. Her father had fought for Charles I and lost most of his lands and possessions to Cromwell. In Charles II's court, her father was a hero. A woman of Julia's distinction could only add to his own importance.

Simeon slid one foot forward to take a closer look, mesmerized by the way the wind ruffled strands of his Julia's hair. His hand ached to tuck the locks into her hood. He liked nothing out of order, not even his betrothed's hair.

A coarse figure moved between him and the window, blocking out the sunlight and his vision of beatitude, and Simeon shouted in rage.

A yellow-haired, filthy-faced mason yelped in surprise and attempted to scurry by, a small pallet of stones propped on one shoulder.

Simeon cuffed him hard against the back of his greasy head as he slipped past. "Haven't I told you not to step so near me?" he exploded. "Haven't I?" He struck him a second time.

Knocked off balance, the workman fell headlong to the floor, his stack of building stones scattering as he went down.

"Get away from me, you filthy turd!"

The mason scrambled to his feet and darted off, leaving the broken stones in a crumble of dust where they lay.

Simeon inhaled again, breathing in calm, exhaling anger, as he returned his attention to the window. He removed a handkerchief from his sleeve and wiped his hand where it had touched the mason's dirty hair. Now he would have to return to his bedchamber and wash with strong lye soap.

Simeon folded the handkerchief carefully so that the soiled part was inside, and returned it to his sleeve. With his clean hand, he smoothed his gray wool coat with the black velvet garniture as his gaze fell upon his betrothed once more.

Julia and her sister sat on a bench facing him. As the women arranged their cloaks around their knees, he took a step closer to the windows that ran the length of the gallery under construction. Julia was laughing now, as was her dim-witted sister. He wondered what had amused her so. He wondered what he himself could say that would be clever enough to make her laugh with him and purse her rosy lips in such a provocative manner.

The clacking of heeled shoes on the Italian marble floor caught Simeon's attention. Who dared interrupt him now?

It was his cousin Griffin; no one else would be so bold. He was dressed in his usual abominable fashion, this morning in lime green and yellow striped breeches with a matching lime green greatcoat with yellow looped ribbons hanging from his shoulder. The heels of his shoes were lemon yellow, as was the hat perched on his black Stuart's wig.

Behind him trotted a Moor close in age to his master, his skin as dark as ebony against his white turban and flowing robes. Griffin had never voiced his relationship to the man, but Simeon guessed that like many of the fops of Charles's decadent court, Griffin retained him as a sexual plaything as well as a personal servant. The thought disgusted Simeon, but he liked Griffin, so he tried not to think about it.

"Good morning, Cousin," Simeon offered.

"Good morning, my villain with a smiling cheek." Griffin removed his befeathered hat and bowed deeply, striking a pretty leg.

Simeon drew back his lips in a near smile. His cousin was impertinent, but at least he knew his place. He liked a man who knew his place, especially when it was below him. "And where are you bound this morning? I hadn't thought you drew your shades before noon."

Griffin chuckled as he replaced his ridiculous hat and took his silver-tipped cane from the Moor. "I've a call to make at Whitehall in high chambers. Care to join me?" He buffed his polished fingernails on the sleeve of his coat.

"No, thank you. I've better matters to attend to than our King's tattletales." Simeon nodded to the window. "Have you seen her?"

Griffin lifted a plucked eyebrow. *"Her,* my lord?"

"My latest acquisition. My betrothed, of course. She's in the garden. Come see." He waved his cousin toward the window.

"Ah, the blessed Virgin Mary, of course." Griffin drew to the window, his Moor a step behind.

The men leaned on the unfinished sill and gazed down. At the same moment, Julia looked up toward the gallery. For an instant her face was without emotion, as it had been for the three days since her arrival from Dover, but then, to Simeon's delight, it lit up with the most angelic smile.

Simeon felt his heart flutter. The smile was for him. So perhaps she didn't dislike him after all, but was simply playing coy as women sometimes did.

Simeon turned his head to speak to Griffin, and his smile turned to a frown. His cousin was staring intently at his betrothed, too intently, a strange light in his blue eyes. Simeon looked back down into the garden and came to the unpleasant realization that Julia's smile was not for him, but for his foppish cousin.

A quick anger bubbled up inside Simeon. *Witless female,* he thought. *Fickle.* And worse . . . *untidy.*

"And yet I love refinement, and beauty and light are for me the same as desire for the sun," Griffin whispered.

For an instant, his cousin's comely face appeared different to Simeon; the light in his eyes reflected a depth in the man he was certain didn't exist.

Simeon scowled. His cousin was always babbling something from obscure literature. "God's teeth, I don't know what *you're* staring at. Everyone knows you prefer the rod!"

Griffin blinked, and the strange light in his eyes disappeared so quickly that Simeon wondered if he had imagined it.

"A might dimber wench," Griffin commented lightly. "But by the stars, that hair! Looks like she just tumbled from your sheets, my lord. Do let Monsieur De'nu see what he can do with her coiffure." Once again he was his silly self.

Simeon took Griffin's comment as a compliment to his manhood and smiled again. "Pleasant tart, isn't she? Nice, firm teats, but then you wouldn't really appreciate that, would you?" He eyed the Moor.

Griffin fluttered a perfumed handkerchief he had pulled from his coat sleeve like a magician. The man couldn't be insulted.

"God rot my bowels, you're lewdly bent." Griffin laughed, and Simeon laughed with him.

Simeon liked Griffin for his wit. That was why he tolerated his vices and was willing to keep him in cloth and coin when his allowance ran short. Simeon liked to keep such men under his thumb. They added to his own notability.

"Well, I should be on my way. I ordered your coach and four. You don't mind do you, Cousin?"

"Take it." Simeon gave a flip of his hand, feeling generous. "Keep it all night."

"Very good, my lord."

Griffin bowed as deeply as a man bowed to the king. The impudent monkey behind him stood stock-still, staring as if he were blind. Because he was in good humor, Simeon chose to ignore the slight.

"Good day." Simeon nodded his head.

"Good day." Griffin backed away, then turned and made his exit from the gallery.

Julia stared at the man in the window. His hat was so preposterous that she wanted to laugh, and yet there was something about the face beneath the feathers that enticed her. His gaze met hers and she felt light-headed, the way she did when a coach went over a bump and remained airborne for a moment. It was the strangest feeling, not bad, just different.

Lizzy glanced up and giggled. "See the man in the funny hat?" She covered her mouth with mitted hands and laughed behind them. "They wear silly clothes in London, don't you think, Sister? I see men in face paint and women hanging their bosoms out of their gowns until you can see their nippies."

Julia didn't answer. She couldn't tear her gaze from the stranger's. She knew St. Martin watched as well. She knew he would think her stare inappropriate, and yet she couldn't help herself.

It was the stranger who glanced away first.

Julia lowered her gaze to her lap. Her stomach fluttered. Who was that man? Surely not a servant in such flothery? A friend? Another distant relative? There were so many members of her betrothed's household that she still had not met them all.

"Sister, I said I'm cold." Lizzy spoke in a tone that implied she'd been forced to repeat herself.

Julia blinked. "Oh, I'm sorry, Lizzy. Let's go inside then and warm ourselves with a cup of chocolate." She rose from the bench and took her sister's hand. She didn't know what on earth possessed her to stare at the stranger like that. Perhaps Lizzy was right, perhaps it was just his preposterous hat.

Julia led Lizzy back up the garden path, beneath a bare arched arbor, and through double doors into the rear of the great, sprawling London house. As they entered the dim hallway, a man approached. To her dismay, Julia realized it was the stranger in the hat.

"Morning, ladies," he called gaily.

Lizzy giggled. "The feathers of his hat are yellow as a daffodil," she whispered.

"Shhht!" Julia reprimanded softly. Once again, she couldn't take her gaze off him.

Like many other men of the king's court whom she had met here in Bassett Hall, his lips were rouged, his high, handsome cheekbones dusted with rice powder, and his chin was decorated with a half-moon-shaped face patch. His head was covered in a monstrous wig, the same coal black hue that was said to be the king's. He looked the part of every dandy she'd met in the last three days, but there was something different about this man . . . something different about his eyes. They were not vacant like the other fops, but filled with a glistening light . . . a secret.

"Out early this morning, are we?" he asked. His outrageously high-heeled shoes clacked on the flagstone floor. "Is it chilly? Shall I need my muff?" He swaggered oddly as he walked on tiptoes, his arms slightly extended.

Never in her life had Julia seen such a theatrical man. She found her voice. "Not . . . not too cold, but windy."

He touched his manicured hand to his breast, still approaching. His well-cut doublet was a most hideous lemon yellow and lime green. *"That time of year thou mayst in me behold when yellow leaves, or none or few, do hang upon those boughs which shake against the cold."*

She turned as he passed her. "Shakespeare, a sonnet, I think."

He met her gaze, a flicker of surprise on his face. "A woman who reads? Gads.'' He struck his chest again. ''Another wonder of the modern world?''

Julia lifted one eyebrow and lowered her hand to her hip. ''I beg your pardon, sir, but of course I can read.''

He raised his palm to her. ''No offense meant—?''

''Julia,'' she offered, too intrigued to be insulted. ''Lady Julia Thomas.''

He struck a leg and bowed, sweeping his hat off his bewigged head. ''My profuse apologies, Lady Julia. You are, of course, his lordship's intended.''

She dipped a curtsy. Lizzy just stood behind her and stared.

''Baron Archer, cousin to the Earl of St. Martin, at your service. Griffin, I am called to friend and foe.'' He straightened and replaced his hat.

''Oh, and this is my sister, Lizzy.'' Julia sidestepped to present her.

He bowed again. ''Lady Lizzy.''

Lizzy giggled and curtsied. ''My, sir, that is an ugly hat you wear. I hope you did not pay a great deal for it.''

Julia sucked in her breath, shocked that her sister would dare say such a thing. ''Lizzy!''

But instead of being offended, the baron threw back his head and laughed. He whipped off his hat and stared at it. ''God rot my bowels, it is ugly, isn't it?''

Lizzy nodded, wide-eyed and frank. ''Ugly, indeed. The ugliest I believe I've ever seen.''

Footsteps sounded in the hallway and Julia saw a dark-skinned man approach. She had only seen a blackamoor once before, and had to force herself not to stare.

''Jabar! Where did I get this atrocious hat?'' the baron called.

''Paris, my master.'' The exotic man with chocolate brown skin spoke in a liquid-soft voice that was mesmerizing.

''And why did I buy such an unsightly beast?''

''Because you liked it, my lord.'' Jabar's English was impeccable.

"Well, Lady Lizzy doesn't like it." With that, Griffin sailed the hat into the air, over Julia's and Lizzy's heads.

Lizzy burst into another fit of giggles.

"Good morn to you, ladies." The cousin to St. Martin bowed again and before Julia could think of anything reasonable to say, he and his blackamoor were out the door.

"Funny man." Lizzy picked up the discarded hat and placed it on her head. She blew at the feathers that dangled over her face and watched them flutter with amusement. "Do you think he lives here with the dark man?"

Julia stared at the empty doorway, utterly perplexed by the exchange that had just taken place. Lizzy was right, the man was funny, and utterly ridiculous, and yet there was something about him . . . something . . .

Julia wrapped one arm around her sister's waist and led her down the hall. "I don't know if he lives here, but it wouldn't surprise me." She glanced over her shoulder. "Nothing would surprise me at this moment."

That evening Julia dressed carefully in one of the gowns her betrothed had presented to her upon her arrival. She tried not to feel hurt that his lordship did not find her own country gowns appropriate for her to wear when she served as his hostess. Instead, she wrestled down her pride and donned the gown he requested she wear. She would have preferred the green velvet, but he had been specific in the note he sent by way of his secretary.

The dress was a magnificent piece of work, far finer than anything her mother had been able to provide for her. The underskirts were a heavy azure brocade trimmed in fur, the bodice and overskirt sewn of the same azure in silk. The neckline of the bodice was fur-trimmed and scooped low over Julia's breasts. Her hair was dressed from the center, parting into wide side ringlets and a single shoulder ringlet on which Drusilla, with the aid of her trusty iron curling rod, had worked long and hard.

Julia stared at herself in an oval free-standing mirror framed in gold gilt. Her grandmother's pearl earrings swung in her ears. She smoothed the bodice of the gown, feeling a little uncomfortable with the way it revealed her breasts. "I suppose I'm ready."

" 'Bout time," Drusilla, the woman who had been her nurse-maid since birth, complained. After all these years Julia had grown used to Drusilla's grumpiness. In fact, here at Bassett Hall, it was a comfortable reminder of home.

Before pushing out the door of her apartment, Drusilla rubbed rouge on Julia's lips and pinched her cheeks hard.

"Ouch!"

"Try not to look like you're bound for yer hangin', eh?" Drusilla warned.

In the doorway, Julia glanced over Drusilla's hunched shoulder to wave goodbye to Lizzy. Although Julia's mother Susanne had been invited to sup with the earl's guests, Lizzy had not.

Lizzy grinned and waved, not understanding that she was being snubbed by her new male guardian.

Julia gathered her courage and took the hallway toward the grand staircase and her awaiting betrothed.

Halfway down the stairs that were wide enough to ride a coach and four, Julia heard footsteps behind her. "Lady Julia . . ." someone called, then softer, "Lady Julia."

The voice was familiar.

She halted and turned, her crackling skirts bunched in her fists. It was Baron Archer . . . Griffin. He was dressed in another ludicrous outfit, this one of pastel blue and pink silk.

"Lady Julia." He fluttered a long pink handkerchief. "Do allow me to escort you below."

Julia watched with fascination as the man tottered down the staircase in his heeled shoes. The height of the platforms added to his own tall stature, making him a rather imposing figure.

She smiled and curtsied as best she could on the stair tread. "Good even', my lord."

"S'death, please, call me Griffin." He took her hand.

"Then call me Julia."

He nodded, his gaze meeting hers. "Julia," he said softly in a voice that didn't quite seem his own.

They paused for the briefest moment, then broke the mutual gaze and started down the steps again.

"I wanted to apologize for my comment in the entry this morning. Anyone will tell you my mouth runs day and night, but I mean nothing by it." It was Griffin's slightly effeminate voice, and yet it wasn't. "I never meant to infer you lacked intelligence."

His arm was warm beneath her grasp. Comforting. "No offense taken. I swear it. In truth few country girls are educated beyond household responsibilities and needlework. As luck, or God's intervention, would have it, my father was a man who believed learning was for all noble families, even the *inferior* females."

He chuckled, seeming not only to catch the tone in her voice when she said inferior, but to agree with her sarcasm.

"Well, I wanted to welcome you to Bassett Hall and tell you that if you need anything, I offer my services."

She dared a sideways glance at Griffin. His offer was of course nothing but a formality, and yet there was something in his tone that made her believe he was entirely sincere.

"This hall, London, and my cousin, for certain, can be intimidating." Griffin halted at the bottom of the grand stairs. "I wouldn't wish to see you frightened or unhappy."

Their gazes met a final time, and Julia was amazed to see not the man in the ridiculous clothing, but the man beneath— the genuine smile and sparkling eyes similar to her own shade of blue. Her grandfather had always said that a person should not judge a man by his cloak, and she was beginning to understand the wisdom of his warning.

"Ah! There she is, my prize," the Earl of St. Martin called from the nearest chamber. "Come, my dearest, and meet our guests."

Julia's gaze flickered from St. Martin back to the man who still held her tightly on his arm.

"Your servant, my lord," she bid formally as she pulled away from Griffin and curtsied to him.

"Your servant, madame . . ." Griffin bowed deeply. ". . . Forever."

Julia lowered her lashes and turned away. The warmth of Griffin's touch still burned her fingertips as she greeted her husband-to-be.

Chapter Two

"Julia, my dear." The earl clasped her hand and lifted it to his lips, but did not quite make contact with her bare skin. She noted that he was wearing white silk gloves, which was odd for a man inside his own house.

"Lord St. Martin." She swept a curtsy.

"Please, please. We are to be married. Let us break through these cumbersome matters of decorum and call one another by our Christian names, shall we?"

He studied her so critically that she lowered her gaze to the floor in discomfort. He smelled heavily of garlic; she feared she might gag. Surely such an educated man would not be so superstitious as to wear garlic to ward off the plague. "Yes, my lord."

Her gaze swept over him. He was an attractive man by contemporary standards, not quite six feet tall and slight in build. He had a handsome, aristocratic face, and pleasant enough brown eyes. "I mean Simeon," she corrected herself.

He smiled, seeming to genuinely be pleased with her. "Excellent, Julia. Now come, let us greet our guests. They've been waiting anxiously to make your first acquaintance." He leaned forward. "But do tame that wayward curl, madame." He pointed delicately to a wisp of hair that fell in front of her ear.

Confused because she had thought the curl charming, she licked her finger and pushed it behind her ear.

He flinched when she licked her finger and closed his eyes.

"There, done," she whispered.

With a nod, he offered his arm and led her into a withdrawing room off the great hall. "I see you've already met my cousin, Griffin."

She glanced over her shoulder at the fop who remained behind them. "Yes. He was very kind . . . to um, escort me down."

The earl whispered in her ear. "Pleasant enough knave, but let me warn you to keep your distance. The man is rather indiscreet in his waning from his marriage, if you understand my meaning."

Married? Julia felt a sinking in her chest, accompanied by an overwhelming sense of disappointment. She had no idea why she'd reacted this way. "A man like that, married?" she couldn't resist asking softly.

The earl raised an eyebrow. "Oh, my dear, it is worse than you imagine. I shan't go into detail with a virgin so delicate as yourself, but suffice to say he does not limit his attentions to females." He shuddered. "I cannot attest to where the man's hands have been."

Julia felt her face grow warm with embarrassment, as self-conscious about Simeon's referral to her virginity as to his houseguest's homosexuality. Everyone in London was so forthright in speech, it seemed they would say anything.

Julia watched Griffin drift past them and into the room to mingle with the crowd of laughing men and fan-fluttering women. Several called to him, and he was drawn into a group of two men and a woman whose face was randomly marked with black moleskin patches shaped like cupids.

Griffin, a homosexual? Julia certainly realized such perversions existed, but she had never known a fricatrice. She was as fascinated as she was horrified. How could he have a wife? Was that why he wore such preposterous clothing? And the dark-skinned man, what was his position? Was he . . . ?

She felt her face grow hotter and swallowed against the lump in her throat, pushing away such thoughts. She needed to concentrate on making a good impression with her betrothed and his friends.

Simeon introduced her to a short, jovial gentleman with a splash of sherry on his cravat. Lord Bottletot, in turn, introduced her to his wife who looked nearly identical to him, down to the hanging jowls and spilt refreshment on the bodice of her gown.

Julia sipped at the glass of white rhenish Simeon pushed into her hand and tried to remember the names and faces as she moved through the crowd. Somewhere she could hear her mother's shrill voice as she laughed with exaggeration. As Julia smiled and spoke to Lord Something-A-Rather, she prayed her mother had not indulged too heavily in spirits before she came down to dine.

Though Simeon had told her it was to be a small dinner party, Julia was overwhelmed. At least a hundred men and women were spread out through three withdrawing chambers. After a half an hour, her head was spinning. Her new shoes were too tight, the wine had made her light-headed, and her mother's unceasing laughter grated on her nerves. Her unseen mother, however, did not grate on her as badly as her intended did.

Simeon was the perfect gentleman, introducing her to his friends, complimenting her clothing and choice of hairstyle. She could find no fault in his manners or his treatment of her, and yet, as the evening wore on, she found herself wishing she could escape from him and disappear into the folds of silk and satin that decorated the rooms.

Simeon spoke kindly to his guests, calling for servants to refill their glasses and their tiny plates of sweet bread nibbles and smoked fish, but there was something about his manner that never seemed quite sincere. It was as if he were playing the part of an earl, rather than actually being one.

In the past three days she had also learned that St. Martin had some sort of fixation with cleanliness and order. Not only did he keep his person fastidious, but he expected the same of everyone and everything in his household. Rooms were constantly being scrubbed floor to ceiling, and lye soap was made by the barrelful in the laundry.

"Oh! There is my darling daughter! Have you met her, Lord Argyle?"

Julia glanced up from her place beside Simeon to see her mother approach, a gentleman on each arm. Her mother's face was beet red, despite the heavy layer of rice powder—positive evidence of her imbibing. "Julia!" She fluttered a paper fan. The bodice of her robin's egg blue gown was so tight that her lumpy breasts spilled over the lace edging.

"Mother." Julia forced a smile as Susanne barreled across the room, dragging the gentlemen with her.

"Let me introduce you to my two new acquaintances. Mr. Rupport here is a merchant, and Lord Argyle, why ... why he's a lord, of course," she twittered.

The two gentlemen, though older than Julia, could have been her mother's sons.

"Please to meet you, my lord, sir." She took a step from Simeon and curtsied to them both.

"Your servant, madame."

"Your servant," echoed the merchant.

"Thank you so much for coming," Julia said, trying to fit into the role of hostess as Simeon expected. "I believe the meal should be served shortly. Could I bring you some more wine, sir, my lord?"

The young merchant appeared relieved to have been rescued from Susanne. "Oh, I should think one more would not harm me."

"Excellent." As if by magic, a young man in green and white livery appeared with a tray of drinks. Julia reached for a fluted glass, but hit the tray instead. "Oh, goodness," she exclaimed as the tray tipped and the glasses tumbled. She tried to catch the glasses, as did the servant, but to no avail.

Glass shattered over the marble floor and instantly every gaze in the room was fixed on her, the room silent.

Before the last glass struck, the servant was on his knees, gathering up shards as quickly as he could.

Mortified, Julia lifted her skirts to help the young man. She had certainly made an impression. Everyone in the room, including her betrothed, would now think her a lumbering country oaf. "How clumsy of me. Let me—"

"You bungling pustule! How dare you!" Simeon exploded. "That was fluted Venetian glass! That was *my* fluted Venetian glass!"

Julia glanced up, shocked by her intended's reaction. "I only meant to—"

"Not you! Stand up, woman, and find your dignity!" Simeon grabbed her arm none too gently.

The heels of Simeon's boots ground the glass into the floor. "How could you be so idiotic?" he raved at the servant. He hit the broken stem of a glass with the toe of his boot and kicked it at the man. "Mine. Mine. Mine!"

The servant, still on his hands and knees, threw up his hand to guard his face as the piece of glass deflected off his shoulder.

"Simeon!" Julia didn't think before she spoke. "I spilled the tray, not the footman. I broke your—"

Simeon turned to her, his face puffed and red. "How dare you speak to me that way in front of my guests. Silence!"

Against her will, tears sprang to her eyes. She didn't want the earl angry at her, but nor would she see someone else suffer for her mistake. "My lord—"

"Let it go," a gentle male voice whispered in her ear. "It's not worth the trouble."

Julia looked over her shoulder to see Griffin pass her. In the confusion she doubted anyone realized he had spoken to her.

Griffin threw up both arms in his theatrical manner. "Come, come, let us say to hell with the Venetians and their glass and eat," he declared to the crowd. He grabbed the servant by his collar and lifted him off the floor. He whispered something in the frightened man's ear and released him.

The servant scurried away.

"Let us eat so that we can fortify ourselves for the gaming tables I know our gracious host will surely provide," Griffin continued, leaving Simeon no place to interrupt. As Griffin spoke he threw open double paneled doors to reveal a large banquet hall set up with buffet tables.

"My lordship, will you kindly lead us to yon laden tables?" Griffin begged Simeon.

Simeon glanced at Julia, who still stood stark-still, then at the servant making his escape. His gaze met Griffin's.

"My lord?"

Simeon smoothed his burgundy velvet coat as he fell back into the role of gracious host. "If my guests are hungry then dine we shall . . ." With that, he left Julia's side and swept into the banquet hall.

Julia hurried to catch up, but as she passed Griffin, she breathed, "Thank you."

He winked at her. "Any time, sweet."

"I mean I don't like him. Ouch!" Julia took the brush from her mother's hand. She knew her mother hadn't meant to pull her hair, but it smarted just the same.

It was half past two in the morning, and Julia was tired and frustrated. She tugged the brush through her hair, avoiding her mother's gaze reflected in the mirror.

Her mother had come to her apartments to help her undress, rather than wake Drusilla at this late hour. Julia had removed her gown and the tight shoes and donned a sleeping and dressing gown, the fabric of both pieces worn, but comfortable.

"I just don't like him," Julia repeated, wishing she hadn't started this conversation with her mother. She knew better. Susanne Elizabeth Thomas tried to be a good parent, but she was selfish and always had been, and her words and deeds always reflected that selfishness.

Susanne plucked her false blond curls from the back of her head and tossed them on Julia's dressing table. Lying atop a pile of ribbons, the curls looked repulsively like a dead animal.

"Well . . . well, that's ridiculous," Susanne hiccuped. "He's an earl. What's not to like about him? He's handsome, and he's got more money than a hatter's got pins."

Tired beyond reason, Julia smoothed back her hair and tied it in a green ribbon. "He smells like garlic, he wears gloves in his own home, and he kisses the air instead of my hand. I think he fears I'll infect him."

Susanne laughed. "Is that all?"

"He doesn't like me."

"Of course he does." Her mother leaned over her shoulder to look in the mirror and blotted at the lip rouge that was smeared on her fleshy chin. "You can't be upset by that little incident in the parlor with the servant. Listen to your mother. Men are like that, Julia. They like their things, and they like to order their servants and women about." She fluttered her handkerchief. "Somehow it makes them think they've got a bigger pizzle than they do."

Julia rolled her eyes. "There's no sense in me trying to talk to you when you're like this, Mother. Why don't you just go to bed and I'll see you in the morning?"

"Like this? Like what?" Susanne plucked at the sleeve of her daughter's robe.

Julia rose from the upholstered stool. "The drink, Mother. You've had too much to drink."

Susanne hiccuped. "Have not."

Barefoot, Julia walked toward the large four-poster bed she would share with her sister until the wedding. Lizzy slept soundly on her back, a ruffled nightcap perched on her forehead. Julia slid out of her robe and climbed beneath the goose-down counterpane.

Susanne followed her daughter to the bed like a mother hen after her wayward chick. "All these years I've been locked away in the country caring for you," she wailed. "All those years without music, or good food and drink, without male companionship, and you can't allow me one evening of pleasure? One evening of enjoyment for myself?"

"Please, I don't want to argue." Julia was on the verge of tears. After the incident with the servant, Simeon had ignored her the remainder of the evening. He hadn't even dined with her, but instead left her with an elderly couple who babbled all night of the appalling food and accommodations they'd had when last in Paris.

At midnight Julia suggested to Simeon that she might turn in because her head ached. In response, he'd pinched her arm viciously, while smiling for any onlookers. He insisted she remain downstairs until the last of his gambling guests had departed, even if it was dawn the following day. The moment the last guest finally departed at quarter after two, Simeon left the room without so much as a good night.

Julia glanced up at her mother, who stood over her bed, her clothes disheveled, her eye paint smeared. "Please Mother, just go to bed. We can talk tomorrow." She offered her hand, but her mother didn't take it.

"Let me tell you something," Susanne said, suddenly sounding far more sober than she had a moment ago. "Your father arranged this betrothal so that you and your sister would be provided for. It was his wish that you marry St. Martin, and marry him you will.'' She shook her finger. ''It's your responsibility to this family.''

Julia closed her eyes to hide the tears that gathered in their corners. It had always seemed to Julia that her mother enjoyed making her cry, even as a young child. ''Yes, Mother. I'll marry him and fulfill my duty to the family. Now take the candle near the doorway so you don't get lost finding your way to your apartments.''

With that, Julia blew out the bedside candle and rolled over in the bed against her sister. It wasn't until her mother's footsteps rescinded in the darkness that she finally gave in to her tears.

Chapter Three

"I cannot order the cook to prepare a meal, nor the house-keeper to air a counterpane?" Julia stood in the front hall, her hands resting on her hips as she attempted to keep her voice even. Medieval armor and weapons surrounded her on three sides, looming above her on the paneled walls like a ghost army. "Are you telling me, Mr. Gordy, that I am not to be in charge of my husband's household?"

The earl's secretary was a strikingly handsome man in his mid-twenties, with inky black hair, devil-dark eyes, and a perfect complexion unmarked by childhood diseases.

Gordy kept his hands tucked behind his back, his gaze ahead. He was as cold as the polished marble floor they stood upon. "I only convey what his lordship told me, madame."

Julia exhaled with exasperation. She had risen this morning with the idea that the best way to make amends between herself and her betrothed was to show him what she was capable of. Once he saw how well she was trained to run his home and scrub his blessed floors, perhaps he would better appreciate her. After all, that was why a man such as the Earl of St. Martin married, was it not? Not just to gain a warm bed and sons, but to have a woman to maintain his household.

She threw up her hands. "What am I to do then, if not run his lordship's home?"

"He did not say, madame, only that he wished the house-keeper to continue her duties without interference." Julia stared at the man, who looked back as if he considered her somewhere below the housekeeper's station. Every hair on his periwig was perfectly arranged.

"Well, I suppose I shall have to ask him myself. Where is he?"

"In his library."

Julia didn't care for his tone of voice, nor the way he painstakingly avoided addressing her with a m'lady or Lady Julia, the title she was born to as the daughter of an earl. Once she and Simeon were married, she would have to discuss the matter with her husband's secretary. Julia wasn't ordinarily concerned with titles, but she expected common respect, something she didn't feel she had with Mr. Gordy.

She turned on her heels and headed toward the earl's library.

Mr. Gordy had to run to catch up with her. "You cannot disturb the master. He is occupied."

Julia would not be dissuaded by a mere secretary, and certainly not by this man who she guessed could easily become her enemy. She followed a long, dimly lit corridor deeper into the catacombs of the massive house. Portraits lined the paneled walls, the eyes of his lordship's primly dressed ancestors seeming to follow her as she passed. "I won't disturb him but for a moment."

"Madame—"

Julia rapped her knuckles on the closed library door.

"What is it?" the earl grumbled from the far side.

Before she lost her nerve, she slid open the paneled door that recessed into the wall.

"Didn't I say I did not wish to be disturbed, Gordy?" the earl shouted.

Julia stepped into the room that was entirely masculine with paneled walnut walls and floor-to-ceiling bookshelves. Heavy crimson velvet drapes hung closed over the great windows, making it dark inside save for the glow of candlelight. The room smelled of acrid lye soap and his lordship's garlic.

"I apologize for disturbing you, Simeon." She spotted the Earl of St. Martin seated behind a massive desk, quill poised. She noticed that the desk was greatly in order for a man busy at work. His lordship was a methodical man in everything he did, and she needed to try and remember that.

He glanced up at her impatiently. "Yet you disturb me anyway, woman."

"I . . . your man, Mr. Gordy, tells me I am not to take command of the household and kitchens . . . not even once you and I are wed."

The earl blinked.

Julia waited, hoping he intended to respond. She was losing her nerve. Why the blast didn't the man say something? She could feel his secretary directly behind her, hovering. "Is it true, sir?"

The Earl of St. Martin lowered his gaze to the ledger before him. "I like organization in my life, Julia. My house is in order. I see no reason to make changes." He dipped his quill in an ink bottle and scratched something in his ledger.

Julia wondered if he was still angry with her over the incident last night. Surely a man as wealthy as St. Martin could not keep a grudge over something so trivial as a few broken glasses . . . could he? "I can assure you, sir, that I'm well trained in household—"

"Madame"—he flipped the page of the ledger—"the decision was made prior to your arrival. I have no doubt of your abilities; I simply do not require them. I am not marrying you to gain a housekeeper."

Then why are you marrying me? she wanted to ask, but didn't, perhaps because she feared the answer. Julia watched as he entered another number in the ledger as if she weren't there. Was that it? Was that all he was going to say on the matter? Well, be damned if that was all she had to say. "Simeon." She dared a step closer to the walnut desk with its carved legs that resembled lion's claws. "Simeon, what is it I'm supposed to do, then?"

He glanced up as if it was the oddest question he'd ever heard. *"Do?"*

She gestured. "When a woman joins her husband's household, it's her responsibility to be sure it runs smoothly. It's how a wife spends her days, overseeing the meal planning and cooking, house cleaning, and laundry."

One corner of the earl's mouth turned up. "Do you stitch, madame?" He spoke now as if she were a child, slowly emphasizing each word.

"Well, yes, of course."

"Then why not make something pretty? Perhaps a cloth for the dining table." He lifted an eyebrow. "That would please me."

Julia crossed her arms over her chest. She had dressed in one of the day gowns he'd presented to her upon her arrival. It was yellow, and though elegant, rather childish in styling. She didn't like it, but she'd worn it because she thought it would please him. The first thing she'd do when she left the library was go directly to her apartments and remove the blasted dress.

It was her turn to lift her eyebrow. "A table linen, sir?"

"Aye." He entered another numeral, his attention returned to his ledger.

"May I not give your staff direction?" When he exhaled with obvious annoyance, she added, "I only ask so that I know what you expect of me."

"You may have what you wish." He waved his hand impatiently as if to shoo her away. "Do what you wish; amuse yourself in whatever manner pleases you, within reason. My servants are at your disposal. Call for a hot posset or a sweetmeat. Call for a coach to take you to buy a ribbon or whatever it is women purchase. I expect you to play hostess when we receive guests, look pretty, remain clean and chaste, and accompany me when I am expected to bring my wife. I simply do not wish for you to take over a household which already functions smoothly. Is that too much for a busy man to ask?"

She ground her teeth. "No. No, I suppose not. It's only that . . ." She let her sentence trail off into silence at his obvious dismissal. It was equally obvious that he was not interested in her opinion on the matter, nor was he going to take it into account.

"Good day, my lord." Julia curtsied and walked out of the room. "Mr. Gordy, close his lordship's door, will you?"

The secretary made a sound in his throat as she swept past him. She knew it galled him to be ordered by her, but he'd heard the earl. His staff was at her disposal.

"Yes," he said flatly.

"Gordy!" the earl shouted. "That is Lady Julia to you, and soon to be Lady St. Martin. Speak thus rudely again, and I'll see you take a dunking for insubordination."

"Yes, my lord." He bowed his head. "My lady."

Julia turned sharply down the hall and made her exit, her head held high, her strides long and confident. *God above,* she thought as she made her retreat. *I need not worry of dying in childbirth or of the plague. I'll die of boredom and frustration in this strange house.*

Hours later Julia sat on a stone bench in the humid orangery. The hothouse, obviously not one of the earl's interests, appeared to have been ignored for years and left to overgrow into a tangled mess.

Julia dejectedly ground one heel into the flagstone tile beneath her feet. The earl didn't want a housekeeper; he didn't want a companion. He'd barely spoken to her since her arrival.

He didn't even seem to be particularly interested in her sexually. She wondered if he thought her unattractive. If he did, it would be just as well. The idea of having to lie with him soured her stomach. She didn't come to Bassett Hall so young and innocent as not to know what would be expected of her in the marriage bed, but she had thought her husband would be interested in her. He seemed to pay her no more mind than one of his hounds . . . or a new piece of art for his gallery.

With a sigh, she stood and stretched. The inactivity of the last few days had made her stiff and irritable. She was used to physical activity. At home on the cliffs of Dover, she had run her mother's household with few servants to aid her. From the age of eleven, she had seen to the cooking and cleaning of her father's dilapidated castle, while her mother gallivanted about the countryside, dining and taking tea with her neighbors.

Julia had overseen the growing of their meager crops and the care of the sheep and horses in the stables. The common folk of the area had come to her—not her mother—in disputes and in time of dire illness. Julia had always risen at dawn, worked through the day, and then fallen into bed tired but content in early evening.

It was probably the earl's impossible hours that caused her to be irritable, much as the inactivity. Because she rose early out of habit, it was difficult for her to participate in evenings of entertainment that did not begin until nine and easily ran until two or three in the morning.

Julia scuffed along the flagstone tiles, her head bowed. She knew it was her duty to marry the earl and make the best of the life he would provide. It had been her father's wish and was her obligation to her mother and sister. But how was she to make her place in this new life? Julia had always known who she was in her father's castle, but who was she here? What purpose would she serve other than to smile at her husband's drunken guests at one in the morning, and breed his lordship's children?

"There you are."

Julia looked up with surprise and then smiled. "Griffin," she greeted, as if he were an old friend.

He was dressed so abominably in an orange saracet doublet that she laughed aloud. Embarrassed by her own rudeness, she covered her mouth with her hand.

He grinned and brushed a hand over his open coat. "You don't care for my choice of garment this morning, Julia?" His tone reflected amusement rather than offense.

Was it her imagination, or did his voice lack its usual high pitch? He strode toward her with less swagger in his walk than she had noticed in the house. He didn't walk on his toes, either.

"I'm sorry," she confessed, laughing behind her hand. "Surely it's my unsophisticated country ways. I must not know what's in good taste and what's not."

"Do you think so?" he asked good-naturedly. Orange ribbons hung from the caps of his doublet sleeves and fluttered as he approached.

She lowered her hand and burst into laughter again. "No," she sputtered. "Actually not. Garish is garish, whether it's in Dover or London."

"Garish, am I?"

"I'm afraid so."

He halted in front of her.

"But it suits you . . . your personality," she told him. "You'd probably look sillier in a plain black velvet doublet and hose."

His brow crinkled. He had the most fascinating laugh lines at the corners of his mouth. "I believe that is meant to be a compliment, but I'm unsure."

"Take it as one." She nodded her head as she folded her arms over her chest. He made her feel uncomfortable and yet giddy at the same time.

"And who are you to talk of fashion, anyway?" he jokingly mocked. "You, in your hatchling chick gown? Gads, that neckline has been out of fashion six months!"

She burst into laughter again, her hands falling to her sides. "Not my choice, sir, but the earl's."

"And you like it?"

"No, but I wore it to please his lordship as he was kind enough to have it made for me and presented it to me upon my arrival."

For a moment Griffin just stood there, returning her stare. It should have been awkward, but oddly, it wasn't.

"Finding your way about Bassett Hall?" he asked after a moment.

She lifted one shoulder. "Well enough." Then she wrinkled her nose. "I find it rather gloomy and grim, despite its cleanliness. Does no one laugh in this household but you?"

"Yes. Now there is you." He offered his hand as if he wanted her to take it.

She didn't dare . . . though a part of her wanted to. She was lonely, and so desperate for friendship, for human comfort. How strange that this man in his garish doublets and tippytoed walk should be the one to offer that hand in friendship. Simeon had not yet once touched her, bare skin to bare skin, or even fingertip to fingertip.

"I don't know that I'll be laughing often in the earl's presence," Julia heard herself confess. "He thinks me a clumsy clod. This morning I was told I would not be taking over my wifely household duties once we're wed. When I asked him what I was to do, he suggested I stitch a tablecloth."

Griffin scowled. "Sounds like my dear cousin."

She groaned. "I don't mean to sound ungrateful. His lordship's been very kind to me and to my family. Very generous. It's just that I can find nothing to do with my time."

They began to walk side by side deep into the tangled orangery. "Mm hm," Griffin intoned.

He was such a good listener that she continued to confide in him. "My mother and sister are content to play at cards, try on new gowns, and make daily trips to various ribbon shops, but 'tis not my inclination."

He reached out to help her push a long hanging vine aside. "What is your inclination?"

She glanced at him and then away. "I . . . I don't know. In my mother's home, I ran the household, cooked, cleaned, tended the ill—women's work."

"What do you *like* to do then? Surely you don't care to scrub floors in your leisure?"

Julia had to think for a moment. No one had ever asked her before what she liked to do. "I . . . I like to read . . . and . . . and . . ." She remembered back to her childhood when her father had been alive. "And play backgammon," she finished, delighted she could name two things she liked to do for pleasure. "And ride, and walk in the garden, and tend to my flowers and herbs."

He nodded. "So if his lordship has given you his leave to abandon all household drudgeries, why not do some of those things? There's a superb library here at Bassett Hall, and surely his lordship has a backgammon board." He frowned. "London is not the place for a lady to ride, but perhaps one day I could escort you outside the city . . . if his lordship is otherwise occupied." Griffin plucked his chin thoughtfully. "As for the gardening . . ." He threw open his arms with a flourish. "What of here?"

Julia glanced at the dry fountain in the center of the glass-walled atrium. Vines had grown up its sides and filled the stone basin. It smelled of rotting vegetation and stagnant water. "Here?"

"My cousin has never expressed any interest in flora or herbage, though I'm surprised he allows it to remain so *untidy.*"

She smiled at his jest, but didn't dare laugh at her betrothed's expense. "I wondered the same."

"His lordship actually only recently came to Bassett Hall— one of his last acquisitions before Cromwell died. Before then, he was living in a smaller home nearer to the palace. There, and at one of his country houses whenever the armies grew restless. I suppose Bassett Hall's previous owners were remiss in caring for their orangery—probably too busy worrying over whether or not they would keep their heads," he finished drolly.

The thought of all the political upheaval her country had experienced in the last twenty years was sobering. "It looks as if it's been years since these trees have been pruned," she said wistfully.

"It would be a mighty task." He glanced at her as if to ask if she was up to it.

Julia grinned. "Do you think it would be all right. I . . . I suppose I'd have to ask his lordship."

He propped one foot on the edge of the dry fountain and gave a wave. "Simeon won't mind. He's given you a monthly purse to spend as you wish, hasn't he? I say, do it. Hire a gardener and get to work."

Slowly Julia turned around, her imagination already at work. It would take time, money, and labor, but the orangery really could be beautiful with time and care. "It would be a challenge."

"One I'm sure you're up to."

She smiled up at him. She hadn't been this happy since she'd arrived at Bassett Hall. "Thank you."

He lowered his leg from the fountain and moved his hand toward her. For a moment she thought he might touch her, but then he lowered his hand to his side.

"Ah, 'tis nothing." He spoke in the high-pitched voice she'd heard before. "Just promise me your first orange." He swaggered on his tiptoes down the flagstone pathway toward the house.

"We have a bargain," she called as she watched him until he disappeared. It felt so good to have a friend at last, for she had the feeling she'd definitely made a friend in Griffin.

Chapter Four

"Oh, Lizzy, couldn't I come later?"

"Not later. Now."

Julia's sister dragged her down the back hall toward the kitchen. The passageway smelled strongly of lye soap and wet wood.

"You have to see Sally," Lizzy continued. "That's what I named her because Amos said she didn't have a name, and everyone should have a name."

Julia couldn't resist a smile. It gave her such pleasure to see Lizzy happy, even if it was only a hound that gave her that happiness. "And who is Amos?"

"The cook. He lets Sally in the back door of the kitchen and feeds her scraps of food because she's going to have puppies." Lizzy lowered her voice to a loud whisper as a child would. "Only don't tell, because the master would be angry if he knew his kidney pie was being fed to a dog." She frowned and crinkled her forehead, obviously mimicking someone. "Kidney pie isn't for dogs, only the master."

Evidently someone had explained the situation to Lizzy, probably this cook she was talking about. Julia knew it wasn't wise for Lizzy to become too friendly with the servants, but what harm would come of it as long as Simeon didn't find out? The poor girl. She needed someone to talk to, and it certainly wasn't as if she'd be making friends with one of St. Martin's many guests.

Lizzy opened the kitchen door. "She's right in here, unless Amos let her out to piddle. No piddling in the kitchen, that's our rule."

"Lizzy." One of the kitchen maids turned to them as she wiped her floury hands on her apron. When she spotted Julia, ner smile fell and she dipped a deep curtsy. "Lady Julia."

"Lady Julia. Lady Julia," the other servants in the kitchen echoed as they dropped what they were doing and curtsied.

"Amos! Lady Julia is here," one of the girls called as if she were sounding an alarm rather than making an introduction.

A tall man with a pocked face and a knit cap perched on his blond head appeared from around the corner of a floor-to-ceiling pie safe. "Lady Julia." He bowed.

"I just brought Sister to see Sally," Lizzy explained, passing the baker. "Have you seen her, Amos?" She brushed her hand against his arm as she passed him.

Julia knew that her sister could be inappropriately affectionate if permitted to do so, and to touch a servant in such a way was certainly inappropriate. She wondered if she need warn the cook, perhaps all the servants. Maybe they didn't understand how Lizzy was. She'd not see her sister taken advantage of because of her slow mind.

"The pup were by the fireplace last I saw her," Amos said nervously. His gaze followed Julia as she passed him, behind her sister.

"Really, Lizzy," Julia laughed. "I've seen hounds before. Father had a pack of them."

"But you haven't seen Sally! Oh, there she is!"

In front of a stone fireplace, wide and deep enough to place a small carriage inside, Lizzy flopped down on the floor and thrust out her arms.

A black, brown, and white hunting hound, obviously familiar with her, climbed into her lap.

"Oh, that's my Sally. That's my girl," Lizzy cooed, smoothing her floppy ears.

The dog wiggled in her lap and licked at her face with excitement.

"See, isn't she pretty?" Lizzy stroked the hound's short, spotted coat. "And look at her fat belly. There's puppies inside!"

Julia rested her hands on her hips and smiled. "She really is a very pretty dog."

Amos rounded the corner, his clothing dusted free of most of the flour. "I . . . I saved the scraps for you, so you could feed her yourself, Lady Lizzy."

Lizzy scrunched her nose. "Lady Lizzy? Why are you saying that, Amos? I'm just Lizzy to you. You never call me Lady Lizzy." She laughed. "You sound silly when you say it."

Julia glanced at the cook, who stared at his holey brown leather shoes. Perhaps they *were* too familiar with each other. Why else would the cook be looking so guilty? She hated to interfere, but thought she'd better say something to him. "Could I speak with you privately for a moment, Amos?" she asked.

"A . . . aye, Lady Julia."

Julia went down on one knee beside Lizzy and scratched the dog behind her ears. "I really do like her, Lizzy. Now don't stay too long in the kitchen. All right?"

"I won't." Lizzy beamed.

Julia rose and walked back through the kitchen to the hallway, with Amos following her. She pushed the door closed behind him so the other servants couldn't hear. She wasn't quite sure what she wanted to say, but for Lizzy's sake she felt she needed to say something. "Amos."

"Lady Julia." He pulled off his knit hat and held it tightly in his flour-dusted hand. She wondered if he had been a handsome man before the pox had scarred his face so severely.

"Amos, I want you to know how much I appreciate your keeping my sister entertained here in the kitchen with the dog. She's been very lonely since we came to Bassett Hall."

"Aye, m'lady."

"But Amos"—she glanced up at him—"I have to ask that you take care with my sister. Though she looks like an adult woman, she's not. Not in her head. She . . . she doesn't understand certain things. Proprieties." She exhaled in frustration. "I'm not saying you can't be friendly with Lizzy, just that . . . that you need to remember that she's—" Julia halted, glanced at the floor, and then back at Amos again. "I won't have anyone take advantage of my sister because of the weakness in her mind. I won't have it."

Amos's eyes grew round. "Oh, no. Oh, no, Lady Julia. I wouldn't never do that. I wouldn't never take *advantage* of Lizzy. She's so sweet and gentle."

"That she is. That's why I feel like I have to watch out for her. Do you understand, Amos?"

He ground the toe of his shoe on the floor, his eyes cast downward. "Ye . . . yer saying you don't want Lizzy in the kitchen, Lady Julia?"

"No. No, I'm not. Although I must admit I'm not sure how my Lord St. Martin would take to the idea." She reached out and gave Amos a squeeze on the arm. He was surprisingly muscular. "I'm just asking that you take care with my sister and not let her sit all day, everyday, at your hearth. It's not seemly."

"That all?" He looked up, brightening. "Ye mean she can still come oncest in a while?"

Julia smiled and shrugged. "She loves the dog and she obviously enjoys your company. Why not? Just take care, Amos."

He nodded his head. "Aye, Lady Julia. Thank ye, Lady Julia."

Julia walked away from the cook feeling a sense of accomplishment. And since she was in such good spirits at the moment, she thought she might as well pay her betrothed a visit.

With a scowl, Simeon's secretary allowed Julia entry into his master's apartments.

"Good morning to you, Gordy," she said cheerfully. "I hope this day finds you well." Despite his obvious good looks, she could barely look him in the eye. There was something about the man that just seemed inherently evil.

"This way, Lady Julia," Gordy answered stiffly.

He led her into one of the antechambers of Simeon's bedchamber. The room was bare, save for a few pieces of necessary furniture. The walls were whitewashed and unadorned, the wooden floors obviously recently scrubbed with sand. It smelled of lye soap and garlic, the two scents she was beginning to associate with Simeon.

The sparse chamber was alive with chatter and movement. Several merchants were displaying their wares of cloth and ribbon, holding up samples for Simeon to study. Because he was such a wealthy, important man, Julia knew that simply being permitted through the doors of Bassett Hall was quite a coup for the merchants.

Simeon stood on a small stool in the center of the room, his arms extended as a tailor moved on his knees and thrust pins into the hem of the velvet burgundy coat. This was the first time she had ever seen Simeon without his wig. His hair was a medium brown and bristly in a close-cropped style.

"Good morning, Simeon." Julia nodded, showing respect but also familiarity, and offered an amiable smile.

Simeon glanced in her direction. She couldn't immediately tell what his mood was.

"I . . . I had a spare moment so I thought I might visit with you . . . if . . . if you're not too busy." She folded her hands in front of her. She wore one of the gowns he'd given her and had taken great care to be certain every hair she possessed was in place.

"Spare moment?" He fluttered his hand, heavy with the signet ring that bore his family crest. "As spare as any moment I have, I suppose. Gordy, get Lady Julia a chair and a cup of chocolate."

"No, no. Thank you." She eyed Gordy who backed away. "Nothing for me. I just wanted to say hello and . . . and ask if you might have some time today. We . . . we could ride; it's a sunny day. Or . . . if you prefer, a game of backgammon. I spotted a fine game board in your office."

From his place on the stool, Simeon looked down on her as if he were a reigning monarch. "I haven't time for games, madame, nor for senseless riding in circles in the park."

He spoke his reprimand so loudly that the merchants turned to stare. Julia didn't back down. She was beginning to suspect that Simeon was a bully. Her mother swore all men were with women. This morning she wasn't in the mood to pretend to be a weak female. "I only thought we might spend some time together to get to know each other, my lord. The wedding is fast approaching."

"Aye. 'Tis. This is my wedding coat. Do you like it?" He turned slowly so that she could fully appreciate the intricate embroidery and fine fabric. "I thought it would look fine with the pink wedding gown I've commissioned for you."

Pink, Julia thought. *Gads. What was it with this man with pink?* But she said nothing. The gown was already commissioned; what difference did it make? It was a small concession to her new husband, wasn't it? "A fine coat, Simeon." She stepped closer. "It's really quite handsome on you." She stroked the sleeve, then touched his hand.

He flinched.

She withdrew her hand. Sweet heaven, did he really deplore her so greatly that he couldn't stand her touch? What had she done to cause him to dislike her so? Surely the incident with the servant and the glassware couldn't have angered him that greatly.

Julia took a step back, her frustration bordering on anger. Obviously her attempt at making friends with her betrothed was not going to work. She glanced at the polished wood floor in indecision.

What did she do now? Retreat? She thought of sweet Lizzy. Then she tried to imagine herself ten years from now in this house . . . with this man. No. She couldn't retreat. She wouldn't.

Julia raised her head.

"My lord, if I could speak to you privately." Then, before he could protest, she clapped her hands. "Gentlemen, ladies. Thank you so much for coming, but the earl has completed his purchasing for the day. Anything he has said he will take, can be left. Mr. Gordy will see you are paid for the items my lord has purchased." She pointed to the hallway. "Thank you again. Good day."

The merchants swept up their bolts of cloth and spools of ribbon and raced for the door, bowing and curtsying as they went.

The tailor, still on his knees, his mouth still full of pins, stared at Julia in obvious indecision.

"Sir," Julia said. "If you could just take a stroll down the hallway, I'll be but a moment and then you can complete the hem. I'm certain you'll appreciate his lordship's fine art. There's a Da Vinci just come from Italy directly over the landing of the west staircase."

"Yes, my lady." The tailor mumbled through his pins. He

rose off the floor and backed out of the room behind the merchants.

Mr. Gordy stood near the doorway, staring at his master.

Julia knew Simeon was not pleased, but after a moment he waved his hand. "Do as she says. Pay them and bring me coffee. Be certain boiling water has been poured in the cup first and drained off."

"Yes, my lord."

Simeon stepped off the stool as the door closed behind Gordy. "For a country girl, you have an air about you," he commented.

She wished her heart wouldn't pound so. "Thank you."

He smoothed his short-cropped hair with the heel of one hand. "It was not intended as a compliment."

"Oh." She glanced down at the floor, then back at him. "I'm sorry. It's just that we never have a moment alone. I think we need time to get to know one another without an audience." Since she was in this far, she decided she might as well take the plunge. If Simeon wasn't going to initiate contact with her, she would do it herself. "For heaven's sake, Simeon." She gestured. "We're going to be wed. Married. Husband and wife. God willing, I will bear your children," she added boldly. "We should know something of each other. Of likes and dislikes . . . of personality."

"You know what I like." He walked to a window draped in heavy cream brocade that added to the austerity of the chamber.

The room seemed so isolated to Julia. Like the man.

"I like order," Simeon said.

She sighed in frustration. "Sir, forgive my forwardness, but my grandfather taught me to speak my mind. Sir, if you're not interested in me in any manner, why marry me?"

"You're mine," he said softly as he fingered the drape.

Confused, she said, "My lord?"

He turned on his heels. "You are mine," he repeated louder, as if she were half-witted.

She felt a chill curl up her spine.

"I signed the betrothal agreement. I agreed to wed you. I fulfill my obligations. *You are mine*. Don't you understand, woman!"

Julia took an involuntary step back at his shout. She *didn't* understand. But seeing the look on St. Martin's face, she thought she never would. The man was beyond understanding, and no matter what her mother said, he was entirely unlikeable.

She knotted her hands at her sides. Her first impulse was to just tell him she wanted to break off the betrothal, but a flash of Lizzy's image in her mind made her bite her tongue. The word *responsibilities* rang in her head. "I'm sorry I disturbed you."

"Yes, well, no harm done." He turned away from her to wash his already clean hands in a washbowl. "Send Mr. Gordy in, will you?"

"Yes." She turned away from him.

"And Julia."

She turned back. For a moment she thought he would attempt to soften his words.

Simeon held his hands over the bowl, dripping water. "Tonight. Nine on the strike, in the great hall. Please don't keep my guests waiting."

She turned away, feeling sick in the pit of her stomach. "Yes, my lord."

It was nearly three in the morning when Julia finally turned in for the night. She shut the door to her apartment, leaned against it, and closed her eyes. Her feet ached, her eyes were scratchy, and she was tired to the bone. Tired of smiling. Tired of making pleasantries. Tired of pretending to all of Simeon's guests that she and St. Martin were the perfect couple.

"Saints in heaven, what am I going to do?" she whispered to the dark, tapestry-lined room. In the next room she could hear Lizzy's soft breathing as she slept.

Julia flipped one high-heeled shoe off her foot and then the other and watched them sail through the air. They each hit the floor with a satisfying clunk. Her hands found the pins of her too tight coiffure and she yanked them out one at a time. Her scalp tingled as she ran her fingers through her loose hair. If it weren't so late, she would call for hot water to soak her throbbing feet.

Julia's eyes flew open at the sound and vibration of a knock on the door she leaned against. Who could possibly be knocking at this time of morning? Had Simeon thought better of his behavior today and come to apologize? She thought not.

She turned around and pressed her palms to the paneled door. Maybe it was Mother. But she always just burst in without knocking. "Yes?"

"Julia?"

Griffin? It was Griffin? She felt a strange surge of excitement. "Griffin?"

She opened the door a crack and peered out. He stood in darkness, but for the glow of a candle at the far end of the hall near the staircase. He smelled of brandy wine, but she didn't think he was drunk. She opened the door a little farther.

"Yes, it's me."

She didn't say anything because she didn't know what to say.

"I . . . I'm sorry to come so late." He sounded nothing like the fop who had been bowling with a leather ball and empty brandy bottles in the gallery only an hour ago. His voice was rich, intimate, disturbing.

"It's all right." She opened the door farther and stepped into the opening, still holding the brass knob for support. "I'm sorry." She ran a hand over her hair that she knew stood out like a witches' mane. "I was getting ready to turn in. I know I look a fright."

He smiled in the darkness—an utterly charming smile—and

Julia felt that she was doing something wrong, something she should be ashamed of, though she wasn't certain what it might be.

"I think you look beguiling." He gazed at her with a far-off look. *"What is beautiful is good and who is good will also be beautiful."*

She felt her cheeks flush as she lowered her gaze to her stockinged feet peeking out from beneath her gown. "I don't know that one, not Shakespeare, though."

"A woman. Sappho."

Embarrassed, yet secretly pleased, she kept her gaze downcast.

He cleared his throat. "I, uh, I came because I have something for you."

He held a draped object, though she couldn't tell what it was in the darkness. "For me?" she whispered. "Now?"

He hesitated. "You're right. I shouldn't have come. It's late—"

"No, it's all right." She glanced down the hallway to be certain no one saw them, knowing she shouldn't let him in, yet feeling wicked in her desire to be alone with him here in the darkness. "Come in."

He slipped inside.

She stepped back to make room, and he closed the door behind him.

"Lizzy's asleep," Julia said softly as she walked to the door between the sitting room and the inner bedchamber and closed it. "I wouldn't want to wake her."

"When I saw this in a shop, I knew you would like it."

She watched as he unwrapped black fabric from the object on a table. Candlelight from a sconce cast his shadow on the wall behind him and made him appear even taller than he was.

She couldn't resist delight at the thought of a gift. She never received gifts except for Lizzy's half-eaten cookies or broken-stemmed flowers. Simeon's ugly gowns didn't count as gifts because they were not given in friendship, love, or even admiration. She wondered under which category this gift fell. "What is it?" She stepped forward to stand beside him and gaze down at a beautifully embossed leather case in his hands.

He unlatched the case and flipped it open.

"Oh," Julia whispered. It was a leather backgammon game with polished ivory and ebony playing pieces. Simple, but elegant.

"It's very old, the shopkeeper told me."

In fascination, she ran her finger along one of the dyed leather triangles of the board. The case had a slight scent of worn leather and time.

Julia glanced up at Griffin. "Thank you. It's beautiful." She was touched not just by his generosity in presenting her with an obviously expensive gift, but by his thoughtfulness.

"Now you don't have to borrow Simeon's. You have one of your own." He seemed as pleased with himself as she was with him.

Her gaze fell on the game board again. "I really do like it." Then she looked up at him. "But I don't suppose I should accept it."

"Why in Hades not?" Then he frowned. "Simeon. Well, just don't tell him. Surely he didn't take an inventory of your possessions when you entered Bassett Hall, and I would guess he's not been to your apartments since you arrived."

"No," she said softly.

"So it will be our secret." He reached out and brushed his hand over her elbow.

It was a simple gesture, utterly innocent, and yet it made Julia feel so good that she knew there was something wrong in it. Of course it was wrong. He was married. Simeon said he was a homosexual. He didn't belong in her apartments so late at night. "Thank you again," she whispered.

He turned toward the door.

"Where are you going?" This time she touched his arm. She didn't know what made her do it.

"To bed, madame. It's nearly dawn."

He spoke with a tinge of sarcasm. It was not her imagination. He really did act like two different people. The question was: why?

"You can't bring me such a beautiful backgammon board and then not offer to be beaten by me at least once."

He laughed and she smiled shyly.

"Just one?" she beckoned.

His hand on the doorknob, he turned back to her. "All right. Just one. But if you think I'm going to allow you to beat me, you're wrong."

She smiled. She liked this man, no matter what Simeon said. "I've a game table."

"Let me help you."

As they picked up the small, round table from near the fireplace and carried it to the center of the room, Griffin's hand brushed Julia's. The sensation was so intensely pleasurable that she almost pulled away.

I shouldn't be doing this, she thought as he offered her a chair. *I shouldn't be making this alliance. It's too dangerous. Nothing good can come of it, and so much bad.*

But even as the thought ran through her head, she was gazing up into his intense blue eyes. After the incident today with Simeon, it was a welcome relief to have someone to talk to who didn't seem to despise her. She needed Griffin's friendship tonight, and somehow he had known.

"Best two of three?" Griffin began to set up her new backgammon board. His hands moved adeptly, but his gaze remained locked with hers.

"Thank you for coming," she whispered.

Griffin made no response but to smile. None was necessary.

"You roll first." He took her hand in his and placed the dice in her palm.

She clasped the dice and rolled. She didn't know what journey she'd embarked on tonight, inviting this man into her bedchamber. But somehow she knew it would be as wonderful as it would be dangerous.

Chapter Five

Griffin stood in one of the two window alcoves of his third-story bedchamber and pushed back the heavy, blue velvet drape. He stared out, lost in thought as rain pitter-pattered on the bubbled glass panes. A loose shutter banged as it swung back and forth, partially obscuring his view of the deserted Aldersgate Street below each time it closed.

Griffin felt as restless this morning as the noisy shutter. He was to meet with the king for tennis at noon so he had much to accomplish before then, but he couldn't concentrate. Each time he picked up a slip of paper with names and dates and attempted to make sense of the muck, his thoughts wandered to a woman.

Wouldn't that shock Cousin Simeon, who thought him to be a homosexual? Griffin and a woman. He smiled to himself, but then his thoughts sobered. He suddenly felt older than his thirty-two years. God in heaven, how long had it been since a woman had occupied his mind as Julia did now? *Too long*.

Julia. Last night, alone in her bedchamber, it had seemed as if they were the only two people in the world. For a brief time, as they played backgammon and talked, there were no politics, no impending wedding. It was just the two of them, friends . . . but more than friends. He knew he shouldn't have gone to her apartments. But he was glad he had.

Now Griffin couldn't stop thinking about Julia's tumble of red tresses, or her brilliant blue eyes, or her laugh that made him giddy in the pit of his stomach. He chuckled aloud at the thought of a woman making him tremble.

"My lord?"

He glanced over his shoulder to see Jabar study him expectantly as he laid out Griffin's wardrobe for the day.

Griffin waved his hand. "Nothing, old friend. Just a silly notion."

The shutter banged.

Jabar nodded with understanding and returned to the task of smoothing Griffin's red and yellow satin coat on the bed.

Jabar and Griffin had been together more than ten years, since they'd met during Griffin's service in the Holy Land. The man sometimes understood Griffin better than he understood himself.

"The woman," Jabar intoned.

Caught. "What woman?" Griffin left the window, relieved to be in the privacy of his room where the falsetto voice and calf-aching tiptoed walk was unnecessary. He tugged absently on the tie of his silk floral dressing gown and stretched.

"The red-haired one with the eyes of jewels." Jabar shook his turbaned head in disapproval. "You should not. She is your cousin's betrothed. Taboo."

Griffin wandered to his desk scattered with papers. Like his chambers, it was in messy disarray. Discovering a sheet under his bare foot, he picked it up and tossed it. It floated in the air for a moment and then drifted onto the writing desk.

"He should never have brought her here," Griffin said. "He no more wants a wife than Charlie, there." He pointed to the black golden-eyed cat curled in a tight ball on his rumpled bed linens.

"Not your trouble." Jabar crossed the room and pulled a pair of yellow clocked stockings from a trunk.

Griffin shook his head.

Jabar displayed a pair of pink ones.

Griffin nodded. "It is not my concern that my cousin should take an innocent woman to his bed whom he does not want? My cousin, a man who is not worth the ground she trods upon?"

"Master cannot solve all problems, only problems given to him by Allah."

Griffin gritted his teeth. He hated it when Jabar called him Master, but in ten years he'd not been able to break him of it. It had been hopeless since Griffin had freed him from that dark pit in the ground so many years before.

Griffin crossed his arms over his chest. "And how do you know that *Allah* has not made Julia my problem?" As a man once in exile, Griffin had long ago learned that God was still God, by any name.

Jabar cut his dark gaze to Griffin as he placed the pink stockings on the bed and added a pair of ribboned green garters. "It has been many years since master has had a woman. I should get you one, yes?"

He frowned. "No. What do I need a woman for?" He indicated the piles of papers that overflowed from his desk to the floor. "Don't you think I've enough to deal with without a woman tied around my neck?"

Jabar nodded. "You are right, Master. You do not need a woman, and this is why you will not interfere with St. Martin's woman, pretty as a morning bird or not."

Griffin knew Jabar was ready to help him dress, but he didn't shed his dressing gown. He would be embarrassed for his friend to know how greatly Julia affected him. Griffin turned away from Jabar to pace.

It felt odd, and yet at the same time a relief to be physically aroused by the mere thought of a woman. It had been so long since Griffin had held a naked woman in his arms that he had almost forgotten its pleasures. It wasn't anything so dramatic as being rejected by love, but that he'd been so occupied these last years. Too occupied finding women for others that he didn't have time to find them for himself.

Griffin chuckled at the irony of it.

Jabar lifted one eyebrow. "You are vexed today, Master, I will pray for your mind's healing."

With another chuckle, Griffin dropped his dressing gown on the floor and walked to the bed. "All right, Jabar. What have we here today?" He blinked theatrically as if nearly blinded. "Uds lud!" He spoke in his pseudo-persona. "There'll be no need for an introduction at Whitehall today, will there? The king will see me before I reach Charing Cross!"

Jabar laughed and Griffin laughed with him, thoughts of Julia set aside, at least for the moment.

Julia raised her quilted yellow and green petticoat and climbed the ladder to reach the book above her head. "Ah, hah. There you are," she said aloud to Simeon's empty library. He was gone elsewhere today, *business,* she was told. "I knew there had to be a book on gardens somewhere." She perched on the top of the rolling ladder and opened the heavy leather cover. "Now let's see . . ."

"Always talk to yourself?"

Startled, Julia glanced down to see Griffin just inside the doorway.

"Oh, you gave me a fright." She pressed her hand to her pounding heart. "I didn't hear you come in."

He was wearing a large, curly wig of the most ghastly red that clashed unbearably with his red and yellow coat and pink stockings.

"I'm sorry. Didn't mean to startle you." He leaned against

the doorjamb. Alone like this, like last night when they'd played backgammon, he didn't seem effeminate, nor particularly theatrical if one could ignore the wig. She wanted to ask him about the differences in his manner, but she wasn't sure how to broach the subject.

Last night he had been so warm, so friendly, and yet utterly masculine in a way Julia couldn't have explained if she tried. Never overstepping the bounds of good taste, he had made her feel beautiful, even sexually attractive. Last night thoughts had crossed her mind that even now made her blush. For the first time in her life, she felt a sexual awakening. Suddenly she was not only aware of her own body and its reactions, but another's body. Of Griffin's.

She avoided his gaze, embarrassed by the wantonness of her musing. Her mother was right; it was time she married. "I . . . I was looking for a book on gardens, on hothouses. I'd like to order some plants to replace those that have died off. I'm not certain what to plant other than lilies in the pond." She indicated the large tome she carried. "I thought maybe this would help."

"I'm glad you've decided to try your hand in the orangery. It will fill your days. It's difficult to come to a new place and find your way."

She rolled her eyes. "Especially this place. It's so different from home. Different from what I expected. I'm a little lonely," she confessed softly. She hadn't seen Simeon alone again since the morning he'd had his coat fitted.

"Ah . . . my cousin. I wouldn't think him to be particularly attentive."

She lowered her gaze to the book. She knew that servants listened in doorways. Simeon's secretary could be anywhere . . . listening. "He's a busy man. I understand."

Griffin glanced out the door, then back at her. "No need to say more. I don't know why you came here to begin with, why your mother would allow—"

"My mother?" She gave a sniff of derision.

He glanced down the hallway again, then back at her. "You could call off the wedding," he said quietly. "It's not too late."

She licked her dry lips. The idea had been tumbling in her head for days, since Simeon had been so abrupt with her in his apartments. But if she didn't marry St. Martin, who *would* she marry? Her family's welfare was dependent upon her making a good match. Lizzy's well-being was dependent on Julia's ability to care for her.

"My father wanted me to marry St. Martin," was all she could say.

"And you? You, Julia?" he whispered with conviction. "Do *you* wish to wed him?"

Julia grabbed the book, turned on the ladder, her layered petticoats swishing as she climbed down. "This isn't an appropriate conversation, sir."

He was silent for a moment. "I'm sorry," he said finally. "I just hate to see a woman . . . you . . . unhappy."

"Oh, I'm not unhappy." Of course she was unhappy. Desperately unhappy. More so since Griffin had befriended her. She glanced up at him, wondering if she would be feeling this way right now if it had been Baron Archer her father had betrothed her to, instead of St. Martin. Even with his ridiculous costumes and silly behavior, he was more a man than Simeon. "I'm certain Simeon will make a fine husband. I only need a little time to adjust."

After a long pause, he nodded. "You're right, of course. It makes no difference. Might as well be St. Martin as the next man. You know what Virgil said: 'A woman is always fickle, an unstable thing'." Then he smiled that silly grin of his. His moment of seriousness passed and he was once again the fop. "Well, good day to you." He swept off his hat and bowed.

"Good day," she whispered to the empty room as she clutched the book to her chest. Tears stung the back of her eyelids. Griffin utterly confused her. He had been so friendly when he'd come to her room and brought the backgammon board. Now, here, he had first said she didn't have to marry St. Martin, and then said she might as well. He just didn't make any sense.

But she was beginning to suspect that there were a lot of things about the Baron that didn't quite make sense.

"You have to at least make an attempt to be civil to him!" Susanne followed Julia down the flagstone path, deeper into the orangery, batting at overgrown bushes as she trotted.

Lizzy trailed silently behind her mother.

Julia kept walking, a heavy wooden crate of plants in her arms. "I am civil." She dropped the crate of plants beside an empty fish pond. "I'm just not particularly nice."

"Well! You're certainly nice enough to that fop, Baron Archer," her mother sniffed.

"Please lower your voice, Mother." Julia sat on the edge of the stone pond and reached for one of the plants. "I'm nice to Griffin because he's nice to me. He's the only one who has shown me any kindness in this dreary house in a fortnight."

Her mother plopped her ample frame on the edge of the pond wall. "But *he's* not willing to marry you, is he?"

Julia glanced up at her mother, then back at the task at hand. She dug deep into the soil with an old trowel she had found abandoned in a gardener's shed. This was it. This was her chance to tell her mother what she thought. "It's just not going to work, Mother," she said firmly. The memory of Griffin's words gave her the courage to continue. "We can call the betrothal off now. It's not too late."

"Impossible."

"Simeon doesn't want me to run his household. He doesn't want my company. He doesn't want a wife."

"He wants what all men want, a healthy breeder."

Julia stabbed the rich soil with her trowel. "Exactly, which is why this isn't going to work. I don't think I can bed a man who can't speak to me except for show in public.''

Her mother threw up her hands. ''Another ridiculous notion from my ridiculous, ungrateful daughter. Oh, why, oh why, sweet Jesus, wasn't I blessed with sons?'' She stared up through the glass-paned roof of the hothouse as if expecting God himself to respond.

Julia pushed a water lily into the hole she'd dug and moved forward to plant another. ''Please, just talk to the earl for me.'' She tried a diplomatic angle. ''Perhaps he feels the same way and is too much a gentleman to say so. Perhaps he could find me a more suitable match. After all, he is our male guardian and that would be his responsibility, if he wasn't marrying me himself.''

''I certainly will not speak to him.'' She crossed her arms over her bosom. She was dressed in an unbecoming pink satin gown with white insets, a gown charged to one of the Earl of St. Martin's accounts, no doubt. ''Your father signed that betrothal agreement, and as long as his lordship is willing to take you off my weary hands, marry him you will.''

''Fine. Then I'll speak to him myself.''

Her mother leaped up. ''You will do no such thing! A woman's place is in duty to her family, first her father's family, then her husband's!''

Lizzy turned from the azalea bush she was examining. ''Mama, the servants will hear you!''

Susanne lowered her voice and shook her finger at Julia. ''You will not speak to his lordship about breaking off the engagement. You have an obligation to your family, to your poor sister. As the wife of an earl you will have great influence and an even greater purse. How else do you think you will be able to care for your sister when I'm gone?''

''Don't holler at Julia.'' Lizzy crossed her arms over her chest. ''She doesn't have to marry that stinky old man if she doesn't want to. I can take care of myself.'' She thrust out her lower lip. ''I know you don't think I can, but I can.''

Julia glanced up at her beautiful sister and her heart felt as if it was being wrenched from her chest. What was she going to do? Her mother was right. She did have an obligation to her sister. Lizzy had been her responsibility since she'd been born . . . and she always would be.

Julia's father had made an advantageous match for her with the Earl of St. Martin. Why couldn't she be satisfied with costly gowns and a great tomb of a house on a fine street in London? What on earth had ever given her the ridiculous idea that she might find affection—perhaps even love—in her marriage? Marriage was to build family and political alliances and produce heirs, nothing more, nothing less.

Lizzy sat down beside Julia and grasped her bare arm where Julia had pushed up her ivory linen sleeves. It wasn't one of the earl's gowns she wore, but a patched one brought from home.

''Don't be upset. Mother doesn't mean the things she says,'' Lizzy comforted. ''You and me, we never listen to her,'' she whispered, though not softly enough for their mother not to hear. ''You don't have to marry the earl for me, I vow you don't. I don't need you to take care of me. I can find my own husband.''

Julia smiled tenderly at her sister and her foolish dreams. Of course Lizzy could never have a husband of her own. What man would want a wife with the mind of a ten-year-old? How could Lizzy ever possibly care for a child?

Julia laid her hand on Lizzy's. She didn't want to upset her sister, or even her mother. She wanted to be dutiful. She wanted to stand up to her responsibilities. If only her responsibilities didn't mean marrying that garlic-smelling, pompous—She cut her thoughts short. ''It's all right, Lizzy. Don't get yourself stewed. Everything will work out fine.''

''It's just wedding fidgets,'' Susanne piped in. ''You'll see that once you're wed, you'll settle in nicely as Lady St. Martin, mistress of Bassett Hall.''

Julia glanced away. She knew her mother thought this was the end of the discussion. For now she would allow her to believe so, but Julia fully intended to speak with the earl on the matter. She would at least try to find out how strongly he felt on the subject. Maybe she could convince him to reject her. The only trick would be to actually gain an audience with her betrothed. It seemed that unless she burst in on him as she had done last week, it would be easier to have an audience with the king than with the Earl of St. Martin.

"Your Majesty." Griffin fluttered a handkerchief as he bowed and went down on one knee. Even after all these years together, he still felt a certain awe in the fact that His Majesty would welcome him so generously into his private life.

King Charles II glanced up from a table where he drank from a cup of ale. "Christ's bones, get up, Griffin. And dispense with the tiptoed nonsense."

Griffin rose and glanced meaningfully at the two servants in attendance.

"Go. Go." Charles waved a hand. "Out of here, both of you. No one may enter my closet until I bid him do so. Any man who enters or is discovered listening at my keyhole will find his head on a stake on tower gates, understood?"

"Yes, Your Majesty." The first liveried servant backed out of the room with the other right behind him. "Yes, Your Majesty. Your servant, Your Majesty."

Charles kicked a stool with the toe of his boot as the door to the private room off his bedchamber closed. He was dressed for tennis this morning in a new black suit, looking remarkably young and handsome without his wig. "No formalities. Sit." He waved his hand before his nose. "God rot your bowels, Griffin. What is that stench? Surely that's not you?"

Griffin chuckled good-naturedly. "A scent newly come from France. It's called *Eu d'floral Romance*. My dressmaker says it will be all the mode."

Charles rolled his dark eyes good-naturedly. "You and your fashion. I've a mind to take that dressmaker for myself before Buckingham bribes him to come into his service."

"I'm certain Monsieur D'Arcy would be honored to serve you, Your Grace." He bowed his head.

Charles groaned. "Please spare me the nonsense, at least in private, Griffin. Here, alone, let it be you and me like the old days in France, when we could walk drunk down a street and clobber a nightwatchman for amusement. I swear, I'm thankful to be home, though it's not as I expected. Nothing and no one is as I expected." He swished the ale in his cup and watched it splash up the sides. "Everyone treats me differently. I no longer know who I can trust and who I cannot."

Griffin lifted his gaze to meet his king's. "You can trust me," he said with utter sincerity.

Charles thought for a moment and then nodded his strong chin. "Aye, that I believe. Now come." He poured a cup of ale for Griffin. "Tell me what you know and let us get to the tennis court while the sun still shines. I fear we're in for a cold, rainy winter. I had forgotten how damned wet London can be."

Griffin pulled a roll of papers from inside his coat and slid his stool closer to his monarch. He couldn't take the chance that anyone might be listening in on the conversation. It could mean the king's life, and surely his own.

Chapter Six

"Ah, there you are." The Earl of St. Martin plastered an unconvincing smile on his face as he beckoned Julia.

"My lord." She dipped as low a curtsy as she dared without needing assistance to rise. She had spent too long in the orangery planting lilies in the fishpond and, for the second time that week, was nearly an hour late to Simeon's dinner party. This was definitely not the way to begin the evening if she intended to discuss the possibility of breaking off their betrothal.

"I feared you were ill when you didn't come down, my darling." Simeon placed a possessive hand on her shoulder and applied pressure with his fingers until it hurt.

Julia could have pulled away, or asked him to remove his hand from her shoulder, but she gritted her teeth and bore the pain instead. She had already embarrassed him in front of his guests by arriving late. She feared that if she challenged him now, he might become furious. Her father had been that kind of man, so she had experience with their ways.

"I apologize profusely, sir." She lowered her head in subservience. "I lost track of the time."

"Let's see that it does not happen again, shall we?" He did not look at her as he spoke between gritted teeth, but toward the gentleman who waited for an introduction.

"Yes, Simeon."

"Lord Boggs, allow me to introduce you to my betrothed, Lady Julia." He spoke in his host's voice, with none of the venom he had displayed only seconds ago. He was an excellent actor. "Julia, Lord Boggs is one of our esteemed members of Parliament."

"My lord." She curtsied, wondering if Lord Boggs detected the sarcasm in which Simeon spoke the word *esteemed*. Julia was quickly learning that though her betrothed was all smiles and proper etiquette, he could be vicious.

"Ah, Lady Julia, you are as beautiful as the gossips say." The round, fiftyish Lord Boggs, with his big belly and a speck of food on his chin, bowed and took her hand. "Everyone in Londontown is dying to receive an invitation to dine with St. Martin, simply to have a look at you."

She smiled, relieved that Simeon had removed his hand from her shoulder. "Why, you flatter me unduly, sir."

Lord Boggs launched into a discourse on the changes in Parliament, absolving Julia of the need to do anything but nod her head and smile. That was all she was required to do at any of Simeon's endless receptions, teas, and dinner parties. In fact, he had instructed her last week that he preferred that she didn't speak any more than necessary. He had explained matter-of-factly that he was the law in their household, and what she thought was of little consequence to anyone.

As Julia moved on to another clump of guests and made small talk with one lord or lady after another, her gaze drifted from one group of laughing ladies and gentlemen to the next, searching for Griffin. A few moments with him had quickly become the highlight of any day for her here in Bassett Hall.

Surely Griffin was here. Simeon had said the previous night at supper that his cousin never missed a chance to overindulge in drink and gambling.

Julia spotted him near the marble fireplace at the far side of the great hall, laughing uproariously as if he were inebriated. He held a woman's painted fan and fluttered it to emphasize each word he spoke.

Julia knew it would be forward of her to seek him out, but she was so excited about the progress she'd made in the orangery that she wanted to tell him. Two nights ago at dinner she had attempted to tell her betrothed about her accomplishments, but he'd simply waved a hand, told her to amuse herself as she saw fit, and ended their conversation by calling for another slice of eel pie.

As Julia nodded and pretended to listen to some baron and baroness's story of a flooded dining hall, she caught Griffin's attention over the baron's shoulder.

Griffin winked and batted his fan. She smiled. Then he motioned with the fan toward the gaming room off the great hall, where gaming tables were always set for guests. Later in the evening everyone would retire there for cards, dice, and more drink, as was the custom at court. This early in the evening, however, the room was still deserted.

Julia politely disengaged herself from the baron and baroness and nonchalantly made her way toward the gaming room. Deep in conversation with a man carrying a cane, Simeon watched her pass, but did not return her smile.

She'd inadvertently angered him again and knew that for the next day or so he would treat her coolly. She was beginning to realize that he operated in just such a cycle as her father had. As long as she did exactly what he asked, exactly *as* he asked, Simeon could be charming, almost pleasant company. The moment she crossed him, though, even in a matter as minor as the dessert to be served at his supper table, he became cross and cold.

So, she thought dismally, tonight would not be a good time to speak to his lordship on the matter of their betrothal.

Julia slipped out of the hall and into the gaming room. The door closed behind her. The unoccupied room was dimly lit with only a few candles, and it took a moment for her eyes to adjust. "Griffin?"

"Julia?" he whispered, a touch of humor in his rich baritone voice. There was no sound of drunkenness in his tone now.

The sound of his voice calling her name made her light-headed, as if she'd had too much wine, though she knew she hadn't. Maybe it was her empty stomach and not Griffin that made her feel this way.

She felt awkward as his gaze met hers, but even in that awkwardness she was thankful to have someone smile at her. "Pretty fan," she teased and pointed.

He glanced at the woman's fan in his hand and set it down with a chuckle. She liked a man who didn't take himself too seriously.

"One must amuse himself somehow among such bores, mustn't he?"

She laughed with him.

"Are you having an enjoyable evening?"

She glanced away. "Y . . . no." She shook her head. "I'm not one for parties. I never know what to say. Simeon says to just stand there and look pretty . . . like one of his blessed hounds, I suppose." She glanced up at Griffin, wondering if he would take offense. She hadn't meant to make a derogatory remark about Simeon, it just came out that way.

"I understand what you mean." He plucked a triangular fruit pastry, frosted with sugar, from a tray that had been set out by one of the servants. "So . . ." he said.

She wondered if he would ask why she'd caught his eye in the other room. She didn't know what she would say. She didn't want him to think her forward, or that she was pursuing him.

"So, what progress do you make in the orangery?" He reached for another tart. "Want one? They're quite good. Not too sweet."

"Oh," she breathed with relief. "It's going wonderfully." It felt so good to be away from Simeon's party's bright lights and boring guests. "I've already cleaned out the big pond in the back, and planted lilies in it. Tomorrow I'll begin piping in water."

"Thought anymore about your upcoming wedding?"

He switched the subject so quickly that it took her a moment to gather her thoughts.

She nodded, lowering her gaze to the toes of her slippers. "I . . . I intend to speak with Simeon . . . to see if this is truly what we both want."

"I see. Here, taste." He lifted the tart to her lips and it seemed natural to take it from his hand.

As she accepted the sweet, his fingertip brushed her lower lip.

"I . . ." Julia's voice trailed off, leaving her sentence to hang in the warm, dark air. His touch made her lose her train of thought. His gesture had been utterly innocent and yet it seemed so . . . so sensual.

She couldn't keep her eyes off him as he licked the cherry sauce from his fingertips. She barely tasted the tart melting in her mouth as she watched him, mesmerized by the way his tongue touched his fingertips again and again.

Julia didn't know what ailed her. Her betrothed was entertaining in the other room, and she was here in the darkness accepting tidbits into her mouth from the hand of another man. There seemed to be a certain strange energy in the air that crackled between them.

Griffin's gaze met hers, and he seemed to feel the same energy, perhaps even the same undeniable attraction she felt.

"Julia," he whispered.

He stood so close that all she had to do was lift her hand

and it found the smoothness of his silk doublet. This was mad. She felt wildly out of control, and utterly drawn to this man. "Griffin," she whispered miserably.

"Ah, Julia. I can't stop thinking about you." His blue-eyed gaze searched her face as she looked up at him. He caught a lock of red hair that had escaped her elaborate coiffure and rolled it between his fingers.

"I . . . I know. I—" She couldn't say what she was thinking. She was ashamed of herself and her newly born wantonness. She couldn't confess that last night in bed she did not fantasize of lying beside her husband, but—God save her soul—of lying beside Griffin. She knew it didn't make any sense. Simeon was her betrothed. Even if he wasn't a homosexual, Griffin was married. There could never be anything between them but a few games of backgammon and a little shared laughter, and yet as she gazed into his eyes, none of that seemed to matter.

He leaned closer, his face close to hers. "This is dangerous, Julia. We shouldn't—And yet if I don't . . . just once . . ." He brushed her chin with his fingertips.

All she could do was nod. His mouth was so close to hers. *Just once,* she repeated his words to herself, knowing what he was about to do. *Just once.*

Julia had never been kissed by a man, but for the dry cheek-kisses of relatives. She didn't know what she expected, but this wasn't it.

As his mouth touched hers, her knees immediately weakened. His mouth was so warm, so insistent, so welcoming . . .

Julia groaned. She could see herself burning in hell for this sin. She could imagine Simeon's fury, and yet she couldn't help herself. If she didn't brush her lips against this man's . . . if her tongue didn't touch the tip of his, she would surely perish, here and now.

"Oh, God, save us both," Griffin whispered against her lips. He pulled her hard against him and delved his tongue deep into her mouth.

Julia was breathless and dizzy. He tasted so good, so manly. She could still detect the faint scent of cherry on his breath. She opened her mouth wider; waves of sensation hit her and took her unaware. Their kiss was so . . . so primal.

Giddy and confused, she pulled away and touched her tingling mouth with her fingertips. "I . . . we can't do this," she whispered.

He ran a hand over his face, looking as disturbed as she felt. "I'm sorry, Julia," he whispered. "I shouldn't have— You're right, we mustn't—" He groaned. "If Simeon knew— It's absolutely vital that I keep up this damned farce . . ."

Farce? What farce? But Julia knew this wasn't the time nor the place to ask him. Someone could walk in at any moment. "It's all right," she whispered. "No one will ever know. It was my fault. I threw—"

"No." He brushed his hand against her sleeve, then pulled back as if he wanted desperately to touch her, yet couldn't allow himself. "It wasn't your fault. It was mine. I knew you were vulnerable and I took advantage. I—"

The door clicked and Griffin spun around. "God's bowels," Griffin uttered loudly. "I do believe the earl has outdone himself this night. Would you care to sample one of the desserts, Lady Julia?"

"There you are, Lord Archer."

Mr. Gordy entered, looking as handsome and as dangerous as ever.

Gordy's gaze moved suspiciously from Griffin to Julia and back to Griffin again. "His lordship requests your presence, my lord. It seems there is a wager to be settled."

"Oh, well!" Griffin spun on his high-heeled shoes and whipped up his fan. As he strutted away on his tiptoes, he fluttered the fan. "Excuse me, Lady Julia, but St. Martin calls."

"I'll see to the refreshments and then be in directly," she lied, trying to cover herself as Griffin had.

Griffin sailed past Gordy. The two men walked into the

hall and closed the door behind them, leaving her in merciful solitude.

Julia gripped the edge of the sideboard to steady herself. She couldn't do this, she thought wildly. She couldn't marry St. Martin. God help her, but she thought she might be in love with his cousin.

Lizzy sat on the edge of the back stair to the kitchen and laughed. "That's the silliest thing I believe I've ever heard, Amos." She reached for another piece of apple tart from the earthenware bowl he held, and popped it into her mouth.

Lizzy liked the kitchen. She liked how warm it was and how good it smelled. And everyone was so nice here. The cooks and servants didn't scowl at her, order her around, or send her to her room. They gave her scraps of sweetmeats and shared their warm buttermilk with her. Amos was especially nice to her. She liked Amos.

" 'Tis the God's honest truth, it is. A dancing bear. I seen it myself in Cheapside market."

She giggled behind her fingers. "And who danced with this bear? You?"

Amos sat down on the step beside her and she slid over to make room for him. She liked it when he sat next to her and their arms touched. Amos was warm and he smelled good, like the kitchen. He was a cook and he made the best apple tarts in all of Christendom—at least that's what he told her.

"No, I didn't dance with the bear. It weren't that kind of dancin'. He stood up and went like this." Amos jumped up from the stairwell and did an awkward jig, his arms in the air like bear paws.

Lizzy burst into another fit of giggles. She knew she ought to get back to the party. Her sister or mother would be looking for her. But Lizzy hated the earl's parties. She hated the earl. He smelled like garlic and he was mean to her sister. He made

Julia cry at night. She didn't say that was why she was crying, but Lizzy knew.

"I think I should like to see that bear," Lizzy told Amos. "Do you think you could take me?"

Amos sat beside her again in his white apron that was powdered with flour. "Don't know about that one, Lizzy. The earl wouldn't like it. Servants aren't supposed to take the ladies of the house places."

"But I'm not the lady of the house." She looked up at Amos. "I'm just the lady's sister. No rules against that, is there? Nobody told me that rule."

Amos laughed. "Ah, Lizzy." Then he touched her cheek with his floury hand.

Lizzy smiled. Amos's hand felt good against her face. "Please? I won't tell, I swear I won't. We could sneak out and sneak right back in. I've never seen London."

Amos grimaced.

She grabbed his hand. "Please, Amos?"

"Aye, all right," he finally said. "Come one of these days, I'll take ye. But if we get caught, ye got to swear it was my idea. I made ye come."

"Oh, goody. I can't wait to go!" She bounced up and brushed the crumbs from her gown. "Guess I got to go back to the dumb party. See you later, Amos." She kissed his cheek. She didn't know why she did it, but she could tell by the look on his face that he liked it.

"Bye, Lizzy," he called after her.

She skipped back down the hall, past Mr. Gordy, toward the sound of music.

Chapter Seven

Griffin sat at a trestle table in a private dining room above a well-known tavern in Bath, and drank deeply from his mug of ale. "How could I have been so stupid?" he lamented.

"I do not know how you could have been so stupid, Master." Jabar stood at the upstairs window and watched the road.

Griffin took another pull from his mug of ale. "One minute I was eating a damned tart," he said miserably, "and the next minute I was kissing her. She was kissing me back. God's teeth, what was I thinking?"

"You were not thinking, Master."

"She's practically Simeon's wife."

"You are married," Jabar added.

"I'm not supposed to be attracted to women! I'm supposed to be this damned fricatrice! *She's* supposed to think I'm a fricatrice!"

"This man tried to warn you that the woman with jeweled eyes was taboo."

"Jabar! Friend." Griffin extended his palm. "You're not helping me."

"I am sorry, Master." He turned back to the window.

Griffin drained his mug. "And what about Julia? What must she think of me now? I kissed her as if I meant it. Hell, I did mean it, and then I traipsed out on my tiptoes fluttering a lady's fan!"

Griffin reached for the pitcher of ale, only to find that he'd already emptied it. He slammed it down hard on the table. "She can't marry him. He doesn't love her, though how the hell a man couldn't love that face, that voice, that smile . . ."

"It is not your place to say who St. Martin will and will not marry. It is your place to watch him."

"I know. I know. I was up all night wrestling with the logic of it." Griffin rose and pushed the chair so hard that it tumbled over with a crash. He righted it irritably and began to pace. "I said something that suggested I wasn't who I appeared to be. I should have kept my damned mouth shut, but for some reason I wanted her to know." He swung his fist. "Hell . . . I shouldn't have just left. I should have tried to talk to her."

"It was important that you be here today, Master."

"I know, but she deserved an explanation."

"Perhaps it is better this way."

"Better how? For whom?"

"Better that Lady Julia not know who you are, what you are. Better that she marry the man her family has bid her to marry. Better because she would be in danger if she knew the truth."

"And she won't be in danger if she marries that bastard? He'll have her dead of childbed in ten years!" Griffin reached the far wall, turned on his heels, and paced in the other direction. He took a deep breath. "You're right. I know you're right and yet—" He clenched his fist in frustration.

"Master!" Jabar stepped quickly away from the window. "The coach comes."

An immediate calm washed over Griffin. He was far more comfortable with matters of politics than matters of the heart—even dangerous politics. "All right. Go to our room and stay until my business here is complete."

"Yes, my master. You have but to call, and I will be at your side with my broadsword drawn." Jabar nodded regally and slipped out the door, leaving Griffin to prepare for the visitor.

Julia stood in the earl's new gallery and listened to the sound of pounding hammers, vibrating saws, and the scrape of mortar trowels. Sunlight poured through the monstrous windows that ran the length of the new gallery and overlooked the bare winter garden.

Simeon stood at the far end of the gallery speaking to the foreman.

She intended to waylay him, before he made his escape to his office that Gordy protected as if it were Newgate Prison.

She leaned against a window frame and stared out at the swaying skeletal trees, feeling as bare and exposed as the limbs. October was well upon them and winter was settling in, which meant that November would be here before she knew it. She and Simeon were to be wed mid-November.

She gripped the windowsill tightly. The more she thought about her impending marriage, the more she became convinced that she couldn't marry the Earl of St. Martin.

Julia brushed her lips with her fingertips as she remembered Griffin's kiss. A heat rose in her cheeks. She'd not seen him today. The ever-lurking Mr. Gordy had informed her that he had ridden out early this morning and was not due back until the week's end. Julia did not ask where he'd gone because Gordy seemed suspicious of her questions, and he did not offer the information.

Julia was so confused. What was wrong with her? Simeon was a good match, better than good. Most young women in her situation would give anything to be engaged to such a man. Who would want the Baron Archer, a married man with no income, a heavy drinker, and a gambler with a supposed attraction to men? A woman was bound straight to hell for such affinities. It was ridiculous that she should feel drawn to Griffin . . . and yet she was. Uncontrollably. What was wrong with her that she would be attracted to such a man? Was she as perverse as he?

But something was not right with Griffin and his effeminate behavior. It was too calculated, too controlled, and, she suspected, false. The man who had kissed her was not the same man who fluttered a lady's fan and wobbled tiptoed on pink shoes.

And what had he meant about a farce? Hadn't he almost come out and said that he was not who he appeared to be?

Julia walked along the windows of the gallery, her stride determined. Once she convinced Simeon that they should break their betrothal agreement, she had no idea where she and her sister and mother would go. Their home and what was left of the lands in Dover had already been sold by Simeon. Julia didn't know how she would care for her family, or even where they would sleep. They had no relatives other than Simeon, but she would deal with that problem when she met it.

Perhaps St. Martin would be kind enough to offer his home until they could find lodging elsewhere. There was certainly plenty of room in this house. It would all work out, she knew it would. As long as she and Lizzy were together, that was all that mattered.

Julia heard Simeon's footfall behind her and turned to face him. "My lord, if I could have a moment of your time?"

He was dressed for travel in a gray velvet doublet and black breeches, a black full-length wool cloak thrown over his shoulders. The cavalier's hat he carried in his hand was plumed with a gray ostrich feather. "I've an engagement at Whitehall, madame. Can it not wait until supper? I've only a few guests coming." He passed her.

Julia ran to catch up. "Actually, sir . . . Simeon, it cannot wait."

He halted to slip his hands into dove gray gloves. "All right, woman, walk with me." He gestured with his hat. "You can go with me as far as the stables."

"Thank you, sir." She walked fast to keep up with him. She knew Simeon well enough to understand his subtle ways. The man or woman who walked behind him was always considered by his lordship to be beneath him. Simeon liked his friends, and his betrothed, beneath him.

"My lord, I've thought long and hard on this matter, and I fear you and I are not suitably matched."

"Matched?" They turned at the end of the gallery into a corridor.

Julia knew this might be her only chance to escape impending disaster. She didn't have any time to waste with subtleties. She knew she couldn't marry Simeon because she had enjoyed Griffin's kiss too much, because the memory of it burned on her lips as she spoke. She yearned too greatly for another. "We are not suited for marriage."

He glanced at her sideways. "Not suited?"

"Our personalities, my lord. I fear that if we were to unite in marriage, it would not be a happy one. For either of us," she added quickly.

He walked down the stairs, his boots pounding on the freshly scrubbed treads. "Happy? Gads, woman, you are an innocent. What does happiness have to do with marriage? I'm in need of a wife, and you, *cousin,* are in need of a roof over your head and food in your mouth."

He was practically calling her a beggar. She wanted to slap him. "I think you could find a woman better suited to your needs. I'm not good at entertaining, and I'm not good at lying about all day drinking chocolate and ordering new gowns."

He pushed open the door at the bottom of the steps and a cold gush of wind whipped through, chilling Julia to the bone. She'd not thought they'd be going outside and hadn't brought a cloak.

He halted in the open doorway, but made no offer of his cloak. "Are you saying you do not wish to marry me?"

She took a deep breath, hugging herself for warmth. "It's not that I don't appreciate your generosity or . . . or the kindness you have shown my family, but . . . yes." She met his cold gaze. "Yes, I'm saying I'd like to break the betrothal agreement."

"No." He let go of the door and the wind caught it so fast that she had to throw her arms up to keep from being hit.

"No?" She shoved the door open far enough to slip out. "No, my lord?" Again, she had to run to catch him. It was so cold outside that her teeth chattered.

"No." He tossed his wool cloak over his shoulders. "I will not release you from the agreement."

"Why not?" She followed him down the flagstone path that led from the rear of the house through a small, stark garden to the stables. "I've said I don't wish to marry you. Surely you'd not want a wife who—"

"No." He repeated firmly. "You are mine."

"Yours?"

He hit his heel on the door of the stable. "Are you addlepated? Mine. Yes, *mine,*" he blustered. "I signed the agreement. I took you and your fat mother and your idiot sister into my house, and now I will have you as my wife!"

Tears stung the backs of her eyelids, but she refused to let them spill. She'd not give Simeon the satisfaction of seeing her as a sniveling, weak female. "You cannot make me marry you."

He lifted the latch on the door. This time he did not raise his voice, which made him seem even more menacing. "Julia, do not cross me."

"I will not have you," she said fiercely between her gritted teeth.

"Oh, you will have me."

She was met with a rush of warm air that smelled of groomed horses and sweet hay.

"I will not marry you and you cannot force me."

He spun on his boot heels. "That dim-witted sister of yours . . ." he whispered.

Julia's breath caught in her throat. Suddenly she wished she'd never started this conversation, never come to London. Never been born. "You—"

He snapped his fingers. "Gone."

Julia covered her mouth with her hand to suppress a cry of anguish. Not her Lizzy. "You couldn't send her away without my mother's approval."

"Wrong. I am her male protector." He stroked his chin with a gloved hand as if in serious thought. "Such vermin do not belong upon the street. She would be better off dead, don't you think?"

His meaning sank in slowly. "Sweet Jesus, you wouldn't—"

"Have you anything else you need to speak with me about, my dear?" He turned away from her and strode into the main hall of the stable.

Two grooms approached them.

"You really should go inside," Simeon told her. "You'll catch your death. I won't have a bride with a dribbling nose on my wedding night. Some believe illnesses are bred of snot, you know."

Julia opened her mouth to retort, for surely this was not the end of the conversation.

Simeon stopped dead. "What is that?" he exploded.

She looked to where he pointed. It was Sally, the dog, nestled in a corner of an unoccupied stall. She lay on her side in the straw; four black, wiggling puppies crawled over her.

"My lord?" The two stable boys came running.

"That!" St. Martin shouted.

One of the grooms peered over the edge of the stall's half wall. "Puppies, my lord. She just whelped them."

"They're black."

"A . . . aye."

"They should be spotted like her. Like the male."

The groom cringed. "We think she bred with that black mongrel that's been hangin' about, my lord."

"Stupid bitch hound." Simeon grabbed up a shovel that leaned on the wall. "The bloodlines are no good! She has sullied herself and her bloodlines. She has sullied me, the St. Martin name."

"Really, Simeon," Julia tried to interfere. "The dog doesn't know any better. She—"

It wasn't until Julia saw Simeon raise the shovel that she realized what he intended to do with it.

"No," she screamed as she grabbed the end of the handle.

But Simeon was too quick, too strong. By the time her fingers clasped the wood, he had already begun the downward motion.

She turned away just in time, pulling her hands away as if they'd been singed.

Julia heard the clunk of metal as it met the dog's skull. Sally yipped and then was silent.

Tears ran down Julia's cheeks, tears of rage, of frustration . . . of sudden, cold fear.

"Drown the pups," she heard Simeon say.

"But my lord," one of the grooms dared.

"Now!"

As Simeon passed Julia, he threw down the shovel. A spot of wet, crimson blood stained the back of the blade. "Let this be a warning, madame." He gestured toward the slain dog. "That which is mine does not betray me without suffering the consequences."

He strode away. "My horse! Where the blast is the horse I called for?"

Julia waited until Simeon was a safe distance from her, and then fled in the opposite direction.

"I can't believe she just ran away," Lizzy chattered as she prepared tea for herself and Julia. Their mother had gone visiting, her absence a relief. "Amos says she just up and took off. Maybe went to live with her man dog." She poured thick cream into her cup, then added the tea. "You think that's what happened?" Lizzy giggled. "Amos says maybe they ran away to the American Colonies, 'cause the babes were out of wedlock. Amos says he's going to get me a new pup soon as he saves enough money. Someday he's going to be the head cook, and then he's going to have lots of money to buy puppies."

Julia let Lizzy chatter because it was easier than having to carry on a conversation. She was so thankful for Amos's help. After Simeon had killed the dog, Julia had gone straight to the cook. He hadn't seemed surprised by his master's cruelty, which Julia found even more disturbing. She had obviously misjudged Simeon and would now pay a price for her own naiveté.

Amos had suggested that he tell Lizzy about the dog rather than Julia, because Lizzy would be less suspicious if he told her. Amos had promised to tell some tale that would satisfy Lizzy. To Julia's relief he had handled the matter better than she could have. Lizzy was disappointed that the dog was gone, but she would have been devastated had she learned the truth.

"Mother said to remind you that the dressmaker will be here at three. She has your gown ready for the first fitting." Lizzy plopped down in a chair and took two tiny iced cakes from a plate in the center of the table. "Isn't it exciting? Your wedding. Mother says I'm to have a new gown as well. The sister of the bride certainly can't come to the church in rags, can she?" she mimicked her mother.

"Of course not." Julia numbly stared at her teacup.

The wedding. It was all she had thought about since the

incident in the barn nearly a week ago. She wasn't stupid. She knew a threat when she heard one. Simeon's meaning was clear. If Julia put up any argument over the wedding, Lizzy would disappear, perhaps to the bottom of the Thames. If Julia further angered him, she, too, would end up as dead as the hound.

For a week Julia had wandered around Bassett Hall in a daze. She appeared at Simeon's side when commanded, but did little else other than sit in her room and stare out at the dreary days that passed one into the other.

Griffin had been gone a week and she missed him. Missed him desperately. That seemed ridiculous to her. She hardly knew him. Yet he was always on her mind.

It wasn't that Julia had any intention of telling Griffin about Simeon's threat. She had told no one. She was too ashamed, too frightened. Who could she tell if she wanted to? Certainly not her mother. Susanne would never believe her. Obviously she couldn't tell Lizzy. No, she didn't want to confide in Griffin. She just wanted to see him. Be near him.

Secretly, she knew she yearned for another kiss, but each time that thought popped into her head she pushed it away and said a prayer for her immortal soul, which surely was in danger.

"I wanted a green gown, but Mother says it must be pink. Hers will be pink. St. Martin likes pink, you know," Lizzy continued through a mouthful of cake.

Julia raised her cup to her lips. The tea was tasteless.

Doomed. She was doomed to marry a man she couldn't help but hate. Doomed to a life of imprisonment . . . fear. If Simeon had only threatened her, she would have walked away right there and then. She would have taken Lizzy and led her out the front door of Bassett Hall never to look back again. But she couldn't endanger sweet, innocent Lizzy.

Julia closed her eyes and remembered Lizzy's cries of frustration when, at three years old shortly after a terrible fever and illness, she had tried to feed herself with a spoon and had been unable to accomplish the task. Lizzy had thrown her little silver spoon down and climbed out of her chair. The illness had done something to her mind. To her body. Suddenly she seemed like a baby again.

Susanne had screamed at Lizzy. She had called her stupid. Lack-witted. "Idiot," Susanne called after the beautiful toddler with her springy blond curls. "I should send for someone from the asylum now and be done with it!"

"No, no," the eight-year-old Julia had cried. "She's not stupid. She can learn." On her knees, Julia pulled Lizzy out from behind a chair where she lay sobbing, her dress thrown over her head.

"Fine!" Susanne had shouted. "You care for the little half-wit. You give up your life for her!"

With that, Susanne had flounced off and Lizzy had fallen into Julia's care. From that day on, only Julia and Drusilla fed Lizzy, clothed her, bathed her. When Lizzy grew up and became such a pretty young lady, Susanne would parade her before neighbors and say she had one pretty daughter and one capable daughter. But Susanne had never again taken responsibility for Lizzy. Lizzy was Julia's responsibility. Julia's. Forever.

Julia glanced up at Lizzy over the teacup she held in her hand. What choice did she have now, but to marry St. Martin?

Lizzy wiped her mouth with her napkin and bounced out of her chair. "Amos is making biscuits, and he said I could make some, too. Want to come?"

Julia shook her head. "No. I think I'll go to the orangery." She forced herself to smile. "See how my water lilies are taking to their new home."

"I'll walk you down." Lizzy grabbed Julia's hand and pulled her out of her chair. "Come along, or I'll be too late for the biscuits."

Lizzy left Julia at the door to the orangery and Julia went inside. With the glass panes repaired on the roof, the room was pleasantly warm, despite the chilling wind that blew outside.

Just stepping into the room that smelled of sweet vegetation and trickling water brightened her spirits a little. At least she would have this orangery. And she'd have Lizzy.

Julia strolled down the path, stepping over dead clippings she'd never had a chance to clean up. It felt good to be alone. Here she felt protected by the trees and bushes, by the distance between her and St. Martin.

"Ah, there you are. I hoped you'd come."

Julia glanced up to see Griffin sitting at the edge of her pond. He was dressed subtly, at least for him, in a red coat and a small black wig.

Julia stood frozen. Then, before she knew what she was doing, she ran into Griffin's arms.

Chapter Eight

Julia felt Griffin wrap his surprisingly muscular arms securely around her waist. Instinctively, she curled her own arms around his neck and pressed her cheek to his shoulder. He was so warm and solid.

"Julia, Julia," he whispered. He smoothed stray wisps of her hair with a gentle hand, and brushed his lips against her cheek. "What is it, dear heart? What's wrong?"

Julia clung tightly to him, knowing it was madness to throw herself at this man, yet not knowing how to stop. "Everything. Everything."

"Shhhh."

He brushed hair from her face that had fallen from her chignon and stared into her eyes with such tenderness that her tears threatened to spill. He was so gentle and yet so indefinably masculine at the same time. No one had ever held her like this before.

"Tell me what I can do," he soothed. "Tell me how I can help."

She squeezed her eyes shut, still holding on to him, making his strength her own. "Nothing. Nothing. Just this. Just hold me another minute. Tell me that everything will be all right."

"Ah, Julia." Griffin pulled her hard against him and held her tightly. "It's going to be all right."

"It's not." She sniffed and lifted her head from his shoulder, feeling much better. "But thank you for saying so." Then she smiled up at him. It was odd how such a bad situation as being forced to marry a man like St. Martin could bring this moment of comfort.

"Tell me." He allowed her to pull back a little, but still held her in his arms.

She made no attempt to escape because she didn't want to. She wanted to feel this secure forever.

Julia hung her head. "I have to marry him. I don't want to, but I have to."

"You don't."

"Yes. I do." She glanced up. "If I don't, my sister and my mother will have no place to go. We have almost no money left. It's the only answer." She exhaled, feeling calmer, her tears dry. "I know you don't understand, but it's a matter of responsibility."

"Ah . . . responsibility." He kissed the corner of her mouth as if it was the most natural thing and released her. "Responsibility is the one thing I understand," he said cryptically.

She watched him walk to the pond to study the new lilies that floated on the water's surface. "Who are you?" she asked.

"Griffin Archer, the Baron Archer, of course," he spoke with a dramatic drawl. "Husband of Lena Thomas. Gambler, drunk, courtier, playwright." He arched one eyebrow. "Fop."

She walked to stand beside him. "The truth."

He glanced sideways at her. "I really am Griffin, cousin to St. Martin."

"I don't mean your name." Julia didn't know what made her think she could speak so frankly with him; she just knew.

"I mean *you*. This man standing beside me is not the man others know. He is not a man attracted to men and young boys," she said firmly. "I know it's not my imagination. The other night you spoke of a farce—"

"Julia, please." He turned to her. "Don't. I shouldn't have said that. I don't know what got into me. In all these years, you're the first one I've ever thought to confide in. But I can't." He took a deep breath. "I shouldn't have kissed you. I should never have allowed myself to . . . to get into this position with you. Talking this way to you." He paused. *"Wanting you."*

He held her gaze for a moment and wordlessly made her understand that whatever his secret was, he could not share it with her.

She glanced away, toward the floating lilies. "You said you understood responsibility," she said, turning back to him. "What did you mean?"

"My entire adult life I've been driven by responsibility."

"And that has to do with *this?*" She tugged at the voluminous laces of his coat cuff. "And this." She touched the black beauty patch on his chin that was cut in the shape of a quarter moon.

"Aye." He smiled the most handsome smile. "And why we must not do this." Then he kissed her again.

Julia gave herself completely to his kiss, understanding in an instant the tragedy of their meeting. Another time, another place, and perhaps they could have had a chance to explore this mad, unexplainable attraction to each other. But he was wed and had his secret . . . and she would soon be the bride of one of the most important men in all England.

He touched his warm, wet tongue to her lower lip and whispered, "You realize . . ." He closed his eyes. *"I* have to realize this cannot be. You and I—"

"I understand." She knew she would probably burn in hell for giving herself so freely to a married man, but at this moment, she didn't care. She would gladly burn for all eternity for the memory of another kiss.

Julia leaned closer to Griffin and caught his tongue between her lips. She was completely inexperienced in kissing and yet her body seemed to know what to do, how to please, how to find pleasure.

He thrust his tongue into her mouth and she savored the feel of it, the texture, the taste. Her legs were weak, her hands trembled, and yet she found a strength within herself, born of their intimate contact. A few moments ago Julia had not known how she could go on and face her marriage to Simeon. Somehow, Griffin was giving her that courage.

"Thank you," she whispered breathlessly as they parted. They were relatively secluded in the orangery. No one ever came here, and no one could hear them from the main house. Still, she felt the need to speak softly, perhaps because she had no desire to share this moment with anyone but Griffin.

"For what?" Slowly he traced her jaw with his finger.

His gentle touch made it difficult for her to answer clearly. "For making me feel as if someone cares what happens to me. Even a stranger such as yourself."

"Am I?"

"What?"

"A stranger?"

She thought for a moment, and then smiled and knew she blushed. "No. I suppose not now."

"Not a stranger, Julia." He took her hand and squeezed it. "A friend. A friend who will be here for you even though he can't be here the way he would like to. The way he fantasizes."

If anyone else had said such an outrageous thing Julia would have been embarrassed, even mortified. But it seemed so right coming from Griffin's mouth. This all seemed so right, and she and St. Martin so wrong . . .

"You know that if there was any way on this sweet earth that I could take you away from this hell—marry you—I would. Here. Now. In this garden."

Her heart soared. Of course he couldn't marry her, not with

a wife, not with his secret, not with her being St. Martin's possession, but the thought that he would have liked to was enough. "Let's not speak of what cannot be."

He nodded, and for a moment held her in his gaze. "I have to go," he said, almost as if in pain.

She tightened her grip on his hand when he tried to pull away. "I wish you wouldn't."

"We can't be seen alone together. Your reputation must remain impeccable. My dear cousin would have it no other way. If he thought there was even a hint of impropriety between you and I, he—"

She squeezed his hand and released it. "Say no more. This week I caught a true glimpse of the man. I underestimated him once; I'll not do that again."

"Julia." He groaned. "I wish that I could—"

She reached out and touched his lips with her finger to silence him. "I wish that you could, too, but we can't alter our paths. To have your friendship is far more than I've ever had before. More than I ever expected." She lifted his hand to her lips, kissed his knuckles that smelled faintly of a floral fragrance, and then released it. "Go, before someone finds you here."

He made a kissing motion with his lips and then strode off. Slowly the sound of his footfall died away.

Julia wrapped her arms tightly around her waist and watched him disappear, her heart full of dread . . . full of joy.

"Oh, hells' bells," she muttered to herself as a thought struck her. "The dressmaker." She lifted her petticoats high and raced up the flagstone walk. "I've got to be fitted for the blessed wedding gown!"

Lizzy giggled softly, her back pressed to the corner of the kitchen. All was quiet in the room save for the crackle of the fire and hiss of steam rising from a pot of boiling potato water.

"Amos," she whispered as she raised her hands to rest them on his broad shoulders.

"Lizzy, Lizzy. I can't."

"You don't like me anymore?" She thrust out her lower lip, but did not remove her hands from his shoulders.

"Oh, no. It's not that," Amos whispered as if he had a bad pain in his belly. "It's just that I swore to your sister that I would look out for you."

"And kissin' isn't looking out for me?"

He groaned. "Lizzy. I don't know how to make you understand."

She looked into his eyes. They were so pretty and dark, as brown as chocolate in a cup. "Julia thinks I'm lack-witted. That I don't know stuff. And it's true. I don't speak French very well and my letters are awful bad, but I know I like you, Amos. I like you more than I ever liked anyone." She took his hand and laid it over her left breast. "When I see you, when you talk to me, my heart feels like this."

His warm hand made her boobies tingle. It felt so strange, but not a bad strange. A good strange.

"Ah, Lizzy." That was all he could say. He still sounded like he was hurting.

"I want you to kiss me, Amos," she whispered.

He touched her cheek with his mouth.

It felt good, but that wasn't what she meant. "No," she whispered and touched her lips with her fingers. "Here."

Amos let out a groan that made her wonder if she'd stepped on his toe or something, but then he brought his face close to her and touched his lips against her lips.

Lizzy wrapped her arms tightly around Amos's neck. He felt so good against her, all hard and strong. His mouth tasted good, like the sweet tea and cookies they'd just shared.

Amos pulled his lips away from hers, but she wasn't done with kissing. She slipped her hand around his neck and pulled him closer again. This time she kissed him hard.

"Lizzy, we can't—" he whispered.

Then she felt his wet tongue against her lips. For a minute she didn't know what to do, but then it seemed like her mouth knew what to do. His kiss felt so good that she just opened her mouth and let his tongue in.

Lizzy was glad she slipped away from Drusilla to be with Amos. Others might think she was a bad girl for this, but she didn't care. She knew she wasn't. How could it be bad to fall in love?

Amos stopped kissing her. "Ye must go before you're missed."

She clasped his hand. "No."

"Lizzy!" His tone was sharp, but she knew he wasn't angry with her, just afraid.

"Just one more kiss?" She lifted up on her toes and pursed her lips. "Please?"

His gaze met hers in the darkness. "One more," he finally conceded.

"Just one more," Lizzy whispered. But as their lips met, she hoped it wouldn't be just one more. Not tonight. Not even next week. She hoped there would be a lifetime of Amos's kisses.

Lifting a candlestick high, Gordy crept up the staircase and down the hallway to Lady Julia's apartment and tapped lightly on one of the two paneled doors. He knew one led to the lady's personal chambers, the other, her servant's.

"Eh?" came a crotchety voice.

He waited a moment, but no one opened the door. He glanced down the dark staircase and banged again.

Inside Gordy heard the scrape of a chair, then the slow shuffle of feet. "What is it?" The door opened and the nursemaid appeared in a sleeping gown and ruffled bedcap. She was an ugly woman with a hollow face and a black wart at the corner of her mouth. Liver spots colored her yellow skin. "What is it?"

Gordy did not make eye contact with the servant, for surely she was well beneath him. "Your charge, madame," he said stiffly. "You should see to her."

Drusilla squinted in the candlelight. "Sir?"

"Your charge," Gordy repeated, tight-lipped. *"The kitchen."*

The old woman's gaze met his and she nodded.

Gordy turned away and hurried back down the staircase before anyone could catch him.

Simeon had outdone himself tonight in celebration of his and Julia's impending marriage. Every crystal glass in the house sparkled. Every bottle of wine was the finest to be had from France and Italy. His buffet table groaned under the weight of exquisite delicacies shipped from hundreds, even thousands of miles away. The most talented musicians in London played from a loft at the far end of the great hall.

The guest list was equally impressive. St. Martin's guests were some of the most important men in England. Even His Grace, the Duke of Buckingham, had made an appearance. Julia had curtsied to the ground when she had met him, and allowed him to take her hand and raise her to her feet. She had smiled prettily, but she had not liked him, nor the way he looked at her.

After nearly two hours of curtseying, smiling, and pretending to be pleased with her forthcoming marriage, Julia finally escaped the confines of St. Martin's company and slipped away to a table of refreshments. As she sipped a punch made with wine and fresh citrus fruits, she peered over the gilded rim of the glass in search of Griffin. Twice they had crossed paths during the evening, but both times they had been unable to do anything but make eye contact.

Julia knew it was ridiculous to dwell on thoughts of Griffin.

No good could come of it, but a heart broken, rather than just bruised as it was now. But she couldn't help herself. The only pleasure she'd experienced in the last few days was when she and Griffin bumped into each other in the library or hall, and were able to converse for a few moments without attracting any suspicion from the staff or Simeon. Twice in the week since they had kissed in the garden, Griffin had played backgammon with her after supper, with Simeon seated in the same room. Both times, it had taken all of her concentration not to stare at Griffin, and she had lost easily to him, much to his delight.

As Julia sipped from her glass, her gaze fell upon her mother, who was making a complete fool of herself as she danced up an aisle of gentlemen to the tune of a country dance. Susanne was laughing uproariously, stumbling, and allowing herself to be caught as she made her way to the far side of the room.

Some of the women raised their fans to gossip behind them. The few male guests who were paying attention to the dancing rather than the card tables, laughed and made crude jests. Julia was embarrassed for her mother, but she knew better than to attempt to intervene. Susanne would only cause a scene, which would surely anger Simeon. Instead, Julia just stood there, wishing she could crawl beneath the linen-draped tables and escape.

"I would give a year of my life for a single kiss from you," Julia heard someone whisper in her ear from behind her. She didn't have to turn to know who it was. Her heart fluttered.

She heard Griffin accept a glass of refreshment from a servant. She kept her back to him.

"Two years," she whispered and sipped from her glass. She could feel the flames of hell lapping at her feet, but she didn't care.

"Three," he challenged.

She continued to watch the room so that anyone who might glance her way would not realize that she and Griffin were conversing rather than simply standing near each other, watching the dancers.

"It would have to be a fine kiss, my lord."

"Oh, it would be."

She felt her cheeks growing warm. This flirtation was dangerous. Julia was never a seeker of danger, nor adventure, but suddenly she understood the thrill she had read about but never experienced.

"I think I should check on the kitchen," she said, having no clue what possessed her to be so daring. "We seem to be running low on those little pigeon pies." With that, she set her glass on a servant's tray and glided across the great hall. She didn't have to look to see if Griffin was following. She knew he would be.

Once she made her escape from the noisy confusion of the great hall, Julia walked slowly down the corridor toward the kitchen. She waited for the sound of footsteps, but heard nothing but her own accelerated breathing. Maybe he wasn't coming . . .

"There you are. I've been waiting practically forever."

Julia gave a little squeak of surprise as Griffin reached out of the darkness of an alcove ahead of her, grabbed her hand, and pulled her into the shadows and into his arms.

"Griffin," she whispered. Her hands fell naturally on his chest, covered with a mountain of fluffy pink lace. "How did you get ahead of me? I just left you in the hall."

"Magic." He pressed his mouth to hers.

"I thought we weren't going to do this," she chastised as she slipped her hands over his shoulders, wondering what it would be like to touch his bare skin.

He crinkled his eyes. "Was that our agreement?"

Her face was so close to his that she could feel his breath as he exhaled softly. His eyes were dark pools of swirling blue that made her yearn to know him more deeply. She barely moved her lips. "It was."

"Then why did you lure me out here?"

"Because . . . because . . ." She lowered her lashes. He was right, she had lured him, with these very intentions.

"Oh, hang it. It's all right, sweetheart. I can't help myself, either. I love you. God, I love you, Julia." He brought his mouth down hard against hers.

She groaned involuntarily. "Don't say it, don't say it," she whispered. " 'Twill only doom us."

Julia parted her lips and thrust out her tongue to taste the brandy wine he had drank. *He loves me. He loves me,* her heart sang.

Griffin raised his hand to the swell of her breast, and she inhaled sharply in awe of the sensation. "Oh."

Immediately his hand stilled. "Did I hurt you?"

"No." She gave a little sigh. "No. It . . . it was wonderful." She gazed into his eyes. "W . . . would you do it again?"

He smiled. "Like this?"

She leaned against him and sighed again with newfound pleasure. "Yes. Oh, Griffin, it's wonderful."

"What of this?" he whispered in her ear.

He slipped his hand beneath the low-cut bodice of her emerald silk gown, and she nearly moaned aloud. Her eyes drifted shut as she experienced another wave of pleasure. She wondered if the heat she felt radiating from the pit of her stomach was from the fires of hell and damnation. "Oh, yes."

"Ah, Julia." He kissed her cheek as he still stroked the side of her breast. "What are we going to—"

"Lady Julia?"

The rhythm of masculine footsteps pounded in the hallway, growing louder. "Lady Julia."

Julia's mouth went dry.

It was Mr. Gordy.

Chapter Nine

A second ticked by, and the footsteps grew closer . . . louder.

Julia gripped Griffin's embroidered brocade coat, her eyes wide with fear. She had to think. Act. It would be impossible for Mr. Gordy to miss them as he passed. Another second ticked by.

A thought flew through Julia's head and she immediately reacted. "Slump down," she whispered in Griffin's ear.

He looked at her as if he wanted to question her intentions, but she grabbed him and pushed him against the wall. "Hurry!"

"Here, Mr. Gordy!" she called as she straightened her bodice. She could still feel the heat of Griffin's hand on her bare breast. "Thank heaven's gates you've come. I believe the Baron Archer is intoxicated. *Again,*" she added for effect.

Griffin relaxed in her arms and slumped down the white plastered wall, playing along as if he were one of the finest actors on Drury Lane.

"You've got to get him to his chambers, Mr. Gordy." She rested her hands on her hips with as much authority as she could muster. "I'll not have this behavior tonight in front of our guests. Not after all his lordship has done to make the evening so fine."

Mr. Gordy came up behind her. "He's pissed, is he?" He sounded as if he doubted her explanation.

She let go of Griffin and he slid to the floor. His head lolled to the side and his eyes drifted shut.

"No, Mr. Gordy," she snapped tersely. "He's not drunk. I always attempt to carry sober men down dark corridors when I should be drinking champagne at my fiancé's side."

She smoothed the skirt of her gown, praying she was convincing. "I'll not have this behavior at Bassett Hall. Do you understand me, Lord Archer?" She poked Griffin with the toe of her satin slipper, dyed precisely the same shade of green as her gown. "Sir! Do you hear me?"

Griffin groaned and began to slip sideways, head toward the floor.

"Well, Mr. Gordy." She motioned with her hand. "Get him upstairs before he embarrasses the earl and me any further."

Gordy grabbed Griffin by both arms and heaved him upward with a groan. "Come, sir," he muttered. "Surely you can walk a few steps."

Griffin righted himself, stumbled, and threw his full weight against Mr. Gordy. Gordy swayed and would have fallen had he not hit the corridor wall.

"And take your bloody shoe with you." Julia picked up the high-heeled yellow slipper Griffin had managed to kick off as he fell, and tossed it at the two men.

Gordy ducked to keep from being struck by the flying missile, then shifted Griffin's weight in his arms and stooped to pick up the shoe. "Come on, my lord. You've got to walk, else we'll both be fried."

"Let me see this behavior again," Julia ranted, "and surely I will be forced to speak to St. Martin. Drunkenness will not be tolerated in this household. Do you hear me?"

Griffin groaned, mumbled something, then punctuated the babble with a loud belch.

Julia almost laughed aloud and had to cover her mouth for fear a sound would escape.

The two men gone, she pressed her back to the wall and heaved a great sigh of relief. She lifted her hand to her pounding heart. That was close. Too close. Proof that even a few innocent kisses were dangerous.

Innocent? She closed her eyes and exhaled a shuddering breath. The kisses she had shared with Griffin were far from innocent—the lewd thoughts that had passed through her head even less so . . .

"Ouch. Stop, that hurts, Drusilla."

Julia walked into the sitting room of her apartments to find Lizzy seated on a stool, Drusilla standing behind her braiding her hair.

"You do that again, and you'll find yourself seeking employment elsewhere," Lizzy threatened, massaging the crown of her head.

Julia knew Lizzy was mimicking her mother's words. That was precisely the same line she gave her servants at least thrice a week. Still, that was no excuse for Lizzy's rude behavior.

"Lizzy! That's no way to talk to Drusilla!" Julia closed the door behind her and stepped out of her green shoes.

Lizzy crossed her arms over her white flannel wrapper and thrust out her lip in a pout. "Drusilla is being mean to me. She pulled my hair."

Drusilla gave a tug of Lizzy's thick blond plait. "Tell 'er," she cackled. "Tell Miss Julia where I caught ye. What I caught ye doin'."

Exhausted, Julia slumped into a chair. After the incident in the corridor, she had gone to the kitchen, ordered more pigeon pies to be brought to the ballroom, and then returned to the guests. She had remained at Simeon's side, the dedicated bride-to-be, and fetched him drinks and smiled until she thought she would go mad.

At two in the morning, she had excused herself, pleading faintness. Simeon had apparently been so pleased with her meek, subservient behavior, that he'd let her go with an air-peck on the temple and a wish of sweet dreams.

Julia leaned over to untie her garters. "What were you doing, Lizzy? Not in the stable loft again looking for kittens? I told you, you must take care with the gowns his lordship has provided for you. As my sister, he expects you to look presentable."

"Lookin' fer kittens, she weren't," Drusilla muttered.

Julia stripped off her silk stockings. She tried to focus on whatever was happening between Drusilla and Lizzy, but her thoughts wandered. The run-in with Gordy had frightened her, but she still felt a strange sense of excitement. Griffin loved her. *He loved her.* Even if nothing could ever come of their love, she wouldn't die a woman who had never known the rich taste of it, the heady scent.

Julia tossed her stockings on the floor beside her shoes. "Want to tell me, Lizzy?"

Lizzy stared at the ragged cotton mules that hung on the ends of her dainty feet. "You can't tell me what to do. None of you can. I'm old enough to do what I want. I'm not a little girl anymore that I need my nursemaid."

Drusilla gave a *harrumph* as she tied off Lizzy's braid with a piece of ribbon and released it. "Looks to this woman like you *need* a nursemaid. That or a jailer!"

Julia glanced up at Drusilla. The old woman had always been gruff, even when they were toddling children. But Julia knew that the woman cared deeply for Lizzy, and that she wanted nothing more than for Lizzy to be safe and content.

"Lizzy . . ."

"Drusilla thinks she knows so much. Let her tell you." Lizzy bobbed up and off the stool, her arms still crossed stubbornly over her chest.

Julia exhaled and the fringe of her hair that fell over her forehead fluttered. It was so late and she was so tired. She really wasn't up to this. But considering the state she guessed her mother was in by now, the responsibility fell to Julia. It seemed as if it always did. "Lizzy. Drusilla."

"Not my place to carry tales," Drusilla declared.

Over her shoulder, Lizzy shot Drusilla an evil look.

"If yer done with me, Miss Julia, I'll have my bed now." Drusilla tugged on her flannel nightcap. " 'Tis too late for an old woman to be about."

Julia considered asking Drusilla to stay until she found out what Lizzy had done, but decided to just let her go to bed. She was right; it was late.

"Good night, Drusilla." Julia rose and patted the nurse-maid's arm as she passed. "I'll talk to Lizzy."

"I ain't seen that girl through this many years to lose her now," Drusilla grumbled. " 'Night."

Julia waited to speak again until Drusilla closed the door. Lizzy stood staring at the blazing fire in the fireplace, her arms crossed over her chest, her lip in a pout.

Julia turned her back to her sister. "With Drusilla in bed, I'll need you to unlace me."

There was a pause and then Julia heard Lizzy move. Her capable fingers soon found the hooks and strings of Julia's gown and underclothing.

"Want to tell me?" Julia questioned softly.

"No."

Julia waited a moment and then went on. "Drusilla is concerned, Lizzy. She's worried about you because she loves you."

"She pulled my hair."

"How can I help you if I don't know what's wrong?"

Lizzy tugged Julia's gown over her head and laid it carefully over a high-backed chair. "Drusilla yelled at me in the kitchen.

Em—embarrassed me in front of Amos. She yanked my ear, too.''

"Why?" Julia faced her sister as she stepped out of her petticoats.

Lizzy nibbled on her lower lip, her gaze downcast with guilt. " 'Cause I did something that she said was bad. She said I'd burn in hell for doing that with a man not my husband.''

Oh, God above, Julia thought. Her throat constricted. Surely Amos hadn't—"Tell me," she managed to whisper as she took Lizzy's smaller hands in hers. "I won't be angry."

Lizzy lifted her lashes. "I kissed Amos."

After what Julia had feared, she almost laughed aloud at Lizzy's declaration. Of course the matter was still serious, but at least Lizzy's virtue wasn't in danger. "He made you kiss him?"

Her eyes widened in surprise. "No! I . . . I told him to do it. I . . . I liked it. I wanted to do it again and again."

"Ah, Lizzy." Julia sank into the upholstered stool and tugged Lizzy down to sit beside her. "Do you understand why Drusilla was upset?"

"I guess because she doesn't want me to burn in hell." She frowned. "Only I don't understand why a kiss could feel so good and send ye straight to hell."

Her words brought tears to Julia's eyes as she thought of the forbidden kisses she'd shared with Griffin only hours ago. "Ah, Lizzy. It's not the kissing that's a sin. Just what it can lead to."

Lizzy studied her sister quizzically. "More kissing?"

Julia closed her eyes and rubbed them. This was neither the time nor the place to try to explain to Lizzy how a man and a woman made babies. Truthfully, it had never occurred to Julia that she would ever have to have this conversation. She had thought Lizzy's mind had never matured enough for such subjects.

Julia opened her eyes and squeezed Lizzy's hand. Perhaps

the best way to handle the explanation was with class differences. Of course Lizzy could never have a sexual relationship with *any* man, because no man would ever wed her with her weak mind, but Julia didn't have to tell her that. She didn't have to hurt her that way.

"Sweetie, you can't kiss Amos because he's a cook—a servant—and you're a lady. It's just not appropriate. Ladies kiss gentlemen. Cooks kiss housemaids."

"But I want to kiss Amos. He tastes good."

Julia groaned inwardly. All she could think of was what would happen if Simcon found out. A servant taking advantage of a feebleminded, but titled lady? Surely he would implode.

"But you can't," Julia insisted. "Maybe you shouldn't go to the kitchen anymore, and that way you won't have to worry about wanting to kiss Amos."

"Oh, no." Lizzy's head bobbed up. "Amos is getting me a new dog. I have to go to the kitchen. Please, Julia, please." She laced her fingers together to beg. "I won't kiss him anymore. I'll just pet the puppy."

Julia couldn't resist a tender smile of relief. Lizzy never purposefully disobeyed. It wasn't in her nature. Perhaps it was even beyond her mental capabilities. "Oh, all right. Just to visit the puppy, but I'll have to speak with Amos."

Lizzy grabbed Julia's hand again. "No."

"No?"

"No, please. Please, please, please. Let me tell him no more kissing." She grimaced. "It was my idea. It was my fault."

Julia slipped her arm around her sister's shoulder. She really thought she needed to speak with Amos, but maybe Lizzy was right. Maybe it would be better coming from her. "Let's go to bed now, and we'll talk about it in the morning. All right?"

Lizzy kissed Julia on the cheek. "I love you, Sister. And I'm never ever going to leave you."

Julia watched her as she sauntered off to bed. Of course she would marry Simeon to protect Lizzy. She had never really had any other choice.

"Do you understand my instructions?" Simeon stood in the armor- and weapon-lined front hallway beside Julia, and waited as one of the maids lifted her ermine-lined cloak onto her shoulders.

"I understand." Julia slipped her hands into her gloves and focused on the floor. She felt so guilty over the kisses she had shared with Griffin that she was trying to behave as she knew Simeon wanted her to—that and to avoid any suspicion. "I'm to purchase the items on the list as you've described in detail."

The list was for her trousseau, and the thought nauseated her. Julia had attempted to send her mother or Drusilla on the errand, but Simeon insisted she must purchase the items herself. Tradition, he told her. Honestly she didn't understand the point. He had already decided what clothing she would bring to their marriage, right down to the lace on her shifts. She had no choice. Of course, perhaps that was the subtle point—for him to demonstrate the complete control he would have over her as his wife, right down to her undergarments.

"Stop at Three Silver Bells Tavern on The Strand when you tire. I'll send word you'll require a private room upstairs to dine, and I'll order your meal."

She wondered if he intended to tell her when she might use the necessary, but she gritted her teeth and held her tongue. "Yes, my lord."

"The driver is to remain with the coach so it's not vandalized, but I've given the footman instructions to remain at your side. You'll be safe."

She started for the front door the footman held open for her. A gush of cold wind blew through the entryway and a swirl of dry leaves blew in.

"And don't dawdle, Julia dear." Simeon folded his pale

hands. ''We'll be entertaining some merchants and their wives this evening.''

She forced a smile as she lifted the hood of her cloak. ''How exciting.''

''Have a lovely day, dear.''

Simeon brushed his lips near her cheek, and Julia made her escape into the chilly morning.

Julia moved mechanically from one ladies' shop to the next. She didn't bother to look at the clothing she purchased, but simply read from the list, waited while the items were wrapped, and then led the footman to the next shop. When his arms became overburdened, she sent him to the coach to unload, then filled his arms again.

Considering the amount of clothing Simeon was having her purchase, she wondered if he ever intended to release her from Bassett Hall to shop again. The thought was amusing, until it occurred to her that imprisoning her was not beyond Simeon's power. Once they were wed, he could legally do what he wished with her.

With that sobering thought, she moved on to the next shop, where she bought French perfume and sachets.

Home in Dover, there had been long afternoons when Julia had sat in a sunny window and dreamed what it would be like to shop for her wedding trousseau. She had fantasized about what it would be like to choose the sleeping gown she would wear to her bridal bed. Now the purchases meant nothing more to her than buying fish or eggs for supper at a market.

After Julia had checked the last item off Simeon's methodical list, she allowed the driver to take her to the Three Silver Bells Tavern. She wasn't really hungry, but she was enjoying her freedom and wasn't anxious to return to Bassett Hall and the smell of its lye soap rooms. Since her arrival in London she'd only been outside the estate's gates a few times. Though she found the city streets to be filthy and noisy, it was still a welcome change from the unnatural silence and cleanliness of her new home.

Julia lowered the hood of her cloak and gave her name to the proprietor, who met her at the tavern door. The pock-faced man bowed twice in rapid succession, chattered that he had been expecting her, and led her through the smoky public taproom toward a staircase that led to private dining rooms above.

Griffin tossed the ivory dice on the trestle table stained with ale, greasy food, and time. He gave a hoot of pleasure as his companion groaned. "Just empty your purse into mine now, Jack, and be done with it," Griffin said.

His companion flipped two coins onto the table and lifted a dusty bottle of sack to his lips. "Cheat. I should challenge you to a duel to defend my good name."

Griffin threw back his head and laughed. "Me, a cheat?" He spoke loudly so that anyone nearby could follow the conversation. To a passerby, they were simply two gentlemen sharing a bottle or two over a friendly game. "By the king's cod, 'twas your die. You initiated the game when I was but an innocent come to quench my thirst in this fine establishment."

A tavern wench sauntered up to their table and tucked a greasy lock of hair behind her ear. "Another, my lords?"

"Nay." Jack tossed a few coins onto the table to pay for the sack, and rose. "I've need of a visit to the backyard, and then home I go before my Katy appears at yonder door and hauls me out by my ear."

Griffin bumped into the table as he rose from the bench and both sack bottles tumbled over.

The maid giggled and retrieved them.

Griffin steadied himself with his hand, adjusted the sword he wore on his hip, and straightened to his full height as if regaining his dignity. "Aye. I believe I've a need to totter in the same direction."

"Come again, my lord," the barmaid called after them as she dropped the coins into her bodice. "Ask fer Rosy."

Griffin dropped his cavalier's hat onto his head and bowed to Rosy. "Farewell, my love, my Rosy."

She giggled as she finished off the last drop from one of the bottles.

Jack elbowed him in the side. "Come on with ye."

The two men walked through the public room, down a back corridor that led outside to the necessary. Halfway down the hall Griffin halted. "Well," he demanded softly. "What have you for me?"

Jack tried to walk away, but Griffin grabbed his velvet sleeve. "You've stalled long enough," he said more forcefully. "I must have information."

Jack leaned against the wall, only half-sober. "Ah, Christ's bones. I didn't get it—but I will."

Griffin tightened his grip on the man's coat and pushed him back to the wall hard enough to make him strike his head and perhaps knock some sense into him. "You shouldn't be drinking like this. It's not safe," he said, tight-lipped. "You know better."

Griffin spotted the glimmer of the knife as the man drew it from his coat sleeve. With one quick motion, Griffin knocked Jack's arm hard enough against the wall to crack bone. The man grunted in pain. The knife fell and Griffin caught it in midair.

"You are a fool, Jack," Griffin whispered harshly, as he pressed the point of the knife to Jack's throat. "I'm not the enemy and you know it. Now get hold of yourself before we're seen."

Griffin turned at a sound behind him. A woman and the innkeeper appeared at the end of the hall to mount the stairs.

Griffin caught a flash of her face beneath the hood of her

cloak and was taken off guard for a moment. He froze. He knew the eyes. She recognized him at the same instant. Her gaze shifted from his face to the knife Griffin held at Jack's throat.

"This way, my lady," the innkeeper muttered as he pretended not to see what he could not have missed.

Julia hesitated on the bottom tread.

Don't stop, Griffin thought. *Please, Julia, keep walking.* He was afraid for her. For Jack. For them all.

Her gaze met his. She was frightened, too . . .

Please, he begged silently, still holding the blade to Jack's throat. For a moment Griffin held his breath. His heart pounded in his ears.

Another long second dragged by. Then, just when he thought there was no hope, she turned away.

Griffin let out an audible grunt of relief. He turned back to Jack as Julia's footsteps echoed on the staircase. He would set Jack straight and then he would go to her. The question was, what would he say?

Chapter Ten

Griffin? Julia caught herself before she breathed his name aloud.

"This way, m'lady," the innkeeper ushered her on as if he had not noticed a man being held at knife point in the back hallway of his establishment. "I've a fine bit of roast duck with leeks coming up directly."

Julia's gaze met Griffin's, and a shiver of fear trickled down her spine. Who was this man she had lost her affection to? What was he?

The moment they made eye contact, she knew what he was asking of her. *Keep walking.*

Julia slid her gaze from the shadowy passageway toward the staircase. It was one of the most difficult things she'd ever done. "I'm sure the duck will be fine, sir." She raised her petticoats and climbed the steps.

At the top of the landing, the innkeeper showed her to a private dining room that was dominated by a large table surrounded by eight mismatched, but sturdy bowed chairs. There were two windows, the painted inside shutters half-closed. A discreetly placed narrow, paneled door no doubt led to a private necessary. A fire crackled in the stone fireplace at the far end of the room, making it warm and cozy .

"Your cloak, m'lady. I hope the room suits. His Grace the Duke of Buckingham rents it often."

Julia allowed the innkeeper to remove it from her shoulders. "It's fine, sir."

"White rhenish on the table." He hung her cloak on a peg near the door. "And your meal should be up directly."

"Thank you." She handed him a coin from the small purse she wore tied at her waist, hoping he didn't see her hand tremble.

He bowed and hurried out the door, closing it firmly behind him.

Once the innkeeper was gone, Julia stood in indecision for a moment. Should she go downstairs? What if Griffin was in danger? Yet from the way he had been holding the other man at knife point, she doubted it. He seemed in complete control—control that came from experience.

Julia walked to the fireplace at the end of the room and thrust out her shaky hands to warm them. No, it didn't make sense to go downstairs. She would wait for him here, for surely he would come.

Julia didn't have to wait long. She heard no footsteps, no turn of the doorknob, no squeak of hinges. Suddenly she just sensed that he was there, behind her.

She turned. "Are you all right?"

He stood with his legs slightly parted, his hands folded in front of him. He was dressed in bright gold and lavender, but there was a sword on his hip, and a look on his face that confirmed her belief that he was not the man his frivolous garb indicated. Griffin's lips were drawn back tightly in a grimace, his blue-eyed gaze intense.

"I'm sorry you had to see that," he said simply.

She folded her arms over her chest. "And what was that I saw?"

He pulled his black woolen cloak off his shoulders and tossed it to the wall, where it caught on a peg beside her cloak. Next he stripped off his brocade and lace doublet, down to his breeches, white linen shirt, and cravat. Apparently he intended to stay.

He took a step toward her. "I can't tell you, Julia."

She took a step back, her gaze fixed on his face. Should she be afraid of him? No, she didn't think so. For, although she had seen with her own eyes that it was Griffin who held the knife, she intuitively knew that it was not he who was in the wrong in that hallway.

"I'm sorry. I shouldn't have asked." She turned away.

"No."

She felt the warmth of his fingers as he caught her wrist.

"I would tell you if I could." He tugged on her arm and forced her to face him. "I want to," he added softly. "I've already told you, allowed you to see more than I should have. I just can't tell you more."

A knock sounded at the door, and she looked toward it anxiously. "My meal. I don't know that you should be seen here. Simeon—"

"It's all right." Still keeping possession of her arm, he called to the door, "Come in, Jabar."

The door opened, and the dark-skinned, turbaned servant entered bearing a large tray covered with a table linen. The succulent smell of roasted duck and freshly baked bread wafted through the air.

"I sent word to our fine proprietor, saying I would dine with my cousin," Griffin explained. "Should word get back to Bassett Hall, which surely it will, no one will think it odd." He led her to the table. "I ran into you here at Three Bells and knew it my duty to dine with you and perhaps escort you home safely."

Julia took the chair he pulled out for her.

As Jabar set the dishes out, Julia noticed him cut his eyes toward Griffin. He was obviously displeased with Griffin for being here with her.

Griffin shot his manservant a severe look and hooked his thumb toward the door. "Keep watch," was all he said.

Jabar nodded his turbaned head and backed out the door without a word.

Standing behind her, Griffin reached for the flagon that had come on the tray. "Ale or rhenish?"

She could smell his shaving soap, the masculine scent of his skin, and she wanted to touch that skin. "Just water." She needed to keep her head about her. She needed no spirits to confuse her any more than she already was by her own thoughts and desires.

"Water it is." He poured her a full cup and then took the seat at the end of the table, so that he was beside her. He placed a healthy portion of duck and leeks on her plate and added a slice of thick bread. "Eat. You look thinner every day. You're wasting away. Eat." He waved one hand and then reached for the flagon of ale to pour himself a draught.

Julia wasn't hungry. Her stomach was flip-flopping. It felt so strange to be alone with Griffin, away from Bassett Hall. Almost frightening. There, within the walls of Simeon's domain, she could retain a thread of common sense. There, she trusted herself not to do anything to jeopardize herself or her sister. But here, they seemed so far from that world. And here, Griffin was so close, so handsome in his rumpled linen shirt and dusty boots. Here, she was so afraid of the wedding that loomed before her. Here, she wanted so desperately to be comforted in Griffin's arms.

"So the keeper let you out. What brings you to the Three Bells?"

She nibbled on the crust of the warm bread. "Shopping. My trousseau."

"Ah ha." He nodded, trying to sound casual, only she could see right through it. "The wedding next week."

The bread was tasteless in her mouth. "Yes."

He lifted his mug to his lips and drank deeply.

He said nothing about the wedding, because she knew nothing could be said.

Julia gave up on the bread and dropped it to her plate. "Could I ask you something? Not about downstairs, something else. Something personal."

He smirked over the rim of his cup. "I'll answer if I can."

She picked up the pointed dining knife and poked at the dark flesh of the duck she had no intention of eating. "The other night . . . you said you loved me."

He was silent, and that was one of the things she loved about him. He was always willing to give her a chance to speak.

"First, I want to tell you what I didn't get a chance to say then. And that's . . . I think I love you, too, though how or why, I don't know, don't understand."

"Julia—"

"My question," she continued before she lost her nerve, "is, how can it be that you love me? You have a wife. Don't you love her?"

He set down his mug. "Yes, Julia, I do love Lena."

Julia felt a jealous tug in her heart. She didn't want to feel it. She knew she had no right. Lena was his wife. He *should* love Lena.

Griffin stilled her hand that jabbed at the meat on her plate. "But I love her differently than I love you."

She lifted her lashes. "How so?"

Griffin released her hand and exhaled through pursed lips. He lowered his gaze to his hands on the table before him and examined his manicured nails. "Women always want words for feelings, and that's so damned hard for men." He paused again.

She set down the knife and waited.

"I love Lena for what she's done for me. I probably shouldn't even tell you this much, but . . ." He took a deep breath. "Years ago, when I was abroad, she sent word that my lands were to be confiscated because of my alleged loyalty to the King."

"Alleged?" Julia raised one eyebrow.

He grinned and went on. "The house and lands had been in my family for six hundred years; I didn't want to be the one to lose it. She proposed that we wed. As my wife, she could petition Cromwell, a distant cousin of hers, to ask that the lands not be revoked."

"It worked?"

He nodded. "We were married in France thirteen years ago."

Julia knew she shouldn't ask any more, but she couldn't help herself. "Children?"

He looked amused. "I hardly think so. Lena was well beyond child-bearing years before we were wed."

Julia's eyes widened in surprise. "She's old?" She didn't know why that delighted her, but it did.

"Elderly." He chuckled and pointed a finger. "But don't tell her that. She hasn't realized it yet."

"But why would she do this for you? She put herself and her own lands and title at risk. Who was she to you?"

"My father's aunt. Held me on her lap. Changed my napkin when I was a babe." He smiled fondly. "She bought me my first man's suit and sword, and probably would have bought me my first whore if my father would have allowed it."

Julia smiled because he was smiling. "She must be very special."

"She is." He tugged at the queue of his tightly curled periwig. "I'd like for her to meet you. She's been invited to the wed—" He halted in mid-sentence, but his gaze didn't stray from hers. "Ah, Christ's bones," he sighed and took her hand. "What are we going to do, Julia? How can I allow you to marry him?"

She bit down on her lower lip to keep it from trembling. "Do? We're not going to *do* anything. You're not going to allow or disallow anything, because it's not your place."

He slid his chair back and reached out for her. She came into his arms and settled on his lap.

"We're going to do as we must. We're going to follow the paths that were already laid out for us before we met." She traced the line of his jaw, feeling the midday stubble of beard that could not yet be seen. "I'm going to wed Simeon because I must. And you . . . you are going to do what you must—whatever that is."

Griffin wrapped his arms around her waist and lowered his head to her breast. She stroked the back of his neck, wishing she could remove his wig and feel his hair between her fingers. She didn't even know what color it was.

"Why?" he whispered painfully. "Why must it be like this?"

She lifted his chin and planted a soft kiss on his lips. She had thought that the kisses they had shared in the darkness would be their last. So now these would be their last. She kissed him again. "Responsibility."

"I know I can't marry you now, but . . . but—" he went on faster than before. "Lena won't live forever. I could take you somewhere. France. Italy. You could—"

She pressed a finger to his lips to silence him. "No. I *must* marry Simeon." She didn't tell him about Simeon's threat, for fear it would put Griffin in danger also. This was her problem and she knew how to solve it. Only by marrying Simeon would those she loved be safe.

"Why must you marry him?"

"Why must you wear star and moon face patches and walk on your toes?" she challenged.

He grimaced. "I deserved that."

"You did. But you deserve this, too." And then she lowered

her mouth to his, closed her eyes, and brushed her lips against his.

Griffin tightened his grip around her waist and thrust his tongue into her mouth.

She moaned as he slipped his hand into her bodice and cupped her bare breast with his hand. It was the most wonderful, wicked feeling.

Julia's heart pounded and her pulse raced as he stroked her nipple with the slightly rough pad of his thumb. She was hot and cold at the same time.

Griffin slid her gown down over her shoulder. The cold air made her skin prickle in gooseflesh, which only heightened the sensation of his warm hand.

She yanked at the drawstring of her corset cover and pushed the linen fabric aside. Griffin caught her breast with his hand and lowered his head.

Julia held tightly to his shoulders and moaned as he took her nipple into his mouth. Nothing had ever felt so good, so right.

She turned in his lap so that she was facing him, her legs straddling his. She lifted her layers of skirts and pushed them behind her. The pressure of his hard groin pressed against hers was maddening.

"Love me," she whispered.

"I do." He covered her breasts with wild, fleeting kisses, his breath coming as fast as her own. "I am."

"No," she whispered, taking his face in her hands so that she could peer directly into his eyes. "Love me. Here. Now. The table." She couldn't believe she was saying such a thing. But it was what she wanted. What she felt. "The floor. I don't care."

She stared into his eyes for a long moment and her heart began to sink. Griffin wasn't going to make love to her. She could tell by the way he looked back.

"Julia." He pulled her against his chest, her head on his

shoulder, and hugged her tightly. "Julia, Julia." He stroked her hair. "No."

"No?" she whispered weakly, hurt by his answer even knowing it was the right one.

"No." He lifted her face so that she could look at him. He brushed away the hair from her eyes. "Not because I don't want to make love to you," he said fiercely. "God knows I do. But because it wouldn't be right. You're right. I can't marry you. I can't give you a home. I have no right to you."

She smiled sadly as tears splashed down her cheeks. The hurt was gone, though the ache of desire still throbbed in her groin. "You're a good man, Griffin."

He gave a dry laugh. "What little good it's done me."

"Oh." She stroked his cheek. "I would venture to guess it's done *someone* some good."

They held each other for another moment, and then she slipped off his lap. She covered her breasts without feeling any shame. The shame would come when she had to bare them for Simeon. "I have to go."

"I, too. I've a message of importance to deliver. I shouldn't have dallied as long as I have." He rose from his chair; the wood scraped wood. "But I must say it was an enjoyable dalliance."

Somehow she found the ability to laugh.

Griffin laughed with her as he fetched her wool cloak and draped it over her shoulders. "The wedding next week. I've business elsewhere. Would you be hurt if I didn't attend?"

She wanted to say that she needed him there, needed his strength, but that sounded ridiculous even in her own mind. "I won't be hurt," she managed bravely. "I wouldn't be there if I didn't have to, either." Then she imitated his grin.

"You're a rare woman, Julia," he said softly, with the saddest smile she thought she'd ever seen. Then he kissed her.

"Farewell, my love."

Her fingers caught his as he walked away. She felt as if she were walking to the Tower steps never to descend again. Next week she would be married. She would never kiss Griffin again, never feel his touch. She felt the last brush of his fingertips as he walked out the door. ''Farewell,'' she whispered, and wished that she was dead.

Chapter Eleven

"And why are you so morose today?" Lena peered over her canvas as Griffin posed in contemplation in the window seat. "No sword fights this morning? No villains to the Tower? London unbearably dull? Hm?"

He cut his eyes at her, but did not stir from the pose. "If I'm morose, which I'm not, it might be because every time I call on you, you make me sit in this damned window for hours on end while you paint lousy portraits."

With a chuckle, Lena drew her brush across the canvas. "Must be serious that you would speak so severely to an old, decrepit woman."

"Old and decrepit, my ass. You can ride astride longer, further, faster than I can any day. And I vow you're better with a sword. Always were."

He glanced out the lead casement window at the dark clouds rolling in off the horizon. It was going to rain. He wondered if that was a bad omen on the day of a woman's wedding. He pressed the pad of his finger against the cold glass and drew swirls in the condensation. He couldn't recall. He wondered if Lena would know.

Lena dipped the tip of her brush into a pot of red ochre paint and stroked again. "You really are upset," she said gently. "What is it, Griffin? Tell me so that I can help."

He shifted his gaze from the window to Lena, his sweet Lena. He had told the truth when he'd told Julia that he loved her. He did. More than anyone . . . until Julia had magically appeared in his life.

Lena looked no different to him than she had when he'd been a child on lead strings. Tall, willowy, and graceful, she had a mane of red hair that was still as bright as it had been in her youth. He sometimes wondered if she dyed it, for surely a woman in her mid-seventies would be gray, but he had never had the nerve to ask.

Though there were a few age lines on Lena's classic oval face—laugh lines, she called them—her brilliant blue eyes still shone with the excitement of a sixteen-year-old. She was still as limber and as active as she had been in her youth, hunting regularly, walking her grounds, and swimming in Bath each summer.

The woman was truly amazing. She had lived through years of civil war, seen one of her ancestral homes burned to the ground by an army, buried three husbands and nine children, and still managed to catch the eye of many a gentleman on a ballroom floor. Whenever Griffin commented to her that she seemed not to be aging, she joked that somewhere in the castle cupboards there was a portrait of her in which she was growing older by the year.

"Griffin," Lena said. "Tell me."

No longer able to hold his pose, Griffin rose from the window seat to pace. "This is one situation you'll not be able to rescue me from." He glanced at her. "Disappointed as you may be."

Lena signaled to a footman standing invisibly near the doorway. "Zeus. Refreshment please. Something sturdy."

"Yes, my lady." He nodded and disappeared through a draped doorway.

Lena set down her brush and came around the easel. She was dressed in hand-painted silk robes from the Orient, with a turban binding up her waist-length hair. Her face, unpainted with powder and rouge, was remarkably youthful and full of life. In many ways she reminded him of Julia . . . or did Julia remind him of her?

"You can't come to my home in a sulk and then refuse to give an explanation." She lowered her hands to her shapely hips. "Give it up, Griffin. You'd not have come if you didn't want to tell me."

"You talk to me as if I'm a child." It was true. She always had, but it didn't offend him. In fact, her mother-henning comforted him. That was one of the reasons he came. This was the only place in the world where he could come and permit someone to care for him, listen to his woes.

"All men are children who want to be suckled at a woman's breast. It's their nature."

He ran his fingers through his shoulder-length hair that sorely needed trimming. Only here in the privacy of Lena's home could he go without a periwig. "Well, thank you," he said dryly. "I feel much better now."

She sighed and looped her arm through his. "Come, if you must pace, let us do it together. I need to stretch these old bones anyway." She started along the wall of windows that faced the west. "Tell me." She patted his arm. "You'll feel better. You know you will."

It was a long moment before Griffin could bring himself to say anything. "A woman," he finally confessed.

"You've hanged her, or simply thrown her into the Tower?"

"Lena!" He glanced at her. *"Neither."*

"Don't look so shocked. It's not as if I don't know what it is you do. I'd certainly hang a woman to protect my king."

He knew she spoke truthfully. Lena was stronger than any

woman or man he'd ever known. "It has nothing to do with the king, dear wife."

Her face brightened. "You? A personal life? Sweet Mary, mother of God, it's about time. I was beginning to wonder if you were *ever* going to have a life of your own beyond *chivalrous duty.*"

He threw up one hand. "I don't know why I come here." They passed another window. Rain was beginning to splatter the glass. "You do nothing but torture me. I come for peace and get nothing but fishwifery."

She patted his arm and cajoled, "You can tell Lena. It's a woman you're in love with, isn't it?"

"Aye. A woman."

"Well, don't sound as if it's the end of your life." She pushed him playfully. "It was what God intended you know, man and woman, not man and king."

He laughed. Another reason why he loved Lena. She knew him so well, she could always make him laugh, even at himself. "All right, all right, I confess." They turned at the end of the gallery and started back in the other direction. "I've met a woman and fallen in love with her."

"And this is why you sulk?"

"I don't *sulk.* Men who have fought in foreign wars, men who carry the king on their backs, do not *sulk.* We . . ." He gestured, searching for the right word. "We . . . *brood.*"

"So, you've met a woman. Wonderful. Divorce me. Have the marriage annulled. Whatever." She gestured with a flourish. "Marry her."

His forehead wrinkled. "Divorce you? I would never divorce you."

"And why not? You don't take me to your bed. I have to find my own men. I was seriously considering divorcing you on those grounds anyway."

He shook his head slowly. "Lena, Lena. You say the damnedest things."

"And you *do* the damnedest things. Or don't do them, as the case may be."

"Even if I could marry her, which I can't, the church is not going to give us a divorce after thirteen years."

"Details. Details. Tell me about this woman. A redhead, I hope."

He had to laugh. "How did you guess?"

"Woman's intuition. I knew that when you finally fell, it would be hard. Only a redhead would ever catch your eye."

"Her name is Julia. Her hair is a lighter red than yours, like the morning sun. She has the most perfect smile, a husky laugh that reaches to my toes. She can beat me at backgammon *and* knap and slur."

"Good heavens, then you'd best marry her. I always said the basis for a good marriage was compatibility at the gaming tables, as well as beneath the bedsheets."

He exhaled with a rush of emotion. "I loved her the minute I first laid eyes on her."

"So divorce me and marry her. Or just go elsewhere and be a bigamist until I make my ascent. It's time you had children, Griffin. You know you're not getting any younger. What's the good of having all this damned land and money if you've no one to share it with?"

To Griffin's chagrin, tears gathered in the corners of his eyes. He looked away with embarrassment. "I can't marry her."

If she saw the tears, she made no indication. "Can't or won't?"

He halted. "Can't."

"Can't, why? Certainly not because of me."

"I can't because . . ." He walked to a window that was dappled with raindrops. The tears dissipated and he saw clearly again. "I can't because she's St. Martin's wife."

"Oh," Lena exhaled, her vivacious energy suddenly deflated.

"Aye. Minor obstacle." He lifted his hand in a weak gesture.

"But who am I jesting? Even if she were free, I'm not. My responsibility is to my king right now. Everyone and their brother is trying to see him dethroned." He clenched his hand in a tight fist. "I vowed to watch over him. I swore to protect him."

Lena stood behind him and laid a gentle hand on his shoulder. "You made that vow to his father a long time ago. You've surely done more than could be expected out of any mortal man. I'm sure His Majesty would allow you to retire from your position. As much as you may hate to admit it, you are not the only competent Englishman on the face of this earth. Griffin, there are others to intercept messages and creep down backstaircases."

He shook his head, still staring out the window into the rain. "Doesn't really matter." He lifted one shoulder in a shrug. Lena's warm hand was a comfort. He had known that if he came here, he would feel better. "She's his—or will be in a few hours."

"Today's the wedding? Hell, that's right. I did receive that invitation months ago."

He nodded, afraid to speak. All week he had told himself over and over again that he had accepted their fates. He thought he had convinced himself that if Julia was strong enough to accept St. Martin as her husband, he was. Only now he felt as if he were crumbling from the inside out. Right now he didn't care about his king, or his England, and he was ashamed. All he wanted was to hold Julia, to run his fingers through her thick hair . . . to make her his own.

"Griffin, Griffin." Lena slipped her smaller hand around his and squeezed it. "Would that I could take this pain from you."

"Doesn't matter anyway. She wants to marry him. Insisted she must."

"Wants to, or must?" Lena led him to the window seat where they sat side by side, she still holding his hand.

"You know." He gestured. "Says she must. Responsibility to her family and so on."

"Ah. Duty. A woman's duty is to marry the man her father chooses, the man who can offer the most money, the most power, the most safety to her family. It's a woman's lot, Griffin. Has been for centuries. We marry to make alliances that will protect our unborn children."

"I can't blame her for marrying him when I can offer her nothing. You did the same . . . more than once as I recall, seeing as how I'm husband number four."

Lena chuckled and rose, slapping him on his knee. "Christ's bones, it's a difficult life we lead, isn't it?"

He drew up one knee and leaned on it, staring out the window. "This is all my own fault. I should have stayed away from her to begin with. I should never have allowed myself . . . allowed her to get to me."

"You men." Lena went to a small table and poured them both a portion of brandy wine. "You think love is something you can control as you control most everything else." She pushed the brandy into his hand. "But you're wrong. I always thought love came when you least expected it." She lifted the glass to her lips. "And when you needed it most."

Griffin took a sip of the brandy. It burned a path down his throat to his stomach. "I left Bassett Hall because I was a coward. I didn't want to see her marry him. I didn't want to see her dance in his arms. Only . . ."

Lena swirled the brandy in her glass. "Only?"

"Only I know she wanted me to stay. She said she didn't, but I know she did."

"You were right to come here. If she has made her choice, you can't interfere. St. Martin is a dangerous weasel of a man. He can't be trusted, never could be, not even as a child. You knew that when you joined his household in those silly costumes of yours."

"Let's not start that again."

"Yes, yes, yes." She fluttered her hand to pacify him. "A place to reside in Londontown and a respected man to hide behind." She smoothed the silk of her gown. "All the more reason why you shouldn't go. Every coat of arms in the kingdom will be represented there. Your enemies will be there cloaked as wedding guests."

"Julia might need me. Tomorrow she will surely need me." He glanced up, trying not to think of her in Simeon's arms. "I'm the only friend she has. Her mother is useless, and her sister is weak-minded. I should go back to London now."

Lena started to say something, then stopped.

"What?" Griffin demanded.

"Nothing." She sipped her brandy.

"Nothing? Since when have you had no opinion? You were going to say something."

"All right, I was. But it's only a waste of my frail breath."

He waited, knowing she would continue.

"As your friend, as your wife," she said, "I have to say you should stay here. If St. Martin ever realizes what has passed between you—"

"We didn't." As he spoke the denial, he wished desperately that he *had* made love to her that night in the tavern. At least then he would have that part of her to carry with him always.

"If he finds out what has passed between you, even in thoughts and words," Lena continued, "he'll have you cut into bits and thrown to the fish in the Thames. There's nothing a man hates more, even than a man who *sleeps* with his wife, than a man who is *loved* by his wife." She took a sip of her brandy. "But," she added more softly.

His gaze met hers. "But?"

"But as a woman." She raised a long, delicate finger. "If it were me marrying St. Martin, I would want the man I loved to be there for me in the morning. To comfort me. To lend me his strength to go on."

Griffin rose, leaving his glass in the window seat. "Thank

you." He kissed Lena as he passed her in his rush to get out the door. "My horse," he ordered the servant. "And a fresh mount as well."

Lena smiled sadly and caught his hand as he went by. "Promise me you'll be careful. You'll be no good to any of us, me, Julia, or our king, if you're at the bottom of the river."

He squeezed her hand and pulled away. He had to get back to London. He had to get to Bassett Hall. He knew he would miss the three o'clock wedding, but at least he would make the evening's celebrations. "I'll be careful."

"Swear it, Griffin."

"I'll be careful," he repeated as he pushed through the draped doorway.

"Do not sleep with her, Griffin!" Lena caught the heavy drapes to hold them open. "Tell me you won't," she called down the hallway. "You sleep with St. Martin's wife, and I'll be a widow again."

"I won't sleep with her!"

Lena let the brocade drape fall as Griffin's footsteps faded. "Right. You won't sleep with her," she declared aloud, tossing up both hands. "And I'm the Queen Mother."

Julia sat stiffly in the carriage beside her husband, surrounded by mountains of pink satin and lace.

Husband. Her face was without expression, her heart without emotion. She was now the Lady St. Martin, wife to the Earl of St. Martin, one of the wealthiest, most powerful men in all of England.

The carriage bounced, sending its occupants swaying. Simeon's leg touched hers before he righted himself by grabbing one of the leather handholds attached to the wall and jerked his leg away from hers.

"If the debt is not repaid with interest in thirty days, the lands will be confiscated." Simeon gestured with his hand to

Mr. Gordy, who was attempting to write a letter in the rocking carriage. "So on and so forth. The Earl of St. Martin, dated yesterday."

Across from them, Mr. Gordy nodded as he dipped his quill in a tiny ink bottle atop the traveling desk and hurried to complete the letter.

"Now, you have the list of whom I expect in my private quarters tonight. Be certain that they are not aware of the others."

Gordy nodded, still writing. "Yes, my lord."

Julia glanced at Simeon, wondering if she had really heard what she thought she'd heard. First her new husband conducted business on the way back from the chapel, and now men in his private quarters? Did that mean he expected her to entertain in her bedchamber on her wedding night?

She touched her hand to her forehead, wondering if she should have taken a little of the laudanum her mother had offered her before they left Bassett Hall for the church. Perhaps it would have dulled her senses, and the smell of Simeon's garlic pouch around his neck would not have been quite so strong.

Simeon must have realized she was staring at him. He smoothed one gloved hand and then the other. He always wore gloves in public to prevent touching others skin to skin. It was one of his personality traits she had come to despise.

"Business matters that won't wait," Simeon explained. "It shan't take long. You don't mind, do you, dear?"

He asked, but Julia didn't think he really cared what she thought. She knew she should have sat quietly and nodded her head, but something snapped inside and she couldn't help herself. "Marry come up," she shouted, startling Gordy. "You're inviting men into our bedchamber on our wedding night?" For the first time this day she felt a flash of emotion. It was anger, hot and all-consuming. "Mind? Indeed I do mind, sir. I will not have men in my bedchamber on my wedding night! I will have my husband, alone, without secretaries, without servants, without his mountains of paper, and without his *futtering garlic!*''

He reached out to slap her, but Julia raised her arm to stop him.

Mr. Gordy's eyes were so round and bulging that Julia thought they might pop out of his head.

''Are you eavesdropping on my conversation?'' Simeon shrilled, lowering the hand he would have struck her with. He gave Gordy a hard kick to the shins.

''No. No, my lord.'' Gordy dropped his gaze to the desk in his lap. ''Of course not, my lord,'' he mumbled.

The moment before Simeon turned on Julia gave her time to realize what a mistake she'd made. She should have kept her mouth shut. She should have just let him hit her once and given him that sense of power, that sense of total possession he seemed to crave.

''How dare you,'' Simeon hissed, drawing his face close to hers.

This time he made no attempt to strike her, but she almost wished he had. Then it would have been over and done with. Then she wouldn't be so afraid.

''How dare you speak to me that way? How dare you suggest that you have any right to say what I will and will not do, whom I will and will not have to my chambers?''

Julia flinched. If the carriage hadn't been rolling so fast, she thought she might have opened the door and just jumped.

''Who do you think you are?'' he screamed, sending spittle flying in the close air. ''And what makes you think that I would have you in my private chambers? You will stay in your own woman's quarters. I'll not have your squalor in my rooms. I'll not have your dusty shoes, your filthy gardening gloves, your woman's blood,'' he raged.

Julia sank back into the corner as far from Simeon as she could get within the confines of the carriage. ''I'm sorry.'' She spoke softly, but she didn't cower. "I assumed that as your wife I would join you in your bed."

"Well, you assumed incorrectly!"

He shouted the words with such conviction that it suddenly occurred to Julia that he was afraid of her . . . or at least afraid of what he was expected to do to her as her husband. The epiphany so amused her that she had to clamp her pink lace handkerchief over her mouth to keep from laughing aloud.

Simeon, the heir to the St. Martin fortune and lands, was afraid to have relations with his wife.

Chapter Twelve

After that, Julia's mood lightened considerably. Simeon didn't really want to bed her. If she was lucky, he would only come to her once every year or so, just enough to get her with child. She could tolerate those circumstances, knowing she would remain in her own bedchambers with Lizzy, where she could look after her. It was certainly better than having a husband she detested pawing over her nightly. If she played her game pieces correctly, Julia surmised, she might well be able to simply ignore her marriage and her pathetic husband.

Saved by their arrival at Bassett Hall, Julia alighted from the carriage on her husband's arm. She understood Simeon well enough to know he would not take their argument inside with them. Appearances were too important to his lordship. She might have hell to pay tonight, but for now she was safe.

They climbed the stone steps that had been covered in fabric in the St. Martin colors of green and white, and entered the front hall. Julia was immediately overwhelmed by the rush of the cheering crowd. Simeon must have invited every nobleman in London.

More than two hundred guests had arrived some days before to celebrate the marriage of the Earl of St. Martin to Lady Julia, eldest daughter of Byron Thomas, the previous earl of St. Martin. For many, she guessed, it was in honor of her father that they came, rather than for Simeon's sake, for he, unlike his nephew, had been a well-respected, well-liked man. Of course there were probably others who were here simply because they feared Simeon and didn't want to cross him by not making an appearance today.

Because Simeon was her father's eldest male relative, Simeon had inherited the title and her father's lands upon his death seven years ago. But he had inherited her father's debts as well as his lands and title. The last Lord St. Martin had been a generous man through the war and the years of Cromwell's reign, giving away money and favors.

From the look of Bassett Hall and some of Simeon's other acquisitions, he had been busy taking while her father had been giving. Although Simeon had sworn allegiance to Charles II upon his return to London, Julia knew from her mother's and father's whispers that Simeon had been a friend and confidante to Old Knoll, and that Cromwell had rewarded those who were loyal to him with the lands of those who were not. It was through Simeon's influence that her father, a barely concealed Royalist, had been able to retain his lands. Now Julia realized that it was not for her well-being or her father's that Simeon had offered that protection, but rather to conserve the wealth that would someday be his.

"Warm wishes," guests offered Julia as she entered the front hall and passed them on Simeon's arm.

"May you have many sons," called others.

Someone tossed dried rose petals at her, and they fluttered through the air.

Because only a few were actually invited to the church for

the wedding ceremony, their guests had found the opportunity to begin drinking hours ago. Many were already rosy-checked and well in their cups. Musicians played in the great hall and every candelabra in the house glimmered with the light of expensive white wax tapers. Everyone was laughing and offering their congratulations. They all seemed so pleased for her good fortune. She wondered if they would all be so happy for her if they knew that St. Martin had blackmailed her into marrying him. What would they think if they knew he had threatened to harm her addlepated sister to make this union? Would they then be grinning like sheep?

"Oh, Sister!" Lizzy burst through a group of women to plant herself in front of Julia and Simeon. Under Simeon's instructions Lizzy had been forced to remain at Bassett Hall and not accompany her sister to the church. For leverage, Julia guessed.

"So it's done?" Lizzy bubbled excitedly. "You're a married woman?"

Simeon gingerly released Julia's arm. "Go, go," he said quietly, waving his gloved hand. "See to her, but if she disturbs my guests, she'll be sent to her chambers."

Julia lifted the pink ruffled hem of her gown and curtsied deeply to Simeon. The gown showed a great deal of her bosom, but he didn't seem to notice. "I'll see you're brought refreshment, my lord."

He gazed at her with a look on his face that made her think he hated her at this moment. "See that you do."

Julia grabbed Lizzy's arm and ushered her through the crowd, thankful to escape Simeon's barely concealed wrath. God only knew how she would face him tonight when he tried to bed her . . . *if he tried,* she thought hopefully.

"Oh, I wish I could have been at the church, but Mother said his lordship said I couldn't." Lizzy held tightly to Julia's arm as they squeezed between two gentlemen deep in argument.

Lizzy thrust out her lower lip. "I wanted to go on my own, but Amos wouldn't let me."

"At least one of you has some common sense," Julia said tartly as she pulled her sister into an alcove beneath the grand staircase. She lifted the mountains of sickeningly pink lace to adjust one of her ribbon garters. "You must never leave the house without an escort, Lizzy. London is a dangerous place. I've told you that time and time again."

"I wanted to go to the church." Lizzy crossed her arms over her chest. She wore the white and pink chintz gown Julia had instructed Drusilla to dress her in. It was utterly becoming on her sister, and, though pink, far prettier than the confection Julia had been forced to wear.

"But I wanted to see you get married." Lizzy pouted.

Julia lowered her skirt, breathing deeply to calm her pounding heart encased in too-tight stays. She was so relieved to get away from Simeon. How was she going to mingle with his guests and pretend she was happily married, when all she wanted to do was slit the man's throat? "I know you wanted to see me wed. I wanted you to be there, too." Julia squeezed Lizzy's arm, hoping to appease her. "But his lordship wished for you to remain here—to welcome our guests."

"His lordship wishes this," Lizzy mocked. "His lordship wishes that." She stomped her small foot. "I'm sick to death of what his lordship wishes. If you ask me, his lordship, the Earl of St. Martin, is nothing but a pile of stinking horse doo!"

"Lizzy!" Julia grabbed her hand and tugged hard, peering out of the shadows, hoping no passerby had heard her sister. "You can't say things like that!" She pulled Lizzy closer to her, into the shadows beneath the stairs. Even the darkest recesses of Bassett Hall smelled of lye soap and damp wood. "He is my husband, and your protector and cousin, and you have to respect him."

Lizzy yanked her hand away. "I don't have to like him."

"No, you don't have to like him," Julia hissed, afraid for

her sister. What had gotten into her? Why was she behaving so boldly? Lizzy had always been so meek and compliant. "But you have to respect him."

Lizzy crossed her arms over her chest and hung her head, tears gathering in the corners of her eyes. "I don't have to like him," she repeated softly.

Julia sighed and rubbed her sister's shoulder. "Ah, Lizzy, don't cry. Not today, please."

"You're angry with me."

"I'm not." Julia continued to rub Lizzy's shoulder in soothing circular motions. "I just want you to be cared for, to be safe. That's all I've ever wanted."

"I'm going to find my own husband to take care of me, and then you won't have to be married to *him*."

"Lizzy," Julia said as gently as possible. "We've talked about this before. You're not going to get married. You're going to stay here with me because I need you. I need you to take care of my babies, God willing I'm so blessed."

Lizzy dropped a hand to her hip and opened her mouth to speak again, then clamped it shut.

Julia ran a hand over the smooth crown of her head to be certain every hair was in place. "Now, Lizzy, I have to tend to his lordship's guests. Why don't you have something to eat? I'm sure there's something wonderful on the buffet table. Pickled quails' eggs maybe," she enticed.

"Can I just go to the kitchen? To . . . to check on the pies," she finished quickly.

Julia knew Lizzy belonged here among men and women of her own station, or even upstairs with her nursemaid, not in the kitchen with the servants. But how could she deny her, today of all days? At least one of them should be happy for a few moments.

"Oh, all right," Julia conceded.

Lizzy squealed with delight. "Oh, thank you, thank you."

She hopped on one foot and then the other. "I won't be long. I vow I won't."

Julia watched her sister dart out of the shadows and hurry down the back hallway in the direction of the kitchen, her skirts swaying on her shapely hips. At that moment she realized someone was watching her.

She met Mr. Gordy's gaze.

How long had he been there? Had he heard any of their conversation? Sweet Mary, she hoped she hadn't said anything derogatory about Simeon. She didn't think she had, but how could she be sure the secretary hadn't taken something she said wrongly?

He stared at her with those cool gray eyes of his.

Julia refused to be intimidated. "Good afternoon, Gordy." She stepped out from beneath the staircase as if brides always hid beneath the steps of their new homes.

He straightened his back, lowering his gaze to the floor as he bowed. "Good afternoon, my Lady St. Martin."

She breezed past him. "See to his lordship's glass, will you, Gordy? Keep it filled." Perhaps if he drank and played cards until the wee hours, he'd be too tired to consummate the marriage tonight. Julia knew their joining was inevitable, but the longer she could put it off, the better.

"Yes, my lady." Gordy stepped out of her way.

Julia smiled graciously and offered her hand to the nearest guest, who just happened to be the lecherous Duke of Buckingham.

"Your Grace." She curtsied deeply.

"My Lady St. Martin." The black-haired Stuart stared at her breasts with obvious interest.

Julia took his arm. "Would you care to walk with me and greet my guests?"

"Flattered, madame."

An utterly predictable man like this Julia could manage. But she was fooling herself if she thought she could ignore or

manage Simeon. He had surprised her by his acts and deeds
on more than one occasion, and that was what made him dangerous. It was that unpredictability that could well get her or
someone she loved killed.

Lizzy led Amos by the hand into the pantry and closed the
door behind them. Inside, the noises of the frantic kitchen
softened.

"Lizzy! I'm very busy," he whispered. "I haven't time to
play games."

She giggled in the semidarkness. The small room was lined
floor to ceiling with shelves, filled with wax-sealed jars, some
of dried fruits and vegetables, others of pickled meats. The
only light inside seeped from the brightly lit kitchen, through
the louvers of the double doors. It made perfect lines across
the skirt of her new pink and white gown.

"I just wanted to see you for a minute," Lizzy chided.
"You've been so busy for days getting ready for this wedding
that you haven't had time to talk to me."

Amos tucked his hands behind him as if he didn't want to
touch her, only they were so close in the tiny room that her
gown brushed against him. She could feel the heat of his body.
She could smell that scent of his she loved. She knew some
of it was just flour and apple tarts, but some of it was him.

Lizzy reached out and grasped his shoulders. He still kept
his hands behind his back as if they were tied there, which
seemed very silly to her.

"Lizzy," he whispered as if he was angry with her, only
she knew he wasn't.

"I want a kiss," she said. "Then I'll go. Then I'll let you
out of my dungeon."

He tried to back away from her, but his foot hit something
and it fell over and rolled into something else, making a cracking

sound. She hoped they hadn't broken the jar of pickled quails' eggs. They were one of her favorite treats.

Lizzy giggled and leaned closer, puckering her lips for him. "You must kiss me, else you'll die in this dungeon."

He groaned as if he was hurt, only she knew he wasn't. It was that "inside his heart" pain that he'd tried to tell her about. That pain that said he loved her, only he knew he wasn't allowed to.

"Lizzy, you're going to get us both in trouble. You told your sister you would stay away from me. That—that," he stuttered, "you wouldn't kiss me anymore."

Lizzy brushed her lips against his. At first he just stood stiff, but then he threw his arms around her and pulled her tightly against him. He kissed her so hard that Lizzy couldn't breathe. She liked it when Amos kissed her so hard she went dizzy.

"I lied," she whispered

Griffin hadn't intended to get drunk. It just happened. A few miles from Lena's, he stopped at a run-down tavern to quench his thirst. He made a detour to the next tavern four miles down the road for another pint to warm himself on the cold, wet ride. At the next inn, he bought six bottles of sack to comfort himself. He had lost his love, his Julia, to Simeon, and there was nothing he could do about it . . . except to drink to forget. Only the more he drank, the more upset he became. The more upset he became, the more ale he needed to soothe himself.

By the time Griffin rode into London, he could barely stay astride his horse. The sun had set and rain fell steadily, soaking him miserably to the bone. He knew he was just feeling sorry for himself, but he didn't care. Every man deserved to indulge in a little self-pity on occasion, didn't he?

Griffin rode up Aldersgate Street, which was deserted save for a few pedestrians and hell carts for hire. As he drew closer to Bassett Hall, carriages appeared, parked on both sides of the street. Footmen and drivers huddled around small fires built to keep themselves warm. Griffin stared at the coats of arms on the coaches as he slowly rode by.

He hiccuped and took a pull from the wine bottle in his hand. He couldn't recall where it had come from. Was it supposed to be a wedding gift from Lena's cellars? He hiccuped again, only this one turned into a satisfying belch. "Damn, Simeon," he said aloud, deciphering the family names as he rode by. "Anyone in all Christendom you didn't invite?"

The bottle empty, he let it slip from his fingers. It hit the ground and rolled under his mount's feet. The horse danced to keep from stepping on the rolling bottle.

"Whoa, whoa, whoa there." Griffin slid in the saddle. He tried to grab the horse's mane to catch himself, but he missed. "Oops."

Griffin didn't feel himself fall, just felt the hard jolt as he hit the ground, tail bone first. "Ouch. Damnation. Winged saints in hell." He tried to think of a more creative curse, maybe a French one, the French were good at cursing, only his mind was too fuzzy.

"Baron Archer?"

Griffin looked up from the muddy ground to see a footman in the St. Martin green and white livery.

"Y . . . Yes?" He pushed up off the street, managing to stand on only the second try. He didn't really need the servant's arm, but he allowed him to assist anyway, just so he would feel needed.

"You are well, my lord?"

Griffin tried to dust off his doublet, but his hands slid over the caked mud. Hell, he must have lost his cloak somewhere. Lena would be sorely vexed. She'd had it brought from the Holy Land for him.

"Fine. Superior." Griffin stiffened his spine and stood upright. He went to tip his feathered cavalier's cap, only to find it was gone, too. "Thieves," he explained, lowering his hand as he passed the servant who held his horse's reins. "They'll rob a man blind on the highways these days." Griffin couldn't recall having encountered highwaymen tonight, but surely it was possible. It *sounded* like a reasonable explanation.

"Yes, my lord." The boy followed, leading Griffin's horse.

"See . . . see to my horse." Griffin caught the iron rail of the front step. He wanted to see Julia. He had to.

"You going to the banquet, my lord?"

"I am. After all, I am the cousin of the groom. Bride, too, somehow." He tried to think for a moment. If he was Simeon's cousin by way of his mother's marriage to one of Simeon's cousins, and Julia was Simeon's first cousin, that made Julia his—ah, piss. He couldn't figure it out.

Griffin took the first step.

"My Lord Archer."

Griffin halted on the step that seemed to sway beneath him. It had been a long time since he'd been this drunk. Years. He'd forgotten how much he hated this feeling. He blinked, wishing the man would stand still when he spoke and stop swaying. It was making Griffin nauseous. "Yes?"

"Would . . . would you care to slip in the back up to your apartments and change your clothes first, my lord?"

Griffin glanced down at his doublet. By the light of torches sunk in the ground on either side of the stone steps, he could see that it was muddy and torn, and one horn button was missing. "So I'm a little dusty from my travel."

The servant lowered his gaze as if fearful to speak. "Your breeches, my lord."

"My breeches?" he asked indignantly. God's bowls, wasn't there a servant left in London who knew his place?

"Your breeches, my lord," he repeated apologetically. Then he pointed.

Griffin looked down, taking care to hold tightly to the rail, his feet firm on the step.

Hmmmm. His breeches were open, his cod swinging merrily

in the breeze. He fumbled with the fabric, tucking himself in. But the ribbon that tied his breeches shut was gone. Had he lost the ribbon the last time he'd stopped alongside the road to relieve himself, or had the bandits gotten that, too?

Griffin eyed the servant. "You think I ought to"—hiccup—"tidy up a bit before I greet the bride and groom?"

The young man nodded. Griffin could have sworn he saw the flicker of a smile on the lad's face, but his voice was filled with an appropriate, subservient demeanor. Must have been the poor lighting.

Griffin backed down the step. "Excellent idea." He stumbled on a loose brick on the walk, but caught himself against his mount's side. He patted the wet, mud-splattered horse. "Good boy. Good horse, good whatever the hell your name is."

Griffin pointed toward a gate that led to the rear of Bassett Hall. "I think I'll go in the back and change before announcing my arrival."

"Yes, my lord."

Griffin tripped only once between the front door and the back, and complimented himself on his excellent carriage. He managed to reach his apartments on the third floor without a soul seeing him. Inside he flopped down on his bed on his back and closed his eyes so the velvet bed drapes wouldn't spin in circles above him.

"Christ's bones, I'm too old for this," he muttered.

Something warm and soft brushed against him. He heard the low hum of a cat's purr.

"Charles, Your Highness." Griffin opened his eyes.

The black cat purred and rubbed his head against Griffin's. Griffin petted the cat. "Are you well, sire, king of all cats?"

Purring, Charlie placed first one front paw, then the other on Griffin's forehead, and began to knead it rhythmically.

"Get off." Griffin pushed the cat off his head, his wig going with it. "Don't you see I'm trying to get dressed?"

The cat placed both paws on the blond wig and kneaded. Purred.

"I can't be bothered with cats. I've more important business to attend to. Secrets to discover. Vicious plots to dethrone our king to uncover."

The cat turned and sat back on Griffin's face.

Griffin gave the cat's rear end a push, spitting cat fur. "That's what I always get, isn't it? The ass end. The first time I've ever wanted something for myself in my life, and nothing but the crust for good old Griffin."

He grabbed the bedpost to steady himself and sat up. "What I need is another drink."

Griffin yanked off his riding boots, dropped them to the floor, and with a heave ho, came up off the feather tick.

"Gotta have a drink. Gotta get dressed." He poured himself brandy. "Gotta let Julia know I'm here if she needs me." He belched and wiped his mouth with the torn sleeve of his shirt. "Here if she needs to be comforted."

Griffin wove his way across the room, shedding his clothes as he went. He would wash and dress, go downstairs, and simply speak to the bride and groom, offer them his congratulations, and return to his bedchamber to sleep off his drunk. With all the commotion of the festivities, few would know he had ever passed through.

Naked, Griffin emptied his glass with one hand as he threw open his clothes press with the other. What was this world coming to that a Baron had to dress himself? Where was Jabar? A man needed a manservant to dress properly.

The glass slipped from Griffin's hand. *Crap. Where was Jabar?* He pressed the heel of his hand to his temple, trying hard to remember. Where was his faithful, turbaned friend? Surely Jabar had not been taken by highwaymen, along with his hat, his cloak, and the string to Griffin's breeches?

Then it came to him in a moment of revelation. He and Jabar had parted at the first crossroads, Griffin taking the road to

London, and Jabar riding west to carry a message. He'd be home later tonight, or in the morning if he chose to take shelter in a tavern's barn.

"Phew, that was close," Griffin threw over his shoulder in the direction of the cat. Charlie was sleeping soundly, curled up inside the cap of his wig. Griffin returned his attention to the task at hand—getting dressed. *Focus.* He had to focus. He reached for a doublet that hung on a peg. A fuchsia floral. Next, a pair of breeches. Pink and orange stripes. *Perfect.*

"There's that blessed shirt I've been looking for." He pulled from the bottom of the press a pink linen shirt with wide lace cuffs. "My favorite shirt. I knew it wasn't lost. Jabar only hid it from me." He tossed the shirt over his shoulder. "Shoes. Shoes."

No shoes in the press.

He crouched to look under the press. No shoes. He tried to stand, swayed, and went down on both knees, which was actually fine because the best way to capture shoes was to search for them on their own level. He discarded the clothing he'd chosen, and crawled across the floor to look under the bed. He found one heeled slipper in bright pink and another in green. Griffin sat up. Where were the matches? Where did Jabar keep his damned shoes?

He crawled across the polished plank floor searching under chairs, piles of papers, and discarding clothing for one of the missing shoes. Damn, it was cold on the floor.

"Where are you when a man needs you, Jabar?" he said finally, sitting back to lean against his bed and allow the room to cease spinning. "I've got to get down there. My Julia needs me."

He took a deep breath and crawled on all fours in another direction. The damned shoes had to be here somewhere . . .

Chapter Thirteen

Julia was surrounded by bantering hens. The painted women with their too tight gowns and fluttering fans all talked at once, engaged in what seemed to be one of London's favorite pastimes, gossiping. As Julia listened with one ear, it seemed to her that the women fought to determine who could ruin whose reputation with the most originality.

"Well, I understand she's been sent to the country to whelp another bastard," cooed a woman with eyebrows drawn in an inverted V. "Second in three years. You think her husband would either claim them or drown them. *He* certainly won't be getting any children with her, not where his interests lie." She fluttered her lashes.

"No!" another woman exclaimed. "Do tell. I heard that he got her youngest sister in *situation,* and she'd had to be married off to a parson's son only last month!"

A thin woman with a mousy, pinched face squealed and fanned her face vigorously. "Emma! How dare you spread such slander about my cousin!"

The women in the catch grew instantly round-eyed. *Caught*.

"Indeed not. I'll not stand here and allow such untruthful babble. It will be the ruination of poor Sarah." The mouse's nose twitched as she leaned closer. "Now, let me tell you who *really* fathered the babe."

Fans fluttered and the matrons drew behind them to hear the latest tidbit. They took no notice as their hostess backed away, knowing she'd not be missed. "Your servant, ladies," Julia said softly.

As she excused herself from the gossips, there was a stir on the far side of the parlor. She heard numerous gasps and a few giggles. Someone cleared his throat to gain another's attention, while a man in a curly periwig laughed aloud. Julia searched the room until her gaze reached the source of the commotion.

Griffin.

He wasn't supposed to be here. Her heart leapt beneath her breast. Thank God he'd come.

But something wasn't right. She recognized it immediately.

Griffin was wearing two different shoes, one green, one pink. Both were heeled, but one slightly higher than the other, forcing him to stand with one knee perpetually bent.

She couldn't take her eyes off him.

He was dressed abominably, even for him. Stripes with florals? Fuchsia with red and green? He looked like a man who had been draped by a dressmaker's scraps from the cutting room floor.

Julia lifted her hand to cover her mouth and trap a nervous giggle. It really wasn't funny. Simeon tolerated his ridiculous fashions because it amused him, but Griffin had pushed the matter too far tonight. To appear at the Earl of St. Martin's wedding banquet dressed like that would be a mockery to his title . . . or was Griffin mocking himself?

Guests immediately encircled Griffin, all talking at once. He was popular among the ladies as well as the gentlemen, and the lords didn't seem to mind how much time he spent with their wives. No doubt they thought themselves *safe* from being cuckolded by him, believing him a homosexual.

Only Julia knew otherwise.

Her first impulse was to go to him. She wanted to touch him, to hear him speak her name, to share a secret smile. She could greet him as she would any guest; no one would think oddly of it. But she didn't trust herself to speak, not yet. She could hear Simeon's distinctive voice nearby. It wouldn't do for him to see her and Griffin together right now, not as vulnerable as she felt. Simeon might sense something, smell it.

Julia heard Griffin guffaw and others followed suit. He didn't sound like himself, not even the Griffin others thought him to be. She watched him sway in his mismatched shoes, and a gentleman offered a hand to right him.

Heavens! Was Griffin drunk? Julia had seen him pretend to be so on more than one occasion, but tonight the slightly slurred speech and lack of balance appeared genuine.

Julia lifted her painted fan to give herself some air. What could Griffin have been thinking? If his "business" was as dangerous as he implied, as dangerous as indicated from the incident in the Three Bells, surely he knew better than to become intoxicated. With Bassett Hall so filled with guests, any one of the men could be Griffin's enemy. How could he be so foolish as to put himself at such risk?

Julia's concern for herself and her impending first night with her new husband slipped a notch in priority. None of that mattered at this moment. She needed to get Griffin upstairs to his apartments and out of the house, out of danger's way until he was sober. The only question was, how?

"By the king's cod!" Griffin's voice startled her, and she glanced up to see him coming directly toward her.

"There she is! Our bride." He pushed through the circle of ladies and gentlemen, his arms outstretched to her. "Your servant, my Lady St. Martin." He bowed deeply, presenting a fetching pink-stockinged leg and green slipper. As he rose, he would have fallen had one of his companions not seized his arm.

"My Lord Archer." Julia curtsied as anger tightened her chest. Griffin was drawing attention to himself. To them both. What could he be thinking?

"Might I offer my grand congratulations." He clasped her hand, and lingered too long with a kiss.

"Thank you," she said from between her compressed lips as she pulled her hand from his grasp. Didn't he realize people were watching? But even drunk, the man had a way of getting under her skin. The memory of his warm lips burned on the back of her cool hand. "His lordship thought your business would keep you from London. I'm pleased that you could come, after all."

"Pity I couldn't make the church." His gaze met hers.

Julia felt her cheeks grow warm. There was too much emotion in his voice. He spoke too familiarly to her. Someone was going to take notice. The gossips in the far corner would be talking.

Damn a man and his drunkenness, she thought. *Was this the only way they could deal with their emotions?* Out of the corner of her eye, she could see the clutch of matron hens watching, whispering. How could they miss the sparks that leaped between her and Griffin?

She turned her back to the women. "My lord, would you care for a refreshment?"

His face lit up in a lopsided grin. "I should think I had enough, my Lady St. Martin"—he emphasized her title with mockery—"but if you insist."

Several guests laughed.

This time she made no attempt to hide her displeasure. "I was thinking perhaps coffee, my lord, or tea. Something *without* spirits."

Again, their audience chuckled.

"Touché, my Lady St. Martin.'' Griffin pulled his hands to his chest and grimaced as if he'd been struck by a sword.

More laughter. Wedding guests were filtering into the small withdrawing room off the great hall, all anxious to see the baron's latest performance. Julia had to get him out of the house before Simeon saw him like this.

She tapped him on the shoulder none-too-lightly with her folded fan. ''I could use some cool air, and I'll warrant you could as well. Care to walk with me, my lord?''

''A pleasure.'' He grinned.

She did not.

Griffin sauntered up to Julia with an awkward gait, thanks to his mismatched shoes. She allowed him to clasp her arm, but steered him toward a balcony door that had been left slightly ajar to cool the room.

She tried to remain calm and in control. In Simeon's world, he or she who retained control prevailed. ''This way, sir.''

''But the drink is yonder.'' He hiccuped, fondling her arm with his fingertips.

''But the cold air and my sharp tongue is this way, my lord,'' she whispered between clenched teeth as she feigned a smile.

He arched an eyebrow. ''Ah, hah. And there is the rub, my lovely, isn't it?''

Griffin opened the door to the outside balcony, and Julia passed him. The air was cold, but the rain had ceased and moonlight illuminated the iron railing.

''What do you think you're doing?'' Julia hissed, the moment she thought they were out of earshot of the wedding guests. She faced him, her back to the rail, her petticoats bunched in her hands so they'd not drag in the puddles on the stone floor.

''Doing, my lady?'' He punctuated his question with a hiccup.

''Coming here drunk! You said you had business elsewhere. You said you would be in the country. You said you would be with your *wife!*'' She hadn't meant to sound accusatory. What right did she have to condemn him for being married? She was wed, now, too, wasn't she? Yet as she said the word, she felt the pain of the truth of their impossible situation.

"My heart is broken, my hopes shattered." He clutched his hand to his heart dramatically. In his drunkenness, he had either not heard the pain in her voice, or was too caught up in his performance to react.

"My true love," he continued, "is all but dead to me now."

She dropped her pink petticoats, not caring if the hem got wet. She hated the damned gown anyway. "Griffin!" She tried to speak softly, but it was all she could do to keep from shouting. She touched his arm. "You need to go upstairs and go to bed."

"Alas"—he touched the back of his hand to his forehead—"there is no sleep without you, no—"

She grabbed his shoulders and gave him a shake. "Griffin! This is dangerous and, even in your state, you know it! You can't afford to behave this way. You'll give yourself away. Or us."

His buffoon's mask fell away. Griffin's bloodshot gaze met hers and his blue eyes filled with sadness. "Julia, I—"

The glass door behind him swung open.

Julia's gaze darted from Griffin to the man in the shadows. She sucked in her breath and exhaled with his name. "Mr. Gordy." She prayed he didn't realize how greatly he'd startled her.

Gordy lowered his gaze, but not before absorbing the intimate way Julia and Griffin stood facing each other, the way she drew her hands from his shoulders and tucked them behind her back. Surely he was setting it all to memory to be recounted in Simeon's office.

"My Lady St. Martin, there is a matter I believe you may wish to attend to."

Griffin whipped around. "Can't you see we're having a private conversation?"

Gordy continued to stare at the damp hem of Julia's wedding

gown, ignoring Griffin as if he didn't exist. "It would be best if you came immediately, my lady."

"What is it?" She sidestepped Griffin. "Simeon? Is he ill?"

"No, my lady." The secretary cleared his throat and spoke so softly that Griffin could not have heard him. "Lady Elizabeth."

Julia felt a trickle of cold fear. She brushed past Griffin. "Where?"

Gordy stepped out of her way to hold the door open for her. "The kitchen, my lady."

"Pardon," Griffin interrupted antagonistically. "But I said this was a private conversation. Whatever *his lordship* wants of the lady could wait another moment."

"Griffin—"

"No." Griffin's hand shot out to catch Julia's arm, but Gordy blocked it.

"Keep your hands off the lady!" Gordy threatened.

"Son of a pox-blind whore!"

Julia spun around in time to see Griffin draw back his fist and punch the secretary square in the jaw. Gordy reeled backward, hit the stone wall of the house, and then lunged at Griffin.

"Griffin!" Julia shouted. "That's enough! Mr. Gordy! I will have no brawling!"

But it was too late. Both men were beyond the point of reason. Gordy swung his fist at Griffin, who managed to duck. Gordy's second throw caught him in the nose. Blood splattered across Griffin's shirt and cravat as he fell backwards against the rail. The rail groaned ominously.

Behind Julia, the doorway filled with curious wedding guests. Everyone was talking at once. No one seemed alarmed by the fight, but accepted it as part of the evening's entertainment.

Julia swung back around to face Griffin and Gordy. She had to do something, stop this somehow before Simeon appeared. And her sister! What was wrong with her sister?

Without considering the consequences, Julia threw herself

between the two men. Griffin drew his fist back to take another whack at Gordy and nearly clipped her in the chin.

"Enough!" Julia shouted above the sounds of the crowd in the doorway. In the excitement of the fray, the lords and ladies of London had become as base as the patrons of a dockside tavern.

"I will not have fighting in my home!" She threw up her arms to block the men from one another. "Mr. Gordy, step back! I will see you in the kitchen."

Gordy stared at her, his shoulders thrown back, defiance in his eyes. For a moment Julia feared he would disobey her. What would she do then? Strike him herself? But then he lowered his gaze and slinked back a step.

"Lord Archer," Julia declared with great authority. "Get yourself to your apartments, sir, or get yourself from Bassett Hall." She pointed over the balcony.

Griffin stared at her as he wiped the blood that dribbled from one nostril. "Julia—" he said softly. Suddenly he seemed sober.

"Your chambers, my lord," she repeated angrily. She was so scared, so damned angry.

He opened his mouth to speak again, then closed it.

Without another word, Julia spun around and rushed from the balcony, through the crowd directly toward the kitchen.

"Where is she?" Julia swept into the kitchen to find Gordy nursing a bloody lip. The entire room was buzzing with activity as servants ran to and fro with heavy trays of foodstuffs, all pretending they didn't see their lady of the house and the master's secretary.

Gordy hooked a thumb in the direction of the rear door.

Julia stared without comprehension. "Mr. Gordy?"

He dabbed his lower lip with a damask table napkin and then at his bloodstained shirt. "Outside." His tone was resentful, bordering on disrespectful. "Either the woodshed or the smoke-house."

"Lizzy's in the woodshed?" The instant the words were out of her mouth, it dawned on her that her sister must be *with* someone. She dashed for the door.

Julia ran along the stone walkway. It was raining again and her breath made puffs of frost in the cold air, but she didn't feel the chill. "Lizzy? Lizzy?" she called frantically. She threw open the door to the woodshed. "Lizzy, are you in here?"

No answer. But the shed was small enough to leave no place to hide. There was no one there, nothing but ceiling-high cords of wood and a few startled rodents. Julia slammed the door closed behind her and ran for the smokehouse.

"Lizzy! Lizzy!" She threw open the door.

Lizzy gave a squeal of surprise.

Even in the darkness, Julia recognized the shape of a man and woman locked in an amorous embrace.

"Lizzy Thomas!" Julia stepped up into the smokehouse.

Lizzy spun around, drawing a wool shawl around her shoulders, but not before Julia caught a flash of a bare breast in the moonlight.

Julia halted in the doorway in shock. She couldn't believe this was happening. Her first impulse was to blame Amos. It was all his fault. He was leading her little sister astray. But she knew it wasn't so. From the look on Lizzy's face, she knew the girl—the woman—was not being taken advantage of. She was enjoying it too much. "Lizzy! What are you doing?"

Lizzy grabbed a large bundle wrapped in cloth from a shelf behind her. "Getting another ham, Sister?"

Amos appeared out of the shadows, dodging a leg of lamb that hung from a hook on the rafter. The smell of the smoky meat was so strong and Julia's concern for her sister so great that her stomach lurched. She hoped she wasn't going to be sick.

She snapped her fingers. "Lizzy! Come here this minute."

Instead of immediately reacting to Julia's command, Lizzy turned and spoke to Amos. "Here's your ham," she said softly. "I have to go."

Julia could have sworn she saw her sister smile coquettishly.

"My lady." Amos came forward, the ham cradled in his arms. "This was my doin'. Not hers. Punish me, not Lizzy, please."

"Amos Wright, you bald-headed liar!" Lizzy accused. "Was not your idea. It was mine and you know it! You wanted to come alone to get the ham, but I said I'd help. I said it because I wanted to kiss you."

Julia grabbed Lizzy's hand. She couldn't believe this was happening. Was Lizzy actually allowing a man to touch her breasts? She had actually encouraged him?

But as Julia pulled her sister from the small outbuilding, she felt a shameful twinge of jealousy. Somewhere deep inside, a part of her wished it was she and Griffin in that smokehouse, and not Lizzy and Amos. "Lizzy, let's go before anyone sees you out here."

"My Lady St. Martin." Amos ran after them, the ham still cradled in his arms.

"Tomorrow, Amos." Julia didn't turn to look at him. "I'll speak with you on the morrow."

"I'll see you tomorrow," Lizzy called over her shoulder, as Julia forcefully ushered her toward the kitchen door.

Upstairs, Julia threw open the door to her apartments and gave Lizzy a push inside. "Drusilla? Drusilla, are you here?" She nudged Lizzy into the closest chair. "Drusilla?"

A door opened off the sitting room and Julia heard the shuffle of the old woman's feet. "Ye ready to dress for your night, are ye?" She gave a cackly laugh. "Early yet. Groom must be anxious, he must."

Julia felt her cheeks burn. She knew she shouldn't pay any attention to Drusilla's muttering, but the nursemaid's words brought thoughts of her wedding night tumbling down on her again.

"No, Drusilla. I'm not ready for bed. Please see to her." She pointed at Lizzy. She knew she shouldn't be this angry. Of course Lizzy hadn't been a willing participant in whatever took place in that smokehouse. Lizzy didn't know what she was doing. She didn't understand. But it was Julia's duty to see it didn't happen again. There was no telling what Simeon would do if he discovered Lizzy was sullying herself with the cook. Julia envisioned the dog and Simeon's shovel.

"Get her dressed for bed and put her in the trundle in your room."

Drusilla turned her attention to Lizzy, squinting her eyes. "What's she done?"

Julia covered her face with her hand in frustration. "I don't have time to talk, Drusilla. I have to get downstairs. Down to my husband." The word stuck in her dry throat. "Please just put Lizzy to bed and be sure she stays there. I don't care if you have to tie her to the bedpost."

Drusilla's eyes grew even narrower as she stared at Lizzy. "Been sinning again, have you?"

"No." Lizzy crossed her arms and stuck out her lower lip.

"You were with that man again, weren't you?"

Tears began to roll down Lizzy's flushed cheeks.

Drusilla grabbed Lizzy's hand and pulled her out of the chair. "Any man that hurts you, I'll kill 'em, I will."

"Don't kill Amos. I'm sorry. I'm sorry." Lizzy broke into full-fledged tears. "Please don't kill my Amos."

"Ah Lizzy." Julia could feel her heart tearing thread by thread. "It's all right." She rubbed her sister's hunched shoulders. "No more of that talk," Julia told Drusilla. "No one is going to kill anyone." She lifted on her toes and kissed her sister's cheek. "Go to bed with Drusilla. We'll talk about this tomorrow, after all of us have had a good night's sleep."

Lizzy sniffed and wiped her nose with the back of her hand. "No one's going to kill my Amos?"

Julia smiled and stroked her sister's cheek. "Of course not, sweetheart."

"Good." Lizzy allowed her nursemaid to lead her away. "Because I love him and I'm going to marry him."

"Marry him?" Julia stared at her sister wide-eyed. Surely those words had not come out of Lizzy's mouth. Lizzy marry? Marry a cook? "Liz—"

A knock at the door cut Julia off mid-sentence. Who could that be? "Yes? What is it now?" Impatiently, she whipped around as the door swung open.

It was Mr. Gordy sporting a swollen lower lip, but a clean shirt. "His lordship, my lady. He has looked for you everywhere. Another guest, a guest of importance, has arrived, and he wishes you to receive her immediately."

"Another guest?" Julia felt as if she were spinning out of control. Would this nightmare of a day never end? "This late?"

"Aye."

"Who is it, pray tell?" She threw up her arms in exasperation. "Surely not the king?"

Gordy fluttered his eyelids. "Baron Archer's wife."

Chapter Fourteen

"His . . . his wife?"

There was a suspicious light in Mr. Gordy's eyes. "Yes, m'lady." He spoke slowly, as if he addressed Lizzy. "Baron Archer *is* married, and has been for many years."

Julia felt dizzy. Of course Griffin was married. She had known that from the beginning. And now *she* was married, married until death parted her and Simeon. So why did the thought of meeting Griffin's wife—his ancient, wrinkled, wife—upset her?

Julia moistened her lips. "I'll be down directly, Mr. Gordy."

The moment he closed the door, she raced from the receiving room into her bedchamber. "Drusilla! Quick! I need help with my hair!"

Julia descended the grand staircase, her bright red tresses redressed in waves down her back and over her shoulders. She had added a spot of rouge to her lips and cheeks and redefined her eyes with a touch of kohl.

"Lady St. Martin," Simeon announced from the hall at the bottom of the steps. He lifted one gloved hand toward her in a regal gesture. "You're not ill are you, dear wife?"

Behind the tender words and implied concern, Julia detected his irritation with her. As she descended the last steps, she tried to remain focused on Simeon and not the woman beside him.

A redhead.

A woman obviously, most delightedly, older than she.

The most beautiful woman Julia had ever laid eyes upon.

"Wife!" Simeon spoke sharply. "I asked if you were ill."

She forced her most charming smile. "Of course not, my lord. I but needed to see my sister to bed."

He caught her hand and squeezed it just a little too hard. "Let me introduce you to an honorable guest." He lowered his voice. "Make a good impression. She's a very powerful woman at court."

He led her toward the redhead in a shimmering sheath of gray and silver. The gown was unlike any gown Julia had ever seen, the material unlike any found in Europe, and yet it was exotically, daringly beautiful.

"Allow me to introduce Lady Archer," Simeon said smoothly. "Widow of the *Duke* of Hampton, once the Dowager Hampton, now *Baron* Archer's wife."

The older woman kept her chin high as she lowered herself into a graceful curtsy. Julia stared so hard that she faltered before bending at the knees to curtsy in response.

"My Lady St. Martin." Her voice, rich and deep for a woman's, exuded sensuality. "I am so pleased to meet you." Then the woman did the oddest thing. She embraced Julia warmly, hugging her as her own mother never had.

For a moment Julia relaxed in the older woman's arms. She needed a hug so desperately that even one from a stranger was welcome. Then, remembering who Lady Archer was, she pulled away. "It is indeed a pleasure to meet you as well. I . . . his lordship and I enjoy your husband's, um, company well. He plays an excellent game of backgammon, Lady Archer.''

"Does he, now?''

The baroness's brilliant green eyes twinkled and Julia wondered if Griffin had lied to her about Lena's age. Surely she couldn't have been anywhere near seventy.

"Please, call me Lena.''

Julia couldn't resist a smile. Lena was so friendly, so warm. How could Griffin not love her? Everyone must love her. "And you must call me Julia.''

Simeon hovered as if he wanted to please Lena, but was unsure how. "Lady Archer will be remaining with us a few days, wife. See that rooms are prepared.''

"Adjoining Baron Archer's, my lord?'' Julia hoped neither heard the catch in her voice. Lena waved a fan painted with half-naked, black-haired women in veils. "Unnecessary, dear. Any chamber will do so long as the fleas are calm and the wine sweet.''

Julia smiled at the woman's sense of humor. "I assure you there are no fleas in Lord St. Martin's house.''

"No, I suppose not.'' Lena laughed lightly, but with a tinge of sarcasm. "What flea would dare cross his pristine threshold?''

So she knew something of Simeon's odd habits, did she?

Lena waved her hand in Simeon's direction. "Go, go. You've fulfilled the required introductions, now make your escape. Drink, eat, enjoy your friends, gird your loins before you retire to your wedding chamber with your beautiful wife, St. Martin.''

Simeon bowed and backed out of the room. If Julia hadn't known better, she'd have thought he was actually intimidated by the older woman.

Lena's splendid smile faded the moment Simeon disappeared from sight. She made a clucking sound between her pearly teeth. "Once a donkey's ass, always a donkey's ass.'' She took Julia by the arm and led her into the adjacent parlor, toward a table of refreshments. "He was never likable as a child, either.

But he's always seemed to worship me from afar. Seek my approval.'' She chuckled and lowered her gravelly voice. ''Something to do with the loss of his mother or his bed-wetting as a boy, I'm sure.''

Julia couldn't help but smile. No matter how hard she tried, she couldn't *not* like Lena. ''You knew him as a child?''

''Aye.'' She plucked two chocolate-dipped strawberries from a silver tray and waved for a footman to bring her a flute of French champagne. ''His mother and I were the best of friends. I suckled him myself when Mary went down with the pox.'' She popped the whole berry into her mouth and chewed with an enthusiasm for the food that Julia thought exclusive to males. ''I'd always wished the good Lord had taken the whelp instead of my sweet Mary.''

Julia tried to stifle her shock at the older woman's words. No one dared mock Simeon for fear of losing their life. Lena was indeed a brave woman.

Lena sighed and took a bite of another confection. ''On her deathbed, Mary asked that I watch over him, see him properly taught, see his father remarried well. I tried to convince her we ought to drown him then, but she wouldn't have it, him being her only child.'' Lena offered the bitten strawberry. ''Do have some, dear. You look as if you could use a meal. Doesn't Griffin see you fed?''

Julia froze at mention of Griffin. What did she mean by that? What had Griffin said to her? Surely he'd not—

''Don't look as if you've seen Hamlet's dead father, sweetheart.'' Lena laughed and took a large swallow of the champagne. ''Your secret is safe with me.'' She plucked another strawberry from the tray, her silvery sleeves swishing as she moved. ''But let me give you some advice.'' She stared directly into Julia's eyes. ''May I?''

Julia nodded, unable to trust herself to speak.

''Resist the temptation. You married the worm, make the best of it. Sleep with your husband or sleep alone.''

"I would never—"

"Shhh," Lena soothed. "I know what goes through the heads of the young and in love. It wasn't so many years ago that I was in love with a friend's son, and me great with my third husband's child. I know what it is to pine for another."

Julia could only stare, her nerves on edge. How much did Lena know? Would she say something to Simeon?

Lena patted Julia's arm. "It really won't be such a bad life. Close your eyes and think of something dull when he's rutting—like clipping your toenails, or changing a baby's napkin. Simeon will be done soon enough and roll off you. I guarantee he'll not come often to your chamber, considering how he is about *bodily fluids,*" she scorned. "Just yield occasionally, and stay out of his way the remainder of the time. You might get lucky one of these days, and he'll leave you a widow. One never knows when fate will strike—a fishbone in his throat, or the running bowels." Lena plucked another strawberry from the tray and motioned with it. "These really are quite exquisite. Did they come from that little sweetshop in Cheapside?"

Julia found it hard to redirect her thoughts. How could Lena speak one moment of hoping Simeon would die a painful death, and the next minute question her on shopping? "I don't know. The housekeeper made the arrangements." Julia knotted her hands together. She felt so inadequate beside Lena. So childish. Perhaps it was better that she had married Simeon. She could never hold a candle to this woman. "I will ask her if you like."

Lena's smile was genuine. "You're a sweet young woman." She brushed the back of Julia's hand with her fingertips. "Griffin was right. You are unusual, especially in comparison to the ladies I generally encounter at court. You seem to actually have a mind that functions autonomously, without the aid of a man. I like you."

"I like you, too, Lena," Julia admitted cautiously. "You say what you think. You speak the truth."

"But I didn't always." Her gaze met Julia's and she became

serious. "There was a time when I, too, had responsibilities, when others were affected by my words and deeds. I bit my tongue then. I did what was best for those I loved. It's only in my old age that I've found the freedom to speak my mind."

Julia nodded, understanding. So Griffin must have told her something about them, about her obligation to marry Simeon. Somehow it was comforting to know that Lena understood, even if Griffin didn't.

"Thank you," Julia said softly.

"For what? An old woman's babbling?"

"Thank you for coming. Thank you for talking with me. Thank you for being here for Griffin. He'll need you tomorrow."

"That was precisely what he said of you. That *you* would need *him* on the morrow."

She knew Lena referred to the consummation of the marriage. "I'll be all right. Simeon won't hurt me."

"He wouldn't dare, the little brat. Else I would rap him on the head with my bony knuckles." She banged on the table with her fist, then delicately wiped her hands with a damask napkin and placed it on a footman's tray. "Now where is that dear husband of mine? I understand from Lady Rolfson that he caused quite a stir prior to my arrival."

Julia removed a handkerchief from her sleeve and blotted her warm face. Time was ticking away on the tall case clock on the first landing of the staircase. It was nearly midnight. She frowned. "Upstairs, sleeping off a drunk, I hope."

Lena grimaced. "I feared he'd do something like that. I shouldn't have let him go. I should have shot him in the leg or something. He didn't do anything too foolish, did he? Declare his love for you before Simeon, or swim in the fish pond?"

"A fight with Simeon's secretary, Mr. Gordy."

She winced. "Ouch. Was Simeon irate?"

"I'm not certain he even knows."

"Oh, he knows. That henchman of his spills every kernel,

I assure you.'' She clasped her ringed hands. ''Well, you'd best have a glass of champagne. It's near midnight, dear. Simeon will be ready to retire.'' She glanced up. ''Speak of Satan . . .''

''My Lady Archer, I hope you've found my banquet table acceptable.'' Simeon approached, retaining the false smile that might have charmed his guests, but didn't fool Julia.

''Quite,'' Lena said coolly.

Simeon turned to Julia. ''It's time we retire, wife. Go to your chambers and I will be with you presently.''

Julia's mouth went dry. So, despite his eccentricities, he intended to bed her. She knew it was inevitable—it was what married couples did—but did it have to be tonight?

Lena rolled her eyes. ''God's bowels, Simeon. Couldn't you be a little more tender than that? You sound as if you're sending your bride to fetch your dirty stockings.''

Simeon's gaze darted to Lena, then back to Julia as if he were a chastised child. ''My lady wife, I apologize. That was crude of me.'' He wrung his hands. ''If you would care to retire above, I should be honored to join you shortly.''

''Yes, my lord.'' Julia dipped a quick curtsy to Simeon and then to Griffin's wife. Her heart pounded. This was it. ''Good night, Lena.''

Lena brushed her fingertips against Julia's cheek in a mother's caress. ''Good night, sweet,'' she whispered in her ear. ''Keep in mind my words. Toenails.''

Julia turned away to keep from laughing aloud as Simeon stood staring uneasily at the two women. She headed straight for the grand staircase, her hands clasped in tight fists at her sides. She saw no one, heard no one's calls of congratulations or good nights. All she could think of was Simeon naked in her bed and how she was going to get through this.

Julia was ready for Simeon by the time he arrived in her chambers. Susanne had been nowhere to be found, so Drusilla had helped Julia to remove her wedding gown and dress her in the delicate pink sleeping gown and dressing robe Simeon had ordered himself.

To Julia's surprise, he came to her by the rarely used rear staircase that opened directly into her bedchamber, rather than the front hall.

"Good evening, my—Simeon," Julia said shyly. Her heart was pounding. She'd married him to protect Lizzy, she told herself. She could do this to protect her sister as well. "Would . . . would you care for champagne? Mr. Gordy sent it up."

They stood in her inner bedchamber, he still near the small panelled door that led to the rear staircase. The room was illuminated by the fire on the hearth and a few candles Drusilla had lit near the bed. The old woman had drawn back the counterpane invitingly to reveal pale pink bed linens and plumped pillows. The chamber smelled of hickory wood smoke, but even at arm's length, Julia could smell the strong soap Simeon had just used to bathe. His hair was still damp at the temples.

He just stood there in his floor-length silk dressing robe.

"Champagne?" she repeated awkwardly, wishing he would say something, anything. Do something.

Simeon shook his head stiffly. "No. It's late. I should . . . we should get to bed."

Julia nodded, swallowing against the panic that rose in her throat. As she approached the bed, she kept repeating over and over in her head, Lena's words. *It will be over quickly, and then he'll roll off. It will be over quickly.*

As Julia shrugged out of her dressing robe, her back to him, and slipped into bed, Simeon moved from one candle to the next, blowing them out.

Julia's eyes adjusted to the dim light from the fireplace as Simeon approached the bed.

It was all she could do to keep from clenching her hands with tension. She wanted to close her eyes, but was afraid to.

How bad could it be? she asked herself. Women had been doing it since time began. They wouldn't keep doing it if it were so terribly bad.

Julia watched as Simeon lowered himself onto the side of the bed. He moved stiffly, as if in great pain.

Simeon started as Julia slid her hand to lift the counterpane for him.

He bounced up off the bed and out of her reach as if he feared she might touch him. "My goodness." He shook his head as if he had a twitch. "My goodness."

Julia didn't know what to say. What to do. For heaven's sake, she didn't want to do this, but if she had to, she wanted to get it the hell over with. If he was nervous, perhaps he just needed a moment to relax.

"Simeon," she said softly. "It's been a long day. Let me rub your shoulders."

He twitched again, as if just the thought of her touching him disturbed him. She waited. Finally he lowered himself onto the bed again, his back to her.

Julia raised up to reach out to him.

"Just lay down," he snapped before she touched him.

Tears sprang in her eyes, but she did as he said. *I can get through this,* she thought. For Lizzy.

"Pull up your gown."

She choked back a sob as she slipped her hands beneath the bed linens and gripped her silky gown. But she couldn't do it. She couldn't pull it up and expose herself.

"You do it?" he asked.

She stared at the vaulted ceiling. She could faintly hear the sound of music from the rooms below. "No."

He whipped around, looking at her for the first time since she'd removed her robe. "No?"

She couldn't meet his gaze. She focused on the dancing flame shadows on the ceiling. "Do it yourself."

With a growl of rage he lunged across the bed and on top of her, still fully clothed.

Julia grunted under the assault and turned her head away so that she wouldn't have to look at him or feel his medicinal breath on her face. This close, he reeked so of garlic that she feared she'd gag.

"Go ahead," she whispered. "Do it and get it over with, my lord."

But Simeon made no move. He laid there on top of her, panting as if he'd just climbed a mountain.

"Well?" she said after a moment. His weight pushed her deep into the feather tick. Though he took great care not to bring his face too closely to hers, she felt as if she was suffocating in garlic. "Are you or aren't you, because you're getting damned heavy!"

He reached beneath them and ripped up her gown. Julia flinched instinctively, but she didn't make a sound. She wouldn't give him the satisfaction. *This is the price I pay for Lizzy's safety,* she thought numbly. *The real price.*

Simeon fumbled against her with his hand, perhaps with himself, but he didn't actually touch her.

"Filthy business," Simeon muttered. "Degrading."

Remarkably, the thought of changing a baby's dirty napkin came to Julia's mind . . . Lizzy's napkin. A giggle escaped her lips. She didn't know what madness possessed her. It just happened.

Julia felt Simeon's cold hand brush her bare stomach.

Dirty napkins.

Toenails. She clamped her hand over her mouth to muffle another giggle.

"Winged saints in hell, woman!" Simeon rolled off her, over the side of the bed, and crashed to the floor. "Are you mad?" he screamed as he scrambled to get up and cover the tiny bit of skin on his chest that had been bared in the fumbling. "Stark raving, asylum-bent, mad?"

"I . . . I'm sorry." She hid a grin with her hand. "I am. I'm just nervous. That's all. I won't laugh again. I swear it. Go ahead, have another try."

He yanked the silk tie around his waist tightly and hurried to her washstand. He poured water into the bowl, picked up a sliver of scented soap, and began to scrub his hands violently. "Have you nothing stronger than this?"

She blinked. "My lord?"

"The soap. The soap." He threw it so hard into the washbowl that water splattered over the sides. "And hot water! I must have hot water. Warm water will clean nothing. Nothing!"

Julia sat up in the bed and drew up her knees. Was he done? Was that it? Was that his attempt at consummating their marriage? It was all she could do to keep from laughing again. "I could call for hot water, or a pan and heat it myself if you like."

He grabbed a clean linen towel from the stand and whirled around to face her. As he spoke he rubbed his hands and forearms so hard that it must have hurt. "You stay where you are! You think you're so clever. You throw your legs open to me like a whore! You open your dirty, wet self to me as if you want it! As if you've had it before!" He shuddered.

Julia set her jaw. "I have never been with another man, and you know it. If you don't believe me, call a midwife and let her examine me. If you don't believe her, have the wedding annulled. My sister and mother and I will be on our way by first light."

"Ah hah! That's what it is!" he proclaimed. "You think to escape me!" He pulled something from the waistband of his dressing gown as he stalked the bed. "This was all just a ploy to keep from me what is rightfully mine."

Julia was close to tears. "Just tell me what you want me to do! You told me I had to wed you. I wed you. You told me I had to submit to you. I have. What do you want *now?*" She rose on her knees, shouting her last words. "You want me to mount you myself to get it over with?"

He seemed not to hear her as he crammed his hands into cotton gloves.

Julia stared, his intention suddenly registering in her mind. Surely he wasn't going to wear gloves?

Simeon stepped toward the bed, and she sat back and pulled the counterpane to her chin.

He grabbed the edge of the blanket and ripped it off her, exposing her naked to the waist. She shrank back, but made no attempt to cover herself. If he hit her, what would she do? Her gaze darted wildly to the bed table, where she spotted a silver candle snuffer. She'd hit him back—harder.

Simeon's eyes glazed as he stared at her pale, naked flesh.

"Go ahead," she dared him. She knew she was treading dangerous waters, but she didn't care. She could only be pushed so far.

He slipped his hand beneath the waist of his own robe.

She crossed her arms. "Well, my lord? Are you ready now?"

He closed his eyes and fumbled beneath the silk of his gown. He gritted his teeth, panted, groaned.

Julia stared at the ceiling through tears. "I'm still waiting, *husband*."

He groaned and yanked his hand out from under his gown. "You think you're so clever? You think you can torment me? Emasculate me?"

The anger that flashed in his eyes frightened her. Had she pushed him too far? Would he kill her here and now? No, he was too cruel for such an act of kindness.

"If you feel emasculated, my lord, I would think that feeling comes from within."

"Oh, you're witty now. Let us see how witty you are before your guests in the morning, *strumpet!*"

He snapped off the gloves and strutted away.

Julia sat up in surprise as he jerked open the door to the rear staircase and disappeared into the darkness. Where was he going? Back to his own bedchamber? *Please, God.*

Julia crept out of the bed as she rolled down the hem of her sleeping gown. Cautiously, she tiptoed toward the staircase.

Was it too good to be true? Was he really gone?

Chapter Fifteen

Julia, hand trembling, closed the door softly behind her husband. "I've certainly made a muck of that." She gave a little laugh that caught in her throat and threatened to become a sob. "A fine wedding night, indeed."

At the hearth, she lit an oil lamp. She desperately wanted light, needed it to chase away the ugliness of the night.

Now what?

She wished she knew what was going on in Simeon's head right now. Did he intend to return to her chambers in another attempt to consummate the marriage? Would he come tomorrow night? Was it too much to hope for that he would never again come to her bed? Of course that would mean no children. Julia had always wanted children. But the thought of being intimate with a man who thought her so distasteful that he needed to wear gloves to touch her made her sick to her stomach.

The hollow sound of a footstep on the back staircase startled Julia, and she grasped the base of the lamp and spun around.

He was back.

For an instant she was immobilized with a sickening combination of fear and disgust. What did she do now? Her duty as Simeon's wife, her duty by God and by law, bid that she lay in his bed and surrender.

She stared at the closed door, the echo of Simeon's slow, steady footsteps pounded in her head like a carpenter's hammer. She had wed St. Martin to save her sister. In willfully exchanging those wedding vows, she had made a bargain—total possession by Simeon, in exchange for Lizzy's life.

If Simeon wanted to lie with her, she would have to submit. What choice did she have? She set her jaw, determined that it would be on her terms.

Julia strode to the panelled door and opened it. Simeon wouldn't expect her to meet him on the stairs. He would expect to find her cowering in the bed. By meeting him halfway, she would catch him off guard. She would establish her own position, meager as it was in comparison to his.

"Simeon?" She stepped onto the first riser and lifted the lamp high to get a better look at her bridegroom. The dark shadow took shape as the yellow light fell upon him.

Julia's blood turned to ice.

"M—Mr. Gordy?" She was unable to suppress the quaver in her voice. Something was wrong. Very wrong.

He was wearing the same silk robe Simeon had worn only a few minutes ago. It fell open as he climbed the staircase. His ugly, cold-hearted gaze locked with hers.

He was naked beneath the silk.

Julia pressed the heel of her hand into the rough wood of the wall and backed up into her room, her entire body shaking with fear. "Mr. Gordy, what do you want? Where is my husband?"

But she knew Simeon had no intention of coming to her aid. She knew it, even before Gordy spoke. This was Simeon's idea. This was what the knave had meant when he had said she would be ashamed to show her face to their guests in the morning.

"The master sent me to do what he couldn't." Gordy's voice was as chilled and lifeless as the November air in the stairwell.

Julia's first impulse was to fling the door closed and run. Scream. But run where? Who would hear her? The half-deaf Drusilla? Sleeping Lizzy? Surely not the drunken guests below. And even if they did hear Julia's cries, who would come? Who would dare cross the threshold of St. Martin's wedding bedchamber?

Julia glanced down at Mr. Gordy as he took his time to climb the long, narrow, seemingly endless staircase. Beneath the open robe she could see his manhood, red and purple-veined, already half-engorged in anticipation.

She trembled from head to foot. A weapon. She needed a weapon. But what? She had no pistol, no knife. Gordy was much taller than she was, much heavier. She would be no match against his strength.

Her fingers gripped the lamp until her knuckles whitened. She didn't care what the laws said of her husband's right to total control over her. She would not lie with his secretary. She would not be raped—not by him, not by any man.

"Mr. Gordy." She gripped the lamp, her voice steadier this time.

"M'lady."

"Stop where you are, or lose your life to the flames of everlasting hell." She took one step down as proof of her sincerity.

Gordy halted and the stair tread squeaked beneath his bare foot. "M'lady?"

"Come a step closer, and I will throw down this lamp." She felt stronger now. In control. "Would you care to hear the details? The oil will soak your robe as well as that hairy chest of yours. It will light quite easily. Even if you can manage to tear off your dressing robe, your flesh will already be on fire.

Once one of our grooms burned to death in a barn fire." She grimaced and wrinkled her nose. "It's rather unpleasant. The smell of burning flesh makes me gag, Gordy. Doesn't it, you?"

He stared at her with anger and fear etched on his haughty face. "The master sent me. I've no choice."

"What of *my* choice? What if I choose not to lie with you or my husband?" She paused. "But I know how angry St Martin can become. I understand that you must fear losing your position." She beckoned him with a crooked finger. "Approach if you must, and take your chances."

Gordy raised one foot to place it on the next step.

Julia lifted the lamp a little higher. It was strange how calm she felt now. How utterly confident.

Mr. Gordy lowered his foot. He was caught. He knew he was caught. It was his mistake not to sneak up the staircase, and her saving grace that he didn't.

He gritted his teeth. "It's not that I want to do this."

"Mm hm."

"You know what kind of man he is. What he's capable of."

She gave a little sigh, as if bored.

"What do I say to him?" He opened his hands beseechingly. "He will be *very, very* angry with me. He expects me to consummate the vows on his behalf."

"Say what you like. Say you did. I care not." She smiled with a clever thought. "Better yet, say you *could* not. Say the thought of touching my filthy body so disgusted you that you went limp." She laughed lightly as if she were mad. *"That* explanation my husband will understand."

He stepped down, his gaze locked on her. His hands found the silken ties of his dressing gown, and he hurriedly covered his flaccid intimate part. "It would be better if you simply submitted. Better for us both. You'll come to regret this, m'lady."

She ran her finger along the warm glass globe of the lamp. "Oh, I think not." She glanced up, unafraid of him now. "Go to bed, Mr. Gordy, and do not take these stairs again. Ever. Not as long as I draw breath in this household. Else I will set you on fire. Then, if I can. Later, if not. Perhaps when you sleep in your bed and think yourself safe.'' She narrowed her eyes. ''I swear by all that's holy, I will.''

Halfway down the steps, Mr. Gordy turned and ran. She closed the door and tilted a chair beneath the knob for good measure.

Then and only then did Julia lower the oil lamp with a shaky hand and dissolve into sobbing tears.

For half the night Julia sat in a rocking chair, rocking rhythmically, staring at the panelled door of the back staircase.

Again, she had underestimated the Earl of St. Martin. How could he be so vile? How could Simeon have sent his secretary to bed her?

Julia had been willing to sleep with her husband to keep up her side of the bargain. And then the bastard did this. As far as she was concerned, the deal was nullified. Simeon had stepped beyond the rules, therefore, she was no longer obligated to them either. If Simeon ever dared show his face to her bed curtains, she would turn him away. If he tried to force her, she would fight with every stone of her strength. She would not lie with St. Martin, even if it meant dying a virgin.

But she was still his wife. Bound to him by law and God until death did part them.

The long case clock on the landing outside her chambers chimed four in the morning.

Julia lowered her face to her hands and sobbed. What was she going to do now? She couldn't run because she had no one and nowhere to run to, not with Lizzy to care for. It was hopeless . . . hopeless. Julia rocked back and forth, filled with an ache of desperate loneliness.

Griffin. His image appeared suddenly in her head as if coming to her rescue. His smile. His laughter. The way he spoke her name. Those ridiculous high-heeled shoes of his.

She needed Griffin.

He was the only one who could ease her grief.

Julia lifted her face from her hands and wiped her eyes with the sleeve of her bride's sleeping gown.

She wasn't even certain where Griffin slept. On the third floor, she knew, east wing.

With a sniff, she pushed away all thoughts of feeling sorry for herself. She rose from her chair and lifted the oil lamp she'd kept burning all night. She slipped her feet into a pair of silk mules and shrugged into her dressing gown.

She wanted Griffin. Now. She wanted to feel his arms around her. She wanted to hear him whisper words of comfort in her ear. The idea was insanity, of course. Simeon was right. She was asylum-bound. What other woman would dare go to a man, not her husband, on her wedding night?

Julia slipped out of her bedchamber, through her sitting room, and into the dark hallway. *What woman, indeed?*

On the third floor, Julia walked slowly down the hallway. She wasn't afraid anyone would see her. So early in the morning the servants were surely still asleep, and the wedding guests who had stayed over still deep in a drink- and rich food-induced slumber.

Julia didn't know which door was Griffin's, but he had once mentioned his view of Aldersgate Street below. She halted at a mahogany panelled door at the far end of the dark hallway. Beside the door stood a full set of armor.

Instinctively she knew the room was Griffin's. When she closed her eyes she could imagine him lying in bed, his hair that she didn't know the color of, fanned across his pillow, his face gentle in sleep.

Julia lifted the lamp and rested the palm of her hand on the smooth wood of the door. She closed her eyes and breathed deeply. She could smell the lemon oil of the freshly polished wood, the hint of rust on ancient chain mail . . . and the heavenly aroma of *him*.

Julia turned the knob. Unlocked.

She pushed the door open. The hinges did not squeak.

The door swung shut behind her with the aid of her foot.

The chamber was dark save for the light of the lamp she carried. The windows were heavily draped. It smelled entirely masculine; rich, dark wood, stoked embers, shaving soap, tobacco, oiled leather, but mostly it smelled of him.

Julia slowly approached the great shadow of a bed to her far left. The chamber was disorderly, with chairs turned on their sides, paper and clothing scattered on the floor and piled on the tables. Her foot met with one of his shoes and she set it skittering across the polished hardwood floor, until it struck one of the feet of the bed and disappeared underneath.

The sound didn't disturb him.

The velvet curtains of the bed hung open so that in the pale lamplight she could see Griffin sprawled on his stomach, arms and legs askew, naked, his bare, muscular buttocks in full view. She had never seen a man totally naked before, and the sight made her smile with wicked warmth. God had created a magnificent thing when he had made a man's body.

Griffin's face was turned away from her, his cheek flat on a pillow, his hair, his *golden blond* hair, fanned out on the dark fabric, just as she had imagined.

Of course. A Greek God, all muscle and sinew, with hair of gold and eyes as blue as the summer sky.

Julia lowered the lamp to the cluttered table beside the bed and stepped out of her mules. As she watched Griffin sleep, her fingers found the ties of her dressing robe. She wasn't sure what she had come for, except his comfort. Now, staring boldly at Griffin's nakedness, she knew.

Her dressing robe slipped to the floor. Lastly came her torn gown. She would not soil what would be between her and Griffin with Simeon's filth.

She thought to blow out the lamp, but decided against it. She wanted to see him. She wanted him to see her.

Unclothed, unashamed, Julia slipped into Griffin's bed. She stretched out beside him, her head on the pillow beside his. Almost afraid to wake him, for fear it would break the magical spell, she stroked his silky blond hair. She closed her eyes, breathed in the clean scent of it. She brushed her lips against the back of his head. He felt so warm, so safe. A haven in this house that had become a hell.

Griffin stirred.

Boldly, she lowered her hand to his bare hip and glided it down his upper thigh. His body fascinated her. He was so muscular. From riding, no doubt. Or perhaps from fighting.

Griffin gave a soft, deep sigh.

With one finger, she traced the ridge of one of his leg muscles to his inner thigh.

He sighed again and rolled toward her.

Griffin's leg fell over hers, trapping her. He now faced her, his lips only a finger's span from hers. His breath smelled slightly of brandy still, but she could tell by his easy breathing that he was no longer intoxicated. His eyes remained shut in sleep.

She stroked the leg that held her down, then hesitantly inched her hand over his hip and up to the light sprinkling of hair covering his chest, crisp and intriguing. Her finger accidentally brushed his nipple and he startled her with a sigh, close to a moan.

Julia stilled her hand.

He mumbled something.

Then she smiled in the semidarkness.

"Julia," he whispered in his sleep. "Julia."

Gently, Julia brushed her lips against his and again caressed the hard nub of his male nipple. "Griffin," she whispered.

He slid his hand over her bare waist. His simple gesture sent sparks of shivering pleasure to every fiber of her being.

This time his lips touched hers.

Griffin pressed his body closer to hers, molding his hard, muscular frame to her softer, rounder one. The curling hair of his groin teased hers. He slipped his hand between them and cupped one breast.

Her eyes drifted shut for a moment as a sigh escaped her lips.

Sin. Everlasting hell. The flames of iniquity were not just lapping at her feet, but consuming her. Married to one man, lying with another. A crime punishable by death here, and everlasting torment in the hereafter. Julia was lost, lost forever.

She didn't care.

Griffin's warm lips found hers and she opened her mouth to his with a groan of bittersweet resignation. ''Love me, love me,'' Julia whispered desperately.

Griffin delved his tongue deep into her mouth as he rolled her onto her back. She clung to him, savoring the taste of him, the weight of his body pressed against hers. Their tongues danced in passionate celebration of a moment neither had thought would ever come.

When both were breathless from the kiss, he slid his warm, damp mouth across her cheek to her ear. Still, he didn't open his eyes. ''If this is a dream . . .'' His voice was throaty and utterly intoxicating. ''If it is, please God, let it never end.''

''Not a dream,'' she whispered, so happy she was near to tears. She gazed at his face, so handsome in the lamplight that it was beautiful. ''Not a dream, my love.''

His eyelids flickered, and she found herself staring deeply into his sleepy eyes. ''How? Wh—''

She pressed her finger to his lips to silence him. ''Shhhh,'' she cajoled. ''It will be daylight soon. There's not much time.''

He stared into her eyes so long that she feared he might push her from his bed. If he did, she would take her life right then and there. But he didn't cast her away. Instead, he drew her into his arms, pressed his hips to hers, his swollen member

against her thighs, and kissed her again. It was a kiss of lovers.
A kiss of man and wife.

"I love you," Griffin told her, brushing her loose hair from
her forehead. "I will love you forever."

She slipped her hands over his broad shoulders. "I ask for
no promises neither of us may be able to keep. Just love me
now."

"Forever," he insisted. Then he reached over her to the table
beside the bed and pulled out a drawer. From the drawer he
removed a small object. "Give me your hand."

"My hand?" Julia raised her left hand.

He slipped something cold and heavy over her middle finger.
She studied it in the dim light. A ring. An extraordinary
man's ring, gold, and encrusted with tiny jewels.

Griffin propped himself over her with his arm and clasped
her hand passionately. "With this ring I do betroth my heart
to yours, Julia. Forever."

She smiled. "With this kiss, I betroth my heart, my soul,"
she whispered. She kissed him softly.

With a groan Griffin lowered his mouth to the base of her
throat and pressed his warm lips to her flesh. She sighed and
closed her eyes. "Love me, love me," she begged.

"Forever."

Again and again Julia cried out in pleasure as Griffin stroked
and kissed her flesh until she thought she would burst into
flames. Their joining was all she had dreamed it would be.
More. She had never imagined someone could make her feel
this way.

He touched her everywhere. Not her intimate parts at first,
but her arms, her legs, her hands, her feet. He pressed kisses
to the backs of her knees, to the crooks of her elbows. He drew
his blunt nails over her back, her shoulders, her calves. He
nibbled from her earlobes to the tips of her toes.

Julia's breasts longed with a need to be touched, stroked,

suckled. Her woman's place ached with such need that she thought she would scream.

"Griffin, please." She parted her thighs and lifted her hips to meet the bulge of his manhood. "I've waited so long for this."

"No need to hurry," he soothed in her ear.

She laughed and rolled her head on his pillow, her eyes half-closed. "Need to hurry—" she panted. "Before—before I— I shatter."

His laughter was deep and husky. "Ah, Julia . . ."

Her eyes opened wide as he took her with a single thrust. "Oh!"

He held still, buried deep inside her.

She opened her eyes to see him staring down at her.

"Still a virgin?" he whispered.

She squeezed her eyes shut against the tears of joy, of sadness that burned the backs of her eyelids. "Don't ask. Swear you'll never ask."

After a moment, "I'll never ask," he promised.

She smiled, her eyes still closed, and lifted her hips against his, fascinated by the new sensation. "Teach me what this is all about." She groaned with pleasure as he moved inside her. "And *hurry* . . ."

Griffin buried his face in Julia's hair and thrust again and again, first slowly, then faster. She rose to meet each thrust, amazed, thrilled by each new sensation that built upon the last.

And this was what Simeon thought so detestable? He truly was a madman.

"Julia, Julia." Griffin called her name as he delved deeper, raising her to a higher plane of sensation.

She clung to him as he lifted her over a precipice from which she could not turn back. "Griffin!" She dug her nails into his flesh as she truly did shatter . . . into a million shards of sparkling bright ecstasy.

Julia's muscles contracted and released again and again. "Oh, oh," she cried.

Griffin thrust once more, groaned, and collapsed over her.

Julia felt dizzy as she brushed his hair from her mouth and gasped for breath. Rivulets of pleasure still trickled through her veins.

After a moment Griffin rolled off her, onto his side, and pressed his cheek against hers. He wrapped one arm around her, drew her close to his warm body, and covered them both with the counterpane they'd flung off sometime during their lovemaking. "You're certain this isn't a dream?" he breathed, nuzzling her neck.

"A drunken dream?" she teased. "Entirely possible considering your earlier state, sir."

He groaned and covered his face with his hand. "I made an ass of myself, didn't I?"

"Mm, hm."

He lowered his hand and opened his eyes. "But you still love me anyway?" He brushed his lips against her cheek as if she could be persuaded.

"Aye. Forever."

"Forever," he echoed.

Chapter Sixteen

Julia drifted with the tide of their lovemaking. She felt as if she were floating in Griffin's arms, snuggled beneath the counterpane of his bed. The sound of his rhythmic breathing, the feel of his warm breath on her cheek, the scent of their satiated bodies, all combined as one sensation.

She had never felt such inner peace. No matter what happened now, she would always carry this peace within her heart. Even if she and Griffin never joined as one again, she would carry, to her grave, the knowledge that she had truly been loved.

As Julia slowly woke, she came to the realization that there was a weight on her legs that wasn't Griffin. She opened her eyes. Early morning sunlight was just beginning to spill through the cracks in the heavy navy velvet of the window curtains.

A cat?

A black cat? She smiled. Griffin had a cat?

Taking care not to disturb Griffin, who slept with one arm flung over her waist, she reached out to stroke the cat. Its long black fur was smooth and silky beneath her fingertips. It began to purr in its sleep.

She would never have guessed that the dangerous man she had seen in that tavern passageway would have a pet—a cat no less. The thought delighted her. This man of hers was many faceted.

Of hers.

Julia laid back on the pillow. Of hers? Had she lost what little sense she'd ever possessed? Griffin was not hers. He was Lena's. Julia was not his; she belonged to the Earl of St. Martin. She would never be Griffin's. Not as long as they lived.

Julia bolted upright at the alarming sound of a doorknob turning. The cat leaped from the bed and disappeared beneath it.

Griffin startled her almost as much as the sound of the door as he rolled away from her and back, sleepy-eyed, a blunderbuss pistol drawn.

"Get up!" came a familiar feminine voice.

The door opened and Lena walked in, closing it behind her.

With a sigh of relief, Griffin fell back on the pillow. "Lena, what the hell are you doing here? I could have blown your head off your shoulders."

"Julia, get up quickly," Lena ordered again.

Julia drew the counterpane up over her bare breasts.

Griffin brushed Julia's arm beneath the coverlet to reassure her. "This is a private chamber, Lena. Get out."

"Oh, no, Lena. I'll not lie with her," the older woman mimicked as she approached the bed.

Julia could do nothing but stare. Griffin and Lena had discussed that?

"I'll not sleep with St. Martin's wife," Lena continued, one graceful hand poised on her hip.

Griffin groaned and switched the pistol from his right to his left hand and set it on the table beside the bed. "It wasn't planned. I had no intentions—"

"It was my fault," Julia confessed, touching the counterpane to her chin. "I came to him." She stared up at Lena, who was dressed this morning in a rich green velvet gown befitting a queen. "I—"

Lena softened as if she found no fault with Julia. "No time for explanations, sweet." She lifted her dressing gown and gave it a shake. "It was fate, pure and simple. Couldn't be prevented any more than the rising sun. Now get up. We've got to get you back to your chambers before your husband finds you missing. He catches you here, and you'll both be swinging from your necks at Tyburn Crossing before supper is served."

Griffin reached out his hand, perhaps to stop her, but she slid out of bed. She hastily slipped into her dressing gown, her eyes downcast, embarrassed to be seen nude by Lena. In her husband's bed, no less—even a husband she didn't sleep with. It was all quite confusing.

Julia pushed her tumbled, red blond hair from her face and tied the sash of the silk gown. On her feet, beyond Griffin's silken reach, she could think more clearly.

She couldn't believe she'd come here last night. She couldn't believe she'd cuckolded her husband on their wedding night. What could she have been thinking? Even considering the circumstances of last night, to sleep with a man not her husband was insanity.

And how had Lena known she was here? If she knew she'd come here, how much of the rest of last night did she know about? The idea that someone might know her husband had sent his secretary to her bed mortified her.

"Come, come, come." Lena straightened Julia's mules on the floor so that she could slide into them, and gently took her arm. "We haven't much time." She glanced at Griffin, who lay on his side, the bedclothes thrown over his waist, but much of his glorious body exposed. "And you, Romeo, get yourself up and bathed."

"That's funny." He grimaced. "Or would be if you weren't in my chamber pulling the woman I love from my bed."

"I'm trying to save her life, and yours. You'd realize that if you weren't still thinking with that handsome rod of yours." She waggled her finger. "Put on one of those silly suits and show your face at the morning table. Apologize profusely to St. Martin for your besotted behavior last night and offer a gift. Expensive. If you can't reach your goldsmith, send a message to mine."

Griffin ran his hand over his face, his facial muscles tensing in anger. "Lena, you don't belong here. You don't belong in the middle of this. I'll take her back to her chamber."

Lena snatched Julia's torn sleeping gown off the floor and balled it in her hands. If she noticed the rent, she gave no indication. Julia couldn't help wondering if she thought Griffin had done it.

"You're madder than I thought, Griffin," Lena said. "Caught with St. Martin's wife in the corridor before the morning fast is broken? With a house full of wedding guests? Would you have me call the sheriff now and save St. Martin the trouble?"

He sat up and threw his long legs over the side of the bed. The coverlet fell away to expose him entirely, but he didn't seem to care. "Julia . . ."

Julia felt as if she were sleepwalking. Thank goodness for Lena's gentle mothering. Otherwise, she doubted she'd be able to move. "Later, Griffin," she said tightly. Her emotions were in turmoil. She loved Griffin this morning even more than she had last night, when she'd wantonly thrown herself into his arms. But the love between them was doomed. Doomed.

"Lena's right," Julia said. "I must return to my apartments." The gravity of the situation was beginning to fall fully on her shoulders. If she was caught, Simeon would have the right to have her arrested. She could be sentenced to die, as could Griffin if St. Martin pursued it. And what about Lizzy? What would happen to her then? Who would care for her, even if St. Martin did spare her life?

Griffin rose off the bed. "Julia." He reached for her hand. "We need to— I don't want you to just leave like this."

Julia turned away before he touched her. If she allowed him to touch her, she would crumble. "Later, Griffin."

"Julia!"

"Later," she snapped.

"He'll calm down," Lena whispered as she smoothed Julia's hair and ushered her toward the door. "That a girl. Let's get you to your chambers and do something with this hair. Have you got another one of those silly pink gowns with the yards of lace? It would please his ass-ship if you wore one."

As he bathed and dressed, Griffin muttered every foul oath he could think of beneath his breath. First he started in English, then advanced to French. The French had such a colorful language when it came to the foul. Exhausting his repertoire of French oaths, he moved on to Italian.

How dare Lena saunter into his bedchamber like that? he fumed. Interfering witch.

Thank God she had.

Griffin didn't know if he would have had the strength to push Julia out of his bed and send her back to St. Martin. He might have allowed St. Martin himself to stride right in and catch them because he was too cowardly to do what had to be done. If Griffin had been a stronger man, he knew he'd never have allowed Julia into his bed to begin with. He wouldn't have allowed her into his heart. Men such as himself had no place in their lives for loving a woman as he loved Julia.

But even now, in the full, cold morning light of reality, his fingertips ached to stroke her silky flesh. He yearned to breathe in the heavenly scent of her hair. He longed to hear her innocent, passionate whispers of encouragement.

Griffin thrust his foot into a yellow stocking and wrapped the ribbon garter around his calf. What the hell had he been thinking? To love Julia only made his life more complicated, decisions more difficult. And it endangered them both. How could he have been so damned selfish? Griffin knew full well that if he was in danger, it could ultimately put the king in danger.

He jerked the other stocking off the chair and thrust his foot into it. But Lena was right. Damn her. She was always right. He hadn't been thinking with his head in the wee hours of this morning. He'd been thinking with his cock. No. It wasn't that simple. This morning with Julia hadn't been a quick tumble. It had been an expression of a lifetime love. A tender surge of emotion tightened in his chest.

Julia had been like an apparition that materialized, a dream that came true. She had come to him a virgin, and though he didn't know what the hell that was about, it made it all the more special.

Now she was his. Not St. Martin's. His.

Maybe the bastard was impotent. If he washed the rest of his body as rigorously as he washed his hands, perhaps all that lye soap over the years had rendered him eternally limp. Griffin chuckled at the thought as he tied up the second garter and picked up his petticoat breeches. One of the looped ribbons caught on the arm of the chair and he yanked the breeches, tearing the ribbon off.

He cursed again and slipped into the breeches anyway. If Jabar had been here, he would have sewn the ribbon back in place in a minute's time.

Jabar. Griffin had forgotten his friend. He glanced at the case clock on the mahogany mantel above the fireplace. Jabar should have been home by now. Last night or early this morning, they'd agreed he'd return to Bassett Hall. He hoped there wasn't trouble.

Griffin pulled on a shirt and a neckcloth, and slipped into a blue and yellow short jacket with deep cuffs. He glanced in the mirror as he laced up the jacket and adjusted the cravat. He was dressed rather subdued this morning, perfect for groveling at St. Martin's feet.

He dipped his hands into the washbowl and ran them over his hair, slicking it back. He chose a nut brown French periwig from a flock of them perched on wig horns on a table. The wig in place, he turned outwardly to the room. If he could just find a pair of futtering shoes that matched, he'd be ready to face that bastard St. Martin now.

Griffin didn't know how she managed it, but Julia beat him to the dining room. Her hair had been brushed until it shone and pulled high into seductive ringlets that teased the bare nape of her neck. She was wearing a gown with a low-scooped neckline, the overskirt looped back to the waist with a fashionable frill that fell from her hips to her mid-thighs over the overskirt. The gown was not in a pale pink as Lena had recommended, but in precisely the same shade of blue that Griffin had selected for his own attire. The bow ties that ran the length of her puffed long sleeves were yellow, as was her underskirt.

Griffin wondered why they would choose the same colors to wear this morning. He knew it was silly to even contemplate, but he couldn't help wondering if there was now some inexplicable connection between them. He had never believed in psychic abilities or the nonsense of astrology that was presently so popular, but a coincidence such as this made him wonder if there wasn't some truth to such notions.

If anyone else noticed that St. Martin's new wife and his cousin, the Baron Archer, wore matching costumes, he saw no indication. The entire dining room was filled with wedding guests. They spilled from the plaster-ceilinged chamber into the parlors on each side, strolling from one buffet table to another. Though tones were hushed—perhaps due to the amount of spirits that had been consumed the night before—there was still an air of celebration.

Julia stood beside her new husband, her gaze downcast. Griffin's breath caught in his throat at her beauty as the morning sunshine highlighted her golden red hair. He couldn't believe that this woman had come to him last night. It was still like a dream.

Either Julia didn't notice Griffin enter the room, or she pretended she didn't. She held a plate for Simeon, from which he nibbled pickled quail eggs as he spoke to a baron and his wife.

Griffin took a deep breath and sauntered farther into the room. Guests made way for him and called his name as if he were someone important. Griffin didn't have the stomach for food, but instead accepted a small porcelain cup of richly brewed Caribbean coffee from a footman. Gradually he made his way through the room, though it took a second cup of the thick coffee to fortify him enough to greet St. Martin.

He had to concentrate on being the character he'd so mindfully created as anger bubbled inside him at the thought that his Julia was this man's wife. Nay, it was deeper than anger. More primal. He had to push his own emotions deep inside, and search for the shallow sanctuary of the fop's persona.

"Good morning, my lord." Griffin bowed. "My lady."

"Ah, Griffin. You survived the night's festivities."

"Morning, sir," Julia murmured, taking care not to meet Griffin's gaze.

Griffin smirked. "Not only survived, my gracious lord, but prospered. My head and lungs are clear. My bowels free. I vow I'm ready to take on any gaming table, even St. Martin's."

Simeon chuckled. "I thought you might have come to apologize for making such an ass of yourself at my wedding."

Griffin grinned boyishly. "Oh, my lord, I do apologize for my abominable behavior, but I vow your wedding will be the talk of London for years to come, thanks to the addition of my fine performance."

Those who gathered around St. Martin and his cousin to eavesdrop chuckled.

Simeon smiled pleasantly, forever on stage before guests. "Your apology is accepted, Cousin. But truly the apology should be directed toward my lady wife. It's women who are offended by drunkenness more than men. They don't understand man's nature or the influence Satan holds over us each day."

"Ah, 'Sathan, that evere us waiteth to bigile.' "

Out of the corner of his eye, Griffin saw Julia mouth, *Chaucer.*

"Chaucer," Griffin said.

She kept her gaze averted, her fingers wrapped tightly around the plate as her lips moved in silence. *The Wife of Bath's Prologue.*

Griffin wished desperately that he could kiss those lips right now. To stand here beside Simeon and know what right he had to Julia was almost more than Griffin could bear. He should never have come to Bassett Hall, not even for the King. He should never have laid eyes upon Julia, never heard her utter that first word. "The Wife of Bath's Prologue," he told St. Martin merrily.

Simeon nodded at Julia impatiently. "An apology, Archer. My wife expects an apology."

"N . . . no." Her gaze darted to Griffin, then back to the pickled eggs. "No apology is necessary. I—"

"An apology to my dear wife, Archer. Now."

Griffin wanted to protest. She had a mouth of her own, a mind of her own. If Julia wanted no apology from him or from the devil himself, she didn't have to take one. His fist ached to crush Simeon's jaw.

But Griffin held his tongue and his fist, and made a vow. There were already suspicions concerning St. Martin and his loyalties, suspicions Griffin had paid little attention to until now. But if there was any truth to the whispers, even a thread, he would see St. Martin in a cage on the Tower wall. He would watch the crows come to rest on his maggot-infested flesh.

Griffin bowed again, this time directly to Julia. "Allow me to offer my profuse apologies, my Lady St. Martin, for my behavior last night. It was base and inexcusable."

She nodded, color diffusing through her cheeks.

"Please, I hope that you will allow me to make up for the incident," Griffin continued when he should have shut up. "By ... by taking you ... hunting ... hunting at his majesty's lodge." He glanced quickly at Simeon, who made no response. "A great lot of us are going and his majesty has promised to pay us a visit. I myself have been invited in a fortnight's time and would greatly be honored by your accompaniment. With your acquiescence, of course, my lord."

"Yes, yes, take her." He flitted a gloved hand, his attention waning. "She could use a few days in the country, I should think."

"You would care to hunt with me, my lady?" Griffin asked her directly. "I ask only you, not out of impropriety, but because I know my cousin detests hunting and the uncleanliness of the lodges."

She kept her gaze fixed on the plate in her hand, perhaps for fear her eyes would betray her. "I'd be honored to go, sir, so long as it pleases my husband that I should go."

Griffin grinned and clapped his hands together. "Good, then it's all settled. Your servant, my lord, my lady."

St. Martin nodded in Griffin's direction, having already moved on to another conversation. Julia never glanced up. Griffin could see that she held her breath.

"Your servant, my lord," Julia whispered. Then she said something to Simeon that he couldn't hear, and walked away.

Griffin watched her retreat. There he went again, thinking with his cod instead of his head. Julia with him at the King's hunting lodge? *Perfect.* Stuart and his court could witness her infidelity. For surely alone away from Bassett Hall he'd not be able to keep his hands off her. Suddenly Griffin lived for the fortnight to pass.

Dismissed, Griffin excused himself from St. Martin's circle. He wondered if he could catch Julia alone, just for a moment. Attempting to follow her from the room, he met Lena.

She smiled charmingly and caught his arm. Julia slipped away.

"My dear husband, how was your sleep last night? Sound, I trust?" She tugged on his sleeve.

Damn, she'd managed to waylay him long enough for Julia to leave the room. Griffin exhaled in defeat and took her hand. "Your servant, my lady wife."

She smiled for anyone who glanced their way, and lowered her voice. "Did you play make-up with the cloven-hoofed one?"

"Aye. All's forgiven." He took her fan and opened it to study the nude harem scene painted across it. "He has no idea he's been cuckolded." He ground his teeth. "I should just run the bastard through with a sword now and be done with him."

Lena nodded to two ladies who passed them. "And would that serve His Majesty?"

He groaned in emotional agony. How had life gotten so complicated so quickly? "No. Obviously I can't risk drawing attention to myself in that manner. I'm too close to the center of the spider's web."

She snatched back her fan and tapped him on his shoulder none too lightly. "Then I suggest you keep your sword sheathed, husband. Both of them."

Griffin opened his mouth to make a retort and closed it again as he caught sight of Jabar in the doorway on the far side of the room.

His friend beckoned him with his ebony eyes.

Griffin knew that look. Something was wrong. "Excuse me." He bowed and hurried toward Jabar.

His friend held one arm unnaturally at his side, as if he'd

been injured. Griffin recognized the pallor of a man trying to conceal pain. "Are you all right?"

"I've already ordered your horse saddled, my master. You must come. Quickly."

Griffin scanned the room. Where was Julia? He couldn't go without speaking to her. He needed . . . he needed to tell her that he loved her. That he would figure this mess out. That he didn't know how the hell he was going to do it, but that he would make that betrothal official and one day make her his wife.

"Master," Jabar whispered. "You must hurry."

The vow Griffin had made so many years ago tugged at him. He laid his hand on Jabar's back and reluctantly gave in. "All right. I'm with you. Let's go."

Chapter Seventeen

Griffin dug his heels into his mount's flanks and lowered his head against the driving wind. "You certain you can still ride?" he shouted above the wail of the storm. He had tried to convince Jabar to remain behind and have his wound tended, but his friend refused. Jabar understood how consequential it was that Griffin get to Jack before their invisible enemies caught wind of his "injury" and sent someone to finish him off. Jabar saw it as his duty to remain at Griffin's side in the face of impending danger.

"We could stop at St. Mary's." Griffin named one of their contacts in the city. "You'd be well cared for until I returned."

Jabar rode up beside him, his left arm held close to his chest. "A flesh wound, Master. You do not think I would give up the chance to draw my sword for a flesh wound?"

Griffin grimaced and focused ahead again, tilting his head so that the wind wouldn't hit him directly in the face. It was beginning to sleet. The muddy ground was icy, and his horse struggled to keep its footing.

"How much farther?"

"Just beyond Goodman's Fields. We carried him to a tavern there and sent for a physician."

"Will he live?"

Jabar thought for a moment, then shook his head. "No. The worst is a sucking wound. The physician will do nothing but dull the pain of dying."

Damn, Griffin thought grimly. Jack had been his vital link in connecting the circle of conspirators plotting to kill the king with the man who masterminded the plan. In Jack's last message he had indicated he may have located the leader behind the elaborate cabal, and that it was vital that he speak with Griffin immediately. Jabar had gone in Griffin's place. It should have been Griffin who took the lead in his arm, not Jabar. Now, if Jack died before he was able to convey what he'd discovered, all those weeks, months, of patience and surveillance, would be lost. Griffin would have to start all over again.

As Griffin rode, he tried to keep his thoughts focused on the king's safety rather than on his own personal life. But he couldn't help thinking of Julia and the warmth of her beside him in his bed. Sweet heaven, it had felt good not to wake up alone in the morning.

"Jabar."

His manservant reined in beside him again. "Master?"

"There was talk when we first arrived and made the decision to stay with my cousin that his vow of allegiance to his majesty was less than sincere."

"Aye. It is true. There was. But it was said of many men."

Griffin tightened his grip on his reins. "When you've time, I want you to look into it."

Jabar's dark eyes widened. "You suspect St. Martin plays a part in the conspirators' plans?"

He shrugged one shoulder. "I know he doesn't have the balls to actually play an active part, but perhaps he's financed someone else, or made promises in the hope of profiting later. I want to know if he has.''

"Did you see something, my master? Do the walls of Bassett Hall speak to you?''

"No. But I don't want to be foolish. Hell, these days no one is exempt from suspicion. The Duke of Buckingham himself could be a conspirator for all I know!''

Jabar glanced at Griffin, his black eyes penetrating. ''But you want only truth, not guilt placed upon an innocent man?''

Griffin knew exactly what he meant. Jabar was asking if Griffin wanted him to set the crime of treason upon St. Martin's shoulders, even if he was innocent, which meant that somehow, Jabar knew of Griffin's relationship with Julia. The idea was tempting. He could think of no easier way to rid himself of St. Martin than to have him tried and sentenced to hang. That would leave the widow free to marry whomever she pleased. So tempting.

"It could be easily done, Master,'' Jabar intoned. ''You have but to say the word and I—''

"You know me better than that,'' Griffin snapped. He felt his gut grind. So tempting. ''I want the truth.''

Jabar fell in behind him again. ''Yes, my master.''

Half an hour later the two men arrived at the ramshackle tavern where Jack had been brought. A lad in an oilcloth cloak met them at the rear of the tavern to take their mounts.

Griffin pushed through the back door, removing his leather gloves as he strode down the narrow hallway. He had not been in this particular tavern before, but in many like it since he came into the service of Charles II fifteen years before. After more than a decade, they all looked the same. ''Where is he?''

A bearded man stood in a doorway. ''Here, my lord.'' He lowered his gaze to the rotting floorboards. ''But I'm afraid it's too late.''

"Too late?'' Griffin exploded. He pushed open the door behind the bearded man whom he recognized, but whose name he didn't know. The elaborate web of men who supported him were often anonymous. "What do you mean, it's too late? You couldn't keep the poor bastard alive for another—" Griffin halted and lifted his closed fist to his mouth as his stomach gave an involuntary lurch. "Ah, hell," he murmured.

Jabar appeared beside him.

Griffin found his voice after a moment. "You didn't tell me he'd been tortured."

Jabar stared at the dead man's body that only faintly resembled a man. "I told you, Master."

Griffin kept his hand at his mouth, partially muffling his words. He couldn't take his eyes off the bloated, bloody heap that had been his major contact for the last six months. Only weeks ago Griffin had played cards with him. Jack had sworn he would soon have information that would see the plot to dethrone the Stuarts destroyed, and the conspirators beheaded. He had sworn he was so close he could taste it.

Now Jack was dead.

Griffin turned away from the bloody bed as he lowered his hand and forced down the bitter bile in his throat. He had been a soldier, for God's sake. He had seen blood in battle. Dead men. He'd even seen tortured bodies. But he had never seen a body like this before. He couldn't comprehend how Jack had lived long enough even to be carried here.

"We've got to cover our tracks," Griffin said quietly, as he forced his mind to move from the pain Jack must have suffered to the realities of their current situation. Griffin's duty now was to protect the living men, and ultimately his sovereign.

Jabar nodded his turbaned head. "Already begun, Master."

The sleet that covered Griffin's cloak melted and puddled at his boots. "Good. I want to talk to Jack's closest man. I want to talk to him myself."

"Already sent for him, my lord," the bearded man said. "The meet's been set for later today, in a public market where you'll be safer."

"Jabar."

"Master."

"You know all who must be contacted. They have to be warned of this . . . development, immediately." He made a fist at his side. "Everyone needs to know they're going to have to take extra precautions. I won't have anyone else die by these traitors' hands."

"Yes, Master."

Griffin lifted his gaze, thankful for Jabar's capability and strength in time of crisis. He never would have survived all the years without Jabar's gentle companionship. "But first I want that wound looked after."

"It is not—"

"You." Griffin addressed the man who covered Jack's body with a linen sheet. His white shirt was drenched in blood, his face honest. "You are the physician?"

"Aye."

"I'll get someone in to take Jack's body. I want you to see to the living." He gestured in Jabar's direction. "He's been shot. I want the wound cleaned and dressed."

"Yes, my lord."

Griffin removed his hat and struck his knee with it. Water drops leaped from the hat to shower the floor and add to the growing puddle. "You stay here, Jabar. Have your arm cleaned up, and your trail as well. Christ's blood!" he exploded. "This could have been you!"

"It was dark still. I was not seen."

Only shot, Griffin thought. *For me. For my cause.* "Just the same, I don't want you in any unnecessary danger. We'll meet later at the Three Bells."

"Where do you go, Master?"

"I'm bound for Whitehall." Griffin stared unseeing across the empty room that smelled of congealing blood, wet leather, and frightened men. Griffin didn't know what he could have done to prevent this, but he felt guilty just the same. Jack shouldn't have had to die. He shouldn't have been tortured. "His Majesty must be informed at once. Without Jack, the entire structure will have to be rebuilt, men retraced. It may be months before the son of a bitch behind it all is traced." He crushed his cavalier's hat onto his head and strode out of the room. "I just hope to hell I'm not too late."

"Not there. His lordship wishes the tables to be placed there, along the wall," Julia indicated to the footman with a sweep of her hand, and then irritably brushed a stray lock of hair from her cheek.

Simeon wanted the withdrawing rooms prepared for another evening of dining and dancing in celebration of their wedding yesterday, and it was already late afternoon. With so many guests in the house it was impossible for the housekeeper to accomplish all her duties. To insure the house was prepared for the evening's festivities, Julia had stepped in to assist, though she wanted nothing but to crawl into her bed and pull the coverlet over her head.

Griffin had ridden out this morning in a hurry, bound for where, she didn't know.

Julia stepped out of the way of the two footmen who moved another table to the wall.

Of course she knew she couldn't expect Griffin to tell her where he went. Nothing that happened last night had changed the cruel truth of the morning. Not his mysterious gold ring that she wore on a ribbon around her neck beneath her underclothing, nor his promise of eternal love. Julia was St. Martin's wife and would be forever.

But rightful or not, Julia still wondered where Griffin had gone in such haste. She couldn't help fearing he was in danger and wished desperately that she knew exactly what he was involved in. Was he in the service of some duke wielding political power? Was he aiding in the buying and selling of illegal trade goods? Neither made sense. His masquerade—the fop impersonation and the fostering of the belief that he lived apart from his wife on a small annual stipend and that he was otherwise penniless—was too elaborate a plot for any of the circumstances Julia could think of.

Julia had cornered Lena privately at noonday and questioned her as to Griffin's whereabouts, but Lena said she knew nothing, and that the less anyone knew, the safer he would be. She refused to tell Julia what he was doing, or why, or for whom, not out of unkindness, but again for reasons of his safety as well as Julia's own. Lena had also warned Julia that she must not see Griffin alone again. She said she feared for their lives.

A chill trickled down Julia's spine as she recalled the tone in Lena's voice. She had spoken not out of wifely jealousy, but out of a genuine concern for both Julia's and Griffin's well-being. Lena probably didn't know how accurate her assessment was. If the earl was capable of sending another man to bed his wife, Julia knew he was capable of locking her in a dungeon until she starved to death.

Julia glanced up, realizing someone had spoken to her. One of the footmen pointed to a small buffet service table that had just been placed in a corner. "Will this do, m'lady?" he asked, obviously repeating himself.

"Fine. Perfect. And then—"

"There you are, my dearest darling!"

Julia instinctively cringed as she heard her mother's high-pitched voice behind her. When Susanne had disappeared yesterday afternoon and never reappeared, Julia had half thought her mother might have been gone for good. She wouldn't put it past her to run off with some elderly, titled lord to a cozy country home to live as his paramour, or something equally ludicrous.

"I've looked for you everywhere!"

I needed you last night when I had to prepare for St. Martin's bed, Julia thought, her back still to Susanne. *Where were you then, Mother?*

"I feared I would have to search his lordship's bedchamber next for my newly wed daughter." She laughed lewdly and a man joined her.

Julia hadn't realized someone else was with her mother. She plastered on a smile befitting an earl's wife and turned to greet her mother. "Good afternoon."

"Oh, good afternoon, Julia." Susanne was firmly attached to a man's arm, and to Julia's surprise, he was not elderly. He couldn't have been more than twenty years and five. "But I suppose I shall have to call you countess now," her mother tittered.

Out of politeness, Julia nodded to the gentleman on Susanne's arm before responding dryly. "I believe you can still call me Julia, Mother."

"Oh, I'd almost forgotten," Susanne burst. "This is Pierre Du'Mois. Visiting from Paris. His father is a marquis." She fluttered her fan over her breasts, that threatened to leap from the yellow embroidered bosom of her too-tight gown. "Pierre, my daughter, the Countess St. Martin."

"Comment allez-vous, Madame?" He disengaged himself from Susanne's grasp and bowed handsomely. As he rose he took Julia's hand and kissed it. "Your servant, my Lady St. Martin."

Susanne grabbed his arm again. "Isn't Pierre the most comely man you have ever laid eyes upon!" She launched into another fit of giggles, as did the Frenchman. "And to think he's wasting his affection on an old bird some ten years older than he." Susanne fluttered eyelashes that were most certainly false.

And Susanne wasn't ten years older? In a pig's eye, Julia thought. That would have meant Susanne would have had to have given birth to Julia when she was ten or twelve!

Julia studied the young man, wondering if he was so

addlepated as to believe such nonsense. The way he gazed into
Susanne's kohl-painted eyes made her think he was. Either that
or he was a very clever fortune hunter. If Susanne told him
she was thirty-some years old, she could have told him she
was an heiress as well.

"I'm pleased that you could join my husband and me on
this joyful occasion, Monsieur Du'Mois. Do stay for music and
refreshment this evening."

"Oh, we can't. Pierre is taking me to the playhouse and then
to join friends, aren't you, darling?" Susanne massaged his
arm.

"You're going now?" Julia needed to talk to her mother
about Lizzy and Amos. After the episode in the smokehouse,
she feared action had to be taken to protect Lizzy not just from
Amos, but from herself.

"I'm afraid I must go, darling. I've a girl coming to do my
hair in that new French style, and then it's off we are. Into the
wee hours, I'd venture."

Julia knew that it would be rude for her to ask Monsieur
Du'Mois to allow them privacy for a moment, but she was
quickly losing her patience for politeness, especially when it
came to her mother. If she didn't catch her now, it could be
days before she found her again. "Mother, I need to speak
with you."

"Well, speak, child." Susanne fluttered her fan. "You know
you can tell Mother anything." She giggled and leaned closer.
"Just so long as it's not *intimate* details of you and the earl."

Pierre's laughter grated on Julia's already raw nerves. Each
time her mother laughed, he laughed like a trained monkey.

"Sir, will you excuse us just for a moment?" Julia asked,
tight-lipped.

"By all means." He bowed to each of them. "Your servant,
Madame, Countess."

Susanne waved her fan at him and then blew him a kiss as
he walked out of the parlor.

Julia rolled her eyes.

"Now what is it?" Susanne snapped the moment Pierre disappeared from view. "It will take me two hours to get out of this bloody gown and into another!" All the sickening sweetness was gone from her voice.

"I wanted to talk to you about Lizzy." She led her mother to the window, out of earshot of the footmen who continued to set tables and add linen cloths.

"I don't have time to talk about your sister." She examined her manicured nails. "I didn't tell Pierre I had another daughter, so keep your mouth sealed."

Julia raised her brows. "Didn't tell him about Lizzy! You disowned her?"

"I didn't disown her. But you know how men are uncomfortable around people like Lizzy. I don't want Pierre to feel *uncomfortable*." She lowered her voice to a frenzied whisper. "His father is a marquis, a very rich, *ill* marquis!"

So her mother was fortune hunting. Any other time Julia might have broached that despicable subject, but considering Susanne's obviously wandering thoughts, she simply ignored the remark. "Mother, I'm concerned about Lizzy and her interest in that cook. I fear it's becoming serious. Last night I caught them in the smokehouse—"

Susanne threw up both hands as if fending off an evil spirit. "God's teeth, I'll hear no more."

"Mother, I'm afraid—"

"Must you ruin any chance of happiness I might have?" Susanne lowered her hands angrily. "I don't want to hear it. I don't want to hear the sordid details." She spun away and waggled her fan over her shoulder. "Just manage the situation. Obviously the sister of a countess cannot be associated with a servant, even a dim-witted sister of a countess. Bribe her, get her another puppy. She's easily distracted."

Julia followed her mother. She truly felt as if she needed

guidance, but she had a sinking feeling she was wasting her breath. "But, Mama, Lizzy—"

"Not another word," Susanne called over her shoulder as she breezed out of the room. "You're the lady of your own household now, a countess. I've gotten you this far. Done my duty. Don't harry me again." She wrung her hands. "I wash my hands of Elizabeth."

Julia started to say something else, then reconsidered, and remained silent. She had been a fool to think she could gain any support from her mother. Julia was alone in the world but for Lizzy, and the sooner she accepted that fact, the sooner she could move on to a solution.

Chapter Eighteen

Julia directed the set up of the buffet tables in the withdrawing rooms, and ordered the footmen to begin lighting the hundreds of candles that would illuminate the evening. By the time the food had been sent for and a mix-up with the musicians settled, it was later than she realized.

She needed to retire to her chambers and change into evening clothes. If she was late, Simeon would be furious. But thoughts of Lizzy nagged at her. Considering Simeon's current displeasure with her, she feared Lizzy was at risk of his wrath as well. This matter between her sister and the servant had to be settled before it went a step farther.

Not surprisingly, Julia found Lizzy in the kitchen, seated on a stool watching Amos cut out pastry dough in the shape of the St. Martin coat of arms. She sat on the wooden stool, her petticoats dusty with flour, her cheeks rosy from laughter. As always, the kitchen bustled with activity.

"Amos, Lizzy, I'd like to speak with you both in the hallway." Julia held open the kitchen door, its hinges allowing it to swing both ways. "Now," she said sharply. Tonight she had neither the time nor the patience for civilities.

Lizzy climbed off the stool with the aid of Amos's beefy forearm. "What's the matter, Julia?"

"What's the matter?"

Her increase in volume caught the attention of several kitchen servants. As Julia's gaze met theirs, they returned to their tasks.

"What's the matter?" Julia repeated, attempting to remain calm. "Please, outside. Amos."

He followed Lizzy in silence into the hallway.

Julia let the door swing shut before she spoke. "This has to cease."

"What?"

Lizzy stared so wide-eyed with innocence that Julia didn't know if she could go on. How could she take away this happiness from her sister, when she herself was bathed in such misery?

She could do it to save her life.

"This has to stop." Julia pointed to the kitchen. "This." She indicated Amos. "It can be no more. It's past the point of innocent friendship."

"M'lady—"

"Amos, I'm not blaming you for this." She studied his ruddy, pockmarked face. "What man wouldn't be infatuated with my sister? She's beautiful, she's lively, she'll listen to your troubles and pass no judgment. She'll also apparently go with you to the smokehouse."

Amos jerked his head up as if he'd been slapped. He opened his mouth to speak, then clamped it shut.

Lizzy just stood there staring, stunned or confused, Julia didn't know which.

"I blame neither of you. I blame myself. I was so intent upon myself and my own troubles that I allowed this friendship to progress too far. Lizzy never belonged in a kitchen. She's the daughter of an earl."

"I don't care if I'm the daughter of the bloody king!" Lizzy emerged suddenly from her stupor and grabbed Amos's arm. "I want to be in the kitchen! I want to be with Amos." She thrust out her jaw with a conviction that surprised Julia. "I *will* be with him."

Julia grasped Lizzy's arm firmly and pulled it away from the cook's. "Lizzy, you're not able to make that decision."

"Lady St. Martin." Amos lifted his brown-eyed gaze slowly. "Now I can't disagree with ye on the matter of her bein' a earl's daughter, and me bein' nothin' but a cook." He took a shuddering breath, as if stringing that many words together had taxed him. "But I got to disagree with you sayin' she can't make a decision like that on her own. She's a lot smarter than you think."

Julia rested her hands on her hips. The minutes were ticking by. She had to get dressed for the evening, or risk St. Martin's wrath. She didn't have time to argue over her sister's capabilities with a cook. "Amos, I never said Lizzy wasn't smart about some things." Julia groaned, trying to find the right words. "But you and I both know she's unable to care for herself, unable to make decisions that would affect the rest of her life."

Amos shook his head. "No, m'lady. I'm sorry, m'lady, but I don't see to yer way of thinkin'."

Lizzy reached out to take Amos's flour-dusted hand, but Julia stepped between them. "Lizzy, you may not come to the kitchen again. If I catch you, you'll be locked in your room with Drusilla."

Lizzy gave a cry of anguish.

Julia avoided Amos's honest face. "Amos, if you continue to court my sister, I'll have you sent elsewhere. This simply cannot be permitted to continue."

"I hate you." Lizzy stomped her foot. "I hate you!" she screamed. Then she burst into tears and raced down the hallway toward the main house.

Amos made a move to follow her, then halted. Of course he

couldn't follow her, because there was no place for him in St. Martin's house, and he knew there never would be.

"It's not right," Amos muttered, his eyes tearing up.

Julia felt as if her heart was tearing in two. How could she make him understand? How could she make Lizzy understand? Even if she tried, would they believe St. Martin was the monster she believed him to be? And even attempting to explain might endanger them both. "Amos, I'm not doing this to hurt you or Lizzy. I care less about Lizzy being a lady and you being a cook than you think." She took a deep breath. "I can't explain myself, but I'm doing this to protect her."

"Protect her? Protect her from what? I would protect her."

Julia turned away. "Not from this," she said softly. "Now go back to your work, and do not make me pay you a visit again."

Julia heard the kitchen door swing open and then shut as she walked down the dimly lit hallway, her head bowed. It hurt deeply to see Lizzy so upset, but Julia knew she was doing what was right. She was protecting Lizzy the best she knew how.

Julia was so preoccupied that she never heard St. Martin approach until she almost bumped into him.

"There you are."

"Oh." She put up her hand to keep her body from touching his, and stopped short. "Simeon."

"Did I not instruct you that I wanted to greet our guests sharply at eight?" He was dressed impeccably in a green silk doublet. "Didn't Mr. Gordy remind you of the time only an hour ago?"

"Yes, Simeon." She lowered her gaze for fear she wouldn't be able to conceal the hatred in her eyes. "I'm sorry. I can get ready quickly."

She attempted to pass him, but he put out his arm, taking care that he touched her with his sleeve and not his bare hand. She noticed that his hand was so red it appeared raw. Had he injured himself or simply been overenthusiastic with his hand-washing this evening?

"I didn't give you my leave."

She pressed her hands to her sides, still avoiding his gaze. "May I go, m'lord?"

"You think you're clever?"

Clever enough to sleep with another man on our wedding night. She had no idea where it came from; it just popped into her head. Then she was ashamed of herself for having such sinful thoughts.

"You think you won because even Gordy didn't have the stomach to take you?"

"No," she said softly.

"Well, you're not clever. Not one bit. You're an idiot bitch like all the other bitches. But you're a pretty bitch, so I'll keep you. I'll keep every bit of you for myself—your mind, your body, your soul. Understood?"

She nodded that she did, but of course she didn't. Who could understand such cruelty, such madness?

He lowered his hand as if he could no longer stand to touch a wall that might be soiled. Then he reached into his coat doublet sleeve and drew out a white handkerchief to dust off his fingers.

"Now get upstairs and put on one of those frocks I spent outrageous sums upon. And for Christ's sake, do smile!"

"Yes, my lord." Julia curtsied and darted past him as he stepped aside.

Bastard, she thought as she hurried away, her petticoats bunched in her hands. Her grandfather always said that every man got what he deserved in the end.

I'm going to survive this somehow, she vowed silently. *Lizzy and I both. And you're going to get what you deserve. We'll see who owns me then, St. Martin—mind, body, and soul.*

Bastard.

*   *   *

That night Julia played the part of the merry bride until she thought she would go mad. She greeted Simeon's friends and foes with a gracious smile and a bubbly laugh. She pretended to be pleased everyone was there to celebrate her wedding. She even pretended to be shyly infatuated with her new husband. It was a deadly game she played now, and she knew she must play it well.

Finally, when she could no longer stand the sound of her own voice, her own deceit, she slipped away from the sparkling music and light into the dark sanctuary of her orangery. Halfway to her fish pond, she spotted the shadow of a man sitting beneath a newly transplanted lemon tree.

Julia halted in the moonlight that streamed through the glass panels of the ceiling. How did he know she needed him? How did he always know? He was dressed not as the fop, but as the man she had seen in the tavern passageway that day.

She took her time before speaking. "I was worried when you left so abruptly. I feared you were in danger."

Griffin touched his hand to his breast, a silhouette in the shadowy garden. " 'She loved me for the dangers I had passed, and I loved her that she did pity them.' "

Shakespeare. He did love Shakespeare, didn't he? Julia caught the trunk of a young sapling, lifted her petticoats, and slowly circled the tree. "You were in danger. I knew it. I felt it."

He raised his palms. "You know I cannot—"

"I didn't ask you where you'd been," she interrupted, "or why."

As he crossed his arms over his broad chest, she couldn't help recalling what his muscular chest had felt like beneath her fingertips. *Had it really been only last night?* She couldn't help but remember what it had been like to tease his nipples with the tip of her tongue.

"You asked Lena."

She smiled as she rounded the tree to study him. "Is there nothing the two of you do not share?"

"Other than a bed, no."

The bark of the trunk was rough beneath her fingertips and she could smell the faint citrus scent its leaves exuded. "I'm jealous."

"You shouldn't be. I love her, but not the way I love you."

Simple words from a not-so-simple man.

Julia stepped away from the lemon tree, but didn't approach him. She was afraid to. Afraid she would throw herself into his arms and never be able to let go of him. She sensed he kept his distance for the same reason. An energy cracked in the air between them.

"I'm jealous just the same," she said softly. "Jealous because she can speak with you in the hall and not fear you'll be seen. Jealous because she can look at you from across the room and not fear—"

"Do you want me to leave Bassett Hall?" He rose from where he sat at the pond's edge. "It would be difficult, damned difficult, but I could make—"

"No!" She raised her hand to him. "Don't leave me. I couldn't bear . . ." She lowered her hand to her breast, realizing how foolish she must sound. How desperate. But she *was* desperate. "I couldn't bear it," she repeated again. "Not now."

Still he stood in the moonlight, his chest rising and falling, his breath coming a little faster than it should have as his gaze caressed her. "Last night, Julia. I shouldn't have made love to you. I shouldn't have endangered you the way I have."

"I came to you. You're not to blame."

"I *am* to blame. I took another man's wife to my bed."

"Another man's wife who climbed naked into your bed," she reminded him gently.

He exhaled. "It's not just us. There are others."

She knew he searched for a way to explain himself without revealing any of his secrets.

"Julia, it was selfish of me to make love to you, to put my wants ahead of the dangers. Not only to you, but to others."

She hung her head, thinking of Lizzy. "You're right. It was selfish of us."

"But I meant what I said last night. When this is over, I want to marry you. I want to be your husband, to protect you, to love you. I want you to carry my child in your womb someday, God willing."

His mention of a child touched her heart. "Only one thing in our way, really." She gave a little laugh, though she saw nothing funny in their situation. "I suppose you could kill *him*," she joked.

Griffin walked toward her, and she took notice that he seemed tired. His face was lined with worry so that he appeared older than his thirty-odd years.

"I would in a moment," he said, "if only it were that simple."

"I said it in jest. I don't want you to kill him for me," she whispered fiercely. "What kind of love would that be, then?"

"Do you think he would hesitate to kill me if he had the slightest inclination?" Griffin halted an arm's length from her. The moonlight fell on one side of his face, masking the other side in shadow. "Do you?"

"No," she confessed with genuine fear for him. "Maybe you're right, maybe you should go." He held her gaze so that she couldn't look away.

"That's what you want?" He reached out and stroked her cheek with his hand. "Tell me. Tell me what you want me to do, Julia, and I'll do it if I can."

She closed her eyes, savoring the light brush of his fingertips on her cheek. Every inch of her skin tingled. Her heart pounded. She wanted him. She wanted him here. Now.

But of course that was impossible. "Yes. No." She squeezed

her eyes shut and then opened them. "Oh, Griffin, I don't know what I want." She covered his hand with hers and held it to her cheek. "I do know what I want. I want to turn back the hands of the clock. I want my father to betroth me to you. I want you to send for me in Dover. I want you to meet me at the church's altar." She took a deep, shuddering breath. "I just want you."

Griffin pulled her into his arms and pressed his lips to her forehead. "Julia, Julia, would that I could change the past, but I can't. All I can do is look to the future."

Her arms tight around his waist, she rested her cheek on his chest. He smelled of horses and brandy, rain and wet leather. He smelled as she always imagined a man would smell. "And what is in our future? Honestly? St. Martin is my husband, and you . . . you have this duty, whatever it is."

He held her tightly against his chest and rocked her gently. "It's possible. All is possible."

Julia wanted to believe him. She wanted desperately to believe him. "And you will not murder him in his sleep? I could never be happy knowing you did something like that for me."

He smiled and kissed her temple. "I promise you, I will not kill him unless he comes at me, sword drawn. Fair?"

She lifted her head from his chest, offering her lips to him. "Fair enough," she murmured against the warmth of his mouth.

They shared a gentle kiss and then he guided her head to his chest again. He smoothed her hair with his hand. "Julia, I have to tell you that matters have escalated . . . become more dangerous. I cannot risk . . . we cannot risk Simeon suspecting that you and I—"

"Oh, no." She raised her head. "No. Of course. He mustn't suspect." She thought of Lizzy again, and for an instant considered telling Griffin the real reason she married Simeon. But how could he help? He had his own matters to attend. Hadn't he just said he was in danger? Julia could deal with St. Martin on her own. She could protect Lizzy on her own, at least for the time being.

"So we must be careful," Griffin continued gently. "We cannot give him any reason, not a touch, not a smile, not—"

"I won't come to you again." She lowered her gaze, feeling her cheeks grow warm. "I promise."

"Oh, Julia." He lifted her chin with thumb and forefinger until she was forced to meet his blue-eyed gaze. "Don't ever regret that. It was the most wonderful gift anyone ever gave me."

"Truly?" She smiled in spite of her fear, in spite of her embarrassment.

He caught her hand and brought it to his heart. "Truly. It sounds ridiculous, but I feel as if you have given me a reason to be, to exist. All my life I felt as if I was waiting for something. Now I realize it wasn't something, but someone."

"Griffin." She wanted to tell him that they were fools to think their love could ever be anything but kisses stolen in darkness and in fear. They would never wed. She would always belong to St. Martin. There was no escaping his iron grip. But she couldn't say it. Not now. Not here.

Julia curled her fingers around the nape of Griffin's neck and pulled his head down. She met his kiss with an open mouth, desperate to feel him, taste him. As their mouths met and he thrust his tongue, his hand naturally found the curve of her breast and her hips naturally pressed against his.

"This . . ." he said breathlessly as he pulled away. "This we cannot do." He released her, shaking his head. "We can't because I'm afraid I'll lose control of myself. I'm afraid I won't be able to stop."

Julia hugged herself for comfort, her own heart pounding, her head dizzy for lack of air. "I know." She nodded. "I know. You're right."

He took a step back, lifting his hand as if to ward her off. "Give me a fortnight or two. Let me see what develops."

"And what of that silly offer to take me with you to the king's hunting lodge?"

His boyish grin appeared. "It was sincere."

"But I shouldn't go."

"I know." The grin fell away. "Not that I wouldn't like the chance to be with you alone, away from here." He spread his arms wide and then let them fall.

She watched him back away from her. Each step he took pained her more deeply than one of Simeon's pinches or slaps could ever hurt.

Again he was in shadow. "You'll be all right with Simeon, at least for a while?"

"I'll be all right. He won't touch me." She smiled wickedly. "I'm too *dirty.*"

To her relief, he asked for no further explanation. "Good, because then I would have to kill him in his sleep, and you would be very angry with me for breaking my promise."

"Go," she told him, pointing toward the house. "Then I'll follow."

"I won't come down tonight to join the festivities. I have business to attend to."

"Good night."

"Good night, my love." Griffin kissed his fingertips and then held up his hand, palm toward her.

Julia let her eyes drift shut and when she opened them again, Griffin was gone.

Chapter Nineteen

A week later, Julia stood at the windows of the gallery, listening to the banging of hammers and the sawing of wood. The sound seemed to go on nonstop during daylight hours, as the workmen rushed to complete the addition before the Earl of St. Martin's birthday in late January. Simeon apparently intended to have his collection of artworks displayed by then, and to throw himself a grand ball.

Julia leaned on the window frame to stare at the cold, dead garden below. Lizzy sat on a bench, the same bench they had shared two short months ago. Julia remembered the way they had laughed together over Griffin's ridiculous hat that day. How carefree Lizzy had seemed, how excited to be in new surroundings. She'd been so happy.

Now Lizzy sat frowning, inanimate, her bare hands folded in her lap, no doubt chilled. Since Julia had put an end to her visits to the kitchen, Lizzy barely spoke to her, and when she did, it was with that same frown on her face. Lizzy hadn't mentioned Amos, not once, but Julia knew that was who she was thinking about. She blamed Julia for their separation, of course. No matter how Julia tried to explain to her that it was better that they stop seeing each other now, before their affection grew out of control, Lizzy refused to listen.

So Julia left Lizzy alone. She was kind to her, but she tried not to disturb her in her grief. She knew that within a few weeks Lizzy would recover from her infatuation with Amos and the feelings she thought she had for him.

In the meantime, life at Bassett Hall was lonely for Julia. With Susanne spending most of her time frolicking about London with the would-be marquis, and Lizzy ignoring her, she had no one to talk with. No one to pass even a few moments a day with in idle conversation.

Since the wedding, Simeon had spent most of his time holed up in his dark office. Men came and went, sometimes mysteriously cloaked, in hired carriages. Other times Simeon actually ventured out. He never said where he was going and Julia didn't ask. As long as he kept his distance from her bedchamber, she was content for the time being.

Of course she wasn't interested in Simeon's foul company anyway. It was Griffin she missed; his pleasant banter of women's fashions and court gossip, his laughter, and his kisses.

Julia spent hours thinking of Griffin and the few precious hours they had spent alone together on her wedding night. She recalled over and over each kiss, each caress, each thrust, until she realized she was going to drive herself mad spending so much time thinking of him.

Though Griffin remained at Bassett Hall, she rarely saw him, and then only in the company of Simeon and his unending string of dinner guests. In public, Griffin was polite to her, but kept his distance. According to the gossip around the punch bowl, the Countess St. Martin was still rather put out with her husband's cousin for making such a spectacle of himself after the wedding. For once, Julia found the hearsay a relief, and had even encouraged it.

Unfortunately, the gossip that offered Julia and Griffin some protection also forced them to avoid one another at Simeon's dining and gaming tables. The few times they had met alone, in the upstairs hallway and once in the library, he had passed her at arm's length, his greeting strained. She could tell he wanted to reach out and touch her as badly as she wanted to reach out and touch him. It was all they could manage to do to restrain themselves.

Below, Julia spotted someone walking up the stone path from the stable toward the house. *Griffin.*

He halted at the bench and greeted Lizzy in his usual flamboyant manner, complete with a bow fit for a queen. Though Julia could not hear them through the gallery windows on the second floor, she could follow the gist of the conversation by their actions.

Lizzy barely responded to his good afternoon. As he attempted to show her his green wool hat with the yellow and purple ostrich feathers, she thrust her lip out in a pout, crossed her arms over her chest, and looked away.

Griffin hesitated for a moment, then sat down beside her. His face seemed to change before Julia's eyes, as he transformed from the ridiculous fop everyone knew to the mysterious man she loved.

Griffin spoke; Lizzy gave no response. Casually he rose from the bench, deposited the absurdly large hat on his head, and picked up a stone from the ground. He tossed it. He picked up another, no longer talking to Lizzy, and threw it. On the third stone, Lizzy glanced up. Her face was still sullen, but she watched Griffin. She said a few words and thrust her lip in the pout again.

Casually he spoke over his shoulder. Then he picked up several small rocks and began to take aim at something and throw them.

Julia leaned closer to the window, wondering what he was up to.

Lizzy rose from the bench and kicked at loose stones on the path.

Griffin tossed her one of the stones from his hand. She didn't put out her hand and it fell at her feet.

"She's not going to play," Julia said softly. "Whatever you're trying, dear heart, it won't work. She can be as stubborn as molasses on a cold night when she wants to be."

As Julia fogged the glass with her last words, to her surprise, Lizzy leaned down and picked up a rock.

Julia smiled. *Bless him.*

Lizzy rolled the pebble between her finger, spoke, then tossed it with little effort. It flew from Julia's sight, but she knew from the look on Lizzy's face that it missed its mark.

Lizzy threw another. And another. On the fourth rock she must have hit the target, because she leaped up and clapped her hands together.

Griffin clapped with her, grinning broadly beneath the hat. He said something encouraging, then scooped a whole handful from the ground, and poured them into Lizzy's hands.

Lizzy was smiling for the first time in days, and Julia was smiling with her. "I love you, Baron Archer," she whispered, touching the cold glass of the lead casement window. "I vow I do."

Griffin said something else to Lizzy, and she pointed toward the windows of the gallery. Griffin immediately looked up.

It was strange to watch him from this far away and have him gaze at her. Even at a distance she felt a warmth radiate from him, a warmth that leapt through her and made her heart flutter.

Griffin tipped his hat to Lizzy and left her to her rocks and target.

Julia knew she should go now before Griffin appeared. If she didn't wait for him, chances were he would seek her out. It would be better that way. Safer. But she wanted to see him, needed to see him, if only for a moment.

Julia waited at the windows and was shortly rewarded by the sound of a man's high-heeled slippers on the newly laid black and white Italian marble floor.

She knew she and Griffin had agreed to avoid each other, but what harm could it do to talk here in the gallery, she rationalized. There were a dozen workmen as witnesses, who would see them, yet not be able to hear their conversation for the noise of their own tools.

"My Lady St. Martin." Griffin swept off his hat and bowed grandly.

Julia curtsied. "Your servant, my lord." A smile twitched on her lips. "Nice hat."

"Your servant." He chuckled and brushed the brim of his hat with a kidskin-gloved hand. "Glad you like it."

"What's she doing down there?" Julia pointed to the window. "She's been in a pout for days. That's the first smile anyone's been able to coax out of her."

"A little target practice." He watched her carefully out of the corner of his eye as he pretended to be concentrating on removing his expensive gloves.

She knew he was thinking what she was thinking. *One kiss. Just one. Perhaps one caress.*

"Target practice. I see." Julia struggled to concentrate on the conversation. He was so damned handsome. Had he been this handsome the day she'd arrived at Bassett Hall?

"So what did you do to make her so angry?" He flexed his fingers and she watched them move with fascination.

"W . . . why do you ask?"

"She decided the tree we were aiming for was you. Wouldn't say why." There was a hint of amusement in his voice.

Julia lifted her hands to her face and laughed. "Me?"

He laughed with her, though not as hardily. "Yes, you. It was her idea, not mine. The target part."

Julia dabbed at her eyes. "The silly girl." She chuckled again, knowing it wasn't really funny, but feeling giddy inside.

Giddy with want of him. "I've done something terrible, at least in Lizzy's eyes." She hesitated to tell him, but what harm could it do? No one could hear them. To anyone that passed they would appear to be making polite conversation.

Griffin waited patiently for her to continue. He was so good at listening, when most men were so poor.

"There was a man . . . a servant here in the house." Julia fiddled with the lace that fell over her sleeve, not because it needed to be straightened, but because she needed to have something to do with her hands. Even as she spoke of Lizzy, she thought of Griffin . . . of his hands . . . his hands on her . . . his mouth on her. "Lizzy thought herself infatuated with him. I caught them kissing."

"You put a stop to it?"

"Of course I did." Julia's gaze darted to the workmen. They were placing molding above the far windows. "It was completely inappropriate. Lizzy's not able to—" Her gaze met Griffin's again. He seemed to know she wasn't telling the entire story. "Simeon would not have it," she finished softly.

He glanced at the workers with a sigh. He was such a good actor. To anyone watching them, one might have thought that the Baron Archer was bored with the conversation, bored with the countess. He was anything but.

"Then it's a good thing you stopped it now before he found out."

She nodded, her hand aching to caress his smooth-shaven cheek.

"And it really has halted?"

"Yes. I told the servant he would be replaced if it continued. I told Lizzy she'd be confined to our apartments if I caught her even speaking to him."

"And she'll do as you say?"

"Of course she will." Julia turned away to look out the window again. Lizzy was still below, throwing rocks now with childlike enthusiasm. "She knows I only want what's best for her. She knows I know what's best."

Griffin took a step closer to her. She didn't dare look at him.

"I miss you," he said, his voice barely audible above the sound of the hammering and sawing. He moved his hand as if he were going to touch her, then recoiled.

"I miss you," she whispered.

"My bed feels empty. Not even Charlie can keep me warm."

"Charlie?" She knitted her brows. "So there's truth to the rumors of Baron Archer's bedchamber preferences?"

A flicker of amusement crossed his face. "My cat. Surely you met him that night?"

That night. "Big and black and furry? Didn't want to share the bedcovers?"

"His name is Charles Stuart, but I call him Charlie." Griffin moved to stand beside her at the window. To her surprise his hand found hers in the folds of her woolen gown. He squeezed it tightly.

"You named a cat after the king of England?" She was smiling, as much for the sake of the cat story as for the warmth of his fingers that threaded through hers.

"Charles has met him. He's not the least bit offended."

Julia frowned as an alarm went off in her head. "The King of England has met your cat? You jest."

He waved his other hand. "Forget I said that."

Now there was something he *wasn't* telling her. Surely the king of England had never entered Griffin's bedchamber, here or anywhere else. Surely . . .

She studied his face for a moment, then peered out the window again. She didn't want any of the workmen to notice anything odd between the countess and Baron Archer. Her mind ticked. Charles II had fled England at the age of sixteen, before his father was beheaded. It was a fact that many young men accompanied the exiled prince. Surely Griffin couldn't have been one of those honored men. Could he? "You told me that you traveled through Europe for most of the war. May I ask where? When?''

''You cannot. I told you. Forget about what I said about Ch— His Majesty. Don't pry, Julia.''

She took a deep breath. He had warned her that he had secrets. He had warned her that she would have to trust him. ''How . . . how is your . . . matter going?''

''Could be worse. Could be better,'' he answered cryptically.

He had promised he would get her out of Bassett Hall, out of St. Martin's clutches. It was that hope she clung to now. ''Do you know how much longer you'll be . . . engaged?'' He stroked her fingers with his thumb, making it difficult for her to think clearly. ''Do you see any finality?''

''Too soon to say, but there's been a great deal of activity.''

The constant motion of his thumb on her hand in the folds of her petticoats was amazingly sensual. Julia's heartbeat increased; her breath shortened.

''I want you,'' he whispered, daring to bring his mouth close to her ear.

His warm breath in her ear made her tremble. ''Aye,'' was all she could manage.

''Care to take a stroll?''

Julia turned to him in surprise. ''Sir?''

''To see what shipment of artwork his lordship has received.'' He pointed beyond the workmen to the heavy curtain of canvas that protected St. Martin's precious artwork from being damaged by sawdust and mortar's sand. ''I understand he's recently received a masterpiece from Rome.''

Julia's breath caught in her throat at his suggestion. He wanted to take her beyond the curtain to kiss her? How did he dare? Hadn't they said only a week ago that they couldn't risk discovery?

Did *she* dare?

''Oh, yes, that shipment.'' She smiled graciously and started toward the workmen, releasing his warm hand as she removed the protection of her petticoats. "Do let me show you the statue of the woman. It's exquisite."

Griffin followed Julia past the long row of windows that ran the length of the fifty-foot gallery. They passed carpenters and masons who barely glanced up. To Julia's surprise, Griffin winked at one handsome blond fellow. She nearly burst into laughter.

At the end of the room, Griffin raised his hand over her shoulder to pull back the canvas curtain for her. Julia walked in, her hand over her mouth to keep from laughing aloud. Griffin followed.

The moment she heard the drape fall, she felt Griffin's hand on her waist. She suppressed a cry of surprise as he spun her around to face him.

"How could you?" She threw her arms around his neck and met him nose to nose.

"Could I what?" His blue eyes glimmered with a mixture of amusement and something darker. Passion.

Giggling softly, her lips met his. "Flirt with that poor mason."

"One has to keep one's reputation." He kissed her again, but this time their mouths lingered.

Their tongues touched and Julia stifled a groan of pleasure. This wasn't a good idea, hiding behind the curtain. Suddenly she didn't trust her own judgment. Her heart was racing, every nerve in her body quivering. She wanted him so badly. Already she could feel herself damp and pulsing.

"We can't do this," she insisted, as she allowed him to back her against the nearest solid wall. She delved her tongue into his mouth, knowing she was losing her sense of good judgment in her desire for this man.

"We can't," he panted, lifting her skirt to press his hand between her thighs. "Can't risk it. Can't be so selfish."

"Griffin . . . Griffin," she groaned as he slid his hand up

her bare thigh above her stocking, then higher until he met with the source of her pleasure.

His fingertips brushed, taunted, teased, then retreated. He kissed her breathless. Dizzy. Again he found the center of her pulsing need.

Holding tightly to his shoulders, Julia rocked against his hand, already so close to that explosion of pleasure she craved. She couldn't believe she was doing this.

"If we are caught, we're dead. Both dead."

"Shhhh," he soothed. "Won't get caught."

With another moan that Griffin muffled with his mouth, Julia parted her thighs. Her legs were so weak she wasn't certain she could continue to stand. A heat rose in her face. Suddenly the cold stone had become fiery.

Julia slid her hand down his chest to the bulge beneath his thighs. Griffin groaned in her ear and trailed a jagged line of kisses down her neck to the swell of her breast that rose above her burgundy gown.

Julia tried to pull the tie of his breeches free, but it wouldn't come undone. Desperately she yanked.

He covered her hand with his experienced one, brushed it aside, and released the flap of fabric. His sex fell hard and hot in her palm.

"Julia," Griffin groaned as she stroked his length.

"Griffin, Griffin," she panted. "Have . . . have to hurry."

He wrapped his arms around her and spun her around so that his own back was to the wall. "Here?" he whispered. "You're certain?"

She fumbled with the oceans of fabric of her petticoats and hitched them high. This was insanity. She knew it was insanity. "Here. Now," she whispered hoarsely. "Now."

Griffin grasped her roughly by her waist, lifted her up, and then lowered her. She groaned as he filled her body, and set her muscles to quivering and her flesh to burning. One stroke, and she dissolved against him. She had wanted him so badly—needed him badly.

Panting against Griffin's purple velvet lapel, guided by his hands around her waist, she pushed up on her tiptoes and then slid down hard upon him.

Griffin gasped, his muscles tensed, and he buried his face in the loose hair that spilled over her shoulders.

"Forever," he whispered as he exploded.

The moment his eyes fluttered open, Julia gingerly removed herself from the position in his arms and shoved her petticoats down. She was still dizzy, her heart pounding. Sweat beaded above her upper lip.

With a lopsided grin on his face, Griffin tucked himself into his breeches and laced himself up.

She tossed him the hat that he had dropped on the floor at some point. He deposited it on his head. Their gazes met.

"Forever," she whispered with a saucy smile.

He reached out and brushed the beads of sweat from her lip and lifted the canvas curtain that separated them from the workmen, who still pounded with their hammers and rocked their saws.

"Quite exquisite," Griffin exclaimed. "Thank you so much for sharing his lordship's treasure. I do hope you'll honor me thusly again, my lady."

She shot him a look that could have seared a lesser man. "Quite welcome, sir, and now if you'll excuse me, I've other matters to attend."

He tipped his hat and bowed.

Julia nodded, still weak-kneed beneath her petticoats.

"There you are!"

Her breath caught in her throat. Her gaze was so intent upon Griffin that she hadn't seen Simeon coming.

"I . . . I was showing Griffin the shipment from Rome."

"Quite exquisite," Griffin picked up the conversation. "I

should love to discuss the sculpture over a snifter of brandy, my lord.''

Simeon scowled at Griffin. As he spoke he tugged a handkerchief from his coat sleeve and brought it to his nose. ''Go on with you, Griffin. Perhaps later.'' His hard gaze fell upon Julia.

She prayed he didn't discover she was shaking in her slippers.

''There's someone in the front hall to discuss a Christmastide donation to the poor. I'd prefer you see to it. Give, but not too generously. I can't be bothered.''

''Yes, my lord.'' She lowered her gaze in silent admission of servitude, all the while thinking of how she had gotten the better of him again. Julia knew she was wicked for her thoughts, but she couldn't help herself. Her wicked thoughts gave her strength—the strength to go on. ''Anything else, my lord?''

Simeon glanced up to see whether Griffin had walked out of earshot. ''Yes, do something about your stench, woman.'' He sniffed into the air and blotted his nose with his handkerchief. ''You smell of something.'' He sniffed again. ''I don't know what it is, but it's rancid!'' With that he trounced off.

Julia kept her back to Simeon and Griffin as they retreated down the long gallery. A secret smile of satisfaction turned on her lips as she breathed deeply the scent of Griffin's love that still clung to her damp skin.

Chapter Twenty

Julia held back a velvet drape with one hand and stared into the darkness, avoiding her own reflection. It was one of those rare evenings when Simeon had invited no guests. Lizzy had taken her meal in her room with Drusilla, and Susanne was gallivanting about Londontown with her Frenchman. She and Simeon had dined alone with Griffin.

Supper had been strained for Julia, even though Griffin put on his jolliest face and kept Simeon entertained with court gossip of the king's mistress, Castlemaine. Julia attempted to appear interested, but each time her gaze inadvertently met Griffin's she looked away, terrified Simeon would suspect something. There had been no afternoon trysts since earlier in the week, but it was all Julia thought of, and she feared that she would somehow betray her infidelity.

"I leave for His Majesty's Hunting Lodge next week," Griffin said, making conversation. "The hunting should be good, as the winter has yet been mild."

Julia struggled not to react to the turn in the conversation.

She couldn't imagine what Griffin was thinking, to mention the lodge. Hadn't they agreed that it would be too dangerous for her to go?

Simeon turned the page of a book he was reading. "I do hope you're still willing to take my wife with you. She's in need of a change of scenery, I think. She has been quite skittish since the wedding."

"Oh, no, my lord. I don't think I can go." She clasped the velvet drapes for support. Of course she couldn't go somewhere alone with Griffin. An impossibility. A wondrous impossibility. "There's much to do for the advent season."

"Nonsense. If Archer is willing to take you, you'll go because I wish you to go. And you'll make a good impression on His Majesty; it's my understanding he likes *pert* women."

Julia caught Griffin's reflection in the window glass. She wanted to go with him. Wanted desperately to go. But she was afraid. Terrified. Was it not worse to give a man dying of thirst a few sips of water, than to just let him die?

Griffin nodded ever so slightly, knowing she watched him. He was telling her everything would be all right.

Julia found her voice. "If you wish it so, my lord, I'll go."

"I wish it so. Now, would you please sit?" Simeon slapped the book down on his lap. "You're making me as vexed as you appear, woman."

In the reflection of the window Julia caught Griffin still watching her intently. She swallowed. Just the thought of his blue-eyed gaze on her made her warm.

"You're right," she said carefully, taking her time to turn to her husband. "I'm unsettled tonight. I should go to my chambers."

"Ridiculous." He returned his attention to his book. "It's too early for sleep. Sit down. Haven't you a bit of needlework or reading material? A bit of romantic dribble, perhaps?"

Griffin leaped up from the French settee he lounged upon. "Play backgammon with me."

She folded her hands in front of her. Being in this small room with Griffin and Simeon at the same time vexed her, all right. Every time one of the men spoke or moved, she startled like a deer in lamplight. "No. No, thank you, sir."

"Sit down and play the game with the boy," Simeon ordered irritably. "Jesus Christ, the son! He entertains you often enough. Amuse my cousin for a few moments. It won't hurt you to at least pretend not to be so contrary, Julia."

Griffin quickly moved to a table only large enough for two to sit across from each other. "Madame . . ." He offered her one of the chairs.

Simeon engrossed himself in his book, and Julia made a face at Griffin. She shook her head as if to tell him they shouldn't be doing this. Griffin nodded and smiled.

I don't want to be here, she thought. *I don't want to play this dangerous game*—and it was not backgammon she thought of. But she sat because she felt she had no choice. To argue might well seem more suspicious to Simeon than refusing to play.

Griffin quickly took the seat across from her and began to set the game pieces into place. As the game began, Julia tried to focus on her moves and not Griffin's hands. But as he smoothed one of his pieces between his fingers, her concentration on the game faltered. She imagined those hands, those fingers, brushing against her nipples, and fought an involuntary shiver of desire. She imagined him taunting her flesh, teasing her. She thought of him touching lower, more intimate places.

"Julia, your play."

Caught. She didn't dare glance up for fear of betraying her thoughts, but scooped up the dice and tossed them. She moved without caring where.

As they played, Griffin kept making eye contact with her. His gazed brushed over her face, the swell of her breasts above the bodice of her gown. He shifted in his hard chair, and she didn't have to guess what was making him uncomfortable.

Once she licked her dry lips quite innocently, and caught him watching her. The look in his eyes told her his thoughts were far from innocent.

Suddenly Julia felt Griffin's hand on her knee beneath the table. She kicked him. He jumped. Grinned.

Stop it, she mouthed.

Stop what?

She couldn't keep from watching his lips move. She felt them on her neck, on her breasts, on her belly. *You know what!* she mouthed back.

He lifted one plucked eyebrow innocently.

"Your turn, my lord," she said aloud.

"What will your sister say?" Amos questioned nervously.

Amos's hand was cold in hers as Lizzy darted through the shadows of the crisp night air. "I don't give a hang what she says." She yanked open the door to the smokehouse, the wind caught it, and Amos raised up his hands to ease it open again.

Lizzy stepped inside. "Close it," she whispered.

Amos closed the door and latched it.

It was so dark inside that she could barely see Amos, but it didn't matter because she could hear him breathing. She could feel him near her. She held out her arms.

"Lizzy, I don't think this is a good idea. The mistress—"

She lowered her arms. "Do you love me, Amos?"

"Lizzy . . . Lizzy, it ain't that simple. I—"

" 'Tis that simple to me, Amos. Either you love me or you don't." She settled one hand on her hip, the same way she'd seen her sister do more times than she could count.

"She is right, Lizzy. About me bein' nothin' but a cook, and you bein' a great lady."

"She's wrong about saying I don't have the head to know if I love you, Amos." She took a step toward him. "Because I know I do. I don't think about anything but you. About how you laugh when the stew bubbles over. About how you wipe the flour off my nose.'' Her lower lip quivered. ''About how I feel inside when you kiss me here.'' She touched her mouth. ''And here.'' She pulled open her cloak and brushed her finger over the bare skin above her bodice.

''Ah, Lizzy,'' Amos said as if he was hurting.

She took another step in the dark smokehouse that smelled of hickory and pork. ''Just tell me if you love me or not.'' She rested her hands on his shoulders.

''She's not foolin' with us. If she catches me touchin' you, I won't have employment. I'll have to go away. We'll never see each other again, Lizzy!''

She looked into his face. It was so dark she couldn't see it well, but she didn't have to, because she knew how upset he was. She knew how he was hurting, because she was hurting, too. ''I'll go with you if she sends you away.''

He laughed. She smiled because she made him laugh. ''Just tell me if you love me,'' she said.

Finally he wrapped his arms around her waist, and she laid her head on his shoulder. Amos was so big and strong. He made Lizzy feel big and strong . . . and smart. Maybe that was why she loved him so much. Because he was the first person who didn't think she was dim-witted. He knew she wasn't as smart as him, as smart as Julia or Baron Archer, but Amos knew she wasn't an addlepate either.

''Do you?'' she insisted.

He touched her hair, smoothing it like she had smoothed her lost dog's hair. ''I love you,'' he whispered as if he were afraid to say it. ''I love you, Lizzy.''

She raised her head from his shoulder. ''Then everything's going to be all right,'' she whispered. ''Because when two people love each other, it just is.'' Then she kissed him. She didn't know how she knew where his lips were, because she couldn't see them in the dark. She just knew.

*   *   *

Julia intentionally made another poor move. She just wanted to get out of this stifling room, as far from Griffin and Simeon as possible.

Griffin made a clucking sound, shook his head in response to her move, and took the dice. Doubles. He moved his last four game pieces home, and thankfully the backgammon game came to an end.

"Another?" Griffin asked, his mouth twitching with amusement. "Surely you'll win next time."

She pushed away from the table, her legs a little shaky. "I promised my sister I would read to her before she turned in." She backed away from him. "Good night, sir. Thank you for the diversion."

She swept toward the door. "Good night, my lord."

Simeon did not glance up from his book. "Good night, wife. I'll be up directly."

Of course he wouldn't be. He said that every night, as if he always turned in with his wife. But everyone in the household knew the earl and his countess did not sleep together. They all pretended otherwise, because it was obviously what his lordship wanted them to do.

"Yes, my lord." She curtsied, and then hurried from the withdrawing room. Taking the lamp from a footman outside the door, Julia went first to the library to fetch a new book to read to Lizzy, then up the back servants' staircase to the corridor that led to her bedroom.

She nearly tripped over Griffin at the head of the dark, winding staircase.

"Oh," she whispered, as the book fell from where she'd tucked it beneath her arm. "You gave me a fright." She pressed her hand to her pounding heart. "And just what is the meaning of bringing up the hunting lodge? I thought we agreed I wouldn't go. That it wouldn't be safe."

Griffin pushed *Morte D'Arthur* aside with the toe of his orange slipper and eased her against the wall. He touched his lips to the pulse of her throat. "God save my greedy soul, I couldn't help myself. And now with your husband's insistence, you'll have to go." He kissed her again, his hot mouth lingering at the pulse of her throat. "I need you, Julia. Let me come to your chamber."

She shook her head wildly, squeezing her eyes shut tightly. She held the lamp out so that neither of them would be burned. "No."

He drew a line with the tip of his tongue between the swell of her breasts. He smelled of brandy laced with desire. "I have to see you."

"No," she panted. "It's not safe. You said so yourself."

"Julia, Julia," he whispered in her ear. "This is making me insane. I can't have you until my task is complete, and yet I can't concentrate on my task for want of you." He kissed her behind her earlobe. "Sweet heaven, do you know how much I want you?"

His plea tempted her. She wanted so desperately to make him happy, if only for a few short, sweet hours. She wanted him so desperately. But then she remembered Simeon's sudden appearance in the gallery the other day. She and Griffin had come close to being caught. Too close.

"It's not safe, Griffin. You have to let me go. Alone. Please let me go." Her voice quavered, her entire being aching for him. "Please?" She didn't dare touch him for fear she wouldn't be able to let go.

He kissed her lips gently, then rested his cheek against hers. "You're right, of course," he conceded softly. "You're far stronger than I could ever be. Besides"—he kissed her again and then stepped back—"we have those days at the hunting lodge to look forward to."

"That's a poor idea." She shook her head. "I shouldn't go. Too dangerous."

"You heard Simeon. He insists. I see no way out of it."

She closed her eyes, then opened them again. Would she be willing to risk everything to spend a few days alone with him, without feeling as if she were walking on shattered glass? "I suppose you're right. I thought I would at least bring Lizzy as an escort. It will look better that way."

"Brilliant." He kissed her lips one last time, his hand lingering on her breast, and then started up the steps to the next floor where his own chamber lay. "Good night, my love."

Julia leaned against the wall to catch her breath. "Good night, my love," she mouthed.

After a moment to catch her breath and retrieve the fallen book, Julia headed for her chamber, illuminating her way with the lamp. As she made the turn in the dark hallway, she spotted Simeon waiting at her door.

Her heart leaped in her breast. *Sweet blood of the Father, where had he come from?* The front staircase, of course.

"There you are." Simeon leaned against the doorjamb. He smelled of the now-familiar garlic, but also brandy wine. He and Griffin must have shared a drink before retiring.

"My lord." Julia halted out of arm's reach of him.

"I was waiting for you." He made a motion as if he were washing his hands. "Where have you been?"

"The library. I retrieved another book to read to Lizzy."

He scowled. "You seemed to enjoy your little game with Archer tonight."

She settled her gaze on the wool mules he wore on his feet. "He plays well, my lord. Better than I."

He chuckled. "Of course he does. He's a man . . . of sorts." Then he did the oddest thing. Simeon reached out and plucked a ringlet of her hair from her shoulder, almost as a caress.

Julia knew she trembled. What would she do if he tried to bed her again? Now that she had lain with Griffin, lying with Simeon was out of the question. She was Griffin's now, Griffin's until death did part them. She would kill herself before she gave herself to another man. No, she corrected, she would kill Simeon. She prayed it wouldn't come to that.

"You remember our little chat in the gallery before our wedding, don't you?" He wound her hair around his finger.

"Our chat?"

He tugged hard on the ringlet and she winced. "Our chat. The ground rules." *Tug.* "You are mine." *Tug.* "No other's."

A chill ran up her spine. *Did he know something? Suspect?*

"Mine until you lay rotting in your grave." He let go of the curl. "Just wanted to remind you of that." He walked away. "Order what you like from the dressmaker for your trip to the hunting lodge." He turned and smiled. "Good night, *wife.*"

Chapter Twenty-one

Julia stood in the front hall surrounded by St. Martin arms and armor and watched with amusement as an entourage of footmen passed, carting the Baron Archer's baggage to the awaiting carriage.

"Make haste, make haste." Griffin led the parade, fluttering an embroidered handkerchief as he pranced on his heeled slippers. "The carriage awaits." He slapped his hand against his cheek. "Why, good morning, my Lady St. Martin." He halted and bowed as if they were at court rather than in the house they shared.

"My lord." She curtsied, taking note of the manner in which his blue eyes sparkled with promise of the days to come. He was as excited about their journey as she was.

Griffin stepped aside to allow the footmen to pass as a liveried coachman flung open the great door.

"God rot my bowels, there's a chill in the air today." He tugged on the ties of his green- and white-checked cloak.

Julia thought him rather bold to choose to wear the St. Martin colors while fully intending to cuckold the earl as soon as they were out of sight. "Chilly, indeed," she remarked.

"Well . . ." In rare form this morning, he fluttered the handkerchief beneath her nose. "I do hope His Majesty is more inclined to play cards at the hearth than to hunt stag. I would hate to catch the ague and die at his feet."

Julia had to look away to keep from laughing aloud. This morning she felt more lighthearted than she had since the day she'd come to Bassett Hall. She was escaping this dreadful house and its master for several days; she was going to meet the king; and most importantly, she was going to be with Griffin.

Even knowing the dangers of going to the hunting lodge with him, her pulse raced with anticipation. She and Griffin had not discussed managing to be alone together at the lodge without arousing suspicion. He had told her to trust him. And she knew that it would happen. He would make it happen.

A third footman staggered past, his arms burdened by a leather trunk and four hatboxes, the baggage stacked so high that he could barely see over it.

"Do you intend to take permanent residence at the hunting lodge, my lord?" Julia inquired teasingly.

Griffin planted one hand on his hip and fluttered eyelashes that she could have sworn had been darkened with the paint pot. "Sweet blood of Jesus, my lady, how should I know what to wear, what events will be taking place at the lodge? What if there's a banquet or a ball and I've nothing fitting to wear?" He wiggled his eyebrows as his hand flitted the handkerchief, daring her to giggle.

Julia managed to keep her composure as a fourth footman passed, carrying a small gilded cage. Inside, Charles the cat sat upon a black velvet pillow, his gold eyes half-closed in contentment.

Julia raised one eyebrow. "The cat, too?"

"Who would feed him properly? And what if His Majesty

is so impressed with me that he calls me to court? Surely I couldn't go without kit-ty."

Heaven above, I love him, Julia thought. All she could do was nod and cover her mouth with her palm.

The footman passed and Julia glanced up the grand staircase. Lizzy had still not come down, though their own two trunks had been loaded nearly half an hour earlier.

"What do you think is keeping Lizzy?" Julia wanted to take her leave before Simeon had a chance to appear. Even knowing what a bastard he was, she still felt a thread of guilt for what she was doing. St. Martin was, after all, still her husband. She wore Griffin's jeweled ring this morning on a long gold chain beneath her shift as a symbol of hope.

"Should I run and fetch her?" Griffin offered. "Perhaps that ogre of a nursemaid has locked her in the hall dungeon."

Julia elbowed him, not caring if anyone saw her. "Hold your tongue. That nursemaid once swaddled me. She would give her life for my sister."

He winked. "Lashing taken, my lady. I shall hold my tongue, though I do still intend to avoid the ogre-ess." He shuddered theatrically. "She frightens me, in all honesty."

"Ah hah." Julia lifted her hand. "Here she comes." But then her smile became a frown.

Lizzy slowly descended the staircase, her head hung, one hand over her abdomen. She was still in her morning gown, without cloak, hat, or gloves.

Julia prayed this wasn't what it appeared to be. "Lizzy, I told you to dress warmly. It's a long ride to the lodge. The air is chilling. The coachman said he saw a flake or two of snow."

"I don't feel well," Lizzy moaned as she reached the last tread of the immense staircase. "My tummy."

Julia felt her heart fall to her feet. If Lizzy couldn't go to the hunting lodge, she couldn't. "Oh, no, tell me you're not ill." She grasped her sister's shoulders, riddled by guilt that her first thought had been for herself and not her sister.

"I think I ate too many biscuits with jam. Drusilla said I shouldn't eat those last two, but I did anyway." She bent over. "Oh, Julia, my tummy hurts."

"What's the matter? Are you still not off?" Simeon approached down the long hallway dressed in a cloak and carrying a walking cane, Mr. Gordy in tow.

"I think Lizzy's ill, my lord," Julia said, hoping her disappointment was not too evident.

"You have to go without me, Sister. I can't possibly travel."

Julia took Lizzy's arm. "Don't be ridiculous. If you're ill, I'll stay."

Simeon frowned. "Insult His Majesty by not accepting an invitation because your half-wit sister ate too many sweetmeats?" he flared. "You'll do no such thing!"

Julia had to grit her teeth to keep from snapping a response. How dare he call Lizzy a half-wit—in front of her no less? "Really, my lord, I think it would be better—"

"It's all right." Lizzy lifted her head quickly. "I'm really not so ill, Julia. I just need to go back to bed. Drusilla can take care of me."

Julia studied Lizzy's face. She did appear pale, but she was awfully lively all of a sudden. She squeezed her sister's hand. "You certain you don't need me?"

"I insist, *wife.*" Simeon grasped her elbow roughly and steered her toward the open front door. "The nursemaid can care for her."

"Lizzy?" Julia called over her shoulder.

Lizzy gave her a little smile and a wave. "Have a good time hunting."

Mr. Gordy took Lizzy gently by the arm. "I will see Lady Elizabeth safely to her chambers, my lady."

"Goodbye, wife," Simeon said, passing her arm to Griffin's. "Safe journey. I shan't expect you until week's end."

Griffin gripped her arm and ushered her out the door. Julia

felt as if she were being handled by all of them—Simeon, Griffin, Lizzy, even Gordy—and she didn't like it, not one bit.

"Go right to bed," she called to Lizzy. "And have some chamomile tea sent up from the kitchen."

Simeon closed the great door abruptly behind Julia, giving her no choice but to climb into the carriage and take her seat across from Griffin.

"Relax," Griffin said with a wink as the footman closed the door behind them. "She's going to be fine. And we're going to have a hell of a week."

Julia lifted her arms above her head and moaned as Griffin sank deep into her. The magnificent royal blue bed curtains swirled overhead. She closed her eyes and clawed at the bed covers, the linen soft beneath her fingertips as she strained against him. Yet another sweet wave of ecstasy washed over her.

"Griffin, Griffin," she whispered as the sensations ebbed. "Enough." She laughed huskily. "No more, else you'll be the death of me."

Griffin covered her damp, quavering flesh with his body and kissed her behind her ear. "Enough?" He thrust and she moaned. "Can there ever be enough of this?" He licked the puckered bud of her nipple, and against her will she moaned again. "Or this?"

Julia opened her eyes and grasped his corded neck. Slowly she lifted her legs until her ankles rested on his shoulders.

"Cheat," he accused with a groan.

She lifted her bare buttocks off the sheets and took him deeply.

"Cheater, cheater," he moaned into the tangled tresses of her hair. "I hate a cheater."

Julia lifted her buttocks again and sighed with her own enjoyment. "Wish to call me to a duel on the issue, my lord?"

He let out a gasp. "A—aye. Just . . . just as soon as I finish here."

She laughed and drew him closer, faster. He was hers now, lost to her feminine wiles. In the four short days they had been at the lodge, she had learned much of the giving and taking of pleasure between a man and a woman.

Julia lifted once, twice more, surrounding Griffin as he spilled into her with a final gasp.

For a moment they were still, panting in unison. Then Griffin rolled off Julia and flopped back on the bed beside her. He tucked his hands behind his head. "Where did you learn that little trick, minx?"

With a satisfied giggle, she rolled onto her side to fetch a glass of refreshment from the bedside table. "You." She rolled back and held the goblet to his lips.

He frowned and took a long drink. "Me? You certain?"

She pulled away the cup and caught a dribble of red wine from his chin with the tip of her finger. She licked the wine from her finger with a calculation that she knew would stir him. "Aye," she agreed innocently.

With a growl worse than any ogre's, Griffin leaped on top of her, sending the goblet flying from her hand to the floor below.

Julia squealed as she tried to scramble away.

"Too late! Too late!" he said triumphantly as he straddled her hips and pinned her wrists to the feather tick. "You're mine now, body and soul. Submit, wench!"

She laughed and tried to wiggle free. "Never, never, never." The heady scent of their lovemaking was still thick and warm in the air.

He lowered his face near to hers. "Submit!" he murmured. "You must submit!"

She managed to free one hand and grasped his flaccid penis. He gave a grunt and was instantly still.

"I believe, my lord, it is you who must submit to me now."

She batted her lashes and then eyed the object in her hand. "Everyone knows that she who has control over the pizzle, has control of the kingdom."

Griffin burst into uproarious laughter.

Julia released him and he rolled off her onto his back. "P— p—pizzle?" he guffawed.

She knitted her brow, knowing he made fun of her, but not certain why. "Y . . . yes . . . pizzle." She sat up and propped her hands on her hips. "Well, what the bloody hell do *you* call it?"

He laughed so hard that tears ran down his cheeks. "Ah sweetheart." He wrapped his arm around her neck and pulled her down beside him.

"It's not funny. How am I supposed to know?" She elbowed him indignantly and squirmed out of his embrace. "What *do* you call it?"

He started to speak and then began to laugh again.

She elbowed him hard this time.

"All right, all right." He threw up his hand to protect himself from her blows.

"Well?" she demanded.

He wiped the tears from his cheek. "Well, men have many names—some general such as rod, or sword, or stem." He kissed her on the forehead and rose. He picked up the empty goblet on the floor and crossed the chamber, lit with a hundred candles, to a table to refill it. "And then there are more personal names."

"Personal?" She rolled her eyes as he sat beneath the bed's high canopy.

"Yes." He walked toward her, glorious in his nakedness.

"Such as?"

"Such as . . . Big mighty . . . or . . . Edward."

"Edward?" It was her turn to burst into laughter. "*Edward?*"

"Well . . ."

She could have sworn she saw his cheeks color with embarrassment.

"Edward was a cousin I once had. Long dead and gone now." He took a sip from the goblet, reminiscing. "Anyway, Edward had the largest *pizzle* my cousins or I had ever seen." He glanced at her with enthusiasm. "Like a horse."

She sniggered.

"So . . ." he finished.

"So you named *it* after your cousin?" She burst into laughter again and threw herself back on the pillows, kicking her legs wildly. "I think I like pizzle better."

He sat down on the edge of the bed and took a drink. "Pretty foolish for a protector of kings, eh?"

Julia halted in mid-laugh and sat up, suddenly sober. His laughter, too, died away.

She paused. "That's what you are, aren't you?" she said softly, knowing it was the truth the moment the words left his mouth.

He stared into the goblet. "I told you my responsibility was great."

She crawled across the bed to kneel behind him, pressing her bare breasts against his back as she hugged him tightly. "You do know him. Well enough to name your cat after him," she whispered. "I'm in awe."

He continued to stare into the cup.

"That's how you were able to arrange this hunting lodge," she said. "The privacy, the elegant food, the servants, but no guests."

He brushed his hand over hers. "Oh, Charles is coming. We just came early. I was afraid we wouldn't have time to be alone together once he arrived."

"So you arranged for us to come early."

"We've nothing to fear from Simeon. The servants here are beyond reproach, many my own men and women. They see nothing, hear nothing, many have heard and seen worse."

Julia crawled over to sit beside him on the edge of the great four-poster bed, her bare legs dangling over the side beside his hairy ones. "You protect the king in secret. That's why you play the fop."

"Men and women both find it easy to confess their sins to me. I'm seen as . . . harmless."

Even though Julia had spent the last four days with this man, making love to him, talking late into the night, she suddenly felt as if she didn't know him. She was almost intimidated. "But how do you protect him?"

He swished the red wine in the goblet and watched it wash up the sides and down again. "There are plots, my sweet."

"Plots?"

"To murder His Majesty."

She sucked in her breath. "I've heard such gossip, but I thought it all nonsense. No one would really kill him, would they?"

He laughed without humor. "More than you would suspect." He paused and then continued. "When our Stuart came home to his rightful throne, all men were expected to pledge their allegiance. Charles had to forgive those who had gone against his father and against him to side with Cromwell, because he had no choice. It was the only way to gain unity once again. It's very complicated, but it all has to do with empty royal coffers and political ties. Anyway, he knew that there would be those who would lie, but—"

"But he had to accept their pledges as truth—"

"Until proven otherwise," Griffin finished for her.

"And that's your role? To seek those who lied, who would plot against him?"

"Who *do* plot against him."

She stared at her hands in her lap, suddenly feeling rather small. "Makes our own trials seem rather trivial, doesn't it?"

He turned slowly to gaze into her eyes. "It doesn't make them any less real, any less painful." He set the goblet on the floor and took her hand between both of his. "And it doesn't mean I love you any less. Only—"

"Only your duty is to our king. I understand entirely." And she did.

"I love you, Julia," he murmured.

She smiled as their lips met. "And I you."

As he pushed her back into the sheets, the dogs in the hallway outside their bedchamber began to bark wildly. Somewhere in the distance, outside the draped windows, a trumpet hailed.

"Ah, hell," Griffin muttered and sat up.

"What? What is it?"

Griffin climbed out of the bed and grabbed his breeches from the back of a chair. "It's him."

She frowned. "Him who?"

He snatched a linen shirt from the floor. "Charles."

Julia's eyes widened, and she grabbed for the nearest corner of counterpane to cover herself as if Charles had actually entered the room. "The . . . the king?"

"Aye." He hopped on one foot trying to thrust the other into a boot. "You might as well get up and dress. He'll want to meet you."

Julia was frozen. "The king will want to meet me?"

"Mm hm." He reached the door and jerked it open, while running one hand through his disheveled hair. "It'll be fun. You'll like him, really." He kissed the air in her direction and, before she could respond, closed the door behind him.

"The king? Fun?" Julia breathed. "Sweet Father." Then she fell back and pulled the counterpane over her head.

Chapter Twenty-two

"Lizzy, where are you taking me?"

Lizzy took Amos's hand and led him through the dark corridor, away from the kitchen. "Somewhere wonderful, you'll see."

He tripped over something on the floor or over his own big feet and laughed. She laughed with him, though she hadn't sampled nearly as much of Drusilla's raspberry wine as he had.

"You can't take me into the big house," he whispered loudly. "Cooks . . . cooks don't belong in the master's house with the ladies. Ye heard your sister's words yerself."

"Sister's not here." She tugged on his warm hand. "And I'm not taking you into the house, just through it."

Amos halted and took a drink from Drusilla's bottle. It was almost gone. Drusilla would be angry in the morning when she woke up and saw the wine was gone, but Lizzy would get her another from the earl's cellar, two if Drusilla would keep her wrinkled mouth shut and not tell Julia when she got home.

"Come on," Lizzy insisted. "We're almost there."

Amos allowed her to lead him through the quiet, dark house to the rear addition, and through the doors into Julia's orangery. The moment they stepped inside and closed the doors behind them, they stood in a puddle of moonlight. Here Lizzy could see Amos's face. The way he smiled at her made her stomach flip-flop.

"Right pretty," he remarked, glancing up at her sister's orange and lemon trees as he took another swallow of the wine.

"Right pretty," Lizzy echoed and wrapped her arms around his waist.

Amos finished off the bottle and let it fall to the stone path and roll into Julia's flowers. Lizzy would have to remember to fetch it later and hide it in the big pile in the cellars.

He wrapped his arms around Lizzy's waist and made her feel warm and safe. "If I didn't know better, if I wasn't a learned man who could read and write his own name, I'd think you got me drunk so's you could have your way with me."

Lizzy thought she knew what Amos meant, though she wasn't sure. She giggled and snuggled her cheek against his rough wool coat. He smelled like flour, cinnamon, and cloves, but he smelled like Amos, too. His smell made her as light in the head as the berry wine. "I wouldn't do that."

He kissed her forehead and spoke softly. "No, I don't guess you would."

She lifted her chin to look into his eyes and he kissed her mouth, just like she wanted him to. "I love you," she whispered.

"You shouldn't . . . we shouldn't say—"

"I love you, Amos," she repeated firmly.

"And I love you." He answered almost as if he didn't want to say it.

"I want to marry you and make babies with you."

He laughed deep in his throat and kissed the side of her mouth. "You even know how babies are made?" He buried his face in her hair and breathed deeply.

"Yes, I know how babies are made . . . sort of. I've seen dogs doing it in the yard."

He laughed, but she knew he wasn't laughing at her to be mean. Amos was never mean to her like others were. "We're not dogs, Lizzy honey."

"I know that." She kissed his chin. "And I'm not saying I know exactly how it's done. I only know I want to do it."

He kissed her neck. "And how is it that you know ye want to do it?"

The way he was kissing her was making it hard for her to think straight. "I know. I just know." She panted like she'd been running a long way. "I know because it hurts . . . not really hurts . . . here." She took his hand and guided it to the warm place that tingled between her legs. Even through her gown and petticoats, she could feel his hand.

He made that sound like he was hurt, but when she took her hand away, he didn't move his. She knew he liked touching her as much as she liked having him touch her.

Lizzy kissed Amos's mouth, hard. His hand down there made her want to kiss him hard. It made her want to wiggle against him.

"I'm a full-grown woman," she whispered in his ear. "A woman who knows what she wants. I'm a woman who wants you, Amos Wright."

He started to say something, but instead he just kissed her with his tongue in her mouth. She liked his tongue in her mouth.

They kissed some more. Amos ran his hand up under her petticoat, and all of a sudden Lizzy's legs didn't want to hold her up anymore. It was getting harder and harder to breathe. Her heart was pounding and her hands were shaking, but she wasn't afraid. "Let's lay over here."

She caught his hand and tried to lead him off the path, but he held her back.

"Lizzy . . ."

There he was, sounding like he was hurting again, but she

understood. He didn't want to get in trouble with Julia. He didn't want her to get in trouble.

"It's all right," Lizzy whispered in his ear. Then she let go of his hand and spread out her cloak on a patch of new grass beneath some kind of tree she didn't recognize. She held her hand out to him, watching his face in the moonlight. "I'm not a child," she said. "I know what I want. You."

Finally Amos came to her and knelt beside her. As Lizzy felt the warmth of his arms around her, she knew everything really was going to be all right. Amos was going to make a baby inside her, and then Julia would have to let her marry him.

Sometime much later, when the pool of moonlight had moved, Lizzy rose from her cloak in the grass and began to tuck her wrinkled bodice back into the skirt of her gown. Shyly she watched Amos as he pulled on his breeches and tied the flap.

"I liked it," she whispered. Then she giggled behind her hand. "Think we could do it again tomorrow night?"

Amos slipped his hand under her hair to her neck and kissed her on the lips. "We done a hell of a dangerous thing here, Lizzy love."

She yanked up her drooping stockings and retied the ribbons. She was so pleased with herself and with Amos, that she was bursting inside. "Seems to me we've done something wonderful here."

He laughed deep in his throat the way she loved to hear him laugh. Even if he was frowning, she knew she'd said something that made him happy.

"Yer such an innocent, Lizzy." He picked up her cloak and shook off any grass or dirt that might have stuck to it. "Ye need a man to look after you."

She let him wrap the cloak around her shoulders. "I need *you.*" She spun inside her cloak and lifted up on her toes to kiss him.

"Come on." He pressed his hand to the small of her back. "You gotta get to your room afore Drusilla wakes and finds you gone. And I got to get out of this house afore I'm caught."

Hand in hand they walked back up the orangery path to the door. "Tomorrow night," Lizzy said. "Meet me here."

"I don't know, Lizzy love." He held the door open for her. "I got to have time. Time to think on this matter. Time to figure out what we're going to do."

"Time? Amos Wright, how much time—"

"Who is that? Who goes there?" A deep, loud voice came out of the dark, startling Lizzy. Instinctively she grabbed for Amos's arm.

"Hells' bells, almighty," Amos whispered under his breath.

Candlelight suddenly filled the stone-walled corridor. "I said who goes there?" It was Mr. Gordy. He lifted the candlestand higher. "Lady Elizabeth?"

Lizzy held tighter to Amos hand. She didn't like Mr. Gordy. He was always watching her, following her when he thought he didn't know it.

"Lady Elizabeth?"

"Mr. Gordy?" Another voice came out of the dark. Lizzy had never realized so many people were wandering in Bassett Hall in the middle of the night.

"Mr. Gordy, what have you found there?" His lordship, Julia's husband, appeared in the candlelight. He was wearing red silk robe with dragons on it, and a turban around his bristly bald head like the rag turban Drusilla wore.

Now Lizzy really was scared. She could do nothing but stare at the two men as she clung to Amos's side.

"God's bloody bowels!" Simeon bellowed so loudly that Lizzy cringed.

Lizzy hated loud mouths, and she hated the Earl of St. Martin and his sour face and stinking garlic smell. Lizzy buried her face in Amos's coat, afraid she was going to burst into tears like a baby.

"I said, what have we found here? Man, what is your name?" He spoke to Amos. "What are you doing with the Lady Elizabeth?"

The earl was making Lizzy's head hurt.

Mr. Gordy lowered the candlestand. "My lord, let me take care of this matter. I should—"

"I said, what have we found here?" The earl shouted so loudly this time that the veins on his shiny forehead popped out like blue worms. He grabbed Lizzy by the hand and yanked her away from Amos.

Lizzy burst into tears. She wasn't afraid for herself, just Amos. "Leave him alone," she blurted into the earl's garlic-smelling face. "It was my idea. It wasn't Amos's fault!"

"Amos?" The earl shoved Lizzy backward, and Mr. Gordy had to catch her with one hand to keep her from falling on the stone slab floor. "Amos, where are you employed here?"

Amos yanked off his hat and lowered his head. "The kitchen, my lord. A . . . a baker."

Lizzy could tell Amos was afraid by the shaky sound of his voice. She didn't want him to be afraid. She wanted to knock the earl down and run to Amos. She wanted to put her arms around him and comfort him. She wanted to protect him.

The earl slowly walked toward Amos, his hands behind his back. "And do you think bakers should be about *my* home in the middle of the night with *my* wife's sister?"

"No, my lord."

The earl stopped right in front of Amos and stuck his ugly face in Amos's. "And do you think bakers should be about *my* home in the middle of the night futtering *my* wife's sister?" Spittle flew from his mouth.

Amos shook with fear. "No, my lord. But . . . but please don't punish Lizzy, she weren't—"

"Silence!"

Amos shook harder. "It weren't—"

"Mine. My property!" The earl hit Amos in the cheek with his fist.

Lizzy screamed as Amos went down.

"Mine, not to be soiled by the likes of you!" The earl kicked Amos hard and Amos grunted with pain.

"No!" Lizzy tried to break away from Mr. Gordy, but he wouldn't let her go.

"Hush. Save yourself," Mr. Gordy whispered in her ear.

"Get him out of here, Gordy!" the earl shrieked, sweat breaking out above his upper lip. He drew back his foot and kicked Amos again. "Get him out of here before I lose my temper and gut him!"

Mr. Gordy let go of Lizzy and quickly set down the candle-stand. Lizzy bolted, but Gordy reached Amos before she did and yanked him to his feet.

"Let go of him!" she shouted, striking the secretary on the back with both of her fists. "Let him be. Don't hurt my Amos!"

The earl grabbed Lizzy by her arm, twisted it, and pulled her away.

Amos put out his hand for her, but he couldn't reach her. There was blood on his hands, blood on his shirt. "Lizzy?"

"Amos!" Lizzy shrilled.

The Earl of St. Martin shook her until her teeth rattled against each other. "Shut up, before I shut you up, you little dimwit." Holding her as far away from his body as he could, he ordered Mr. Gordy, "Get him out of here." He swung his foot as Mr. Gordy half-carried, half-dragged Amos past them.

"What do you want me to do with him?" Mr. Gordy grunted as he fought to control Amos's flailing arms and legs.

"Don't hurt Lizzy! Don't hurt her," Amos moaned. "Send word for Lady St. Martin."

"My lord?" Gordy passed Lizzy and the earl, carrying Amos further and further from her.

"Kill him!"

Lizzy stopped struggling against the earl and turned to face him. Suddenly she was numb from her toes to her lips. She couldn't speak; she couldn't move. Surely she couldn't possibly have heard what she thought she'd heard.

Mr. Gordy must not have heard right either, because he stopped beyond the circle of light cast by the candlestand on the floor. Lizzy couldn't see Amos any longer, but she could hear him breathing hard.

"My lord?" Gordy questioned.

"Are you deaf? Kill him!" St. Martin stomped one foot, still holding tightly to Lizzy's arm. He punctuated each word with another stomp. "Kill him. Kill him. Kill him!"

"Yes, my lord." Mr. Gordy dragged Amos away into the darkness, and Lizzy fell on her knees at the earl's feet.

"No, please, no," she begged, hands clasped.

But even as the prayer passed her lips, she knew it would go unheard.

Julia poured three glasses of sweet claret and carried them across the cozy withdrawing room on a silver tray. "Your Majesty." She offered him a goblet, which he accepted with a regal nod. "My lord."

Griffin took his wine and hers as well. "Sit." He patted the crimson velvet cushion beside him on the floor.

Julia welcomed his hand and settled beside him, petticoats flared around her. She still couldn't believe she was in the presence of the king. Sitting on the floor playing a three-handed game of putt with him, no less.

"Ah, exquisite," the king remarked, drinking heartily from his goblet. "And now, madame, it's your turn to deal. I've a mind to win back at least ten pounds of what I owe you before the evening is done." He passed her the deck of cards. "That or else I'll be forced to sleep with you myself to pay my debt, for everyone knows my coffers are empty." He winked at her.

Julia's cheeks grew warm, but she laughed at his jest. From

anyone else she might have been insulted by such a bawdy remark, but after three rainy days spent in the company of His Majesty, she could only be flattered.

In the last few days she had become enchanted by Charles. He was handsome, charming, witty, but most importantly, he was Griffin's friend. Here at the lodge she had witnessed an amazing relationship between the two men that ran far deeper than that of king and servant.

The two men were actually comrades. And though, in public, Griffin retained a certain air of appropriate reverence, in closed quarters, alone, the men acted as if they were childhood friends. They quarreled and competed like brothers.

Julia shuffled the deck, listening as the two men continued their conversation.

Griffin casually slid his arm around Julia's waist. By now she was comfortable with his displays of affection in the presence of His Majesty. Apparently the king had known about their clandestine relationship before his arrival.

"Jabar reports that promising information surfaced in a London tavern only last night," Griffin said. "And our investigation of several puritans magically-turned-loyal-subjects continues."

The king picked up his cards from the wool tapestry he'd ordered pulled off the wall to make a cozy spot before the fireplace. "And the lady's husband?"

Julia focused on her cards. Griffin had said nothing of investigating Simeon. Surely he didn't think Simeon was part of some master plan to murder the king? It wasn't possible. Just the same, her heart skipped a beat. Men found guilty of treason were hanged. Hanged men left widows free to marry another.

She immediately felt guilty for wishing such a fate upon anyone, but the man was such a bastard. Perhaps he really was capable of treason.

Griffin paused and Julia glanced up to find his gaze fixed on her.

"Oh, hang it," the king muttered. "I've stuck my stocking

in my mouth now, haven't I?'' He shrugged one broad shoulder. ''I only assumed that you and the lady had made plans for the future . . . should the earl be suspect.''

Griffin's gaze slowly shifted to his sovereign's. ''I thought it better that nothing be said. I'm certain naught would come of it, and I don't want to offer . . . false hope.'' As he spoke he squeezed Julia's hand.

She squeezed back, sharing his emotions. They wanted so desperately to be together—to be man and wife. They wanted so desperately what they could not have.

The king lifted his hand casually. ''You want him thrown in the Tower anyway?'' He reached for his goblet. ''I can do that, you know. One of the privileges of being king.''

''No.'' Julia was surprised by her own forwardness with His Majesty, but she spoke before she had the good sense to consider her words. ''Please don't. I wouldn't want a man falsely accused on my account.'' She lowered her lashes. ''Not even for Griffin.''

The king gave a snort of derision. ''The man's a snake, Julia, and by my own blessed cod, he reeks of garlic.'' He waved a hand in front of his prominent nose. ''I despise it when he pays homage. The entire hall must be aired.''

She couldn't help but smile. If she didn't laugh over her situation, she would do nothing but cry. ''If my husband is indeed treasonous, he should go to the Tower. But in my opinion, Your Majesty, no man, not even a snake,''—*not even a man who sends another to bed his wife,* she thought—''deserves to be falsely accused of such a heinous crime.''

''Very well.'' The king sighed. ''I suppose I couldn't expect differently. I should have known you would carry the same high moral standards as Griffin. A pity my court is not filled with Baron Archers and Countess St. Martins.''

A knock sounded at the door and the king reached for his goblet. He didn't bother to look up, but began to rearrange his cards in his hand. He had stretched out on the many cushions strewn across the small withdrawing room floor and removed his riding boots. "Aye."

One of the entourage of men who had accompanied His Majesty to the hunting lodge appeared in the doorway. He held a folded piece of paper. "A message for the Countess, Your Highness." He kept his gaze fixed on some invisible spot high on the plastered wall.

"For me?" Julia rose with the assistance of Griffin's arm. "From Bassett Hall?"

"Aye, my lady."

Julia accepted the missive and the servant backed out of the room, closing the paneled oak door behind him.

Julia broke the green wax seal with the St. Martin shield. A letter from Simeon?

> *My Lady,*
> *A matter of urgency concerning the Lady Elizabeth*
> *requires your immediate presence.*
>
> *Your Servant,*
> *Mr. Gordy*

"He's not broken his neck in a bucket of soapsuds or choked on his garlic, has he?"

Both men chuckled at the King's jest.

Julia folded the paper, a sense of dread washing over her. A matter of urgency? Gordy didn't say she was ill. Immediately Julia thought of the baker. Surely Lizzy hadn't been kissing him again. "I have to return to Bassett Hall. Tonight." She glanced up. "By your leave, of course, Your Majesty."

"Pity." The king moved one of the cards in his hand, his long legs stretched out before the fireplace. "You're better at cards than my companion here, and a damned sight more comely."

Griffin laughed with him, but his face was lined with concern. "What's wrong? *He's* called for you?"

She fiddled with the paper. "Will you excuse us, Your Majesty? I've only need of Griffin for a moment."

"Take him, take him. Why not?" He tossed down his cards, face up. "You've already taken my coin and my heart, why not my comrade as well?"

She forced a half smile and curtsied. "Your servant, Your Majesty. Griffin?"

He rose from the velvet cushions and followed her out of the withdrawing room and into the high-ceilinged passageway. Here the stone went unplastered, and their voices echoed off the walls.

"What's wrong, sweet? What does Simeon want?"

She bit down on her lower lip. "Something with Lizzy." She held up the note. "Mr. Gordy sent word, not Simeon. My guess would be that Simeon knows nothing of it."

Griffin took notice of the broken wax. "He used Simeon's seal without his permission? Takes Bullocks."

"I have to go. Now." Julia felt as if a bucket of icy water had been thrown in her face. She knew she shouldn't have left Lizzy. She refolded the note. "Can you come, too?"

Griffin reached out and lifted a lock of golden red hair off her shoulder. Here in the privacy of the lodge she wore it down over her shoulders, as he preferred it.

"I'm sorry, sweet. I can't."

She compressed her lips tightly. "Why?"

"You know why. Jabar returns here tomorrow. He may have word of the conspirators."

"You could send Jabar a message," she offered hopefully. "Tell him you've gone home to London."

"Impossible. Besides, I belong here right now. At His Majesty's side."

Julia felt tears sting the backs of her eyelids.

"I'm sorry, sweetheart." He tried to touch her shoulder, but she pulled away.

She knew she was being foolish. Griffin was protecting the

king of England, for God's sake. He couldn't be at the beck and call of a woman, not even the woman he loved.

Griffin folded his arms over his chest. He wore her favorite blue velvet doublet, the one that matched the color of his eyes. "I can join you in a few days, perhaps."

"It's all right." She turned away.

"Julia—"

"Griffin, I have to pack. Could you call for the carriage?"

"I could help. Charles can wait on his cards."

"I'd rather be alone." She knew she was being childish, but she couldn't help how she felt. Lizzy might be sick or hurt. She needed Griffin. She didn't want to share him. Not even with the king of England.

As she hurried down the hall, a servant who stood in a doorway so still that he was nearly invisible, leapt to light the passageway.

"Julia," Griffin called with obvious exasperation as he followed her, his footsteps echoing on the stone. Then he halted. "At least let me see you off."

"I'd rather you didn't." She halted at the turn in the corridor and looked back. God, she loved him so much it hurt. "Just let me go, Griffin. It's over. It's back to our responsibilities, both of us. Back to Bassett Hall I go, to my sister . . . and to my husband."

Griffin watched her leave in a silence that she knew broke both their hearts.

Chapter Twenty-three

Julia stood at the window of her bedchamber and stared out at the dreary January sky. Christmas had come to Bassett Hall in a flurry of gifts and parties, but without the warmth of a family's love. Now, the cold, wet rain of winter had settled in, and Julia felt trapped. She felt as if nothing was ever going to be right again.

Lizzy had spent the advent season in bed, her eyes closed, her face pale. Julia had arrived at Bassett Hall from the king's hunting lodge too late to save poor Amos, but in time to rescue Lizzy. It had taken two days of begging for Julia to convince Simeon not to put Lizzy in an asylum. No one ever spoke of Amos again, and out of fear for her sister, Julia did not ask how Simeon had disposed of him. She feared to ask more would push him beyond his limit of tolerance.

So, Lizzy's baker was dead, and there was nothing Julia could do to console her sister. Lizzy barely spoke, barely ate, barely slept. For a month she did nothing but lie in bed, her eyes closed. At first Julia had tried everything. She'd coaxed

Lizzy with delicacies of food, wooden toys, even a kitten. Nothing could take the dull-eyed stare from her face. Now after two months, Lizzy rose each day and went through the motions of living, but there was no life in her eyes.

Julia was overwrought with concern for her sister, but she didn't know what more she could do for her. She blamed herself for Lizzy being caught with the baker by Simeon. It was her fault for not sending Amos away when she'd first caught a hint of the illicit affair. It was her fault Lizzy had been left alone to sneak about Bassett Hall in the middle of the night.

While Julia had been lying in bed in Griffin's arms at the hunting lodge, Amos had been sentenced to death. Of course there was no proof but Lizzy's word, so there would be no legal recourse, even if Julia dared seek it. In the eyes of the law, Amos was an insignificant baker who had run off from his employer.

Julia set down the napkin she was embroidering. She'd torn out the same row of green stitches three times this morning. Her heart just wasn't in stitching napkins with the St. Martin crest on them.

Julia had seen little of Griffin. There was no quarrel that separated them, only the harsh realities of their lives. Griffin knew nothing of Amos's death. Julia lied and told him Amos had run away, and that she'd had to return from the hunting lodge to Bassett Hall to comfort Lizzy. She hadn't told him the truth for fear of the danger to Lizzy and to herself. Simeon had made it clear the night she returned that he could still send Lizzy off to an asylum at any time, or worse. Even if Julia had thought it safe to tell Griffin, she wouldn't have. His responsibility to the king was too great right now. He needed to concentrate on protecting his majesty.

Lately, Griffin spent much of his time away from Bassett Hall, with the king, she guessed, though he never said. She liked to think that every moment he was away would somehow bring an end to this nightmare of her marriage, but she wondered if she and Griffin were both fooling themselves. When Julia did see him, it was only for brief snatches of time. Only twice since their return had they met alone, and both times she had been so afraid they would be caught, that she'd not really been able to fully enjoy their lovemaking.

Julia slowly drew her first initial in the condensation on the inside of the window glass. With Lizzy not herself and Griffin gone most of the time, she was so lonely. Griffin's promise that somehow, someday they would be together seemed less and less real each day. Even the heavy ring she wore on the ribbon beneath her shift seemed unreal.

"Here's another napkin." Lizzy offered Julia a piece of white damask. "Should I start another?"

Lizzy's face was pallid, her eyes sunken in from the weight she'd lost. But at least she was on her feet.

Julia smiled, though she didn't feel like it. "Would you? We've still at least twenty to stitch, and the party is less than a week away."

Lizzy stared dull-eyed. "Should I send Drusilla to fetch more?" Since the incident with Amos, Lizzy had barely left the privacy of the apartments they shared.

"No." Julia rested a hand on her sister's bony shoulder. "I'll do it. Why not make us a pot of tea and I'll bring up something special to eat with it. Would you like a ginger cake if there's any?"

Lizzy drifted away. "Whatever pleases you. I care naught."

Julia watched Lizzy wander away. She wasn't really up to food either. The tea would be enough. For the last fortnight her stomach had been queasy on and off, day and night. She wasn't ill, no fever, no chills, no headache, just the nausea. Somewhere in the back of her mind, Julia knew there was one possibility she need consider, but she refused to even think about it. To become pregnant with Griffin's child when her husband did not bed her would be the end to them all. It was too terrible a possibility to even consider.

"I'll get the napkins," Julia said as cheerfully as possible. "And you pour the tea to steep. I'll be back directly." She halted at the door. "I don't suppose there's any need to pour Mother a cup. We haven't seen her in three days."

Lizzy reached for the kettle of hot water a servant had left on a spider on the hearth. "I saw her last night."

"Did you?"

"She said to tell you goodbye." Lizzy poured the water, using the hem of her petticoat to protect her hand against the heat of the iron handle.

"Goodbye?" Julia's brow creased. "What do you mean, goodbye?"

"She went to Paris to marry the Frenchman."

Julia was nearly as shocked by her sister's lack of facial expression as of the news. "Married? And she didn't tell me?"

"You were with the earl, occupied. Mother didn't want to disturb you." Lizzy carried the teapot to the table and set it on a woven rag mat that protected the finish from the heat.

Julia raised her voice unconsciously. "And *you* didn't tell me until today?"

She raised a thin shoulder, her back to Julia. "Didn't think it mattered."

Julia opened her mouth to blurt, *Didn't think it mattered?*, but she restrained herself. Lizzy couldn't be held responsible for what she said and did right now.

Shaking her head, Julia left her bedchamber. "Mother married?" she said to herself as she descended the steps. "Incredible."

In the front hall, Julia crossed paths with Simeon. She did her best to avoid him whenever possible, but when she did see him she tried to remain cordial. Lizzy's presence in the house was too unstable not to. "Good noon day, my lord."

Simeon glanced up from the book he carried as he walked. A pair of glass and wire spectacles rested on the end of his nose. "Good noon. How are the preparations for the table linens coming? I want nothing left uncrested."

In less than a week the earl would be fifty. Since Christmas everyone had begun working in a frenzy to prepare for the ball he would throw in his own honor. "Well, my lord." She kept her eyes downcast, taking notice that his hands were so raw from washing that they were streaked with dry and oozing blood. "And the gallery. Will it be ready in time?"

"It had better be, else I'll be stringing up masons by their necks to adorn the walls."

Julia never flinched. After what Simeon had done to poor Amos, nothing he said could shock her. "I'm quite certain it will be completed by then, and just to your liking."

"We've already begun to hang some of the artwork. I should like you to take a turn later in the gallery and see if they're placed to their best advantage. You should consult me, of course, should you have a suggestion for change."

"Of course. Yes, my lord." She dipped a curtsy. That was enough conversation with her husband for one day. "Good day, my lord."

She started to walk off, but he stopped her.

"Wife?"

"Aye?" She turned around.

"Are you feeling well?"

Something in the way he said it made the hair on the back of her neck bristle. "Aye, fine, my lord."

He frowned and turned his head one way and then the other. "Just wondering. You look a little peaked." He closed his book, studying her thoughtfully. "You really should get that worthless cousin of mine to take you riding. The fresh air would do you good."

Julia touched her palm to her cheek and forced a smile. "I'm fine. Really. Good day, my lord." Then, before he could stop her again, she lifted her petticoats and made a hasty retreat.

What did he mean she was looking peaked? She patted both

cheeks to bring color to them as she headed for the house-keeper's quarters where the linens were kept. Since when had Simeon begun taking notice of her appearance? What was he watching for? And why on earth did he bring Griffin into the conversation? Surely he didn't suspect she and Griffin were—

A sudden wave of nausea took Julia by surprise, and she gripped the cornerstone of the wall for support. Fighting the dizziness and nausea, she realized that she could no longer avoid the possibility of pregnancy. If she was pregnant, she didn't have much time. Waiting for Griffin to rescue her from her marriage wasn't going to work. She was going to have to come up with her own means of saving herself, Lizzy—she rested her hand on her abdomen—and her unborn child.

"A little to the right." Julia rested one hand on her hip, watching with a critical eye as the workmen lifted the precious Italian painting to the height she desired. "There. Excellent."

Although upon her initial arrival at Bassett Hall Simeon had made it plain that he didn't wish her to participate in the daily running of the house, he had begun to rely on her when he entertained. With his birthday ball only three days away, there was more than enough work for the housekeeper, and Simeon and Mr. Gordy spent most of their time locked in the library attending to whatever business it was her husband was so involved in. That left Julia with the task of seeing the new gallery completed.

"See that one hung and we'll have to start again at daylight," she told the men.

"Aye, m'lady."

Julia walked to the windows. She had met Griffin in the great hall nearly an hour ago and told him she needed to talk to him. She'd done nothing for days but contemplate her possible situation. She'd come up with no definite plans yet, but her mind was sifting through the possibilities. Julia was hoping

Griffin would join her here, where there would be witnesses to an innocent conversation she would have with her husband's cousin. After what Simeon had said the other day, she was hesitant to meet alone with him.

"There you are."

At the sound of Griffin's voice, Julia closed her eyes with relief. "My lord."

"My lady." He was dressed in a suit of the most obscene turquoise and yellow. A smile twitched on his face as if he could read her mind. "Like it?" He tugged on the sleeve of his doublet. "Just delivered. I'll be the envy of every man in London, won't I?"

"The envy of every parrot."

That boyish grin again.

Julia walked along the lead casement windows that ran the length of the gallery, drawing Griffin away from the workers, but still in plain sight.

"You needed me?" he asked softly.

"Aye . . ." She fiddled with the gold ring she wore beneath her clothing. Today it felt as if the metal burned. "I . . . I was wondering . . ." She glanced out the window, afraid her face might give away some of the emotions inside her. "Griffin, I need money and I have no one else to turn to."

"All right."

"Mother's run off with the Frenchman," she continued without really hearing him. "And what little dowry there was, Simeon invested with his goldsmith."

"How much?"

Still, she didn't hear him. "I imagine there would be some way for me to contact the goldsmith and see if I could remove some of the money. I should have been saving some of the household allowance Simeon gives me, but I just didn't think." She lifted one hand. "It didn't occur to me that I would need—"

"Yes, Julia," Griffin said firmly, taking the hand she gestured with.

Julia pulled away from him and glanced in the direction of the workers. Busy putting away their tools and ladders, they took no notice of her or Griffin.

She crossed her arms around her waist. "I'm sorry. This blessed ball has me on edge."

"I can have the money for you in a few days. How much? A hundred pounds. Two? I like everyone to think I live on an allowance from my wife, but I really have coin of my own. Lena's taken it upon herself to invest for me over the years."

"You don't even want to know what it's for?"

When she turned back to the dark windows, his blue-eyed gaze followed her. "Must be for a good cause. You'll tell me when you want to." He shrugged his broad shoulders and the yellow fringe on the epaulettes of his doublet shimmied. "I'm certain you have good reason."

"I don't need it now. Yet. But . . ."

Griffin glanced over his shoulder. The men hanging the artwork were retreating down the long gallery. At the other end, the masons were hard at work on the last wall. That wall would separate the room from a series of small storage areas and join the addition with the main house.

Griffin covered her hand on the window frame with his own. "Tell me what's wrong, Julia. I've been so busy I've barely had time to talk with you in weeks, but that doesn't mean I don't think about you. It doesn't mean I don't care."

"Lizzy and I, we may have to . . . go."

The muscles of his jaw tensed. "Go? Go where? Julia, what's wrong?"

She had no plan yet to give Griffin, and she didn't want to tell him she suspected she was pregnant. She hadn't thought that far ahead. She just knew that when the time came she might have to flee, and would need money to book passage to somewhere far from Bassett Hall.

"Tell me," he said softly.

She wasn't ready to tell him. Not yet. And she still had weeks to make plans, months probably. By her calculations, if she were pregnant, she was only two months along. She still had time to plan, and Lizzy had time to get stronger. All those weeks in bed had made her so fragile that Julia feared moving her now would be the death of her.

Her gaze met his. "Could we not talk about it now?" She was begging him, and somehow he knew it.

After a pause that seemed endless, he nodded. "Not now, but soon." He wasn't asking her, he was telling her.

"Soon."

"But if you're in danger," he said quickly, "I could get you out tonight. I don't know how or where, but I could do it."

"No. There's time. Lizzy's just beginning to recover. I'd be afraid to move her just yet."

"Julia." Griffin seemed to be debating whether or not to tell her something. Finally he conceded to his inner turmoil. "We've made progress. Letters have been distributed asking for financial support and otherwise. Not only do they plan to kill our king, but replace him immediately with their own."

Julia's eyes widened. "You know who it is?"

He scowled. "No, but we're close. He's becoming impatient. His own foolishness may lead us right to him."

"Is . . . is Simeon involved?"

"Julia—"

"Never mind." She lifted her palms. "Don't tell me. No false hope today. I couldn't bear it."

He sighed and stared out the window. Darkness was settling in on the city, and the glass reflected his own image. "I want to hold you so badly. I want to—"

"Shhh," she whispered, running her fingers over the freshly painted window frame. "There'll be time enough for that later."

"Time enough. Years."

"Years," she repeated with a smile.

"Tonight, will you come?" He beckoned her with a glistening light in his eyes.

"No. Not tonight. It's not safe."

"Tomorrow night?"

She hesitated.

"The night after?"

"It's foolish to take chances," she whispered. "Now go on. I need to check the progress on the west wall. His lordship will give birth to kittens if the wall isn't done by the night after next."

Griffin eyed the wall. "They may finish it, but it certainly won't be dry."

"I've convinced him that we can hang velvet draperies to shield the unplastered stone. The rail's already been hung from the ceiling. Green and white draperies, of course."

Griffin broke into a grin as he walked away. "The St. Martin colors, of course."

The two laughed as they parted, and for the briefest moment all seemed to be right in the world.

Lizzy sat in the darkness on the top step of the servant's back staircase. She didn't know how long she'd been there. She'd never been really good with time, and since Amos had gone, time hadn't really mattered anymore.

Lizzy supposed she should get up and go back down the hallway to her apartments, before Drusilla sounded an alarm and sent an army of footmen searching for her. Julia was downstairs with the earl, dining, making plans for the big ball. Lizzy just wanted to get away from Drusilla and her mother-henning. She just wanted to be alone.

A fat tear ran down Lizzy's cheek. She was so lonely without Amos. She missed him so much that her tummy hurt all the time. The earl . . . it was his fault Amos was gone. His fault Amos was dead. If Lizzy knew how to shoot a pistol, if she knew where to get one, she'd take that pistol and shoot him right between his ugly, garlic eyes. Lizzy wasn't silly enough to think that would bring Amos back, but seeing the Earl of St. Martin's blood all over his clean floor might make her feel better.

Lizzy wiped at her tear, but another ran down her other cheek. It wasn't fair. She loved Amos so much. She hadn't done anything wrong. Amos hadn't done anything wrong. He wanted to marry her.

It was a moment before Lizzy realized someone was watching her from behind. She glanced over her shoulder. It was Mr. Gordy. He was always watching her.

Lizzy folded her hands in her lap. Drusilla had dressed her for bed in her sleeping gown, but Lizzy had put on her night rail before she'd slipped out of the bedchamber. She didn't care if Gordy saw her in her sleeping clothes. She didn't care who saw her. It would just give Drusilla one more thing to ramble about.

"Lady Elizabeth?"

It was the first time he had ever spoken to her when he was watching her. Usually he just stared.

"Yes?" Lizzy sniffed and wiped at her tears with the back of her hand.

"Are you all right, Lady Elizabeth?" As always he sounded funny, like there was too much starch in his breeches. That's why Lizzy figured he always stood so straight. He couldn't bend.

"I'm all right," Lizzy said.

She heard him walk hesitantly toward her, but Lizzy wasn't afraid. There was nothing left in the world to be afraid of. The worst thing that could ever happen to her had already happened.

"Miss Elizabeth, you cry too much."

She sniffed again. "I can't help it. I'm sad."

He was very close to her now. "Why? Why are you sad?"

Lizzy's lower lip trembled. "You know why."

Mr. Gordy was quiet for a moment. He looked around to see if anyone was coming. "Could . . . would you mind if I sat beside you, m'lady?"

She scooted over a little on the step. "Sit if you like. I never saw you sit. You must get tired."

Mr. Gordy folded his long legs stiffly and came to rest beside her. She glanced sideways at him.

"Tell me why you are sad, Lady Elizabeth."

She twisted her hands in her night robe. "Because"—*sniff*— "my Amos is dead. The earl had my Amos killed because he touched me." Another tear trickled down her cheek.

"Lady Elizabeth, if I told you a secret . . ." He breathed deeply, as if he were out of breath. "If I told you a secret, could you keep it a secret forever?"

She glanced at him with interest. "A secret about Amos?"

He nodded solemnly. "A secret that would make you stop crying. I'd do anything to make you stop crying. You don't eat, you don't sleep, you just cry. But you have to swear. If you told—"

She shook her head wildly. "Oh, I wouldn't tell." She ran one finger over her compressed lips. "Swear," she mumbled from her closed mouth.

Mr. Gordy stared down the dark stairwell. "He's not dead, Lady Elizabeth."

Lizzy's mouth flew open. Her heart fluttered. She felt like somebody had lifted something heavy off her chest. But then she frowned. "You wouldn't lie to me, would you? People lie to me all the time."

"I would not lie to you. Not you. Not ever."

"How do you know he's not dead?" she whispered, trying hard not to squeal with happiness.

"Because the earl told me to do it, and I didn't. I didn't because I knew it would hurt you," he breathed.

"Where is he?" Lizzy clasped the secretary's arm.

He stared into her eyes. "At a farmhouse in Essex, milking cows."

She scrunched up her nose and giggled as she released his arm. "Amos hates cows."

"Cows are better than an early grave."

"Amos is alive and milking cows," Lizzy said to herself. "My Amos is alive."

"I must go before I'm missed."

He started to get up, but Lizzy grabbed his arm and pulled him back down so that she could look him squarely in the face. "This isn't a trick."

"No. But he cannot come back. He can never come back, else the earl will find out and kill Amos himself."

She nodded gravely. "I'm not stupid. I know he can't come back."

Gordy smiled. Lizzy never remembered seeing him smile before.

"I'm glad you're not sad anymore," he whispered.

"Thank you." Then she kissed Mr. Gordy on his smooth-shaven cheek.

Gordy stretched out his long legs and rose from the stair tread. Lizzy watched him as he disappeared down the hall, his hand on his cheek where she'd kissed him.

"Amos is alive," she whispered to herself. "He's alive, and now I just have to find him!"

Chapter Twenty-four

Griffin rolled over and buried his face in the warm, soft cleft between Julia's breasts. "Wife," he called her.

She laughed and ran her fingers through his hair, making his scalp tingle ... his entire body tingle. "Husband," she said.

Griffin breathed deeply. The dream was so real. He could smell her hair. He could feel her hands.

"Griffin ... Griffin," she whispered in his ear.

"Griffin?"

He opened his eyes, but she was still there. He squinted in the darkness. "Julia?"

"Shhh," she whispered. The room was so dark he could barely see her, but he could smell her hair, he could feel her warmth. "Move over, it's cold," she told him.

Still not quite awake and a little confused, Griffin slid over in his bed. Charlie meowed in protest. "Sorry." He pushed the cat off the bed. "Checkmate. My woman takes your cat."

Charlie scurried under the bed.

Julia slipped naked under the counterpane, and he drew her into his arms. "I was just dreaming about you." He closed his eyes and nuzzled her neck.

"Were you?" Her lips were warm on his.

"I wasn't expecting you." He kissed her earlobe, her neck. "When I asked the other day, you said you wouldn't come."

"Want me to leave?"

She made a move to go, but he grabbed her and pulled her back. "No. Never." He pressed his mouth to the ridge of her collarbone. "I'm just pleasantly surprised."

"I know I said I wouldn't come. It really is dangerous." She laid her cheek on his chest. "But I couldn't help myself. All night I lay in bed beside my sister unable to sleep. I had to come." She ran her hand over his shoulder. "I don't know how much longer I can stay at Bassett Hall. How much longer we can be together."

He heard the catch in her voice and it reverberated in his own heart. He felt so damned useless. All he wanted to do was take her away, make her his own. But he couldn't, not now, not yet. He was too close to finding the snake. Despite his overwhelming desire to protect and care for Julia, his commitment to His Highness still gripped him. Griffin pressed his lips to hers again. "If you would tell me what's wrong, maybe I could help."

She turned over on her side to face him and brought her mouth to his. "Hush. We haven't much time before the household awakes, so if you intend to ravish me"—she was already breathing heavier—"do it now."

Griffin welcomed her hot, wet mouth on his. He'd missed her so badly these last few weeks, wanted her so badly . . . It was all he could do to concentrate on his work. It was all he could do to hear what the king said when he spoke.

His Majesty had already given him permission to take his leave when this was all over. Once the ring of traitors had been discovered, Griffin would take Julia away from England, somewhere far from here, where no one would know she had a husband. He would take her sister, too.

"I love you, I love you, I love you," Julia whispered, drawing her lips over his chest.

Griffin groaned as she caught his nipple between her teeth and tugged. Over the years he'd bedded many women, but no one had touched him like this. No one had ever loved him as his Julia did.

Griffin reached with both hands to caress her full breasts as she climbed onto his chest, kissing, rubbing, teasing.

Already he was rock hard. Ready. But they made love so infrequently. He wanted it to last for hours, until dawn, until sunset.

She must have sensed his urgency because she shifted astride him.

"Oh, no," he said huskily. "Not yet."

She ground her groin against his. "You don't care for this, my lord?"

"Oh, I care for it, but I care for this, too."

Griffin flipped Julia over onto her back, and she had to cover her mouth with her hand to keep from laughing aloud. She didn't know what had possessed her to come tonight. After what Simeon had said in the hallway, she should have stayed as far from Griffin as possible. But suddenly she felt as if time were running out. She was beginning to fear that either she would not make it out of here alive, or that once she escaped, she'd never see Griffin again. The weight of impending doom had sent her through the darkness of the corridors from her chambers to Griffin's.

Julia sank back in the warm bed linens and sighed with pleasure as Griffin ran his hands over her breasts and down her rib cage.

As fingers of pleasure curled around her limbs, she wondered what Griffin would think if she told him she might be with child. He had mentioned children. Surely he would be pleased.

But she knew he would also be afraid for her. Knowing she was pregnant might affect his duty to the king. Julia never wanted to feel responsible for taking him from his duty.

Griffin kissed her navel and she tightened the muscles of her abdomen, feeling the warmth of his touch lower. With a soft groan she threaded her fingers through his silky blond hair.

But he deserves to know, she thought, drifting with the tide of pleasure. *Of all the things I've kept from him, this is the one thing I have no right to keep.*

Griffin's warm mouth met with the soft down of curls at the apex of her thighs, and all reason slipped from her mind. *I'll tell him,* she thought. *Later . . .*

Julia heard Griffin sigh and she relaxed against the pillows, giving herself fully to him. For once she didn't worry about being caught. *What if this was the last time?*

The warm tip of his tongue sent a shock through her entire body, and she grasped the knotted bed linens piled around them. Waves of sensation washed over her. He always knew just how to touch her, how fast, how slow . . .

Julia moaned. She felt his fingers, massaging, delving . . . It was too fast . . . too soon . . .

She arched her back and surrendered to his touch with a shuddering cry of relief.

Griffin muffled her groans with his mouth, sharing the taste of their lovemaking. He whispered her name in her ear. He told her he loved her.

But still Julia wasn't satiated.

She parted her thighs, lifting up to move against him.

"Greedy witch," he teased. But he knew what she wanted . . . what she expected.

As he slipped inside her, she pulled on his neck and brought his mouth down hard against hers. She arched her hips, taking him in fully as she thrust her tongue into his mouth. They kissed until they were both breathless and gasping for air.

"Julia, Julia," Griffin panted in her ear.

"Griffin."

He sensed her burning need and drove deeper, faster.

She wanted it to last forever, but it was over in seconds. Julia rose and fell over the precipice, taking Griffin with her.

When they had both caught their breaths, he rolled off her and onto his side.

Little bursts of pleasure still exploded inside her as she rolled onto her side and snuggled her buttocks against his groin. Griffin wrapped his arms around her waist, his hand on one breast, and pulled her even closer.

"I'll get you out of this, and we'll be together," he promised softly. "Soon. You just have to be patient with me."

"How soon?" she whispered when she could find her voice.

"Very soon." He kissed a damp spot behind her ear and pushed up on one elbow. "Why? Simeon hasn't shown up in your bedchamber, has he? I know I said I wouldn't kill him in cold blood, but if he—"

"No. He avoids my bedchamber as if it were plagued. Only . . ." She hesitated to go on. She wanted to tell him about the baby. She wanted to tell him about her premonition of doom. She wanted to tell him she was afraid not just for herself, but for all of them.

"He doesn't suspect?" Griffin rolled her onto her back.

In the darkness she could only make out the outline of his face. His breath was warm on her lips. Should she tell him what Simeon had said? Why worry him? She could do enough fretting for the both of them. "I don't think so. But there's something else. Something more pressing."

He still held her in his arms. "Yes?"

"Perhaps . . ." She lowered her lashes, suddenly feeling shy. "Perhaps I'm with child."

The moment she waited for his reaction seemed an eternity. But then, even in the darkness, she saw his smile. "A child?" he breathed, as if it were a miracle.

"Surely you knew it was possible." She smiled back. "This *is* how you make babies, my lord."

"Oh, Julia, that's wonderful. A bit earlier than planned, but wonderful." He released her suddenly and sat up. "But I have to get you out of here. If Simeon discovers—"

"How would he discover anything? Drusilla is the only one who could possibly suspect, and she'd never tell." She caught his hand and pulled him down beside her again. Suddenly she felt it was her place to reassure him. To comfort him. *"We have time."*

He grimaced. "I don't like it. I need to get you out of here. Today."

"I'm not going."

She couldn't see the crease in his forehead, but she knew from the tone of his voice that he was frowning. "What do you mean you're not going? I've been meaning to talk to you about this. It's the right thing to do. I should have done it sooner. I'll find a safe haven, and join you when my work here is done."

"I'm afraid to take Lizzy anywhere right now. She's still so fragile. She wouldn't fare well traveling by ship or coach. She laid in bed so long that it tires her to walk the length of our sitting room."

"And you won't leave without her." His deflated words were a statement, not a question, because Griffin knew Julia too well.

"A few weeks, and she'll be better, stronger. That will give us time to make arrangements."

He laid back on the pillow and tucked one arm beneath his head. With the other arm, he drew her close. "That was what you wanted the money for. You were going to try to escape— without my help. Without telling me."

"I would have told you, but I thought it would be better if I did it myself. I won't come between you and the king. He needs you."

He squeezed her arm. "You need me," he said heavily.

"And there'll be time enough for both." She spoke with such confidence that she was nearly able to convince herself. Julia understood Griffin's sense of responsibility. He needed to see his duty through with the king. She didn't want Griffin to ever have any regrets.

He hesitated. "I don't know." He ran one hand through his tumbling hair. "I don't like it."

"Like it or not, it's the best we can do. The safest for all of us." Julia kissed his cheek and climbed out of his warm bed into the chilly morning air. Gooseflesh covered her skin as she reached for her night rail on the floor. "I have to go. Tonight's the big birthday ball. We have to keep up appearances until the very end."

Julia froze at the light tap on the door. Lena was not here. It wasn't her this time. Then Julia realized the knock had come not from the outside door that led to the main corridor, but from an inside door that led to a dressing room.

"It's all right, it's Jabar," he soothed. He sat up in bed. "Come in."

Jabar entered the dark bedchamber, carrying a candle.

Julia squinted as her eyes adjusted to the light. "Good morning, Jabar." He was an odd man, but she liked him. She liked him because Griffin did, and because she knew he protected Griffin.

"My lady," Jabar said in his satiny voice. "A message, my master." He offered a small silver tray with a sealed note upon it. "Just arrived."

Griffin accepted the missive and waited for Jabar to light the candles beside his bed. "The lady wishes to return to her chambers unseen. See her there."

"Yes, my master."

Julia heard Griffin break the wax seal of the message as she turned to go. As he took a deep breath, she turned around. "What is it? What's wrong?"

He stared at the note in his hand, his face suddenly pale despite the shadow of a beard. "Lena," he said.

Julia started back for the bed. "What? Lena's ill?"

His hand fell to his side. "Dying. Her heart."

"Oh no, not Lena." Julia felt an overwhelming sense of sadness. Lena meant so much to Griffin. Julia hated to see him hurt.

"It was sent in the middle of the night. She may already be dead."

"But perhaps not." Julia grabbed the bed linens and threw them back. "You have to go to her—now."

He crumpled the message in his hand, in obvious mental agony. "But I can't leave you here. Not knowing . . ."

"Don't be ridiculous. I've known for weeks. Nothing has changed except that now *you* know. You have to go to her, Griffin. Lena needs you. She's your wife, for heaven's sake."

He sighed heavily. "Not really my wife, but—"

"Really your wife. You love each other far more than most of the married couples in London. Lena is who is important now. I'll be fine. I told you, we've months before there's anything to fear." She turned to his manservant. "Jabar, get him traveling clothes and something to eat. Call for his horse. You go with him. He shouldn't be traveling alone."

Jabar moved without waiting for Griffin's approval.

"Griffin, you haven't time to waste feeling sorry for any of us." Julia tugged at Griffin's hand and stood him up. *"Lena needs you."*

"I don't want to leave you."

"What harm can he do me today? It's his blessed birthday!" She wrapped her arms tightly around his waist and hugged him.

Griffin slowly tightened his grip and hugged back. "I'll be back as soon as I can. I swear it."

"Give her my love." She kissed him, wiping a single tear that trickled from the corner of her eye. She knew it seemed preposterous that she should be sad that her lover's wife was dying. But these were preposterous circumstances, weren't they?

Charlie curled around her bare ankles and then Griffin's.

"Oh, the cat," he said, exasperated. "I may be gone a couple of days. Who's going to feed the damned cat?"

"I'll take him." Julia lifted the black cat into her arms and headed for the door. "I have to go. It will be daylight soon. If a messenger has come, someone's awake in the household already."

"I'll see you as soon as I return." Griffin walked her to his door.

She lifted up on her tiptoes, the cat cradled in her arms, and kissed Griffin lightly on the lips. She hated to see him distraught with worry. It made him look so much older. "It's going to be all right," Julia whispered on her way out the door that Jabar held open for her. "We're going to be all right."

She only wished she felt as confident as she sounded.

Jabar saw Julia safely to her chambers. She closed the door behind her and released the cat into the semidark sitting room off her sleeping chamber; it sprang to the floor and disappeared beneath a chair.

Lizzy appeared sleepily in the doorway. The sun was just beginning to rise, illuminating the bedroom, but still leaving the inner sitting room in darkness. Lizzy looked like a blond angel with the first rays of golden light behind her. "Are you all right, Julia?"

Julia lifted her hands to her cheeks, wondering if she was flushed. "I'm fine. Just couldn't sleep."

Lizzy rubbed her still sleepy eyes. "Is the Baron Archer well? He's not sick or hurt is he?"

Julia stared at her sister. "Why do you ask?"

Lizzy shrugged her shoulders as she walked toward the fireplace, the hem of her white sleeping gown trailing behind her. She lit a lamp on the mantel with a straw. "You came from his room. You look worried. You've looked worried a lot lately."

That was the most Julia had heard Lizzy say in two months. "How . . . How did you know that's where I've been?" There was no need denying it. Lizzy apparently already knew the truth and didn't seem alarmed.

Lizzy lit another oil lamp and then began to stoke the fire. "I sleep with you, Sister. You think I don't know when you get up in the middle of the night and come back in the morning?" She rolled her eyes, then giggled. "I certainly didn't think you were going to the earl's bed."

Despite her better sense, Julia laughed aloud. Her sister's revelation wasn't funny. If Lizzy knew, Drusilla knew. She prayed it stopped there. On one hand she was concerned that Lizzy knew her secret. How long could she keep it? On the other hand, she was relieved to see Lizzy acting like herself again.

"Let's not talk about this right now." She picked up a silver-handled hairbrush Lizzy had left on the chair last night, and began to brush her hair. "I'm not ready to talk about Griffin."

"Just tell me when you want to." Lizzy swung a pot of water for tea on a spider over the stoked coals. "I understand about loving a man you're not supposed to love."

Lizzy sounded so innocent, so childlike in one way, and yet so experienced and all-knowing in another. In a way, it was a shock for Julia. Suddenly she was beginning to see her in a different light. "I'm so glad you're talking again, Lizzy. I'm glad to have you back."

"I'm not sad anymore," she said triumphantly.

"No?"

Lizzy shook her head, grinning. "No."

"Can I ask why?"

Lizzy looked up from beneath a veil of blond lashes. "Can I ask how the baron is beneath the sheets?"

Shocked, Julia's eyes widened. "Lizzy! Indeed not! That's personal, and certainly not something young ladies discuss."

Lizzy sashayed away. "Then you can't ask why I'm not sad." She headed through the doorway, back toward their bedchamber. "But you'll know soon."

Flabbergasted, Julia shook her head. She didn't have time for Lizzy's nonsense now, but sooner or later she'd get to the bottom of this. She just prayed her sister's happiness didn't involve another man. She wasn't sure either of them could survive it.

"Lizzy, we've a lot to do today to prepare for the earl's ball. Guests will be arriving by noonday." She followed her into their sleeping chamber, still running the brush through her hair. It had gotten so tangled when she and Griffin were making love. "I could really use your help if you feel up to it, but I want you to rest so you can attend the ball. Drusilla's already picked out the prettiest gown. Perhaps you'll even catch the eye of a gentleman." She didn't think any lord would serious consider courting Lizzy, but the idea might interest her. She winked. "You never know."

Lizzy made no response, but pulled back the brocade drapes that partially covered the window. She leaned on the sill, as deep as Bassett Hall's three-foot-thick stone walls. "There he goes."

"Who?"

"Baron Archer and his black man." Lizzy waved. "They're going somewhere on their horses fast. Will the baron be back in time for the ball? Everyone likes it when the baron comes. He's funny. And his clothes are so funny." She giggled into her palm.

Julia pulled the brush through her hair, unable to resist a smile at the thought of Griffin. Maybe everything really was going to be all right. He was happy about the possibility of a baby. He wanted to take her and Lizzy away from here, to be with her forever. Even if they could never be legally wed, they could be together far from Bassett Hall and St. Martin. Maybe they would go to the Caribbean islands, or even the American Colonies.

"No, I don't think he'll be back tonight. His wife is very ill."

"I'm sorry." Lizzy hung on the sill. "But if she dies, it will be easier to wed the baron." Matter-of-factly, she flipped back one of her thick blond braids over her shoulder. "Soon as you get rid of you-know-who."

Julia didn't know where Lizzy was getting her ideas. But it was quickly becoming apparent that Lizzy knew more than Julia gave her credit for. And she certainly paid closer attention to the world around her than Julia realized.

"Come out of the window," Julia said, hoping once again to change the subject. She wasn't ready to talk about the possibilities for the future, not even with her sister. Not yet. "It's drafty. Let's dress and get to our tasks. I told you, we've a lot to do if we're to be ready for the birthday ball tonight."

Lizzy swung around away from the window, and her eyes were suddenly wide and frightened.

Julia halted the hairbrush in mid-stroke. Someone was behind her . . .

She turned, her heart sinking to her knees. She already knew who it was. How could she not? There was no mistaking the overpowering stench of garlic.

Chapter Twenty-five

"Well, isn't this a comely portrait? Two whoring sisters, making plans to murder a husband." The Earl of St. Martin stood three paces from Julia. He was clothed in his silk dressing gown and skull cap with a tassel, but did not appear to have just climbed from his bed. Julia suspected he'd been up a long time.

"We make no such plans, my lord," Julia insisted. Survival came instinctively. "You know my sister is not responsible for what she says." Julia placed herself between the earl and Lizzy, spreading her arms to keep her sister back. "I would not murder . . . *not even you.*" The anger in her low voice surprised her.

"No?" He shot his red-raw hands out of the silk gown sleeves. "You'd not kill your husband? *Not even if he knew you carried a bastard child?*"

Lizzy gave a squeak of fear as Simeon took a step closer.

Julia shuddered. *He knew! God help them all.* She didn't know how, but he knew.

"Not even if your husband knew the culprit?" Simeon continued to rant. "Housed the culprit, fed him, called him *cousin?*" He shouted the last words so loudly that his voice echoed off the stone walls despite the wool tapestries that covered much of them.

Julia did not shrink back. It wasn't that she was not afraid— for her sister, for Griffin, for her unborn child. But she'd had enough. And backed into a corner, she would not cower. "How did you know?" she demanded, not knowing where she found the voice. "A peephole in the wall?" The thought made her skin crawl. "Were you watching? You or your henchman, that is, because we all know you send him to do what you cannot."

His palm flashed so quickly that Julia had no warning. It stung hard across her cheek.

"No, I wasn't watching!" He shuddered. "Who would want to watch such a disgusting, filthy act?" He drew back his hand as if soiled by the physical contact. "But do you think that I don't know what goes on in my own home?" He pulled a rag from the pocket of his gown and began to rub the hand he had slapped her with. "Do you think I am not told what goes about?"

"No one ever saw me." Still Julia didn't know where this defiance was coming from. She should have been down on her knees begging the earl for mercy—for Lizzy and Griffin, if not for herself and her unborn child. But somewhere in the back of her mind she knew she couldn't beat the earl on her knees. She had to stand up to him. It was her only possible chance. "No one could have told you anything."

His brown eyes flashed with delight. "Your sheets, madame. You think the laundress would not report the mistress's sheets, clean for more than three moons?"

Her woman's cycle . . . of course. Betrayed by clean linens. Julia nearly laughed at the ridiculousness of the thought. Slowly she lifted her gaze, her mind racing. "Let me send Lizzy to my mother in Paris. Do what you will with me, but you must spare my sister."

"I must? I *must?*" Spittle flew. "There is nothing I *must* do, *wife,* but die and pay taxes!" He pointed a raw finger. "You are the culprit here! You committed the infidelity! You have no right to make demands upon me!"

Julia lowered her gaze to her husband's boiled wool mules. "You could divorce me, my lord. I'll just go."

"Divorce!" He waggled the raw finger. "There has not been a divorce in the St. Martin family in nine hundred years!" He took a step closer, his tone venomous. "You are mine. I would see you dead before I would divorce you."

Dead. The word rang in Julia's ears with a clarity that was heart-stopping. "Let my sister go," she said softly. "Your cousin as well. I seduced him. It was me. Me all along."

The earl tipped his head back and laughed. "You and the sodomite. It's rather humorous, isn't it?"

At least he didn't know Griffin's true identity. At least that secret was still safe.

Julia stared at Simeon's face. And to think she had almost believed him handsome the first day she'd come to Bassett Hall. Could it only have been five months ago? It seemed an eternity.

"Please," she beseeched again. "Do not blame a man for what a woman is guilty of."

"Eve and the apple, eh?" He smirked. "Well, Adam will get his comeuppance sooner than he thinks."

Julia felt a cold numbness spread upward from her toes. "What have you done?"

He stuffed his rag into his pocket and clasped his hands. "Pity he had to ride to his wife. He'll miss my birthday ball." His forehead creased. "The guests will be disappointed when my dear cousin doesn't arrive . . . ever again."

"What are you talking about?" Pushing her sister back, Julia took the step forward this time. "What have you done?"

He began to back out of the bedchamber toward the sitting

room door. "No need to try your rear staircase. Barred. The snoring nurse's door—barred."

"What have you done to Griffin?"

"You are to remain in your apartments until I can decide what plan of action I intend to take." He shrugged his thin shoulders. "When our guests ask where you are, I'll have to say you're ill. All of you ill." He shuddered theatrically. "A pity if you died. A worse pity if we suspected the pox. Your bodies would have to be burned, destroyed to kill the disease. No one would ever know the sad truth, would they? No one would have to know my dear wife cuckolded me, and I had to see her punished for giving away what belonged to me." He struck his chest. "Me!"

"What have you done to Griffin?" Julia repeated, stalking Simeon to the door.

"A surprise." He drew his thin lips back in a sneer. "Dear wife Lena, not ill at all. Healthy as a horse when last I sent word to her. She's actually interested in providing financial support for a little project I'm intent upon. She likes me. Respects me. Always has."

Julia reached out and grabbed Simeon's dressing gown. He wasn't making any sense. What was he babbling about? "What have you done to him?" she screamed.

The earl shrank back at her touch. "The highways are rather dangerous these days, don't you think? Thieves everywhere . . . They'll kill a man for his saddlebag." He clicked between his teeth. "Sad. Tragic."

Julia released Simeon's gown. "Bastard," she whispered beneath her breath. She looked up. "He might surprise you. He's good with a sword. It may be your man who comes back in a coffin."

"Man? Oh, I'm no fool." He opened the door just wide enough to slip out. "When I want a man dead, I send an army."

* * *

Hours later, Julia paced her sitting room. Drusilla sat quietly darning socks, while Lizzy made animal shapes with the last of the embroidered linen napkins meant for the ball.

After Simeon barred the door behind him, Julia had tried to shout for help. Simeon had returned to warn her through the door that if he or anyone heard her, he would shoot the three of them, without hesitation. There would be no mercy. He would not have her embarrass him before his guests, who were already beginning to arrive for his birthday.

Julia had considered trying to wave someone down or call to someone from the window, but Simeon had thought of that as well. He positioned a man below the window to watch. If the guard so much as saw the drapery move, he was to alert the earl. Again, Simeon said he would not hesitate to use the pistol from his desk. And the walls were so thick, he reminded her, that no one would hear the shots. As an extra precaution, he would not allow any of the guests to use the wing of the house her apartments occupied. She was imprisoned.

Lizzy picked up Griffin's cat and sat him on her lap. "He has to let us go someday, Julia," she said, trying her best to comfort her.

Julia took deep, even breaths. She'd been nauseous for hours. She wanted to cry, to shout at the unfairness of her situation, but she couldn't. She had to be strong for Lizzy. She couldn't scare her.

Drusilla seemed to understand the gravity of their situation, but, as always, she took it with quiet, grumbling dignity.

Julia appreciated Drusilla's loyalty, especially when the old woman now knew that Julia had cheated on her husband, that she was pregnant by her lover. But Drusilla's loyalty was not to what was right or wrong, not to honor, not even to God's laws. Drusilla's loyalty was to her charges, and it seemed she would defend them and their actions to her grave.

Julia was so distraught she couldn't think. She couldn't form a plan in her mind, because there seemed to be no chance. Simeon had been contriving this for days, perhaps even weeks.

And Griffin—every time Julia thought of him riding into a trap, her breath tightened in her chest until she thought she would suffocate. He thought he was going to his dying wife's aid, and he was riding into a trap. Julia could only hope and pray desperately that Griffin and Jabar could fight off their attackers. Perhaps someone would happen upon them on the road. Perhaps Griffin would take a different way. Perhaps, perhaps. Her head was full of a million hopes, but none gave her comfort.

Julia lifted her gaze to Lizzy. Her first responsibility was to her sister, of course, and to Drusilla. They had played no part in her infidelity. Simeon had no right to hold them accountable for her sins.

"What are you doing, Lizzy?" Julia asked with a chuckle that bordered on hysteria.

Lizzy had taken one of the linen napkins and tied it around the cat's neck so that the St. Martin shield was displayed on his back.

Lizzy looked up and smiled. She seemed not to understand how desperate their situation was. She had heard Simeon as much as say he intended to kill them, and yet she seemed unafraid, insisting Julia would think of something.

"Making him a doublet. Isn't he fine?" She petted the cat and it purred in response. "He's a fine cat, Julia. Do you think he could live with us when the baron joins us in our new house with the baby?" She scratched the cat behind its ears. "I do miss my dog, Sally. A cat would be nice, don't you think?"

Julia massaged her pounding temples. She had to find a way for them to escape. "We'll see, Lizzy."

A knock sounded at the door, and all three women looked up expectantly.

"Yes," Julia called. It couldn't be Simeon, he wouldn't knock.

"A tray, my lady," came a voice she didn't recognize. "Sent by his lordship."

As he spoke, Julia heard a metal bar scrape. Before she could rise, the door opened, a tray slid on the floor, and the door slammed shut again.

Julia made no attempt to try and gain the servant's help, or to push her way through the door. Surely Simeon was smart enough to send up a servant he held in confidence. No, Julia knew that if she was to beat Simeon it would have to be not with muscle, but with her mind.

"Want that I should fix it?" Drusilla asked, making no move to rise.

Julia's stomach tumbled at the scent of the mutton sausage and egg pie. There was a small pitcher of cider as well. She gripped her stomach. "No food for me. I think I'd best lie down."

Lizzy pushed Charlie off her lap and walked to the tray. She didn't bother to pick it up. "Mutton." She wrinkled her nose. "I hate mutton. Drusilla?"

The old woman pushed a lump of fresh tobacco under her lower lip and went back to her darning. "Think I'd eat his slop? Liable to be poisoned!"

Lizzy wandered away from the tray as the cat sniffed it curiously. "I'm not much hungry anyway." She glanced at the retreating Julia. "Want me to sit with you?"

Still holding her stomach, Julia lifted the other hand to stop Lizzy. She needed some quiet time to think. Perhaps to sleep an hour or two. "No. I'm fine. Just let me rest. Drusilla." She eyed Lizzy.

"I'll keep her."

"Thank you." Julia closed the door between the two rooms and climbed onto her bed. Resting her wrist on her forehead, she fell asleep in seconds.

Julia heard Lizzy scream and immediately bolted upright. The morning shadows of the room had shifted to noonday shadows. "Lizzy?" Julia's head was muddled. Had the scream been real or imagined? "Lizzy?" She leaped out of bed and raced for the sitting room.

"Julia! Julia!" Lizzy cried as if she were in pain.

Julia flung open the door.

Drusilla held Lizzy in her arms as she sobbed. There was no one else in the room.

"What's wrong? Is she hurt?" Julia peered into her nursemaid's wrinkled face, still disoriented from sleep. "Drusilla?"

Drusilla pulled Lizzy against her lumpy breasts and stroked her silky hair. With one gnarled finger she pointed to the floor near the fireplace.

Griffin's cat lay on its side twisting in pain, its eyes rolled back in its head. It had vomited and its mouth was foaming white. Strangled, gurgling sounds came deep from Charlie's throat. The cat was dying.

Julia's gaze locked with Drusilla's. "What happened?"

"Ate the pie."

Julia stared at the cat again, her heart going out to it. She didn't like to see anything suffer. Poison? she mouthed in disbelief.

Drusilla nodded, still holding Lizzy tightly in her arms.

Poison? There had been three plates. The tray had been meant for her and Lizzy and Drusilla. Simeon had tried to poison them . . . kill them. It was beyond belief, and yet somehow it was not.

Julia stared at the cat in indecision. Instinctively she knew nothing could be done for it. Nothing but comfort it in its last moments.

Suddenly Charlie's entire body jerked and then went still, its eyes staring, but unseeing. It was dead before she reached it. "Oh, poor kitty," she whispered. A sob escaped her throat as she kneeled and stroked the silky, black fur. "Poor kitty." Feeling foolish for her tears, she wiped at them with the back of her hand. How could she cry for a cat, when she hadn't cried for herself, or for her sister, or even for Griffin? It made no sense.

Her tears spent, Julia wiped her nose with the handkerchief she pulled from her sleeve and rose. "Let me take her," she told Drusilla. She felt better now. Her tears had actually seemed to give her strength to go on. "Will you get a sheet or something and wrap up poor Charlie?"

"Aye." The old woman gently passed Lizzy's arms from her shoulders to Julia's. "Go on, sweet." She smoothed Lizzy's cheek with her gnarled hand, as tender as any mother could have been with her child. "Go with yer sister."

Sniffing loudly, Lizzy hugged Julia. "Bastard," she muttered. "Garlic-stinking bastard!"

Julia led Lizzy toward the bedchamber. She had never heard Lizzy speak so angrily.

"Killed the cat. Bastard."

"Shh," Julia soothed, closing the door between the two rooms with her foot. "It's all right."

Lizzy pulled away and stomped her foot. "I want to go. I don't want to stay here anymore."

Julia pushed her hair from her eyes. She had to keep Lizzy composed. Hysteria would do none of them any good, and it might provoke Simeon. "I'm going to get us out of here, Lizzy," she said calmly. "I swear I am."

* * *

The sun shone brightly on the road to Lena's country home. As Griffin rode, he thought how unfair it was that the day should be so bright and clear when his fair Lena lay in bed dying, perhaps already dead. What right did the sun have to shine when his Lena no longer would?

Griffin urged his mount faster. Behind him he heard Jabar make a sound of disapproval. Jabar thought they were riding too fast, taking chances that might lame their horses before they reached Lena. Griffin ignored him.

He'd not related to Jabar the depth of his conversation with Julia that morning. He'd only confessed that he needed to get her out of Bassett Hall. Jabar had protested. He had found several indications that St. Martin was somehow tangled in the web of traitors intent upon dethroning the king. Only there was no positive proof yet. Jabar insisted Griffin should wait until Simeon could be arrested. Left to the legal system, the Lady St. Martin might be a widow in months, and free to marry without drawing attention to Griffin or his position.

Griffin pulled his cavalier's hat lower on his head. He was torn between wanting to be at Lena's side, and wanting to be with Julia. If she felt Lizzy couldn't be moved, at least he could remain close at her side. Maybe Jabar was right. Maybe evidence against Simeon would surface and solve the entire dilemma.

It was amazing to Griffin how overwhelming his desire to protect Julia had become now that he knew she might be pregnant with his child. All of his life he'd considered himself a soldier, and suddenly he wanted nothing more than a warm hearth and his woman and child safe in his arms. If Simeon was convicted of treason and hanged and Lena died, Griffin would be free to marry Julia.

Lena. His dear, clever, witty Lena. He didn't want her to die. He didn't want his own happiness to stem from her death.

Griffin groaned. Life used to be so easy when he'd not had these confusing emotions to deal with. In the old days with the king, wandering the streets of Rome and Paris, he'd felt that strong sense of responsibility, but he'd never felt this damned scared . . . afraid . . . overjoyed.

"We will be there soon, Master," Jabar said, appearing magically at his side. "Let us slow our mounts and give them rest. If you wish to return to Bassett Hall, you must have a horse to ride upon."

"I'll take one of Lena's horses if I need to. I can—"

A flash of movement in a hedgerow along the well-traveled road caught Griffin's eye. Instinctively, he released his reins and reached for the two long-barred German pistols he carried in his saddlebags.

Jabar must have seen the movement at the very same moment. "Ride, Master!" the manservant shouted as he drew a broadsword from his side. "Ride!"

Ambush.

Gunshots cracked the air as horses poured over the hedgerow. Six, eight, ten, a dozen men bore down on them.

Sweet God, Griffin thought as he took aim at the nearest rider bearing down on him. *How will we ever take on so many?* But even as the thought raced through his mind, he squeezed firmly on a trigger and sent the man to his maker.

The cool, sunny noonday air was filled with the sound of gunfire, screaming horses, and the stench of blood and burnt gunpowder.

Preferring the curved blade of his broadsword to a firearm, Jabar bore down on a man and severed his head with one clean swoop. Blood spurted, splattering Jabar, and Griffin turned away as he fired his second pistol into the gut of the next attacker.

"Into the woods, Master!" Jabar shouted.

Griffin felt his body jerk as something seared his arm. A lead bullet, no doubt. There was no time to look down. He could feel burning pain, so he knew his arm hadn't been blown off. His single-shot pistols fired, he dropped them into the open saddlebags and drew his own shorter sword. "I'm behind you!" he called to Jabar.

Suddenly his horse reared and screamed as only a horse hit by lead did.

Damn, Griffin thought as he rode the horse to the ground. Doomed now.

As his horse fell, Griffin lunged free of the crushing weight, dragging his sword in his weakened arm.

"Master!" Jabar shouted. "Run!"

Griffin knew that less than a minute had passed since the unknown assailants ambushed them, but time seemed to lose all meaning. Each second dragged on as a singular eternity as he rose from his knees and spun to face the next attacker. On foot, he was at a definite disadvantage, he thought, feeling oddly disjointed, accepting. On foot, he would likely die.

The sound of pounding hooves on the road tore Griffin from his calm.

"Forward! Attack!" came a feminine voice Griffin recognized.

The approaching horsemen were dressed in the red and blue colors of Lena's late husband. At point, rode his Lena in men's breeches and a blue and red cloak. She held a sword high over her head, leading the charge, a sword far too heavy for a woman with a failing heart.

Griffin didn't know what was happening exactly, or who was responsible, but he knew he'd been set up.

More gunfire exploded in the mid-afternoon air. Griffin's attackers fell rapidly around him. The eight men still astride were no match for Lena's thirty-odd soldiers, trained to fight in her late husband's army. Men screamed as they went down on their wounded and dying mounts.

Leave it to Lena to come to my rescue, he thought as the

last of the attackers fell. A smile crept across his blood-spattered cheek. *My sweet—*

Before his eyes, the bullet hit her square in the chest. No warning. Only that determined look on her lovely face, and then the shock that came with knowing you've been mortally wounded.

Griffin bounded toward her as she fell, her horse dancing artfully away from her as it had been trained.

"No! Lena!" Griffin cried. Once again time slowed to an agonizing *tick . . . tick . . .* It took minutes, hours, weeks to reach her.

"Lena, Lena!" Griffin fell on his knees and lifted her into his arms. Her thick plaits of red hair fell over her shoulders and brushed the gravel road. "Lena!" He shook her and magically her eyes opened.

She smiled. "Griffin." It was barely a whisper, just a breath. The wide, wet wound in her chest bubbled.

"Good you could come," he choked. He knew she was dying. She knew she was dying.

Again came the smile. She didn't look as if she were dying, just sleepy. Her eyelids fell shut and then blinked open again.

"Tried to send word . . . but then . . ." She took in a rattling breath. "Then, knew it was too late. Had . . . had to meet you."

"Who were they?" Griffin leaned closer so he would not miss a word.

"S—Simeon's men. Simeon."

An iron vise gripped his chest. "He knows about me and Julia?"

She nodded and closed her eyes. "One of his new footmen was a spy. Mine. Old trick. Worked."

"I've got to get back to Bassett Hall."

Her eyes remained closed. "Worse."

"What?" He leaned closer. "How could it be worse? Julia's not safe in that madman's house."

Lena tightened her grip on Griffin's neck. "Worse," she repeated.

"How?" He didn't mean to be harsh, but he was so afraid. He was losing Lena. He couldn't lose Julia and his child, too. "How?" he asked more gently.

She took a long moment to answer, so long that Griffin feared she didn't have the strength. But then her eyelids flickered, and for a moment he was looking into the same brilliant green eyes he had looked into so many times over the years. Eyes he trusted. Depended upon. Loved.

"Traitor," she said firmly. "B—bastard knave is the traitor. W—wanted gold from my hold to help finance an army." She laughed, and then jerked in response to the pain. "Promised me a duchy when he was king."

When he was king? Icy tendrils gripped Griffin as tightly in his gut as if he'd been shot there, too. Simeon *was* the master of the spider's web.

And Julia was tangled in the midst.

Griffin took a moment to let this new revelation sink in before he met Lena's gaze again. She was staring up at him.

"Go," Lena whispered. "Go to her. Save her. Save yourself. No time."

She was right, of course. If they were to have any chance at all, he had to go now. But he couldn't leave Lena dying here on the side of the road. The sound of her breath told him she only had minutes to live. "In a moment." He brushed his lips against her dry cheek, fighting the tears that stung the back of his eyes. "I love you," he said. "Always have. Always will."

"No goodbyes. We'll meet again, you and I." She closed her eyes and smiled. "Sweet dreams."

Griffin held Lena as she took her last breath and died in his arms. He choked back a sob as he stroked a lock of her bright red hair. "Sweet dreams, my lady wife."

He kissed her cheek one last time and ever so gently laid her down. He wiped at his eyes and rose to beckon one of Lena's soldiers. It was time to take action; there would be time to mourn later. Now Griffin had to get to Bassett Hall and Julia, before it was too late.

Chapter Twenty-six

In late afternoon, Julia observed the door creak on its hinges and slowly swing open. Simeon crept into her sitting room. With the door ajar, she could hear music drifting from the new gallery on the floor below. The ball had begun.

He squinted into the dark room. Julia had settled Drusilla and Lizzy in the bedchamber and closed the door so that the last of the sun's rays did not penetrate the sitting room. The light from the hallway cast a long shadow of Simeon's form across the tapestry on the wall.

"I wondered how long it would be before you checked on us." Julia sat relaxed in the chair, her hands folded in her lap. She would not be beaten by this man. She would *not*.

Simeon was unable to hide his surprise. "Ah, you're . . . *awake.*" He slid his pristine, gloved hand down the front of his new green and white doublet, made especially for his birthday ball.

"I think you mean ah, *still alive.*"

His gaze shifted to the food tray still on the floor near the door. Drusilla had covered its contents with a crested napkin. "Not hungry, wife?"

"Not very."

"And the others?" He glanced at the closed door.

"Weren't hungry, either."

To Julia's complete surprise, Simeon's thin lips drew into a smile. "You're a clever woman. More clever than I thought." He nodded, seeming genuinely pleased.

Though her blood boiled, she remained calm, her hands still folded. "This isn't going to work. You have to let us go, Simeon."

"I think not." He raised one gloved hand to his chin. "But you have certainly altered my plans." He tapped his chin with one finger. "I've an idea." He held up the finger. "As a reward for your intelligence, you can come to my party. Everyone's so disappointed you're not there. They're looking for you, and we can't have that, can we?" He scowled, lifting on eyebrow. "You would almost think they came to see *you* and not *me*."

Her first impulse was to say that she wouldn't come to his birthday ball if it was the last stop on the road to everlasting hell. Thankfully, her logic prevailed. If she wanted to escape Bassett Hall, obviously she had to get out of this room.

"I should like to go to the party, my lord," she said carefully, rising. "I've so looked forward to it." She wondered if he could see through her lie.

He watched her. "I suppose you would. The refreshment is quite fine. You're probably hungry after your long day."

She started for the bedchamber. "Lizzy and I can be down in an hour."

He laughed so loudly, so obnoxiously, that she turned to face him.

"I said nothing of the dimwit," he declared. "She will stay here." Seeing her blanche, he added more gently, "With her nursemaid, of course. For safekeeping."

Trapped. He had trapped her again.

Julia hesitated, her hand on the doorknob. Did she remain here to protect Lizzy, or take her chances beyond the doors? What if he attempted to have Lizzy removed while she was below? Could Drusilla save her?

Julia's gaze met Simeon's, and she realized she had no choice. "I can be dressed in an hour's time."

"Excellent. I'll be up to escort you in forty-five minutes' time. I'd like you to wear your wedding gown rather than the one you were to wear."

Julia felt a strange shiver of premonition. "My wedding gown?"

"Now, now." Simeon held up his finger. "You are not in a position to argue." He lowered the finger she wanted to sever at his knuckle. "Mr. Gordy will remain behind to watch over your sister," he continued. "Should there be trouble, with her or the crone . . ." Simeon stared, deadpan. "He will slit their throats."

Julia stood at the far end of the gallery, engaged in conversation with a handful of guests. The room was brilliantly lit with hundreds of candles that glimmered off the wall of window glass. Ladies and gentlemen drifted, goblets in their hands, admiring the new gallery and its art collection and remarking as to what an impressive, powerful man St. Martin had become. If anyone noticed that she was dressed in the same gown she had worn for her wedding, they did not mention it.

Julia felt as if she were dreaming. Nothing around her seemed real. She was going through the motions of serving as Simeon's hostess, but she felt as if she were standing back watching herself, rather than actually participating.

She was frantic with worry over Lizzy and Griffin's safety. Would Simeon try to kidnap Lizzy while Julia was at the party? Had he really sent an army to attack Griffin? Where in heaven's name would Simeon get an army?

There were so many unanswered questions, and she didn't know where to begin finding the answers. She'd thought she had some idea what kind of person Simeon was, how he would react, but she was utterly confused now. Why had he released her from her bedchamber? Surely he'd not forgiven her for her transgression. But had he truly released her from her bedchamber prison so he would have a hostess for his birthday party? The idea seemed absurd. But at this point in the evening, what didn't seem absurd?

Someone spoke to Julia, remarking on the splendor of the painted plaster ceiling. Golden cherubs with harps and flutes danced above them in fresh gilded paint. Over the guest's shoulder, she caught a glimpse of Simeon. He was watching her. It was all Julia could do to nod and make some nonsensical response to her guest.

She'd been carrying a glass of wine with her for more than an hour, but it was still full. She knew it was foolish to be afraid of the food and drink. St. Martin certainly couldn't poison half of London. But despite the irrationality, she couldn't bring herself to sip anything but a little water.

As the guests that surrounded her chatted merrily, she studied their faces. She needed to make known her situation, beg for aid, but who could she tell? Who was not allied to St. Martin in one way or another? And even if she knew who she could confide in, how would she tell them? Simeon's beady brown eyes followed her every movement.

Julia felt so weak that she wondered if she were going to faint. She didn't even have a wall to lean against, as they were now behind the curtains she herself had seen hung only two days ago. Behind the curtain was the rear gallery wall, still wet from mortar filled in by the masons as late as this morning.

"If you'll excuse me," she murmured to the circle of ladies and gentlemen around her.

"Your servant, madame. Your servant," the men echoed.

Julia set her glass on a passing footman's tray and walked

alongside the wall that was floor-to-ceiling windows. The music that played from the musicians' balcony high above them seemed to carry her along. She had no idea how she was going to get Lizzy and Drusilla and herself out of here so she could find Griffin, but she was going to do it. Tonight with a house full of people would be their best chance. Tonight before Simeon sent poisoned water to her bedchamber, or Mr. Gordy with his blade.

Lizzy lay completely still in the bed and opened one eye. Drusilla sat slumped in the chair, her eyes closed, her mouth open so that Lizzy could see the gaping holes in her mouth where teeth had once been. Drusilla exhaled in a noisy snore.

Carefully, quieter than any mouse she'd seen in the cellar, Lizzy slipped out of the opposite side of the bed and tiptoed into the sitting room. She closed the door without so much as a squeak of the hinges.

Lizzy had a plan. The earl had made Julia go to the ball. Julia said she was going to figure out a way to get help and come back for Lizzy and Drusilla. Lizzy didn't argue with her sister because she was already upset, but Lizzy had a plan of her own and her plan was better.

She stepped into a pair of quilted petticoats, not bothering to remove her sleeping gown. She stuffed the gown into the petticoat and tied it behind her. Without her corset she'd never fit into her bodice, but she could wear Julia's blue wool jacket. She snatched up the discarded garment and thrust her hands through the armholes.

Lizzy's idea was perfect. Julia was tired and worried about Lord Archer. It was going to be so hard for her to find help to get them out of Bassett Hall with the earl watching her. So Lizzy would get help. She would go to the farm where Amos milked cows and bring him back. He would know how to get Julia out of the house, because he was a smart man.

Lizzy tucked her unbound hair beneath one of Drusilla' silly mob caps. Now all she needed was a cloak. But they wer in the clothes presses in Drusilla's chamber. Lizzy would hav to walk through her own bedchamber to get to Drusilla's. To risky, she decided as she rolled on a pair of stockings. She' borrow one from the stable when she got the horse.

Lizzy found her shoes beneath the chair where she'd lef them, and slipped them on her feet. Quietly, ever so quietly she tiptoed to the door. It wasn't locked. She knew it wasn' locked or barred because when Mr. Gordy had checked o them after Julia left, he never locked it.

He must have forgotten, silly goose.

Lizzy turned the knob and opened the door. She peeke outside. The hall was dark and quiet. She stepped out an closed the door behind her. Light as a feather, she tiptoed dow the hall. She passed the grand staircase. She was too smart fo that. She'd take the back stairs to the servants' hall. Out th kitchen. To the barn. It was a perfect plan. Julia would be s pleased.

Lizzy slipped down the steps, still quieter than a mouse. Sh was so happy. She was going to find Amos. He was going t save her sister and marry Lizzy and make babies in her. Mayb they'd even go to the American Colonies and look for Sall the dog.

It was so dark at the bottom of the staircase that Lizzy ha to feel her way along the wall. But she wasn't afraid. Thinkin about Amos and his kisses kept her from being afraid.

Lizzy found the doorknob of the door that led from on hallway to another. She had thought it was silly to have a do there, but Amos said it had something to do with the hall bein added so servants could get to the new gallery without bein seen by guests.

Lizzy turned the knob.

She didn't expect light.

She didn't expect Mr. Gordy.

"Oh." Frightened, Lizzy took a step back.

"I knew you would come to me," Gordy said, taking a step toward her. "I prayed you would come." He took another step. "He said to kill you, but I could never do that. I could never—"

He put his hand out to touch her hair, and Lizzy opened her mouth to scream.

Mr. Gordy moved so quickly that she didn't have time to get out of his way. He grabbed her around the waist, and his hand clamped down so hard on her mouth that no sound came out.

Lizzy struggled in his arms, trying to scream. She kicked him in the legs. He grunted, but held her tighter.

"Shhhhh," he whispered, his breath hot in her ear. "You mustn't fight me. You mustn't draw any attention, Lady Elizabeth, else how will we escape?"

Julia drifted through the gallery, toward the servants' rear entrance between the main house and the gallery. Just when she was beginning to think there would be no hope in escape, sweet luck had struck. She'd not seen Simeon in half an hour. She didn't know where he'd gone or what he was doing, but he was definitely not in the gallery.

He'd been there beneath a Dutch still life around half past nine, watching her, and then when she looked up again, he was gone. For half an hour she had laughed and smiled and pretended to sample the exquisite menu. All the while she had watched for her husband.

Simeon often slipped out of his parties to meet with one or two of his guests privately in his library. Julia didn't know what business they discussed, and didn't care. She only prayed that this was the case tonight and that the business was lengthy.

Her plan was simple, and perhaps not the best, but it was the only thing she could think of. Without knowing who she

could trust, she decided she could trust no one. She had no one
to rely on but herself. With Simeon gone, she intended to slip
into the front hall, take down one of the weapons, and go to
the cellar and get gunpowder and musket balls from the locked
armory. Thank the sweet Lord she'd had the sense to bring the
household keys she'd borrowed from the housekeeper. With
the loaded pistol, she would go upstairs to release Lizzy and
Drusilla. Gordy had backed down once, she only prayed he
would back down again. If he didn't, she'd shoot him.

With Lizzy and Drusilla free, they would make their escape
out onto the street. They wouldn't take time to have horses
saddled. She doubted the old nursemaid could ride. Instead
they would flee to a busier street and hire a coach. They'd
ride from London toward Lena's and pray they found Griffin
unharmed.

Julia turned to respond to a gentleman in a blond periwig
when Simeon appeared directly beside her.

Julia's heart skipped a beat. She hadn't seen him coming.

"Wife?" Simeon smiled so pleasantly that she knew he was
up to something.

"Husband?"

"Excuse us," Simeon said to the guest as he took possession
of her arm. "Household business."

The guest bowed and turned away.

Julia attempted to remain at the man's side, but Simeon
tightened his hold on her and forcefully steered her away.
"I think that's quite enough dancing and dining, my dear,
considering your delicate condition. I'm certain you're
fatigued." He nodded, smiled, and spoke to guests as they
passed.

"Oh, no, I'd prefer to stay." Julia tried not to panic. "I'm
quite fine. I'm not tired at all."

The music burst into a lively country dance, and Julia could
barely hear herself speak. "Really, sir."

They reached the rear curtained wall and Simeon glanced

around to see if anyone was watching them. All the guests had turned to observe the first dancers lining up in the center of the gallery.

Julia tried to prevent Simeon from drawing her beyond the curtain, but her own strength was no match for his. She opened her mouth to cry out, to cause a scene, anything to keep Simeon from dragging her away, but he was too quick. Everything was happening too quickly. Almost as if he'd planned it.

Simeon clamped his hand down on her mouth, spun her around, and shoved her against the stone wall. It was still wet with fresh mortar, and she could smell the wet stone.

"You really didn't think you were going to get away with what you did, did you?"

Her head banged against the stone and stars of light and pain burst in her head. Her hand fell to her breasts, where Griffin's ring hung beneath her undergarments.

"You didn't truthfully think I would allow you to give away what was mine?" He grasped her by the shoulder and slammed her against the wall again, his hand still on her mouth. "And get away with it?" He punctuated his last words by throwing her against the wall. Her hand that held the ring jerked, and the ribbon snapped.

Julia groaned as pain shot down her spine and she felt the jeweled ring fall through her clothing. She tried to struggle. She didn't want to lose Griffin's ring. But she was so weak from no food or water all day that she could barely stand. Stars exploded in her head again and the ring was lost.

Julia's thoughts came in dull pulses. She couldn't believe this was happening. Not with so many witnesses so close. Surely he didn't think he could kill her with so many people so near, did he?

"You didn't think I would let you cuckold me and live to laugh at me, did you? Did you?"

Her head hit hard against the wall, and her teeth slammed together again and again.

He lowered his hand from her mouth. She tried to scream but she couldn't. Her head throbbed with blinding pain. Her mouth wouldn't move. Her voice wouldn't rise from her throat.

He's really killing me, she thought, her mind drifting with an amazing calmness. *Lizzy . . . Griffin . . .*

"I keep what is mine," Simeon continued to rant.

Julia thought it strangely ironic that she could still hear the music. How many souls could say they died to such a lively tune?

"And you are mine." Simeon drew close to whisper in her ear. "Always were, always will be."

Slam. Again. Again.

"Mine. Mine to keep. A great treasure. Mine forever."

Julia felt her head slam against the stone, only this time the pain was dull. Simeon's voice grew soft. She heard one last shrill violin note, the laughter of the guests. Then there was nothing, nothing but blackness.

"Lady Elizabeth, you must not struggle."

Lizzy lay on her side on a narrow cot, in a small room somewhere within the servants' quarters of Bassett Hall. Mr. Gordy had led her through the darkness down so many winding halls that she wasn't sure where they were in the house. He had tied a handkerchief around her head and across her mouth so that she couldn't speak. Her hands were tied behind her with another piece of fabric.

Gordy sat stiffly beside her on the bed. A single tallow candle illuminated the cold, drab room. There was no furniture but the rope bed, and the walls were bare, save for a few cracks in the plaster wall. The only evidence that the room was occupied by someone was Mr. Gordy's clean, starched shirts and cravats that hung on pegs protruding from the wall.

"Please," Mr. Gordy whispered. He touched her hip to comfort her, then pulled his hand away as if he was afraid of her.

"I did not want to do this. But it was the only way. If anyone heard you, surely the earl would have been told." He stared at her with his gray eyes. "And then we would both be dead."

"Let me go," Lizzy tried to say against the dry handkerchief in her mouth. But the words didn't make any sense in her ear. It was just a jumble.

Lizzy was so afraid. She was afraid of Mr. Gordy. She didn't understand why he was doing this to her. She was afraid for Julia. Where was Julia?

"Please," Lizzy said. "This hurts."

Gordy stared at her as if he didn't know what to do next. They had been in the room a long time. Lizzy wasn't a good judge of time, but she knew it had to be more than two hours. "Please," she begged.

He clasped his hand. "If I take the gag off, will you speak softly?"

She nodded.

"Lizzy, I mean what I say. He will not hesitate to slit our throats and toss our bodies down the well."

Lizzy felt sick to her stomach. Why did the earl want to kill her? Because she loved Amos, or because Baron Archer had made a baby in Julia? She didn't know. But if the earl was this angry with her, how angry was he with Julia? He had sent that food to make Julia sick, maybe even die like the kitty. What if he tried to make her die again? Lizzy's lower lip trembled, and she had to concentrate hard not to cry. Julia needed her.

Lizzy looked up at Mr. Gordy. If she was going to get away from him, she was going to have to do whatever he wanted her to, or at least pretend she would. "I'll be quiet," she mumbled against the handkerchief. "Please?"

After staring at her for a moment, Mr. Gordy stood up and carefully sat her up. He stooped in front of her. "Promise? To save us both?"

She nodded.

Mr. Gordy removed the handkerchief, and Lizzy took a deep breath.

"Are you all right, Lady Elizabeth?" He stared at her so strangely. Like she was someone very important. "If there was any other way I could have gotten you here, I would have. I didn't want your nursemaid to hear you. If she had, I would have had to kill her. That's why I left the door unlocked. If I'd had to take you from the room, I would have had to kill her, and I knew that would make you cry." He took her hand gently in his. "I don't want to see you cry."

Lizzy tried to slow her breathing so that she didn't get light headed. She was so afraid, but she knew she couldn't let him know how afraid she was. "I won't scream," she said softly. Her voice sounded strange . . . wavy.

"I won't hurt you," Gordy repeated. "I would never hurt you. I did it all for you. I betrayed the master to protect you."

Lizzy didn't know what he was talking about. "Where is my sister?"

He glanced away. "I'm sorry. I couldn't save her." He clasped her hand again. "But I can save you from the earl I've coin. I can take you anywhere you want to go." He took her hand in his cold one. "I can make you happy if you'll allow me."

Lizzy didn't understand. What made Gordy think she would go anywhere with him? What did he mean he couldn't save Julia? She watched him as he rose from the floor.

"I think it would be better if we went now," Mr. Gordy said. "The master will be looking for me soon. When he discovers I didn't kill you and the old maid, he'll be enraged." He pulled a lumpy canvas sack from beneath the rope bed. "If he tries to harm you, I would have to kill him. The earl has been good to me. I don't want to have to kill him." His gaze met hers. "Are you ready, my love?"

Lizzy stood because she didn't know what else to do. She

ad to get away from Mr. Gordy. She had to save Julia from
e earl.

"Come." Gordy held out his hand to her.

She hesitated, trying hard to think. What would Julia do if
1r. Gordy was trying to steal *her?* Julia was smart. Lizzy just
ad to think like Julia. "Could . . . could you untie my hands."

He hesitated.

"Please. It hurts." She tried to talk in a soft voice she knew
me men liked.

"You won't try to run?"

She turned her back to him so that he could release her
ands. "Of course not." She told him what he wanted to hear.
You're saving me. Why would I run?"

"That's right, Lady Elizabeth. I'm saving you. I just want
protect you. Care for you. Love you," he whispered.

Lizzy glanced up. She didn't like him close. She only liked
mos this close, whispering in her ear. "Let's go," she said,
ying to sound as if she wanted to go with him.

Gordy took her hand and led her out of the room and into
dark corridor. Here the walls smelled dirty and musty. Lizzy
dn't know where she was, so she couldn't tell where he was
king her as they went through doors and down more dark,
rrow hallways.

Finally they stepped through a door out into the night air.
zzy shivered.

Gordy immediately slipped out of his black coat and laid it
er her shoulders. "There are cloaks for us in the barn, where
e'll get the horses. It's not a pleasant night to ride, I'm afraid,
t it is the quickest way I know to get out of London."

Lizzy stared at the barn looming in front of them. She
uldn't leave Bassett Hall while Julia was still inside. What
s she going to do? Then a thought came to her.

Lizzy halted on the stone path to the barn. "Oh, dear," she
id sweetly, as if she were trying to wheedle something out
Drusilla. "I fear I can't ride without stopping at the necessary

first.'' She lowered her lashes like some women did when talking about such things.

''The necessary?'' Mr. Gordy seemed startled, as if he didn' realize women needed to use it.

Lizzy nodded. ''I can't possibly ride. It's right through the hedgerow there.'' She pointed. ''I won't be but a moment.''

Mr. Gordy glanced in that direction. ''You won't try to run?''

''I promise.'' She smiled and squeezed his hand before she let go of it. ''I'll be right back. Wait for me here.''

Chapter Twenty-seven

Griffin rode behind the king's soldiers up the stone drive that led to the rear of Bassett Hall. Another regiment of soldiers had been sent to enter by the front. There were coaches everywhere, lined up along Aldersgate Street. Every window on the first story of the great stone house glimmered elegantly in candlelight. Footmen and coachmen gathered at the coaches and stared as the king's soldiers rode by.

Griffin had to find Julia. He had to get her out of Simeon's—the traitor's—clutches. He only prayed he wasn't too late. On the long ride back to London he had tried innumerable ways to convince himself she was unharmed. Surely St. Martin would not have thought his wife's infidelity was punishable by death, even if he thought Griffin's was. And even if he believed her crime so heinous, he'd not have tried to kill her tonight, not with the house full of guests. Not with so many witnesses. Not on his birthday.

It had been difficult for Griffin to leave Lena's body on the road at the site of the ambush. But he had to remind himself that she was dead, and that his duty now was to the king, to Julia, and to the baby she carried. Lena's last words before she died in his arms had been to wish him and Julia happiness.

Griffin had left Jabar behind with Lena's men to carry her body back to her castle. Jabar had wanted to tend to his master's wounded arm, but there was no time. It was only a graze. It hurt like hell, but it would heal. Griffin had ridden back to London, straight to Whitehall. Within moments of securing an audience with the king, troops were dispatched to Bassett Hall. Griffin needed Simeon taken alive to gain what information he could from him before he lost his head in the Tower, but they were not to risk allowing him to escape. The king's orders were to take the earl alive, dead, or maimed, depending upon Simeon's degree of cooperation.

As Griffin rode up the stone drive, he tried not to think about all the mistakes he had made in the last six months. Why hadn't he suspected Simeon sooner? How could Simeon have been leading the plot to dethrone the king beneath his nose, and Griffin not see it? How could he have so misjudged the Earl of St. Martin? How could he have left his Julia wrapped in the man's talons? Had his damned honorable sense of duty cost her her life, cost him the only romantic love he would ever know?

"Help! Help!" came an oddly familiar voice from a hedgerow. "Help me, please."

Startled, Griffin, riding at the rear of the regiment, reined in his horse. A woman ran up a small embankment toward them, her petticoats flapping in the wind.

"Help me!" she cried.

Griffin squinted in the darkness. The soldiers had ridden ahead and were dismounting to surround the house. In moments it would be secure. Simeon would not escape.

"Lizzy?" Griffin called in amazement.

Just as she crested the embankment, a man appeared, chasing her.

"Lady Elizabeth! Lady Elizabeth," the man hollered, sounding as if he were in tears. "Please don't. Please don't run. You promised."

Lizzy caught sight of Griffin as he swung out of the saddle, taking a pistol with him. "Help me!"

"Lizzy!"

"Lord Archer!" She threw out her arms. "Help me! He's trying to take me away."

"Lady Elizabeth," the man sobbed. "Don't do this. Don't abandon me. I can't live without you."

Griffin opened his arms and caught Lizzy. Her face was tear-streaked and her hair was tangled, but she appeared unharmed.

"Lizzy, what is it? What's happened? Where's Julia?"

"Set her free," the man shouted. "Set her free or else—"

Griffin saw Mr. Gordy draw a pistol from the canvas bag he carried. "Where's Julia?"

Lizzy clung to Griffin, making it difficult for him to raise his weapon. Gordy was still charging them. If Griffin had to shoot, he'd have a hell of a time taking aim with an hysterical woman in his arms.

"I don't know," she cried, shaking her head wildly. "Mr. Gordy said he couldn't save her from the earl."

"Let her go!" Mr. Gordy halted twenty paces from them. He lifted an old wheel lock pistol. "Let her go, or I'll shoot."

Lizzy covered her ears with her hands. "I don't want to go with him. I want Amos. I want my sister!"

"Put down the weapon, Mr. Gordy," Griffin said. He still wasn't certain what was going on, though he suspected Gordy was trying to kidnap Lizzy without Simeon's knowledge. "You wouldn't want her hit in the cross fire."

Two soldiers with muskets emerged from the darkness. "Lay down your weapon," one of them ordered Gordy.

The pistol shook in the secretary's hands. "She's mine. All these months I protected her. I watched her. I kept her safe," he sobbed. "She's mine and I want her now." His voice cracked with gut-wrenching emotion. "I love her."

Lizzy spun around in Griffin's arm to face her kidnapper. "If you love me," she screamed angrily, "tell me where my sister is."

Tears ran down the secretary's handsome face. "I don't know. I couldn't save her. Only you. Only you, Lady Elizabeth."

"Put down the weapon in the name of the king," the soldier ordered again. "Or we shoot."

Gordy's gaze drifted in the direction of the soldiers. "I saved her. Why doesn't she want me? Why doesn't she love me?"

The soldiers advanced toward Mr. Gordy. "Your pistol. Lay it aside, and you'll not be harmed."

Mr. Gordy took one last look at Lizzy and then pulled the trigger of his pistol, firing on the closest soldier. The king's man went down. The second soldier fired on Gordy.

Lizzy screamed and covered her ears again. Griffin pulled her against his body to shield her from the sight.

The lead ball hit Gordy in the chest and threw him backward onto the ground. Griffin somehow knew Gordy had fired on the soldier because he wanted to die.

Griffin led Lizzy away from the dead men. "Come, Lizzy. Hold on for me." He hugged her. "You have to tell me what happened. You have to help me find Julia."

Led by Griffin and Lizzy, the soldiers reached the gallery and were lining up the guests for questioning. The bright room was a noisy chaos. Lizzy had related to him what she knew. There were still more questions than answers. But Griffin knew that the last time Lizzy had seen her sister, Julia was still alive and here in the house.

Griffin immediately found the captain in charge. The entire house was being searched. So far, no one had found St. Martin or Julia, but the earl had been seen not a minute before the soldiers arrived.

Out of the crowd of ladies and gentlemen Drusilla appeared, dressed in a flannel, striped sleeping gown and cap.

"My baby." She took Lizzy into her arms. "My baby."

Griffin turned away from the captain, who had begun shouting orders again. "Drusilla, have you seen Julia? Do you know where she is?"

Fat tears rolled down the ugly, old woman's face. "I woke up and Lady Lizzy was gone. The earl, he took Lady Julia away hours ago. Took her to the ball, he did. Made her wear her wedding gown."

Her wedding gown? Griffin rubbed his temples, trying to think. His wounded arm ached like hell. *Her wedding gown?* That was odd, even for Simeon. What were his intentions? At least Griffin knew he had to still be here. Bassett Hall was surrounded by soldiers. No one could escape.

Griffin squeezed Lizzy's hand. "You stay with Drusilla."

She nodded, her face streaked with tears. "Please find my sister. I want my sister."

"I'll find her," Griffin vowed as he rushed to the front hall and instinctively climbed the grand staircase, dodging soldiers who seemed everywhere at once, their boots soiling the earl's freshly scrubbed floors. At the top of the first landing, Griffin raced for Julia's apartments. He flung open the door and rushed in, nearly tripping over a tray of food and a bundle of dirty linens.

"Julia!" The sitting room was lit by several candles. No Julia. "Julia," he called again and again as he hurried through the adjoining rooms. He even checked the back staircase. She wasn't there.

"I've found him," someone called from the hallway. "Get Captain Leander. The earl has been found!"

Griffin charged through the door down the hall. At the landing, he came upon two soldiers dragging Simeon by his green and white silk doublet.

"Unhand me," the earl ordered. "Take your filthy hands off me. I'll have you strung up for this!"

"Simeon!"

The earl glanced around and his lip turned up in a sneer. "Cousin, what a surprise. I thought you . . . indisposed."

Griffin yanked Simeon from the soldiers' grasp, surprising himself. Until this moment he had been able to remain a soldier and use his head. Even with Lena dying in his arms, he'd been able to keep a certain emotional distance that allowed him to function. To do his job. He had lost that distance. "Where is she?" he demanded, tightening his fingers on the earl's windpipe. "Where is Julia?"

"My wife?" Simeon cackled despite the grip Griffin held on him. "You seek my wife? *My* wife?"

"Your life is already forfeit, you treasonous bastard, but tell me where she is now, and I'll see your death is a merciful one."

Simeon seemed unshaken. "She's mine," he spit. "Always was mine. Always will be."

Griffin roared in frustration and lifted Simeon off the floor. In one motion, he spun around and lifted him over the railing of the staircase.

Behind him, Griffin heard the soldiers shouting to send someone for the captain.

"Where is she?" Griffin shook Simeon by the shoulders; the earl's legs were dangling in the air high above the marble floor of the great hall below. "Tell me, Simeon. Tell me!"

He laughed. The bastard laughed.

Griffin was tempted to let him go. Let him fall. Let his skull splatter on the floor below and dirty its pristine marble with his blood and brain matter. But the king needed St. Martin. He needed information. And the earl was the only one who could tell Griffin where Julia was.

"Baron."

Griffin felt a hand on his arm.

It was the captain. "Baron Archer," he said calmly. "Let my men take him. He's better off to us alive. We've ways of extracting information from men who do not think they wish to talk."

Griffin stared into Simeon's face. The bastard was smirking.

Griffin allowed four soldiers to haul the earl back over the rail.

"Secure him in one of the chambers until we can take him to the Tower," Leander ordered. "I want six guards inside with him."

The soldiers, giving Griffin wide berth, dragged Simeon down the hall toward Julia's chambers.

"She's here," the captain told Griffin. "She must be. My men will find her. Just give us a few minutes."

They'll find her, Griffin thought heavily. *But will she be alive?*

Julia could see nothing through the blindfold.

She tried to shift her weight from one foot to the other. She was tied, standing, to a stone wall. She could feel the uneven rocks against her back. She was so weary she could barely stand, but whenever she slumped in exhaustion, the pain in her wrists tied over her head was unbearable. So she stood.

Julia didn't know how much time had passed since she'd become conscious again. Everything was so fuzzy. Getting fuzzier. But she knew it had to be hours. When she'd first awakened, there had been music. She had faintly heard laughter.

At first she couldn't figure out where she was in relation to the gallery. She could feel a wall close in front of her. There was space on either side. It wasn't until she realized it was fresh mortar she smelled that she knew where she was.

The wall.

She was sealed in the new wall of the gallery!

She didn't know how Simeon had managed it. The mason should have filled the space with rubble, as was usually done with walls this thick. But somehow Simeon had gotten inside. He had dragged her in and tied her up, and then escaped before she awoke.

Of course she couldn't scream. She was gagged. Clever son of a bitch. She knew he'd planned it this way. He had planned it so that she could hear the music, hear the guests, yet not be able to call to them.

At some point, the music had suddenly ceased. There had been screaming and men shouting. She could almost feel the vibration of marching footsteps.

Julia prayed that the commotion had been Griffin's arrival. She had to believe that he'd escaped Simeon's trap and returned to rescue her.

He would probably never find her.

Simeon would never tell where he'd put her. Not even if they tortured him.

It wasn't that Julia was afraid to die. She wasn't. But her heart ached for those she loved, Lizzy, Griffin. And what of the tiny babe that grew in her womb?

A lump rose in her throat and she choked it back. Tears stung her eyes. "No," she shouted inside her head. "I won't do this. I won't do this to myself or to Griffin. He's here. I don't know how, but he'll find me."

Please God, let him find me.

Griffin paced the marble-tiled floor of the empty gallery, up one side and down the other. *Think. Think,* his mind screamed. *Where is she? She has to be here. Simeon never left the property.*

The soldiers had been looking for Julia for hours. There was no sign of her. She had just vanished.

A candle sputtered in a candelabra on a small buffet table and went out. All the candles were burning out. Soon the entire gallery would be in darkness.

Griffin felt like those dying candles. Without Julia, life would never burn in him again.

But where was she? Griffin's gut was so twisted with fear that he couldn't think.

He turned sharply on his heels, his fists clenched at his sides. That son of a bitch Simeon. The captain said that in the Tower they had ways of abstracting information from prisoners.

Images of Jack's body flashed through his head, and a rage he'd never known bubbled up inside him. He struck his fist so hard into his palm that a pain shot up his injured limb. Perhaps he'd give Simeon a taste of his own tactics. A few strips of skin peeled off a man's thigh tended to make him talk. Simeon would tell Griffin where Julia was then, wouldn't he?

Footsteps echoed in the gallery, and Griffin immediately attempted to quell his emotions. He couldn't let anyone see him like this—so nearly out of control. He forced himself to unclench his hands, and glanced up.

It was the captain. He was scowling.

Griffin drew his mouth tight, still wrestling his anger. He turned sharply at the end of the gallery near the green and white draperies. Julia had ordered them hung only days before. *Julia.* Another emotion threatened to surface, but this one was the worst of all—despair. He stared out the dark window that reflected his own wavy image. "What news have you?"

The captain shuffled closer. "Haven't found her." There was a catch in his voice, as if there was something he wasn't saying.

Griffin turned to him, his voice hoarse. "You haven't found her?" He had to say it. "Not her body?"

Leander shook his head, keeping his gaze fixed on the toes of his shiny boots.

Frustrated, Griffin tucked his hands behind his back to restrain his impulse to hit something, anything, even the captain. He just felt so damned helpless. "So, what have you found?"

The captain removed his hat and ran his fingers through his

short, bristly hair. "You're going to be damned angry, my lord. You might as well take my head to the king on a platter now."

"What are you talking about?" Griffin snapped.

"The earl, my lord."

"Aye?" Griffin took a step closer. He felt as if he were a band of cloth stretched too tightly. Anything might make him snap. Then there was no telling what he would do, but Simeon would surely lose his life.

"He"—the captain drew in a breath—"killed himself, my lord."

"He what?" Griffin exploded as he grasped the green and white draperies and yanked them hard. Yards of silk in the St. Martin colors fluttered down. "He did what? How?" he shouted. "How the hell did he do it with an entire futtering army guarding him?"

The captain stood stiff-backed. "Poison, my lord."

Griffin kicked the piles of silk that had fallen at his feet. "Poison? Wasn't he searched?" he raged.

Leander grimaced. "Aye, my lord. It was the cider, we think."

"Cider? What the hell are you talking about!"

The captain's voice quivered, but he continued. "There was a food tray left in the chamber. The earl drank from the pitcher of cider. The whole thing. Said he was thirsty from dancing. The next thing my men knew, he was writhing on the floor. Groaning and gripping his stomach. He's dead, my lord."

Griffin felt his heart falling . . . falling. Tears welled up in his eyes, and he turned away. How would he find his Julia now? How?

Griffin stepped over the fallen draperies into the space behind. He and Julia had made love here.

Behind him he heard the weary footsteps of the captain as he took his leave. Griffin knew he couldn't blame the soldiers for this. Who would have thought poison would be left in a bedchamber . . . in Julia's?

Oh, God. His stomach knotted, and he feared he'd be ill. Had Simeon poisoned his love? Had he left her body somewhere in the cellar to rot? His Julia. His baby.

A sob rose in his throat. No. No. He placed his hands on the new wall of the gallery, still damp to his fingertips. His legs were suddenly weak. His arm felt as if it were on fire.

His knees buckled under him, and he slammed onto the floor.

He saw a glimmer and blinked.

A glimmer?

He swallowed the acrid bile in his throat as he reached out with his bad arm. His fingers found the cold metal, and he turned to face the room where candlelight still burned.

It was his ring. The ring he had given Julia.

Hope.

Griffin rose to his feet and spun one way and then the other. She would never have given up his ring voluntarily. Either Simeon had taken it from her, or she had lost it. But she'd been wearing it last night. She'd been wearing it when they made love.

She had been here. *Tonight.*

Please, God, please let her be alive. He had never been a praying man, but he prayed fiercely now.

"Julia?" Griffin shouted. "Julia?" She had to be here somewhere. She had to be alive.

He turned again slowly in a circle, trying to think like Simeon. Trying to think like a madman.

What had he done with her?

Griffin rested his hand on the new wall. It was still damp and a little gritty beneath his fingertips.

Still damp. Still wet.

Griffin stared at the wall. Surely Simeon wouldn't have . . . But it had been done so many times in the past. It was said that all the great halls of England were built of the bodies of their enemies.

"Julia!" Griffin shouted. "Julia!" He slammed his fists

against the wall, once, twice, three times. Pain seared up his injured arm.

Panting, he pressed his cheek to the rough wall. "Please," he whispered.

As if an answer to his pitiful plea, he heard a sound. A faint sound. Not necessarily a voice.

There it was again.

It *was* a voice!

"I'm coming, Julia," Griffin shouted at the wall, cupping his hands to amplify the sound. Then he dashed off to find a hammer. "I'm coming, sweetheart. Hold on!"

Julia's heart skipped a beat. She must have drifted off. Had she heard voices again. A voice?

Then she heard it again. A man's voice. Tears dampened her blindfold.

"Griffin," she said again and again. "Griffin, I'm here." She knew he probably couldn't hear her with his ears, but she prayed that somehow he would hear her with his heart. "I'm here, my love."

The first bang of the hammer and the tumble of rocks frightened Julia. Irrationally she feared that it was Simeon. He'd come for her. But it was Griffin's voice she heard. Not Simeon's. It was Griffin, coming for her. Griffin alive!

She heard the pounding again, and more rock fell to the left and in front of her.

She heard Griffin's voice again. Stronger. Louder.

"Julia? Julia!"

"Griffin," she cried against the gag. Her throat was sore. Her head throbbed with pain at the effort. "Griffin."

Then suddenly he was there. Touching her, calling her name in a calm, soothing voice.

"Julia, I'm here," he said thickly.

He untied her blindfold. Even the dim light that came through the hole in the wall hurt her head. But she kept her eyes open so she could see him. See her Griffin. She stared at the moisture gleaming in his eyes and wanted to touch them. Baron Archer, protector of kings, was crying.

Next came the gag. "I knew you would come," she croaked.

He untied her hands from above and caught her as her knees buckled.

"Julia?"

Her tears stung her eyes and blurred her vision. Spots of light spun in her head and made her dizzy.

He went down on one knee to hold her in his arms in the midst of the rocky rubble. "You're not going to faint, are you?"

She wrapped her arms around his neck. She felt weak, but she had no intention of fainting. She didn't want to take her eyes off him. Not for one moment.

Julia smiled as his warm mouth sought hers. "I've been waiting for you," she whispered against his lips. "Waiting forever."

Epilogue

Six months later

Julia smiled and accepted one of her guests' congratulations, her gaze straying. Where was Griffin? As she returned her attention to her guest, she absently ran her hand over her extended abdomen and smiled as the baby kicked. "Thank you so much," she said. "If you'll excuse me, I believe I'll go in search of the bridegroom."

Halfway across the great hall of Lena's country house, Julia met Lizzy and Amos.

Lizzy took both of Julia's hands in hers. "Sister, I know you wanted us to spend the night, but Amos really wants to get back to his shop." She glanced over her shoulder at her new husband. "He said that I should stay, but I'd rather go back with him." Her eyes shone with happiness.

Griffin had assured Julia that with enough money behind them, Lizzy and her baker would be accepted in any drawing room in the country. But where Lizzy was most comfortable was in her husband's little bake shop near London Bridge. There above the shop, she had made a cozy home for herself and her husband of nearly six months, and for the baby she was expecting.

Julia squeezed her sister's hands. "Oh, Lizzy. I was hoping you would stay a few days." Her sister's smile was infectious. "But you go. I'll be fine."

"I'll be back for your confinement. Swear I will."

Julia kissed Lizzy's cheek and then Amos's. "Take good care of her."

He blushed, almost handsome in his dark blue doublet and starched white cravat. "Yes, m'lady. You can be sure of that."

Reluctantly, Julia released her sister and watched them go. It had taken Griffin less than a week to find Amos Wright. And despite Julia's hesitation, Lizzy and the cook had married in less than a fortnight. Now she was glad Griffin had insisted that it was the best thing for Lizzy. He was right. Lizzy truly was happy, and that was what was important.

Julia turned away as they disappeared from sight. Now where had Griffin gotten to?

Jabar approached her, dressed all in white, as always. "My lady, the master seeks you. In the withdrawing room." He pointed to a panelled door off the great hall. "A special guest," he said softly. "One that did not wish to be announced at the front hall."

Perplexed, Julia lifted the emerald green petticoats of her wedding dress and followed her husband's manservant to the door. Jabar slid the door open, then closed it behind her.

Julia broke into a grin at the sight of her husband's broad shoulders. He was dressed rather subtly for his usual taste, in a sapphire blue coat and black breeches. As a joke, he wore one black and one blue shoe made especially for this occasion, though this time the heels were low and of equal height.

Griffin's back was to her as he spoke to a guest.

"You called, husband?"

"Julia." He turned to greet her, revealing the hidden person.

"Your Majesty, what a surprise!" She curtsied deeply.

Griffin caught her hand and drew her up. "Whoa, there. You shouldn't be doing that. If you don't mind, I'd prefer my son or daughter was not born on the floor."

Charles laughed and put out his long arms. "I'd rather have a hug, if Griffin will allow it."

Still a little intimidated by the fact that Griffin was a friend to the king of England, Julia allowed His Majesty to place his arms around her shoulders and hug her.

His embrace was strong.

"That's enough." Griffin took her hand and pulled her away from the king. "I fought too damned hard to make her my own. You'll have to find your own wife, Charles."

The three laughed, and Julia rested her cheek on Griffin's arm. "Tired?" he asked and kissed the top of her head.

"A little."

"Sit. Sit," Charles instructed. He indicated an embossed leather settee. He took a brocade chair directly across from them. "I apologize for not making the ceremony, Madame, but I was needed elsewhere. The damned Dutch are just aching to go to war with us."

"That's quite all right, Your Majesty."

"Charles. I asked you to call me by my given name, at least in private."

She felt her cheeks grow warm. "I'm honored by your presence at all, *Charles*. It wasn't necessary that you come."

"Wasn't necessary? Griffin's wedding, and it wasn't necessary that I come?" He laughed, his dark eyes sparkling. "The man who broke the ring of conspirators who could have taken my throne from me? I'd not have missed seeing the two of you today if I'd had to fight the Dutch myself."

She gazed into Griffin's eyes, a smile just for him. She was so proud. "Thank you for coming, just the same."

The king rose, and Julia and Griffin started to rise as well.

"No, no, sit, Madame." The king raised his palms. "I insist. I'll just slip out the back."

Julia settled down on the settee again, thankful for the reprieve. Her back had been aching for hours, and her feet were weary. By her calculations the baby would be here in a few weeks. "Please come again when the house is not quite so full, Charles. We'd like to have you stay with us a few days."

"So you intend to remain here?"

Julia's gaze met Griffin's. "We're both happy here," she said. "It will be a good place to raise our children, and we think Lena would have liked us to stay."

"Just so long as you promise to come to London often. I'll be lonely without my favorite drinking and gambling companion." The king slapped Griffin on the back, his voice filled with sincerity. "Lonely without my favorite big brother."

Julia stared, knowing she couldn't have possibly heard what she thought she heard.

The king looked at Julia, then at Griffin, then back at Julia again. He snapped his fingers. "Ods fish, don't tell me I've done it again." He hooked his thumb in Julia's direction. "You mean to tell me the woman wears a Stuart ring, and you didn't tell her?"

Julia stared at the jewel-encrusted ring on her middle finger, the same ring she had once worn on a ribbon beneath her underclothing. She was speechless.

Griffin glanced sheepishly at Julia, then back at the king. "No, no, of course I didn't tell her. I've never told anyone."

"Tell your wife, Griffin." The king of England dropped his hat on his head and nodded a farewell.

Julia could do nothing but stare at her new husband as the king made a hasty exit. "The brother to the king of England?" she whispered, thankful she was already sitting down.

The night Griffin had rescued her from the wall, they had remained awake until dawn. Wrapped safely in each other's arms, they had revealed to each other the secrets they had felt forced to keep all those months. Julia had confided in him what happened on her wedding night with Gordy, and told him about Amos. Griffin had told of his years of travel with the king. But never once had he mentioned any blood relationship to the throne.

Griffin sat down beside her on the edge of the leather seat and took her hand in his. "What I say cannot leave this room. If it is ever repeated, I will deny it."

She stared into his blue eyes.

"I am the illegitimate son of Charles Stuart I. I made that pledge—"

"To your father," she breathed. "To protect your brother. No wonder you took that vow so seriously."

He nodded.

"But, your parents? They were married."

He kissed her knuckles, one at a time. "My mother had an affair with the king. He could never claim me, though he saw me well provided for."

Julia brushed Griffin's shoulder-length blond hair from his chiseled face. "Royalty," she said. "I should have known."

He laughed. "Royalty born on the wrong side of the sheets is no better than being born the candle-maker's son."

"But no one ever knew, not in all these years?"

"No one but Charles and me, after my mother and my true father went to their graves."

Julia kissed him softly on the mouth. "I would love you just the same if you *were* the candle-maker's son."

He slipped his hand over her round belly to draw her close, and the baby kicked heartily . . . the grandchild of a king.

Julia and Griffin laughed and kissed again.

"I love you," he whispered.

"Say it once more."

"I love you, forever."

ABOUT THE AUTHOR

Colleen Faulkner lives with her family in southern Delaware and is the daughter of best-selling historical romance author Judith E. French. She is the author of nineteen Zebra historical romances, including *Angel in my Arms, Fire Dancer, To Love a Dark Stranger, Destined To Be Mine, O'Brian's Bride* and *Captive*. Colleen's newest historical romance, *If You Were Mine*, will be published in August 1999. Colleen loves hearing from her readers, and you may write to her c/o Zebra Books. Please include a self-addressed stamped envelope if you wish a response.

BOOK YOUR PLACE ON OUR WEBSITE AND MAKE THE READING CONNECTION!

We've created a customized website just for our very special readers, where you can get the inside scoop on everything that's going on with Zebra, Pinnacle and Kensington books.

When you come online, you'll have the exciting opportunity to:

- View covers of upcoming books
- Read sample chapters
- Learn about our future publishing schedule (listed by publication month *and author*)
- Find out when your favorite authors will be visiting a city near you
- Search for and order backlist books from our online catalog
- Check out author bios and background information
- Send e-mail to your favorite authors
- Meet the Kensington staff online
- Join us in weekly chats with authors, readers and other guests
- Get writing guidelines
- AND MUCH MORE!

**Visit our website at
http://www.zebrabooks.com**

ROMANCE FROM ROSANNE BITTNER

CARESS   (0-8217-3791-0, $5.99)

FULL CIRCLE   (0-8217-4711-8, $5.99)

SHAMELESS   (0-8217-4056-3, $5.99)

SIOUX SPLENDOR   (0-8217-5157-3, $4.99)

UNFORGETTABLE   (0-8217-4423-2, $5.50)

TEXAS EMBRACE   (0-8217-5625-7, $5.99)

UNTIL TOMORROW   (0-8217-5064-X, $5.99)

Available wherever paperbacks are sold, or order direct from the Publisher. Send cover price plus 50¢ per copy for mailing and handling to Kensington Publishing Corp., Consumer Orders, or call (toll free) 888-345-BOOK, to place your order using Mastercard or Visa. Residents of New York and Tennessee must include sales tax. DO NOT SEND CASH.

ROMANCE FROM HANNAH HOWELL

MY VALIANT KNIGHT   (0-8217-5186-7, $5.50/$6.50)
In 13th-century Scotland, a knight had to prove his loyalty to the
King. Sir Gabel de Amalville sets out to crush the rebellious Mac
Nairn clan. To do so, he plans to seize Ainslee of Kengarvey, the
daughter of Duggan MacNairn. It is not long before he realizes that
she is more warrior than maid . . . and that he is passionately drawn
to her sensual beauty.

ONLY FOR YOU   (0-8217-4993-5, $4.99/$5.99)
The Scottish beauty, Saxan Honey Todd, gallops across the English countryside after Botolf, Earl of Regenford, whom she believes killed her
twin brother. But when an enemy stalks him, they both flee and Botolf
takes her to his castle feigning as his bride. They fight side by side to
face the danger surrounding them and to establish a true love.

UNCONQUERED   (0-8217-5417-3, $5.99/$7.50)
Eada of Pevensey gains possession of a mysterious box that leaves
her with the gift of second sight. Now she can "see" the Norman
invader coming to annex her lands. The reluctant soldier for William
the Conqueror, Drogo de Toulon, is to seize the Pevensey lands, but
is met with resistance by a woman who sets him afire. As war rages
across England they find a bond that joins them body and soul.

WILD ROSES   (0-8217-5677-X, $5.99/$7.50)
Ella Carson is sought by her vile uncle to return to Philadelphia so
that he may swindle her inheritance. Harrigan Mahoney is the hired
help determined to drag her from Wyoming. To dissuade him from
leading them to her grudging relatives, Ella's last resort is to seduce
him. When her scheme affects her own emotions, wild passion erupts
between the two.

A TASTE OF FIRE   (0-8217-5804-7, $5.99/$7.50)
A deathbed vow sends Antonie Ramirez to Texas searching for cattle
rancher Royal Bancroft, to repay him for saving her family's life.
Immediately, Royal saw that she had a wild, free spirit. He would
have to let her ride with him and fight at his side for his land . . .
as well as accept her as his flaming beloved.

*Available wherever paperbacks are sold, or order direct from the
Publisher. Send cover price plus 50¢ per copy for mailing and
handling to Kensington Publishing Corp., Consumer Orders,
or call (toll free) 888-345-BOOK, to place your order using
Mastercard or Visa. Residents of New York and Tennessee
must include sales tax. DO NOT SEND CASH.*